I0637518

SKYWORLD

The Unmaking Tide

Dane Stewart

Just For Boys Publishing

For permission requests, contact justforboyspublishing@gmail.com

ISBN: 979-8-9986083-1-5

First Edition

Published by Just For Boys Publishing

For my children

PROLOGUE

S elene had said they would drift gently to the ground.

She had been wrong.

They plummeted like a dying star, a streak of metal and ruin slicing through the endless sky. The clouds swallowed them whole, thick and blinding, but they never seemed to end—just layer after layer of choking mist. Then, without warning, the world beneath them wasn't sky anymore.

Branches, titanic and gnarled, loomed out of the fog. They didn't land on them. They tore through them. The impact sent a sickening shudder through the falling district, steel and stone snapping like brittle twigs. Elysra's stomach lurched as the ground beneath her fractured, entire streets ripping apart in an instant. Buildings crumbled, bridges snapped, and a deafening, metallic groan split the air as the remains of Aetherium's District 145 crashed into the jungle below.

El was thrown—violently. Her fingers clawed for something, anything, but gravity and momentum had other plans. She was yanked sideways, smashing through a crumbling walkway before tumbling into the chaos of debris and dust. She glimpsed flashes of fire, of people screaming, of the world breaking apart around her. Another impact sent her spinning, her body slamming against something hard—then another.

And then—cold.

Frigid, breath-stealing, bone-deep cold.

She hit the water with such force that for a moment, she didn't know which way was up. Darkness swallowed her. The roaring crash above was muffled now, distant, but the current seized her instantly, dragging her down, down, into the unknown depths below.

Few in Aetherium had ever known a body of water vast enough to swim in. The city's reservoirs were carefully contained, its canals too shallow, its baths too small. But El had learned. And not just learned—she was a good swimmer.

The shock of the cold had stolen her breath, but instincts took over. Her limbs moved without hesitation, cutting through the frigid water as she twisted to orient herself. Up. She kicked hard, fighting against the pull of unseen currents. Her chest burned, her muscles shuddered in protest, but she pushed forward.

Then—air.

She broke the surface with a gasp, dragging in a lungful of precious oxygen. Water streamed from her face as she blinked rapidly, shoving her soaked hair from her eyes.

The sky above was chaos incarnate. Burning fragments of the fallen district rained down, screaming as they struck the water's surface. Massive slabs of stone and steel plunged like meteors, sending towering waves rippling outward with every impact. The distant screams of survivors—scattered voices lost in the vastness of the storm-tossed sea—were nearly drowned out by the roar of destruction.

El treaded water, gasping, her chest still heaving for more air. Her limbs ached, bruises already forming where debris had battered her during the fall. She twisted in the water, her violet eyes darting across the churning surface, searching desperately for any sign of the others. El barely had time to take a breath before the wave slammed into her, rolling her violently beneath the surface. Darkness engulfed her again, the cold biting deep, her body tumbling in the chaos. The weight of her soaked clothing threatened to drag her down, but she kicked hard, pushing against the force of the water.

She eventually surfaced, coughing up water, her vision blurred by mist and stinging droplets. For several agonizing moments, she treaded water, turning and dodging as debris rained down around her—splintered beams, shattered glass, entire sections of buildings breaking apart as they struck the waves. Each impact sent violent ripples rolling across the water, threatening to pull her under again. Exhaustion creeped into her muscles, but she forced herself to move, to keep going.

Then—there. A shoreline.

It was barely visible through the mist, a dark smudge against the endless, restless expanse of water. Her body groaned in protest, but she gritted her teeth and swam toward it, pushing through the churning waves with desperate strokes. The closer she got, the more details emerged—

twisted roots clawing at the water's edge, massive stones jutting from the sand like the ribs of some long-dead beast.

At last, her feet found purchase on the uneven, muddy ground. She staggered forward, half-wading, half-dragging herself out of the water. The moment she reached solid ground, her knees buckled, and she collapsed onto all fours, coughing as she expelled the last of the water from her lungs. Every breath burned, but she gulped in the air greedily, letting the shuddering gasps fill her aching chest.

For several seconds, she stayed there, head bowed, hands sinking into the damp earth. The world still felt like it was spinning, like she was caught in the lingering momentum of the fall.

Finally, her breath steadied.

She was alive.

She pushed herself upright, her legs unsteady beneath her, and turned to take in her surroundings.

Behind her was more water than she had ever thought possible. It stretched endlessly, vanishing into the misted horizon, its surface rippling and heaving from the wreckage still crashing down. Massive chunks of what had once been her home jutted out like broken teeth, steel beams and shattered towers half-submerged, their edges slick with water and draped in strands of debris. Most of the wreckage, however, had already been pulled beneath the surface, swallowed by the depths without a trace.

The sight sent an icy shiver down her spine. District 145 had been torn apart, its shattered pieces and broken fragments sinking into the unknown. The sheer vastness of it all made her stomach twist. The idea that she could swim for days and never reach the other side terrified her in a way she couldn't name.

She forced herself to turn away, her soaked clothes clinging uncomfortably to her skin as she faced the land before her.

Trees.

Not just trees—a jungle, but unlike any she had ever imagined. Towering, titanic in scale, their dark brown trunks thicker than entire buildings, their roots curling through the earth like the limbs of sleeping giants. Their canopy was impossibly high, so far above that it blurred into the clouds and mist, leaves of mostly dark purple shifting with the distant sway of the wind. Thick vines cascaded down from unseen heights, draping the trunks like living bridges, their surfaces glistening with moisture, and a heavy mist clung to the branches like a shroud, twisting between the vines and curling around the wreckage.

And tangled within them—District 145. Or what remained of it.

Chunks of the city had lodged into the trees as they fell, massive slabs of stone and metal tangled in the branches like the skeleton of a civilization that had tried and failed to take root here. Walkways dangled precariously, split buildings tilted at unnatural angles, entire balconies and broken staircases half-swallowed by the jungle's hungry grip. Mist curled through the wreckage, blending the city's remains with the wilderness, as if the trees themselves were claiming what remained of District 145 for their own.

It was unlike anything she had ever seen. Terrifying. Unfathomable.

And absolutely incredible.

In a moment she thought of her friends. The others had to be here. They *had* to be.

"Jonathan!" she called, her voice raw. "Valera! Israel!"

Silence answered her—silence and the slow, rhythmic creak of the branches overhead as they settled under the weight of the fallen district.

And then—movement.

Not from above, but from the water itself.

A figure broke the surface a few yards away, gasping, coughing. Valera.

El knew that cats hate water, but she was not prepared for what she saw next.

Valera exploded out of the water like a demon escaping the depths, her claws digging into the wet sand as she scrambled onto the shore. She was soaked from head to tail, her normally sleek fur plastered against her body in a wild, sopping mess. Her ears were flat against her skull, her green eyes blown wide with sheer panic.

She let out a deep, guttural *HISSSS*—one of pure rage, pure terror, pure *betrayal*—spinning to face the water like it had personally wronged her.

A wave, small and harmless, rolled lazily toward the shoreline. Valera lost her mind.

She screeched, leaping backward with all the grace of a startled housecat, her tail puffing out like an overgrown dandelion. *"NO!"* she bellowed, swiping at the water like she could physically fight the sea itself. Another tiny ripple dared to touch her toes, and she yelped, full-on bolting away from it, scrambling up the nearest patch of dry land.

El stood frozen, dripping wet and exhausted, watching this legendary, battle-hardened warrior—one of the fiercest, deadliest fighters she had ever known—reduced to a frantic, waterlogged mess.

Valera whirled around, eyes blazing, panting, and still trembling with the raw horror of what she had just endured. Her soaked fur stuck out in awkward patches, making her look more ridiculous than fearsome, but the fury in her expression was real.

"The water... IT TRIED TO DROWN ME!" Valera spat, her voice shaking with rage.

El blinked. "Well… yeah, that's kind of how water works."

Valera hissed again—*at her* this time, as if El personally had something to do with this treachery.

El wiped a hand down her face. "Oh, come on, you act like it hunted you down and—"

"IT DID!" Valera cut her off, teeth bared, tail lashing. "I FELT ITS MALICE!" She gestured wildly at the lake, as though expecting it to rise up and fight her.

Another wave rolled in, barely grazing the sand near her feet.

Valera screamed.

El lost it. She doubled over, wheezing with laughter, unable to contain it anymore. She had never—not *once*—seen Valera rattled, let alone terrified.

"I fail to see the humor in this!" Valera growled, shaking out her fur furiously, still glaring daggers at the water.

"I— I just—" El gasped between laughs. "You fight machines, Valera! You fight *monsters*! You fight *an entire army* without hesitation! But—" she wheezed, trying to catch her breath, "—one swim and you're—"

"I did not swim," Valera interrupted, her voice dangerously low. "I *suffered*."

El nearly collapsed from laughing. "Oh my—"

Valera sulked, shaking out her fur again like a disgruntled housecat. "This is a cursed place," she muttered, ears flicking with distaste. "I do not trust it."

"Because of the water?" El wheezed.

"Yes," Valera growled. She shot one last venomous glare at the lake—just in case it got any ideas—before stalking away, tail flicking, dignity in shambles.

El wiped tears from her eyes.

This was going to be so much fun to tell Jonathan.

Jonathan…

Fear seized her.

The laughter, the absurdity of Valera's water-induced meltdown—it all vanished in an instant.

Jonathan.

El's stomach twisted. If she had survived, and Valera had survived, then he had to be here somewhere. He *had* to.

She forced her aching limbs into motion, shoving aside exhaustion, cold, and the lingering taste of lake water as she stumbled forward. Valera, still scowling at the world, seemed to pick up on her urgency. Without a word, the tigress warrior fell in step beside her, shaking out the last remnants of her ordeal and turning her sharp gaze toward the ruins.

They searched.

Through the wreckage of the fallen district, through the shattered remains of once-proud buildings now impaled on the massive trees, through the tangled mess of stone, steel, and jungle, they looked. The city had been tearing apart for miles before the final impact, pieces flung who knew how far.

El had no way of knowing if they were even in the largest part of the wreckage.

A handful of other survivors had begun to stir from the rubble. A few called for help, their voices weak but alive. El and Valera pulled out who they could, but every moment stretched unbearably long without a sign of Jonathan.

Then, finally, movement and a familiar face.

El and Valera snapped toward it, muscles tensed, hearts hammering. A figure shifted in the wreckage, stirring from beneath a collapsed section of stone and wood.

Israel.

He was half-buried beneath a section of collapsed balcony, a mess of twisted metal and shattered glass around him. His coat was torn, blood streaked his forehead, and his bionic arm sparked faintly at the shoulder joint. And yet, somehow, the man was still alive.

He groaned, shifting, his human hand moving to rub his face as if waking from a particularly rough nap rather than surviving a city-wide catastrophe. El and Valera rushed toward him, shoving debris aside. Israel winced, cracked his one good eye open, and let out a deep, gravelly sigh—the kind that said he was far too old for this nonsense.

El let out something between a laugh and a sob. "Israel, you stubborn, *stubborn* old man—"

"Careful." He exhaled sharply as they pulled the last bit of rubble off him. "I'm injured, not deaf. No need to get sentimental on me."

Israel stood, his bionic hand flexing as sparks flickered from the damaged joint. His good eye squeezed shut for a moment, then he let out a breath. "Right. Well. That feels like getting drop-kicked by a warhorse."

El ran a hand through her soaked hair, equal parts relieved and exasperated. "What hurts?"

Israel gave her a flat look. "Lass, we just fell out of the sky. *Everything* hurts."

Valera grunted, dragging him to his feet in a manner that was not entirely gentle. "If you can jest, you can move."

El's smile faltered. "Jonathan," she pressed. "Have you seen him?"

Israel's expression sobered slightly. He glanced around, then back at them. "No," he admitted. "Last I saw, we were all still fallin'. And then, y'know—impact." He gestured vaguely at the wreckage. "The lad could be anywhere."

El swallowed hard, a sharp pain starting in the back of her throat. That was what she was afraid of.

Valera, ever practical, turned toward the trees, scanning the jungle with narrowed eyes. "Then we keep looking."

El nodded. "We keep looking."

They searched tirelessly for the rest of the day, combing through the wreckage, calling Jonathan's name until their voices grew hoarse. Every shattered street, every half-sunken building, every twisted piece of metal was a reminder of just how far they had fallen—both literally and figuratively. More survivors joined them, but still no sign of their friend. As the sun dipped below the canopy, plunging the world into eerie twilight, they were forced to accept the inevitable: they would not find him before nightfall.

Israel grumbled as he dropped a bundle of wood onto the clearing they'd chosen for camp. "That boy better be alive," he muttered, rubbing his shoulder as if the day's exertion had finally caught up with him. "I did not survive falling out of the sky just to get dragged through a jungle looking for a corpse."

Valera's lithe form crouched low as she stacked the wood into a proper pile, and she flicked her ears in irritation. "He is alive," she said flatly, her voice brooking no argument. "If he were dead, I would know."

A silence stretched between them.

El pulled her knees to her chest, her mind replaying every moment of the fall, searching for something she might have missed—a clue, a direction, anything. Jonathan had to be out there. Somewhere.

"He'll be fine," Israel said gruffly with a glance in El's direction. "Boy's too bloody stubborn to die."

El exhaled a slow breath, watching the embers dance in the darkness. "Yeah," she said softly. "I hope you're right."

Israel and the handful of other survivors soon drifted off to sleep, exhaustion weighing them down like stones. But not El. And not Valera. The pair of them sat around the fire, staring into the flames like their lives depended on it.

The tigress warrior sat beside her, slit-pupil eyes glowing faintly in the firelight, tail flicking idly as she stared into the jungle. She was silent, as always, but there was a weight in her presence, a kind of quiet companionship that El had come to appreciate.

Then, out of nowhere, Valera broke the silence.

"I told you," she said, her a rumbling purr in the dark. "You should have wed Jonathan."

El nearly choked on air. She sat up so fast she almost fell backward. "What?" she sputtered, her face burning despite the cool night air. "I'm only fifteen!"

Valera's ears flicked in mild irritation. "You turn sixteen in two weeks."

15

El flushed deeply and felt grateful for the darkness. "That's not—! That doesn't—! That's still too young!"

Valera made a dismissive noise in the back of her throat. "Stupid," she said. "A strong mate is chosen—one who can protect, hunt, and endure. Jonathan is all of these. He would make a perfect mate for you." She shot El a pointed look, as if the very idea of debating this was beneath her. "You should claim him before someone else does."

El's heart gave a traitorous thump at his name. "He's also reckless," she argued, though there was no real force behind it. "He's cocky. Hotheaded," she added. She shook her head. "He's... ugh. He's Jonathan."

"I agree, he has many strengths," Valera countered, accent thick but words forceful. "But most of all, he is brave. He would die for those he loves. He fights even when he knows he will lose. And when the world breaks, he is the one still standing. You are small, She-Cub. Clever, yes, but small. You will need a strong mate."

El folded her arms, scowling. "I don't *need* a mate."

Valera turned her glowing eyes on her, unamused. "Everyone needs someone."

El opened her mouth, ready to argue, but the words never came. Because the truth was... she wasn't sure Valera was wrong.

Jonathan *was* reckless. He *was* impulsive. He infuriated her half the time and exasperated her the other half.

But when she thought of him—his stubbornness, his fire, the way he never gave up, never stopped fighting—there was a warmth in her chest that had nothing to do with the fire in front of her. Jonathan had always been there. Standing in front of her when danger loomed, pulling her from the edge of disaster, making her feel safe even when everything was crumbling around them. Even thinking of him made her feel safer...

Still.

"I'm too young," she said, but even to her own ears, it sounded weak.

"Humans," she muttered, this time speaking more to herself. "Always making things difficult. Just bite him and be done with it."

El groaned and buried her face in her hands. "Can we please talk about something else?"

Valera gave a satisfied *harrumph* but said nothing more.

Eventually, exhaustion won over conversation, and the pair finally drifted into sleep.

Morning arrived thick with warmth and humidity, the air clinging to Elysra like a second skin. Despite the heat, a cold weight sat in her chest—a hollow, gnawing ache she couldn't shake.

Jonathan was still missing.

The thought followed her like a shadow, dull and persistent, tightening around her ribs with every step.

Without Jonathan, the entire group felt hollow, their every movement subdued. After a brief meal of whatever salvaged rations they had scrounged up, they set out. Higher ground was their best bet—if Jonathan was out there, they needed a better vantage point. The handful of survivors they'd found clung to the wreckage like shipwrecked sailors to driftwood, as if the broken remains of their fallen city could somehow shield them from the vast unknown surrounding them.

Israel, ever resourceful, had managed to dig up a pair of binoculars from the wreckage. "A little cracked," he muttered, adjusting the lenses, "but I ain't picky. Burn me, I once scouted a whole battlefield with a dented soup can and a prayer."

Valera blinked. "That... does not sound real."

Israel just smirked and handed her the binoculars.

When they finally reached a decent overlook, they took turns scanning the landscape. And that's when El realized something about this place was very, very strange. From this height, she could barely see the far end of the lake, but what she *could* see made her stomach drop. The water stretched further than she ever imagined—easily a hundred miles wide. But that wasn't the strangest part.

Beyond the lake, rising in the distance, were mountains... except they *weren't* mountains.

They were *wrong*.

Not jagged peaks or rolling hills, but massive, cylindrical structures, smooth and impossibly straight, like great branches reaching up into the sky...

El lowered the binoculars.

"That," she said slowly, "is not normal."

Israel took the binoculars from her and had a look himself. After a long moment, he muttered, "Rust and ruin, that is strange."

Israel handed the binoculars back to El and she adjusted the focus, scanning the shoreline with growing desperation. The thick mist blurred the distance, making it difficult to see clearly. But then—movement. A lone figure, barely more than a smudge against the sand.

Her breath caught.

There.

Several miles away, Jonathan was making his way up the shoreline.

"I see him!" she gasped, gripping the binoculars tighter. "He's alive—he's moving!"

Israel was at her side in an instant. "Where?"

She didn't lower the binoculars, but her voice turned urgent. "The shoreline—three, maybe four miles out." Her stomach twisted. "He's hurt."

Israel growled anxiously. "How bad?"

Even at this distance, she could see Jonathan's injuries—his tunic was torn, his body smeared with blood and dirt. He was running, or at least trying to. He was hurt— badly. His steps were uneven, every movement sluggish with exhaustion and pain. Blood streaked his arms, his clothes were torn, and even from this distance, she could see how he was barely holding himself together.

Then she saw them.

The jungle behind him shifted, and figures emerged from the shadows.

Malrics.

Not just a few. Twenty at least.

El's voice turned to ice. "He's not alone."

And the Malrics were gaining on him. Jonathan slowed—then turned to face them. El's breath caught in her throat. "No, Jonathan, don't—"

But of course, he did. For a heartbeat, El dared to hope. If anyone could beat twenty Malrics, it was Jonathan.

But hope was a fickle thing.

The Malric that stepped forward was a behemoth. Larger than the others, heavier, his armor reinforced with thick plates that made him look less like a man and more like a walking war machine. Several hundred pounds of muscle and steel. His movements were slow, deliberate—like he knew there was no chance of losing.

Jonathan, bleeding, panting, still met his gaze without flinching.

The Malric cocked his head, considering his opponent. Then, without warning, he struck. El saw the blade before Jonathan did.

"Jonathan!" she screamed.

The jagged steel plunged through his stomach.

Jonathan jerked—his body going rigid, mouth parting in a silent gasp. The Malric twisted the blade, and Jonathan crumpled in a pool of his own blood.

El's scream tore through the jungle.

And then the Malrics were coming for them.

CHAPTER 1
EYES OF THE NIGHT FATHER

O NE YEAR LATER

Jonathan crouched in the crook of a massive branch, one hand gripping a dew-slicked vine. Around him, the jungle of Ydrathar rose around in towering layers—wild, vast, tangled, and alive. During his time in the wild he had learned the dangers of this strange world: venomous creatures in the undergrowth, the gleam of predator eyes in the dark, plants that killed with a single touch. But survival had become second nature. He knew which trees whispered of death, which paths to take, when to run and when to go still.

The jungle no longer felt like an enemy. It wasn't home—not quite—but it was close.

And from this height, nearly all of Ydrathar unfurled before him—alien, endless, and still impossible to fully understand.

Ydrathar. The World Tree.

Even after a year living in its branches, the scale still defied reason. A tree so vast, it held an entire world in its limbs. Forests, rivers, valleys—even inland seas—all cradled in the arms of its ancient wood. He'd once thought the distant peaks on the horizon were mountains. They weren't. They were branches—some nearly as large as Aetherium itself—reaching skyward like the ribs of some forgotten god. And the inland seas? Dozens of miles across, scattered through the flatter portions of the canopy like jewels. Strange, teeming with vibrant life, they were cradled in the tree's embrace, watering its people and sustaining its wild, impossible world.

He'd always thought Aetherium was large, but this? The World Tree was so large it still made his head hurt to think about.

Jonathan took a slow breath, steadying himself. It was easy to get lost in the sheer impossibility of it all. Behind him, the clouds rolled—familiar now, a reminder of the skybound city he once called home. Before him, the canopy stretched beyond sight, a wild ocean of green and purple and silver leaves. Rivers coiled through the branches, holding more water than all of Aetherium combined. This world—suspended in primordial limbs, vast beyond reason—was a marvel. But today, wonder would not serve him.

Today wasn't about marveling at the impossible.

Today, he barely noticed.

Today was about something far simpler.

Today was his last day of servitude.

Assuming he could complete this one final task…

23

Drekkar pushed aside a curtain of purple leaves and emerged from the underbrush like a whisper, not a sound betraying his steps despite the gnarled vines and brittle foliage beneath him. He was ancient—at least by Malric standards—the oldest tiger Jonathan had ever known. His long gray hair and beard were bound in leather cords, his weathered hide etched with a lifetime of tribal ink and old wounds. Both of his eyes were now clouded, weary old clumps of fool's gold, and lately they seemed to see far less than it used to. A heavy cane supported his weight as he walked, but he moved with the easy grace of someone who had nothing left to prove to the world or its dangers.

"You ever wish you'd just stayed in bed? Because I do. A lot," Jonathan said.

"If you walk only where you wish," the old tiger said, voice low and calm, "you'll never arrive where you're needed."

Jonathan snorted. He knew Drekkar was right—but that didn't mean he had to like it. As if reading his thoughts, the elderly tiger added, "In your life, young Jonathan, there will be moments when you will be able to choose your own path, and others where you must walk the required one; the path of duty. Honor is doing what must be done, even when it cuts deep. The tree doesn't grow straight unless the roots fight the stone."

Drekkar purred softly and placed a warm and rough hand on Jonathan's shoulder. "Besides. I will let you sleep in tomorrow… Provided you don't get turned into serpent droppings today."

Jonathan bit back a smile. It was hard to tell with Drekkar—sometimes his wisdom and sarcasm came so closely wrapped, you weren't sure if you'd just been given a life lesson or the punchline to a terrible joke. Maybe both.

"Tomorrow, I can do whatever I want, regardless of what you say or don't say. Tomorrow, I will be a free man," answered Jonathan.

"Free man? If I were you, I'd be more worried about keeping both your legs attached to your body."

Jonathan started to reply but was interrupted by a shadow that suddenly fell across him and Drekkar. Jonathan turned, and he looked up—and up—and up.

Varg, son of Drekkar, was unlike any Malric Jonathan had ever seen. He was massive, easily the largest of their kind Jonathan had ever encountered. Broad-chested, thick-limbed, his fur was a deep, burnished gold streaked with dark stripes—and around his shoulders and jaw spilled a heavy mane, more like a lion's than any tiger Jonathan had ever seen. His paws were enormous, claws half-sheathed, the kind of hands that could crush skulls like fruit. One ear was ragged, a jagged notch torn clean through it, but somehow the scars only made him look more handsome, not less. There was a wildness to him—like a raw piece of untamed jungle trapped in flesh, barely held in check.

The giant tiger crouched low on the branch beside Jonathan, the wood groaning under his weight. When he shifted, one massive hand settled against a nearby limb for balance. The limb—thicker than Jonathan's torso—snapped under his massive weight. Varg exhaled in mild annoyance, brushing splinters from his mane as though swatting at a gnat, unconcerned.

Jonathan had known Varg for a year now, but the Malric's sheer presence still unsettled him. No matter how familiar, it was impossible to grow comfortable around someone who broke tree trunks by accident.

"Remind me never to get on your bad side," Jonathan said as he looked at the shattered log beneath him.

Varg looked genuinely perplexed, tilting his massive head as if Jonathan had spoken nonsense. "All sides of me are bad," he said with total sincerity. "That is why enemies die when they surround me."

Jonathan blinked. "That's not… okay. Sure."

Jonathan exhaled through his nose. There was no winning with Drekkar and Varg, and he felt a headache coming on from the conversation.

Silence settled between them as they watched the clearing below, the humid air heavy as stone. Jonathan's chest tightened, every breath a reminder of the weight pressing down on him. One last mission. That was what they had promised him—one final task before his chains were cut. But instead of relief, all he felt was just… nervous. Nerves stacked on nerves, until it was all he could feel.

His mind began to drift.

One year ago today, after being left for dead on the beach, it was Drekkar's Malric pride who had taken him in. Jonathan remembered little of those first days—just fevered flashes of pain, shadowed figures speaking in ominous tones, and the bitter sting of strange salves smeared across his wounds. They'd kept him alive—though he wasn't sure if it was out of mercy or morbid curiosity.

They rarely spoke the common tongue, but he'd learned theirs, picking it up in pieces through grunts, gestures, and the occasional thrown object when he got something wrong. It hadn't taken long for him to become one of them. Or close enough. Life among the Malrics was brutal but fair. They demanded hard labor, and he gave it willingly. He hunted, hauled supplies, trained, and fought beside them.

It wasn't until two months living with the pride that they informed him—casually, over dinner—that he was, technically, a slave.

Drekkar had chuckled, his silver hair flashing in the firelight. "You are property, boy. Bought with blood and debt." He tore a chunk from his meal with sharp teeth and chewed thoughtfully. "Did you think we were feeding you out of generosity?"

Jonathan had choked on his food. "I'm *what*?"

"You work. You fight. You eat. You live. That is the way of things." He waved a clawed hand lazily. "You did not run, so we kept you. You did not die, so we trained you. You did not listen, so we beat it into you." He shrugged. "And now, you are one of us. More or less. We've made worse investments. Like that idiot who tried to ride a sky serpent."

Jonathan stared at him. "You're telling me I've been a slave *this whole time*?"

Varg snorted. "Strange how humans always need a word for things. You have food, shelter, strength. Is that not enough?" He smirked, showing far too many teeth. "But if it makes you feel better, we paid almost nothing for you. You're definitely more valuable than a hunting knife. Maybe two knives. I mean, you obviously smell weird. But at least you can lift things."

It was as close to a compliment as the Malrics got.

27

It hadn't really made him feel better.

A year and a day—that had been the price. And now, with the sun sinking behind the distant branches, only one thing stood between him and freedom. Drekkar had told him if he completed one last task, he would release Jonathan from service, and he would be free to search Ydrathar for his friends, for the other Sky People.

The wind shifted, pulling Jonathan from his memories, and he felt it—an unnatural stillness that settled over the jungle like a held breath. The birds quieted. The insects vanished. Even the leaves, always swaying in Ydrathar's eternal breeze, seemed to freeze in place.

Then the sound came.

A low, rising tremor in the air—not thunder, not wind—but something powerful, primal. The kind of sound that made the hairs on the back of his neck rise and his heart forget how to beat.

Branches groaned. Leaves tore loose and spiraled upward instead of down.

And then it came.

The sky serpent tore through the canopy like a lightning bolt unbound, silver scales flashing in the morning light, wings outstretched in a sweeping arc that spanned nearly the width of the entire clearing. It landed, massive talons sinking into the mossy earth with a thunderous *whumph* that sent dust and pollen billowing like a fog around it.

It was a juvenile sky serpent, Drekkar had said—but Jonathan had rarely seen anything so massive. Twice the length of one of Aetherium's transport barges, its tail coiled and uncoiled with hypnotic menace. Muscles rippled beneath iridescent scales that shifted from liquid silver to deep sky blue as it moved. Eyes like twin moons locked onto the field, bright and unblinking.

This was not a creature meant for taming. This was a living force of nature, a study in contrast—graceful and terrible, majestic and lethal. Its wings, thin but edged in jagged ridges, flared wide to dry in the sun. Each breath it took sent a shiver through the air, like a volcano dreaming beneath the surface.

"So what's the last mission you've got for me?" Jonathan asked quietly.

Drekkar shifted uncomfortably—a rare sight for someone usually as unshakable as bedrock.

"I'll be honest, young Sky Cub... I didn't think he'd be quite this... big."

Jonathan sighed as his headache worsened. "Just get to the point."

Drekkar's gaze swept the beast. He pointed slowly.

"There," he whispered, voice low and reverent. "The Eyes of the Night Father."

Jonathan squinted. "Where?"

Drekkar hesitated. "Ah. Yes. That's the thing. I probably should've mentioned—it's, uh... under its tail."

Jonathan blinked. "I'm sorry—what?"

Drekkar pointed to a small black object, no bigger than Jonathan's hand, nestled just beneath a ridge of scaled flesh. Smooth, cylindrical, and utterly ordinary-looking—except for the faint gleam that hinted at something that didn't belong. Something powerful.

"Long story," Drekkar said. "Some fool tried to trap the sky serpent. The Eyes went flying. Lodged itself right under the third scale behind its left hind leg. Perfect fit, really."

Jonathan stared at him. "You're telling me the mythical artifact I need to retrieve to earn my freedom… is currently jammed between the scales of a sky lizard the size of a small mountain?"

Varg nodded without blinking. "Yes. Be swift."

Jonathan exhaled. "This is the dumbest day of my life."

"Not if you die," answered Varg. "Then it's just your last."

Jonathan turned back to the clearing, heart thudding. The serpent's tail shifted slightly, massive coils twitching with the lazy menace of something that could crush a house without trying. Each of its slow, slumbering breaths stirred the jungle floor like distant thunder.

And there it was. The Eyes of the Night Father.

A myth. A relic. His path to freedom.

Lodged in the hide of a creature that could eat him in a single bite.

Jonathan was fast. But was he faster than a sky serpent?

He was just about to move when Drekkar raised a hand.

"Wait," the old tiger said. "One more thing. Very important."

Jonathan paused and turned to him, studying the wizened Malric. Malrics were strange. In so many ways, they were nothing like humans. Wild, feral, brutal. They lived by instinct and honor, spoke more with action than words, and believed loyalty was something proven, not claimed. They were blunt, ferocious, and often terrifying.

But they were also loyal to the bone. Courage ran in their blood. They didn't lie, didn't scheme, didn't pretend to be something they weren't. If a tiger gave their word, it was carved in stone. They protected their own, shared what they had, and stood beside you in battle without needing to be asked. Fierce, yes—but fiercely good in the ways that mattered most.

Drekkar met his gaze, his normally cloudy eyes now gleaming like amber.

"Remember," he said, voice dry as bark, "don't die. It's a mess to clean up after."

Then—just barely—he smiled.

And Jonathan did too. But even as he did, he knew. His freedom—his future—was sitting right there in the coiled shadow of a nightmare. And if he wanted it... he had to take it.

But now, there was no more time for wise words.

Only the hunt.

He bolted.

No hesitation. No second thoughts. Just raw instinct and pounding feet, heart hammering, arms pumping, he ran for the object, eyes locked on the small, dark cylinder. During his time with the tigers of Ydrathar he had learned to run as silent as a whisper, and he had never been more grateful for that fact. He reached the serpent in a breathless blur, the heat radiating from the coiled serpent like the world's largest oven. Jonathan didn't dare slow down. His hand shot out. Fingers closed around the object. Lighter than he expected.

He yanked it free—and the moment he did, the ground seemed to shudder beneath his feet. The serpent stirred. A low, thunderous exhale rolled through the clearing, and Jonathan's stomach dropped as he ran back toward Varg and Drekkar.

The sky serpent exploded into motion behind him—wings snapping open with a deafening crack that split the air like lightning. Its roar followed, a bone-shaking bellow that stripped leaves from trees, and the entire jungle seemed to reel from it, the very world tearing at the seams behind him.

Branches slashed at his arms. Vines clawed at his legs. His lungs burned. His heart slammed against his ribs. A glance over his shoulder confirmed what instinct already knew: the serpent was coming fast. Insanely fast. Like a living storm with teeth.

No way he could outrun it. A dozen seconds—maybe less.

Plan B.

He veered left, leapt over a fallen trunk, and sprinted toward the cliff edge just ahead—an abrupt drop into green mist and open sky.

He jumped.

The jungle vanished beneath him, swallowed by open air and the vast shimmer of a lake below. Wind howled past his ears. The water rushed up to meet him.

He hit like a stone.

The impact knocked the breath from his lungs. Cold closed in, swallowing him whole. He sank deep, deeper, the weight of the lake muffling the chaos above. His lungs burned, but he stayed under. Counting heartbeats. Letting the silence wrap around him.

Only when his lungs threatened to mutiny did he kick toward the surface.

He broke through with a gasp, sucking in air, blinking water from his vision.

Silence.

The sky serpent was gone.

Later, long after the adrenaline had faded and the weariness had set in, Jonathan stumbled back into camp— dripping wet, scraped, bruised, and clutching the prize like it might vanish if he let go. *The Eyes of the Night Father.*

He dropped the black cylindrical object into Varg's lap, then collapsed onto a mossy log. "So go on, enlighten me. What's so great about this ridiculous little thing that you risked my glorious, irreplaceable life?"

With theatrical reverence, Varg opened the case.

Inside, nestled in a velvet lining, was...

A pair of sunglasses.

Jonathan stared. "No. No, no, no."

Varg, solemn as stone, lifted the shades with both clawed hands. Then, with deliberate weight, he slipped them onto his broad, striped face.

"What do you think?" he asked, voice low, suppressed grin on his weathered face.

Jonathan blinked. "You've got to be kidding me."

Varg remained motionless, radiating gravitas behind the tinted lenses.

"This—*this* was the mission?" Jonathan threw his hands up. "I nearly got eaten alive by a sky serpent—for *sunglasses?*"

"Yes. Now I am invisible. You cannot see my eyes, therefore I cannot be surprised."

Jonathan's hands curled into fists as frustration flared hot in his chest. This wasn't the first time Varg had gifted him a splitting headache. He sighed and rubbed at his temples, as if sheer willpower could ease the pounding behind his eyes.

Varg sat in silence for a long moment, the sunglasses perched precariously on his broad muzzle. Then, slowly, his ears flattened, and a deep scowl creased his scarred face.

With a growl, he tore them off, the thin arms snapping like twigs in his massive hands. In one smooth motion, he hurled the shattered pieces into the jungle, where they vanished into the undergrowth with a faint clatter.

"I hate them!" he snarled, shaking out his mane as if to rid himself of the last trace of the glasses. "No one told me they would make everything darker."

Jonathan blinked at him, speechless.

Varg crossed his arms, still glowering. "What kind of cursed artifact makes the world worse when you wear it?"

Jonathan pinched the bridge of his nose. "…They're sunglasses, Varg. That's literally their purpose."

Varg grunted. "Then they are evil. Good riddance."

Varg and Drekkar began to trek back to their camp. Jonathan sighed and followed after his friends. The great quest was over, the prize destroyed, and Jonathan wasn't sure if he wanted to laugh or cry—so he settled for neither. Sunglasses or not, he had survived, and that meant the chains were broken. His freedom was his at last.

Now he just had to claim it.

CHAPTER 2
THE UNMAKING TIDE

As Jonathan, Drekkar, and Varg neared the encampment, the familiar blend of weathered hides, charred meat, and damp earth hit them like a welcome mat soaked in smoke and sweat.

Home.

The pride's territory was a sprawling mess of rough-hewn wooden huts, stretched-hide canopies, and lounging Malrics draped across heavy logs, gnawing on massive bones. Others busied themselves sharpening weapons, and a pair of younger tigers wrestled near the fire, growling and snapping at each other.

Dinner passed in the usual way: loud, messy, full of tigers shouting over one another, and lots of red meat. (Jonathan had long since learned that the second he so much as glanced at a piece of fruit, they mocked his "weak prey guts" and acted like he was about to sprout antlers and flee into the underbrush.)

And then, just as they were finishing their meals, Drekkar addressed Jonathan in front of the pride.

"You have served your time," he said, tearing a chunk of meat from the bone. "Tomorrow, you are free to go."

Just like that. No fanfare, no ceremony, no dramatic speech about honor or duty.

Jonathan stared, half-expecting more. Another test. One final challenge. A ritual. A fight to prove himself. Some grand moment of reflection beneath the stars. But no—just a simple statement, delivered as casually as a weather report.

He idly poked at the last of his food, exhaling slowly.

So. That was it, then. Tomorrow, he would be free.

He should've felt relieved. He should've been enjoying his last night among the Malrics—these fierce, wild, impossible people who had become, in their own way, a kind of family. But instead, his chest felt tight.

It wasn't hesitation. He *wanted* to leave. He needed to find his friends—El, Valera, Israel—all the people he'd been separated from for so long. And yet, after a year in this place—working, fighting, surviving alongside Varg, Drekkar, and the rest of the pride—walking away suddenly felt more complicated than he'd expected.

And underneath it all was something else. A growing unease. He knew the Tiger King and the Unmaking Tide were drawing closer. Drekkar's pride had survived on the far edges of the Wild, mostly untouched by the king's reach. But that wouldn't last. The storm was coming. And part of him wondered if leaving now was abandoning the very people who had saved his life.

Varg dropped down beside Jonathan with all the grace of a falling boulder, his great mane spilled over his shoulders in a thick, untamed curtain. He said nothing for a long time, just chewed, watched the fire, and let his tail flick lazily across the dirt.

Then, out of nowhere, he spoke.

"You may touch it."

Jonathan blinked. "Uh… what?"

Varg didn't look at him. He just nodded toward the massive war axe strapped across his back. "Once."

Jonathan sat up straighter, eyebrows raised. "Wait. Seriously?"

Varg sighed, like he was already regretting the decision. "One time. No more."

Jonathan hesitated. This had to be a trap. Malrics didn't share their weapons—didn't even let others look at them too long. He'd once seen one snap a man's wrist for brushing against a hilt. But Varg wasn't joking. Slowly, Jonathan reached out and ran his fingers along the weapon's scarred handle. The wood was warm. Worn smooth from use. Varg's shoulders tensed like steel cable, his jaw clenching—but he didn't move.

The gesture was generous. Terrifying, but generous.

Varg picked a piece of meat from between his teeth and flicked it into the fire. "Try not to be useless while you're out there."

And so it went. Every member of the pride had their own way of saying goodbye.

Ruhn shoved a bundle of dried meat into his hands without a word, barely glancing at him before grumbling, "You eat like a dying animal. Try not to starve." She stalked off before he could even attempt to thank her. Kareth One-Eye chose a different approach—he nearly dislocated Jonathan's shoulder with a "friendly" punch, smirking as he said, "Try not to get yourself killed. Or do. More food for the rest of us." Jonathan was still massaging his arm when Torvek, the grizzled old Malric who had never spoken to him a single time, walked up without warning and flicked Jonathan's ear. Hard. Then he just grunted and walked away, leaving Jonathan completely baffled.

That night, Jonathan's throat was tight as he crawled into his sleeping roll and stared up at the dark sky. A year ago, he had been nothing but a half-dead outsider, a burden, an amusing pet at best. But now? Now they were sending him off the only way Malrics knew how—by pretending they weren't going to miss him at all.

And the truth was, he could stay if he wanted to. He had known that for some time. Beneath all their gruff posturing, they had accepted him as one of their own. No different than any other member of the pride. And if he chose to remain, they would let him. He could carve out a life here—he already had, piece by piece, hunt by hunt, one backbreaking task at a time.

But tomorrow, he was leaving. He wanted to leave.

Still, stars help him, he was going to miss these insufferable brutes.

But fate had rarely been kind to him, and by the time the sun rose, his path would be soaked in blood.

Jonathan woke to a hand clamped tightly over his mouth.

He jolted, instinctively reaching for the knife at his waist, the one his father had given him long ago, but stopped when he saw the eyes staring back at him—wide, urgent, unmistakably Ruhn's. She shook her head, slow and firm, and pressed a finger to her lips.

His heart was pounding. Not from the wake-up, but from her expression. Something was wrong.

She lifted her hand, and Jonathan slowly sat up. Around them, the rest of the pride slept in scattered heaps, the soft grumble of feline breathing rising like the distant growl of a mountain storm. The fire had long since gone to embers. Shadows loomed thick between the roots.

Ruhn motioned for him to follow into the underbrush. Jonathan rose and followed, each step careful, slow—

Too slow.

A distant *snap* of undergrowth. A huff of breath. A low, guttural growl—wrong, unfamiliar.

Ruhn froze mid-step.

It was too late.

Shapes poured into the clearing like a wave of darkness: hulking bodies, glinting fangs, snarls like war drums. Malric warriors—but not Drekkar's. Their fur was painted with war sigils, and their eyes shone wild and silver in the moonlight.

Jonathan had never seen them before, but he knew exactly who they were. Drekkar had spoken of them often—

and always with venom. He believed they were infected, tainted by the same Rot that was corrupting the World Tree from within. They called themselves the Unmaking Tide— Malrics twisted by darkness, granted strength and power in exchange for something far worse: Bloodlust.

Prides like Drekkar's followed the Old Ways— hunting, feasting, guarding their territory, settling disputes with claw and blade under the watchful eye of sacred customs. But the Tide was different. They had abandoned the Old Ways long ago. While other prides bickered over borders and rites, the Tide marched. They absorbed the fallen into their ranks, conquering pride after pride until their numbers swelled beyond anything Ydrathar had seen. And with that growth came something unheard of among the Malrics—a structure. A hierarchy sharpened by war. The Tide was no longer a pride. They were an army. Trained. Ruthless. Obedient. And worst of all, they no longer served custom, tradition, or even pride. They bent the knee to something else entirely: a king.

The Tiger King.

And rumor had it, the Unmaking Tide killed all humans on sight.

Jonathan barely had time to process that thought before they had surrounded Jonathan's pride. The Malric warriors were at least a hundred strong, their sheer numbers blotting out the moonlight as they filled the jungle clearing. And they didn't wear the patchwork hunting leathers of Drekkar's pride. No—these tigers were clad in battle armor, dark and jagged, built for war rather than survival. Their weapons gleamed, cruel and heavy, designed for breaking bones rather than skinning kills.

Drekkar's pride wouldn't stand a chance.

From the formation of Tide warriors, one stepped forward. He was taller. Broader. His fur, once the same color as fire, was now streaked with grime and sickly patches where some dark disease had taken hold. Half his jaw was gone, consumed by the Rot and replaced with a grotesque construct of fused bone and dark metal, bolted directly into his skull. The rest of his face was a collection of battle scars and injuries, one of them twisting his muzzle into a sneer, another across his eye that left it discolored.

But his presence drew the eye not through flourish, but through stillness. Every movement he made was precise and controlled, the kind of economy born from discipline, not hesitation.

He stopped at the center of the clearing and lifted his gaze.

"I am Prince Raulg, sky serpent's bane, blood cousin to the Tiger King, and warlord of the Unmaking Tide" he declared. "And I will speak to Drekkar."

To Jonathan's surprise, Raulg's words were flat, devoid of weight or intent. Not angry. Not cold. Just *empty*. His voice fell into the night like dry stone on wet earth, neither loud nor soft—just disturbingly neutral, as if even tone had been stripped away.

A hush fell over the camp. The sleeping pride stirred, ears twitching, tails lashing. One by one, they rose, tense and wary.

Then, slowly, Drekkar emerged from his hut.

His cane tapped softly on the earth, his frame stooped but unbowed. Age had settled on him, but it had not broken him. His eyes were sharp beneath his heavy brow, his jaw set with the quiet fury of a warrior who had survived too long. He sighed, then rubbed a clawed hand down his muzzle, as if exasperated.

"Ah. There you are," Drekkar muttered. "Thought I smelled something rotten."

"You will join the Tide," Raulg said, his blackened jaw making strange wet, clicking noises as his voice echoed through the clearing.

Drekkar snorted, tilting his head. "Hnn. Knew one of you would come scratching at my den sooner or later." He sighed, stretching his back like this whole thing was an inconvenience. "And now I get to say what I been meaning to say for years. You and every one of your friends can shove your tail between your legs and leave. There. Told you. Now off you go."

Raulg showed no anger at the disrespect, and instead thundered calmly, "Join us, Drekkar. The Tree cannot save you. Not any more. Join us. Join the Unmaking Tide, and you will receive power beyond anything you've ever known. Refuse... and you will not leave this place alive."

"Ydrathar take you," Drekkar answered, though there was more resignation in his voice than anger. "You think you can conquer her? Rule her? Twist her children into your little army? But Ydrathar doesn't bow. Not to kings. Not to armies. And sure as vines strangle slow, not to fools and cultists like you."

Raulg's face made no expression at all.

43

"Ydrathar—the World Tree—is dying. And with it, your religion," he said simply. "Not by accident. The Tiger King means to kill her, and he will soon accomplish his designs. That is why you no longer hear her speak. Can you not feel it? The Rot is winning; the Tree is dying. The prophecy is unfolding, and there's nothing left to stop it. Join the Tide… or drown in it."

Jonathan felt something shift inside him as the words sank in. The rumors had never been clear—some said the Rot had birthed the Tiger King, others claimed he had risen and claimed the Rot for himself. But now, as Raulg spoke, the pieces clicked together. The Tiger King wasn't simply another victim of the Rot. He was steering it. Feeding it. Turning its corruption into a weapon as he hunted for more—and the World Tree itself was his ultimate goal.

Drekkar's eyes narrowed, a flicker of sorrow passing through them. "She doesn't speak as often as she once did, it's true," he admitted quietly. "But she has seen worse days than this. She will outlast even you."

The warriors laughed. But to Jonathan's surprise, Raulg's ugly eyes held as much emotion as if he were watching grass grow.

"The Tiger King has already set his course. He has entered the Hollow. He has found the Sunken City. He will strike at the heart of Ydrathar itself. Before the next full moon rises, your religion will die. And with it will come the End of All Things."

A hush fell at Raulg's declaration. Not that it mattered. Jonathan wasn't listening anymore.

He saw something he hadn't expected.

Raulg stood motionless in the clearing, and in his hand—

Jonathan's breath caught.

It was his sword.

Jonathan's sword.

He recognized it instantly. Valera had given him that blade in what felt like another life. It no longer shimmered green, and whatever power it once held had long since gone quiet, but he would have known it anywhere. That sword was part of him.

And so was the memory of the one who had taken it.

The past hit him like a tidal wave—blood, pain, the fight on the beach. That hopeless, savage struggle. He'd been outmatched from the start, a boy swinging at a storm. He hadn't even left a scratch on the Malric who faced him. Jonathan's heartbeat pounded in his ears. He forced a slow breath, willing his fingers to unclench.

That fight had nearly killed him. And now, the warrior who'd nearly ended him stood before him—with Jonathan's sword in hand. And Jonathan felt something flare inside him—sharp and stubborn.

Defiance.

Defiance. Resistance. Pure contrariness. The memory of that blade going through him, the helplessness on the beach, the shame of losing—it all boiled up at once. He knew he was severely outmatched and outnumbered. Knew that rushing into the clearing would be suicide. But none of that mattered. Someone had to stand up to this brute. Someone had to see that justice was done. And for some infuriating, irrational reason, Jonathan wanted to be that someone.

Ruhn seemed to sense what was about to happen and she grabbed Jonathan by the arm, but he slipped away and stepped forward, out of the shadows and into the glow of the dying fire.

Every eye turned to him.

The enemy warriors blinked in confusion, ears flicking back in mild surprise as their gazes shifted toward the brush.

"Aww," Raulg said, recognition flashing briefly across his scarred muzzle. "The Skywarrior." His voice oozed recognition, laced with something colder, darker. "It would appear you've made quite a name for yourself since I gutted you with your own sword a year ago. What a pleasant prize we've stumbled upon this fine evening."

He took a slow step closer, his gaze gleaming with cruel amusement.

"Normally, the Tiger King executes your kind the moment they're found. His hatred for your species runs deep—deeper than blood, deeper than root. He dreams of a world purged of Skyborn entirely, where no trace of your kind remains on the branches or roots. But you..." Raulg's lip curled into something that might've been a grin. "For you, I suspect he'll make an exception."

He paused, savoring the moment.

"Indeed, he's been searching for you for quite some time. He'll be most pleased when I deliver him such a prize."

Jonathan didn't flinch. "Been a year and he's still looking?" he said, tone dry. "Sounds like your king's got a lot of muscle—just not much upstairs."

Raulg growled, a deep, gravelly sound that rumbled in his chest. His hand dropped to the hilt of his stolen sword.

"Have a care with your tongue," he said, voice low. "Not all insults end with breath left to regret them."

"Oh, I've got plenty more where that came from." He stepped forward slightly, eyes locked on the towering warrior. "But right now, I can do you one better."

He squared his shoulders, meeting those cold, hollow eyes with a fire of his own.

"I challenge you to a duel."

Raulg looked at Jonathan, but there was no reaction. No flicker of recognition, no shift in expression. It was as if he hadn't even registered that the boy had spoken at all. His gaze passed over Jonathan like wind over stone—impersonal, indifferent, utterly void of meaning.

"To the death," added Jonathan.

CHAPTER 3
A VERY SMALL BLADE AND AN EXTREMELY OVERCONFIDENT PLAN

J onathan reached to his waist, fingers closing around the knife he had carried most of life, the only relic of his father. He drew it and held it out in front of him, steady despite the pounding in his chest. Firelight danced along the blade's short edge—three inches of honed steel.

Three inches. The same length as one of his opponent's fangs.

The corrupted Malrics exploded in uproar—growls, roars, laughter, a storm of hisses and frenzy.

"He is a slave!" one snarled. "His life is owned. He has no right!"

"A Skyborn cannot challenge a Malric!" another spat, fangs bared. "It is forbidden!"

Jonathan clenched his teeth. They were probably right. Malrics lived by custom and law—deep-rooted traditions passed down in blood and battle. Even the Tide still clung to a few of the Old Ways, twisted though they were. But those rites rarely extended to outsiders. Certainly not to Skyborn.

Jonathan gripped the blade tighter. If Raulg refused the challenge, there would be no duel—just a slaughter. Him. Drekkar. The rest of the pride. None of them would join the Tide, which meant none of them would survive the night.

Somehow, he had to make the monster believe this mattered.

But the warlord did not react. Did not move. Jonathan felt it—that horrible, creeping stillness. The deadness in those pale, unblinking eyes.

"What's the matter? You afraid?" Jonathan taunted, letting the words settle. "Or do you only fight battles when you outnumber your enemy three to one?"

"Listen to it squeak!" one of the Tide cackled. "Thinks it can stand among us!"

"What's next? Will it claim a pride?" another scoffed. "He is nothing! A pet!"

"He should be on his knees, not holding a blade!"

But Jonathan ignored them and pressed forward, forcing his voice to carry above the din.

"I claim rite by the Law of Blood and Flame," Jonathan called, the words Drekkar had once muttered in passing now burning in his memory. "I offer my life for the lives behind me. Let the Tree decide who stands."

"The Law of Blood and Flame? But you are no Malric. You have no right to claim such," growled Raulg. There was no anger in his voice, only the tone of one speaking to something so far beneath him it didn't warrant his attention.

"He *is* Malric," Drekkar growled, and bared his fangs at Raulg. By freeing him, Jonathan had become one of them, and Drekkar would respect that until his dying breath. "More Malric than you, you water-logged, bark-chewing, soft-pawed disgrace to your kind."

But still they scoffed. It wasn't until Jonathan's voice cut once more through the murmuring crowd they silenced.

"The stakes," Jonathan said, leveling his gaze at the emotionless leader. "If I win, you leave. But if you win…" Jonathan rolled his shoulders, like he was settling in for something inevitable. "We march under your banner. No fights. No resistance. We'll fight for you."

A ripple passed through the gathered Malrics. Some scoffed. Others growled low in their throats. Even in Drekkar's pride, warriors shifted uneasily, tails flicking, ears twitching. None of them—not even his own pride—had ever seen Jonathan fight in direct combat. They had seen him hunt, seen him endure, seen him survive. But fighting? Fighting was different.

Especially against one such as Raulg.

Drekkar hobbled closer, his cane pressing into the dirt with each slow and limping step. His gaze was heavy, unreadable, but Jonathan could feel the weight of it.

A pride fought together, hunted together, bled together. Stood together. Honored each other's agreements and challenges.

And if Jonathan had issued a challenge… then they would stand by it.

Drekkar exhaled, the sound more sigh than growl. He looked at Jonathan for a long moment, something like resignation in his eyes, then turned to face Raulg.

"The challenge has been made," Drekkar declared, and turned to face the Tide. "And family is more than blood; more than lineage. Jonathan is a part of my pride. And a pride stands by its own."

For a long, suffocating moment, Raulg simply stared at him, his deadened eyes flat and empty. Then, at last, he inclined his head.

"So be it," Raulg said. His voice was a low, grinding growl, like stone breaking under immense weight.

The warriors around them rumbled—some in approval, more in protest—but they all obeyed. Clawed feet scraped against the packed earth as they widened the clearing. Weapons were lowered, but no one sheathed them. Not yet.

Drekkar exhaled beside him, the firelight carving deep shadows into his face. "Hope you have a plan."

Jonathan rolled his shoulders, adjusting his grip on the knife. "Working on it."

Across from him, Raulg stood still, waiting. Watching. There was no more room for talk—only the fight. And now that it was just the two of them, Jonathan finally took a good, hard look at his opponent. Six and a half feet of muscle and armor. Predator's teeth bared in the flickering firelight. Claws that could shred through steel. A sword— Jonathan's sword—gripped effortlessly in one massive hand. Rot deep in his flesh, a warped lattice of blackened growths, raw and slick, as though corruption itself had been hammered into bone.

And the eyes. Cold. Empty. Unfeeling.

It was the same Malric who had driven that blade into his gut and left him to rot on the beach. And he had done it without hesitation. Without effort. Like putting down a stray dog. Jonathan knew he should be afraid. Any sane person would be.

And yet... he wasn't.

The fear never came.

Not because Raulg wasn't terrifying—he was. But Jonathan had spent a year in Ydrathar, in the company of creatures just as deadly. He had learned their ways, learned how to still the tremor in his hands, how to steady his breath when stalking prey far deadlier than himself.

And he had changed.

He was taller now, heavier, every ounce of weight earned through blood and labor. His body had hardened with the brutal demands of the life of a hunter—dense bone, thick muscle, the kind of strength built from survival, not comfort.

Fear had its place. But not here. Not now.

He shifted his stance, rolling his shoulders, exhaling slow and steady. He wasn't the same boy who had fallen on the beach a year ago. And this time, he wouldn't be the one left bleeding in the dirt. Because this time, he *did* have a plan.

To everyone's surprise it was Jonathan that attacked first.

Raulg was strong—Jonathan had expected that. He was massive, a walking wall of muscle and armor, and the brute moved like an earthquake given form, each swing of his sword cleaving through the air with enough force to split stone. Jonathan barely dodged, twisting away at the last possible second. A fraction slower, and he wouldn't have survived it.

Jonathan could feel it in his bones—if this turned into a contest of raw power, he'd lose. He couldn't block, couldn't go toe to toe with a creature three times his weight.

But he didn't need to.

He was faster.

Jonathan inhaled sharply, reaching for the pull of gravity beneath his skin. The weight of the world shifted around him, and suddenly, he was lighter—just enough. He moved—faster than before, faster than any of those watching expected. He dodged another crushing swing, barely managing to roll out of the way before the sword carved a trench in the ground where he'd stood. He lashed out with his knife, striking at the gaps in the Malric's armor—his side, his leg, anywhere unprotected.

But it wasn't enough. The armor was too thick. His blade barely left a scratch.

Think. Adapt.

Fortunately, he had something else up his sleeve.

His knife was worthless against the Malric's plating—but the sword in his opponent's hand? That was a different story. And it wasn't just any sword. Jonathan knew that blade. He had a bond with it. He could feel it, humming just beyond his reach, calling to him, aching to be in his hands once more.

And so, he went for it.

The next time the Malric swung, Jonathan twisted to the side, darting in close. He wasn't aiming for the body this time. He was aiming for the hand.

His knife found its mark, sinking deep into the Malric's wrist.

Not a killing blow—not even close—but it was enough.

The sword betrayed its new owner. The beast snarled, and for the first time, stumbled. And just as Jonathan had hoped—the sword flew from his grip.

The sword had betrayed Raulg.

Everyone saw it.

For a heartbeat, the battlefield was silent. Stunned. Disbelieving. Even Jonathan could barely process what had just happened. He had struck the first blow.

Malrics did *not* lose their weapons. They did not fumble. They did not—could not—be separated from their blades so easily. And yet, there it was, stuck in the dirt twenty yards away.

All those gathered around stared. Some in awe, some in shock, others in a deep, unsettled horror.

Raulg moved first.

A snarl tore from his throat as he lunged—not for Jonathan, but for the sword.

He was closer. He should have reached it first.

Jonathan had two seconds. Maybe less.

But he was smiling.

The Malric didn't know it yet, but this fight had never been fair.

Jonathan didn't even reach with his hands. He didn't need to. Instead, he reached with something deeper—the pull of gravity that had whispered to him for years, the invisible force that had always been there, waiting. He grabbed hold of it, twisted it, called to the blade.

And the sword answered.

It ripped from the ground in a burst of motion, black steel cutting through the air. The Malric barely had time to react before the blade flew past him, straight into Jonathan's waiting hand.

The moment his fingers closed around the hilt, the world shifted.

Power roared through him, wild and untamed, a surge of raw energy that sent a shockwave rippling outward. It was like finding a part of himself he hadn't even realized was missing. The sword recognized him. Welcomed him. Green fire erupted along the blade, searing through the air with an eerie, untamed glow. Runes flared to life, timeless and brilliant, burning like embers whipped into a storm. The very air around him hummed, alive with something fierce, something righteous.

Jonathan blinked, staring at the weapon in his hand. "Whoa," he breathed. "Okay… that's new."

The battle resumed in an instant.

Jonathan barely had time to register the surge of energy flowing through him before the Raulg lunged again, faster, more furious than before. But, with gravity as his ally and the sword as his friend, Jonathan was faster.

The sword moved with him, like an extension of his own body. The green runes along the blade flared, burning bright as he met the Malric head-on. He twisted, sidestepped, slashed—his blade singing as it bit into the Malric's armor. Sparks flew as black steel met plated metal, and piece by piece, the armor fell away.

The Malric was strong—unbelievably strong—but Jonathan was faster. Smarter. More precise. He didn't waste a single movement. Every dodge, every parry, every strike was calculated, stripping away the Malric's defenses one layer at a time.

The watching warriors had fallen into stunned silence.

None of them had ever seen a human fight like this. None of them had ever seen their leader—this giant, this unshakable force of destruction—bleed.

And he was bleeding.

From his arms. His legs. His sides. A dozen cuts, none of them immediately fatal, but all of them real.

Jonathan could feel the battle turning, feel the way his opponent's movements slowed ever so slightly, how his breathing grew heavier, the telltale signs of fatigue setting in. But still, the monster showed no emotion. No anger. No frustration. No pain.

Nothing.

Blow after blow, wound after wound, the Malric didn't even flinch.

Jonathan gritted his teeth, tightening his grip on the sword. *What are you?*

Jonathan saw his opening.

He surged forward, blade flashing green, and slashed—low and fast. His sword carved into the Malric's leg, slicing through sinew and muscle. The monster staggered, its knee buckling beneath its own weight. Jonathan didn't hesitate. He rolled to the side as the beast stumbled forward. Then, with every ounce of strength in his body, he drove his boot into his back.

The Malric crashed down onto all fours, and rolled onto its back. Jonathan moved in an instant, closing the space in a single, fluid motion. His sword gleamed as he brought it down, aiming precisely—not for the kill. Not yet.

The black steel, alight with green fire, rested against Raul's throat. Not deep enough to cut him, but deep enough that if he so much as twitched, it would.

Jonathan's chest heaved, sweat mixing with the blood splattered across his skin. His grip on the hilt was steady as he stood over his fallen enemy, the firelight from the surrounding warriors casting jagged shadows across them both.

"Yield!" Jonathan roared.

Silence fell like a hammer.

Raulg went unnervingly still. Jonathan's grip on the hilt tightened. He had expected more—another desperate struggle, a snarl of defiance, a final, brutal effort to rise. Instead, there was nothing. His stomach twisted. Something was wrong. His blade was still resting against the great tiger's throat, but none of his strikes had been fatal. Not by a long shot. He had fought to submission, not to kill.

Jonathan didn't move, didn't blink. The Malric's heavy chest should have been rising, breath ragged with pain, muscles trembling with exertion. Instead, the massive warrior simply lay there. His face didn't look as though he was hiding fear; more like there was simply nothing there.

And then—he turned his head.

Their gazes locked.

Jonathan braced himself for another attack, for fury, for something. But instead, the Malric's eyes dimmed...

And then, he simply died.

It was like an unseen hand had flipped a switch. One second, he was there. The next, he wasn't. But before the lifeless body could go completely still—before the last flicker of movement left its form—the Malric's mouth parted.

And it spoke. Not in his own voice. Not in any voice Jonathan had ever heard.

"Bring me the Skywarrior."

Jonathan's blood turned to ice.

The dead Malric's blackened eyes remained locked onto his. The voice that rasped from his unmoving mouth was hollow, distant, like an echo from the depths.

"Kill the others."

And then—silence.

A dreadful, choking, absolute silence.

And then the rest of the Tide moved.

Jonathan barely had time to ready his sword before the first one lunged.

CHAPTER 4
DRINK DEEP, THEN DIE

The night shattered with Drekkar's roar.

"Run! To the Sacred Well!"

And just like that, the battle was over before it had even begun.

The Tide warriors surged forward, but Drekkar's pride scattered like shadows in firelight, slipping into the jungle with the fluid grace of hunters who knew every inch of the land. Jonathan was already moving, sprinting between the thick trunks, weaving through the tangled undergrowth. He didn't need to look back to know the Tide was in pursuit. But pursuit was a fool's errand.

Drekkar's pride would never win in open combat—but this wasn't combat. This was a chase. And here in Drekkar's home territory, the Tide were chasing ghosts.

Jonathan moved through the jungle like a shadow, masking his tracks where he could, doubling back when necessary. The towering, ancient trees and the darkness of night devoured him whole, and the deeper he ran, the quieter it became—just the distant howls of the Tide warriors, the rustle of disturbed foliage, the soft whisper of his own breath.

He had no idea how long he ran. Time lost meaning in the dense wild, swallowed by the rhythmic pounding of his feet against the earth, the sweat dripping down his back, the constant push forward. Hours passed in fragments—blades of grass bending beneath his weight, the distant glimmer of predatory eyes in the dark, the slow creep of exhaustion in his limbs. By the time the sky began to shift from the deep purple of night to the pale blue of morning, he had made it.

The Sacred Well.

Jonathan exhaled, stepping cautiously into the clearing.

He was the first to arrive.

The Sacred Well was nothing grand—just a simple spring tucked into the jungle's vastness, its name carrying more weight than the place itself. No towering ruins, no archaic carvings, no mystical aura. Just a quiet pool of clear water, its surface rippling gently as it fed a narrow stream that disappeared into the undergrowth. But for generations, it had been a waypoint, a meeting ground when hunting in this part of the territory—a place of safety, of regrouping.

Jonathan dropped to his knees at the water's edge, cupping his hands and drinking deeply. The cold, crisp rush of it steadied him, washing away the burn in his throat, the ache in his muscles. He let out a slow breath, wiping his mouth with the back of his hand before lifting his gaze.

The jungle around him was alive with its usual murmur—the rustle of leaves, the distant cries of unseen creatures, the steady thrum of life. The Sacred Well might not have looked like much, but at that moment, it was exactly what he needed.

From here, he could see much of Ydrathar.

The jungle stretched endlessly in every direction, a vast, living ocean of emerald and shadow. Towering titan trees loomed over the canopy, their massive limbs tangled with vines as thick as ship ropes. In the distance, a herd of thunder-beasts grazed, their long necks reaching for the highest leaves, their low rumbles reverberating through the humid air. A massive sky-serpent coiled through the clouds, its scales catching the dawn light like shifting shards of glass. Further off, near the banks of a lake fed by a roaring waterfall, a pack of saber-backed prowlers lapped at the water's edge, their massive, muscular forms moving in eerie synchronization.

And beyond it all—Arenthil.

Many of the largest branches of Ydrathar—colossal branches that rose so high their peaks vanished into the clouds above—had names. And now that he was a free man, that was where he intended to go. If his friends were alive, that's where they would be.

The thought surprised him with its intensity. After all this time—after everything—he hadn't let himself feel the weight of their absence. But now, standing here, staring toward the horizon, it hit him all at once. He wanted to see them. To see her…

The survivors trickled in, one by one, but the numbers were fewer than they should have been. Too few. The air was heavy with the absence of those who hadn't made it, the silence filled with the weight of names that would never be spoken again. Jonathan felt it settle deep in his chest, but he forced himself to stand, to watch the tree line, to count every familiar face that emerged from the jungle.

And then, at last, Drekkar appeared.

Jonathan's stomach clenched at the sight of him. The old Malric moved with deliberate steps, his cane dragging slightly, his breath coming in short, shallow bursts, deep pain in his clouded eyes. His fur was matted with blood—too much blood. He was hurt, badly.

The pride rushed to him, instinctively moving to support him, to help, but Drekkar let out a low growl, baring his fangs.

"Enough," he rasped. "I still walk."

Jonathan stepped forward, fists clenched at his sides. "Drekkar—"

The old warrior lifted a hand, silencing him. His eyes, clouded but still sharp, turned toward the well. "Let me drink."

No one spoke as he stepped forward, kneeling with great effort. His claws dipped into the water, cupping it slowly, reverently, as if savoring the weight of it in his hands. He drank deeply, his throat working as he took in the cool water.

Then, with a long, slow sigh, he shifted back, leaning against the thick trunk of a nearby tree. His breath was still shallow, but his expression was calm, content.

Jonathan swallowed hard, his chest tight. "Drekkar?"

The old Malric exhaled, a rough, rumbling chuckle rolling from his chest. "Hnn. Keep your whining to yourself, Sky Cub. I've swiped death across the nose more times than I can count—sooner or later, it was bound to bite back. And a hunter knows when the chase is done."

Drekkar let out a slow breath, lifting his weary gaze to the remains of his pride. Fewer than should have been— many of them ragged and battered, but alive. He studied each face in turn, his expression unreadable, until finally, he gave a small, approving huff.

"You live," he said simply. "That is what matters." His gaze swept over them, sharp despite the exhaustion dragging at him. "You will keep living. Hunting. Fighting. You will not be prey." His lip curled slightly, revealing a flash of fang. "You will not be leashed. Find the Pride of Toth in the shadow of Grimveil. Tell him what has happened. They will take you in, I am sure. He is a great warrior. Together, you can stand against the Unmaking Tide and the Tiger King."

A murmur rippled through the group, low growls and quiet affirmations.

Drekkar nodded once. "Go now. Scatter. Hide your scent, cover your trails. Find the others, the ones who fled. Regroup." His voice hardened. "The Tide have their numbers, but we have Ydrathar. They do not own these lands. They will never own us."

The pride didn't wait for more. No cheers, no questions, no farewells. Just motion—silent, swift, disciplined. It was the way of the Malrics.

They vanished like mist into the trees.

And then there was only Jonathan.

Drekkar's voice grew softer, more strained, and he beckoned for the youth to come closer. Jonathan obeyed, kneeling at the old warrior's side, close enough now to feel the fading heat of his body. For a long moment, Drekkar said nothing. He simply studied him—his foggy eyes still sharp beneath the weight of death, like a burning that refused to go out. Then he exhaled, slow and steady, as if releasing something he'd held onto for far too long.

"Ydrathar is dying, Jonathan," he murmured.

Jonathan's breath caught. Drekkar's hand closed around his wrist—still surprisingly strong—and pulled him closer. "Raulg was right about many things. But he was wrong about one: the Tree still speaks… And what she speaks is agony… She screams of death... Dying… Corruption… The World Tree is beginning to Rot… and I fear she does not have much time."

He paused, gathering what remained of his strength. "There's something at the heart of it. A sickness. It runs deeper than the prides know, deeper than the roots themselves. This Rot—it's not just decay. It's not natural. It's something… Something more."

His breathing grew ragged, the weight of his words thick in the air.

"You must find it," he said, voice a rasp now, rough with urgency. "Go where the Tree runs darkest. Into the Great Hollow, where no light dwells, where even the old ones refuse to tread. There, you will find the Sunken City. The corruption has a source, Jonathan, Ydrathar has told me. Something feeding it, spreading it. And unless you find it—

and kill it—this world will fall. Not just the prides. Not just the jungle. The *entire* World Tree... will die."

Jonathan started to protest. It was an impossible task, and he knew he would never be able to do what his old friend wanted. He shook his head and started to argue, but Drekkar's hand trembled in his grasp, and the old warrior's gaze stayed fixed on him, fierce and unyielding. He coughed again, harsher this time, and a shudder passed through his body. "Promise me, young Jonathan. *Promise* me you'll see it through. Find the source of the Rot. End it. Or all of Ydrathar is doomed."

"I... I can't. That's impossible!"

"For some, maybe. But not for you," said Drekkar.

Something twisted inside him—tight, painful, like roots wrapping around his chest. He wanted to scream that it wasn't fair, that he wasn't strong enough, that this wasn't supposed to be *his* burden. He was just a boy from a broken city in the clouds, not a savior. But as Drekkar's trembling hand gripped his wrist, Jonathan felt the weight settle on his shoulders. It wasn't just the request of a dying friend—it was the last will of a people, a forest, a world trying not to vanish.

"Why me?"

"Why you?" Drekkar echoed, and a fit of coughing overtook him. Blood touched the corners of his mouth, but his voice, when it returned, was low and steady. "Because you don't have the size of a tiger. Or its strength. You lack its instincts, its fangs, its claws."

Of course—of course even on his deathbed the old tiger would insult him. Jonathan wanted to protest, to shoot back some sarcastic retort, but nothing came. His throat burned, and his voice caught somewhere behind the lump rising there.

Drekkar's ears twitched. His breath came shallower now, but the corner of his mouth curved. "Don't look like that. Thought you'd be used to my insults by now."

Jonathan snorted, rubbing a hand over his face. "You're dying, old friend."

"Doesn't mean I have to be nice about it," he said. And though his face was pained, there was still a friendly smile hidden in his wrinkled face.

"What I'm trying to say is… you may not look like a tiger. But you've got the heart of one. And Ydrathar… while she cannot see the future with a perfect clarity, she can see things the rest of us do not. And she has chosen you… She spoke to me, Jonathan. And she has summoned you…"

But Jonathan shook his head, voice breaking. "I don't know the way—I can't fight an *army!* I don't even know where to start!"

Drekkar looked patiently at his young friend. He paused, considered his last words carefully. "There will be moments when you may choose your own path, my young friend. And there are other moments when the path chooses you, and you must walk the path of duty."

Then Drekkar reached out and gripped his wrist.

Before Jonathan could react, the old tiger pressed his hand into the soil.

The world vanished.

In the blink of an eye, a torrent of images slammed into Jonathan's mind in a vision—raw and vivid, as if the World Tree itself had reached into him and pulled open his soul.

First came a vision of the Rot. And for the first time, Jonathan understood. It offered power—but demanded a price. Freedom was the first to fall. Then will. Then thought. What remained was hunger. Bloodlust. A hollow strength bound to something far darker.

Then came a vision of the future. The Rot spreading, devouring branch after branch, root after root. The flowers blackened. The creatures twisted. Spores thick as smoke choked the air, and blossoms bloomed with teeth. Tigers, humans, beasts, all warped into monsters. And at the center of it all, the Tiger King, drunk on power, his body aflame with the corruption he had willingly embraced.

Then Jonathan saw the entirety of Ydrathar the World Tree transformed—not dead, but reborn as something monstrous. The World Tree, once radiant with life, had become a towering engine of ruin. Its branches curled like claws against the sky, blackened and smoldering, oozing with veins of rot. Where once it had cradled life, it now exhaled death. The Tree had become something else. No longer mother, no longer guardian, but a ravenous demon, a towering, thinking extinction event.

The Tree no longer gave life. It *hunted* it.

And then Jonathan watched as the mighty tree turned its gaze upward.

One by one, the floating cities of men—the last known remnants of the old world—were dragged from the heavens like prey, their engines sputtering, their citizens screaming as they fell. Aetherium collapsed in a storm of ash and flame, its remaining towers shattering like glass against the twisted canopy below. Lights went out. Skies turned black. Screaming voices vanished in fire and fog as Aetherium and all its people were swallowed whole by a guardian-tree gone mad.

Finally, Jonathan saw the Heart of the Tree, and he understood that this was how it existed now, in this very moment: a glowing green light, pulsing weakly within the hollow of the trunk—faint, fragile, and pure. It shimmered with light, goodness, memory. With *life.*

But it was flickering. Dying.

And then, a voice—soft and aching, full of beauty and pain—whispered in his mind.

"Save me!"

Ydrathar was calling.

And then, in a flash of green light, the vision ended.

The world around him snapped back into place, and Jonathan fell backward, landing hard against the jungle floor. His breath came in short, ragged gasps, his shoulders trembling as silent tears streamed down his face. The vision had struck like a tidal wave of images and sound, threatening to drown him in its sheer intensity. Ydrathar had spoken not in words, but by overwhelming his senses—sight, sound, sensation.

But as Jonathan lay there trembling, he realized that wasn't the part that truly broke him. He was crying because, in her desperation, Ydrathar had spoken in the raw, timeless language of the heart: pure feeling, unfiltered and overwhelming.

She had let him *feel* it.

And she had spared him nothing. Everything she felt, he felt.

Jonathan had felt, in perfect clarity, her pain as the Rot chewed through her roots, twisted her branches, defiled the life she had nurtured. He felt her helplessness as her children—those who lived in her canopy and called her sanctuary—fell one by one to corruption. And worst of all... her sorrow. The deep, ancient sorrow of a being who had watched generations thrive in her care, only to see their future consumed by darkness.

That emotion—pure, undiluted—had struck harder than anything else.

Jonathan curled forward slightly, arms wrapped around his chest, as if trying to hold himself together. The weight of it was too much. His shoulders shook. His eyes burned. And for a long time, he simply lay there, hollowed out by a grief that wasn't his... but now lived inside him all the same.

And worse—deep down, he knew he was expected to help her.

He didn't want to. Stars above, he didn't want to. Not again. Not more. Not this.

The task was impossible, and questions without answers swirled in his mind. Fight the Tiger King? The thought alone was madness. The creature commanded the Rot itself, wielded power enough to enslave prides and shatter armies. What chance did a single, broken boy stand against that? And how do you kill a sickness that twisted everything it touched into monsters? How do you fight an enemy that wasn't flesh and blood, but hunger itself? He had no army of his own, no city, no kingdom—only his own two hands and the will not to die.

The burden seemed unbearable, and his head ached at the thought of it all. The task was impossible. He felt like a child again—small, lost, drowning beneath the weight of something far too big to carry.

And yet—beneath the fear, something stirred. Deep, quiet, and wild. He felt the crushing weight of responsibility settle on him like a mantle. Not asked for. Not earned. Just given. It was more than a dying friend's final plea—it was the inheritance of a world on the brink. And beneath the ache of grief, something colder and heavier took root: the realization that duty doesn't wait for permission. It calls. And dares you to answer.

Drekkar's breath hitched—a flicker of pain he barely allowed to show. His gaze, though dimming, held steady to the last. Then, with a long, final exhale, he leaned back against the tree and closed his eyes.

For several moments, the jungle held its breath. Only the distant rustle of leaves stirred the silence, a whisper overhead like the World Tree mourning one of its own.

After a time, Drekkar's voice rasped through the hush.

"...Water."

Jonathan moved quickly, fetching a drinking bag and filling it from the Sacred Well. He knelt beside Drekkar, pressed the cool leather to his lips. Drekkar swallowed, then choked slightly, coughing against the taste. He exhaled, shaking his head. "Hnn. Always liked this place. Memories and all that." His voice was thin, but his lips curled, just slightly. "But Ydrathar help me... this water tastes like a drowned rat."

A pause. Then, with tears in his eyes, Jonathan couldn't help a small laugh.

Drekkar smirked weakly. "Hah. Knew I'd get the last word."

A heavy silence followed, the kind that seemed to stretch between the roots and stars.

And then he simply... stopped being.

CHAPTER 5
THE PATH I DID NOT CHOOSE

Jonathan didn't know how long he stood there, staring down at what remained of Drekkar. The jungle had already begun reclaiming the old warrior—vines curling softly at his limbs, leaves drifting down like a gentle shroud. The rest of the pride was gone, vanished into the depths of Ydrathar. That was their way. No graves. No markers. Only the roots to remember them.

And yet, somehow, leaving him here, letting the jungle claim him, felt... wrong. Come to think of it, *everything* felt wrong.

The weight in Jonathan's gut was heavier than any wound he had ever taken. Drekkar had saved him. And together, they had lived, fought and hunted. And through that relationship, Drekkar had forged Jonathan into something stronger. And when he had given the order to run, Jonathan had listened without thinking. But that was the problem, wasn't it? He had listened, when he should have known better. When Drekkar had needed someone to stand at his side, Jonathan had run. And now, there was nothing left of him but silence and the blood soaking into the earth.

The guilt hadn't even finished sinking in before something heavier settled on his shoulders—responsibility. Drekkar hadn't just died. He'd passed something on. A task. A burden. A dying wish wrapped in myth and madness. Jonathan didn't even understand it fully—save the World Tree? Kill the Rot? Stop the Tiger King? It felt impossible. Like trying to hold back a flood with bare hands.

And now, that impossible thing rested squarely on his shoulders, pressing down like a mountain he hadn't asked to climb. His eyes drifted toward the distant peaks of Arenthil, where he prayed his friends were waiting. He could go to them. He wanted to. He could almost see them—El, Israel, Valera. That life was still possible. He could choose it. He could walk away from this madness. The temptation hit him like a wave—warm, familiar, safe. But Drekkar's words echoed back: *there will be moments when you may choose your own path. And there are other moments when you must walk the path of duty.*

He didn't want to be a hero. He wasn't ready to carry the weight of a world.

But Ydrathar was bleeding. The Rot was spreading. The Tiger King was on the move. If no one stood up, then the sky would fall again—and this time, it wouldn't stop with one city.

He drew a breath. Slow. Shaking. And then he turned away from the Sacred Well.

He turned away from the peaks.

The choice was made.

His friends would have to wait.

Ydrathar needed him. And he would not fail his friend.

A shadow suddenly fell over him. Heavy. Familiar.

"Mm," a low rumble came from behind. "He looks worse than usual."

Jonathan spun, relief and grief crashing together in his chest. "Varg…"

The Malric loomed at the edge of the clearing, mane glinting gold in the morning light. His golden eyes swept over the scene, lingering on Drekkar's body. For a long moment he said nothing. Then, slowly, he lowered himself into a crouch beside his fallen father. Varg's claws brushed the earth near Drekkar's hand, careful, reverent in a way Jonathan had never seen from him before. He exhaled—a sound almost like a growl, but softer. "My father fought well," Varg said at last. "That is all a tiger can ask for. To fight. To bleed. To die with teeth bared."

Jonathan swallowed hard. The ache in his chest deepened.

Varg stood again, shoulders broad, expression grim. "Do not look so heavy, Little One. This is not sorrow. This is honor." Varg's notched ear flicked, his mane shifting as the wind stirred. He grunted. "I will miss him. He owed me money."

Jonathan blinked. "What?"

Varg straightened, dead serious. "A bet. He said you would not survive the first week. I said you would last at least a year. I have now won. But…" His eyes softened slightly. "I would rather never have made the bet at all, if that meant I could see him again. Just one more time."

Jonathan couldn't decide whether to laugh or cry.

Varg's golden eyes lingered on Drekkar's body one last time before shifting back to Jonathan. His mane tumbled in waves as he straightened, broad shoulders rolling like shifting boulders. "I will be leaving soon," he said, voice low. "My path must be my own now. I will wander, fight, and find my way. That is what comes after a father's death. And you, Little One. May you enjoy your life among the Sky People." He gave a faint snort, though there was no mockery in it—only something that sounded almost like regret.

Jonathan swallowed the ache in his throat. He drew a breath and said, steady and certain, "Later, maybe. For now—I'm going to the Hollow."

Varg went still, his bulk stiffening as if Jonathan had just suggested leaping willingly into a fire. A deep growl rippled from his chest, and he stepped closer, claws flexing against the dirt. "The Hollow?" he rumbled, voice rough with shock. "That is madness, Little One! Utter madness. No warrior walks into that place and comes out the same—if they come out at all."

Jonathan explained his vision, that Drekkar's final request had been for Jonathan to save the Tree.

Varg shook his mane, pacing like a caged storm. "Visions, Wells, Hearts—nonsense! I trust only claw, only steel, only things I can punch!" he snarled. Jonathan tried to protest, but Varg was having none of it. "You cannot stab a vision! You cannot wrestle a god-tree! You cannot bite a Tree Heart. I don't even know what that is!" He stopped pacing just long enough to glare at Jonathan, notched ears flat.

"My father released you from his pride. You're free. No more duty, no more chains," he said and took a step closer, urgency creeping into his tone. "Go! Find your people. Live among them. Be happy. But do not go to the Great Hollow, Little One. It is madness!"

Jonathan shook his head. His voice was quiet, but steady.

"I'm sorry. I have work that needs to be done," he said, and turned to leave.

Something like panic flashed across Varg's golden gaze.

"Don't do it, Little One! Come with me. Live free! Ydrathar will provide for us—food, water, shelter. Two outcasts, no chains, no obligations." He stepped into Jonathan's path, desperate now. His shoulders stiffened. He looked at Jonathan with a weight in his gaze as heavy as a coming storm.

"You will die," he said.

"Maybe," Jonathan said. He met the tiger's gaze without flinching. His voice was steady now—hard and bright as tempered steel. "But even so, I will *not* be deterred. I *am* going to the Great Hollow. I *am* going to find the Sunken City. I *am* going to kill the Rot and save the World Tree. And then I'm going to find the Tiger King… and stop him."

Varg was silent, his bulk as still as stone. Jonathan could see the cogs of thought grinding behind his gaze. Finally, he gave a slow nod.

"Very well." Then his grin split wide, fierce as a scar. A booming laugh ripped out of him, so loud the birds fled the canopy in a flurry of wings. "You are mad, Little One! Utterly insane. You speak like a warrior twice your size with a death wish twice as large." He cracked his knuckles, teeth flashing like ivory daggers. Then, with a gleam in his golden eyes, he added: "Lucky for you—I like mad things. I would like to have retrieved my axe from camp, but it belongs to the Tide now, and you seem to want to hurry. So let us be on our way. If you believe you know the path, then I shall follow you. For you are tiny. But I am very large, and before your journey is through, you will have need of me. There is nothing in all of Ydrathar I cannot defeat in battle."

"You can't—" Jonathan started to say.

Before he could finish, Varg reached down and grabbed him by the back of the neck, lifting him effortlessly off the ground like a wayward cub. Jonathan dangled there for a moment, arms crossed and scowling. He couldn't remember ever having felt so helpless.

"I'm ten times your size," Varg rumbled, grinning up at him. "I can pretty much do whatever I want."

Still chuckling, Varg set him down—none too gently—then dropped to one knee in the dirt with a loud, exaggerated sigh. He swept one massive paw across his chest in mock solemnity.

"I, Varg the Handsome, son of Drekkar, do hereby vow to follow this tiny madman into certain death. Wherever you go… I'll be there. Even if I don't understand why."

Varg stood and slapped a heavy paw onto Jonathan's shoulder— knocking him off his feet in the process—and bared his teeth in something between a grin and a snarl.

Jonathan and Varg spent the rest of the day pushing through the jungle in the direction Jonathan believed led to the entrance of the Great Hollow. Entrances to the Hollow were rare, but he'd heard of one near the edges of the pride's territory. By late afternoon, he parted a curtain of thick vines—and the wild swallowed them whole. It was nothing like the outer groves he knew—this was the deep green, the unwalked wild, where even the Malrics avoided traveling alone. He took another step around a wide bend—

—and stopped cold.

He stood at the edge of a gorge. A gorge that was most definitely *not* supposed to be there.

It cut through the jungle like a wound, jagged and impossibly deep, the bottom swallowed in shadow. The opposite side was far, farther than would be smart to attempt to jump across, and sheer cliff walls lined both sides, crumbling and treacherous. But it wasn't the size of the gorge that stopped Jonathan in his tracks.

It was what it was made of.

The walls of the gorge weren't just stone or earth or wood—they were layered, a strange fusion of the natural and the impossible. Thick roots twisted downward, and woven between them—partially buried, partially exposed—were enormous girders of metal and steel, curved beams and columns that shimmered faintly, unmistakably of human make. Glowing veins of circuitry ran like rivers along the metal, merging into the surrounding wood so that plant and steel became indistinguishable. It was like the World Tree had grown around the skeleton of something else—something built—and then become one with it.

"I don't know what that is," came Varg's voice, a low and rumbling sound, like a storm rumbling beyond the horizon, "but I want to punch it. Just to be safe."

Jonathan blinked, not sure what to say.

The brute took a step closer to the edge, eyes narrowed in scrutiny. "I'm very good at punching things," he added, matter-of-fact. "Especially things I don't understand. I like to punch things when I don't know what the things are."

Jonathan arched a brow. "I'm not sure punching is going to solve this sort of problem." He paused, inhaled, and added, "Besides, I've always preferred stabbing."

Varg nodded solemnly. "Yes. Stabbing makes sense for you. Your arms are very... not strong." He tilted his head, studying Jonathan. "I am large and mighty, but you are small and brittle. Like a bird's bones. Stabbing is safer for your kind."

"Rude," said Jonathan.

Varg looked genuinely startled, lifting his hands in confused apology. "I meant no offense, Little One! In fact, being weak and pathetic is a great advantage. Enemies will ignore you and focus on me, which increases your chances of running away and surviving." He smiled, as if he'd just paid Jonathan a generous compliment.

Jonathan sighed. "You sure know how to lift a guy's spirits."

Varg blinked, genuinely puzzled. "I could lift you. But not your spirits. They are invisible."

Jonathan stared.

Varg held up both hands, completely sincere. "Unless they make a sound or leave tracks, I do not know where they are. But I could look."

Jonathan's headache throbbed harder. He forced a breath, pushed his focus back to the gorge, and leaned out over the edge. Shadows writhed far below. "This must've opened during the rootquake a few days ago."

Varg grumbled and shook his head. "This was no simple rootquake," he muttered, voice low and grim. "This was the World Tree cracking open. And it was the Tiger King's doing."

"What? How?"

Varg crossed his arms. "I have seen him fight, the Tiger King… he speaks, and the beasts obey. He roars, and the roots move. Even the bones of Ydrathar crawl to serve him. It is unnatural. I do not like it."

Jonathan stepped closer to the edge, peering into the dark split. "What's down there?"

Varg didn't move. His voice was flat, matter-of-fact. "The Great Hollow. Also darkness. Probably death. Definitely a bad smell. But mostly Hollow."

"The Great Hollow?" Jonathan asked. "I thought there were only a few entrances to it."

Varg finally turned toward him, squinting down into the gorge. "All the big branches are hollow. Giant tree tunnels. Some you walk through, some you squeeze like a stuck marmot. But openings like this don't last. The Tree hates visitors. She always tries to keep the top world and bottom world from mixing. Mixing the top and bottom world is bad. It's like mixing oil and.... Something else. Exploding oil, maybe."

"Mixing oil and exploding oil?" Jonathan asked and tried not to smile. "I could see how that would be bad." He once again stared down into the gorge, brow raised. "But if I understand correctly, you're telling me—we've got one of those entrances *right here*? I thought we'd have to hike all the way to the edge of the Wilds just to find one. Why not just climb down right here?"

Varg crouched beside the edge. He peered into the chasm with a thoughtful grunt. "Too steep. You would fall. Then hit rocks. Then die. Then hit more rocks."

He stood and pointed across the divide. "I know another entrance. Less falling. Less dying. But we'll have to go around this gorge. Might take days. Maybe longer if we stop for snacks. I would prefer not to die hungry."

Jonathan shifted his gaze to the far side. It was distant—but maybe not *impossibly* distant. "We could jump it."

"Not a big deal to walk a few extra days, Little One," Varg said and yawned, teeth bared in a lazy stretch.

Jonathan stood at the edge, measuring the distance. It was right at the edge of possible—just far enough that he wasn't certain if they could make it, but he was feeling reckless enough to try it out.

"I think I could make it," Jonathan said slowly. "And you're—"

"What if there's water at the bottom?" Varg's gaze flicked toward the gorge, calculating. "That's not something I'm willing to chance."

Jonathan shot him a look, disbelief cutting through his growing annoyance. The mighty Varg would rather plummet to his death than get wet? Jonathan opened his mouth to protest again when the undergrowth behind them rustled.

Varg's ears twitched sharply. "Did you hear—"

A sound tore through the humid air, feral roar that rattled Jonathan's ribs. His blood went cold.

Varg's head snapped toward the sound, his claws unsheathing with a sharp, metallic click. "Raptobeast."

Jonathan felt his pulse quicken. Raptobeasts were monsters—hulking, reptilian brutes covered in jagged scales, gaping maws lined with rows of needle teeth, and with long, muscular limbs that ended in sickle-like claws, perfect for climbing—or rending. They packed enough strength to crush a Malric without trying. He and Drekkar's pride had once faced one that had wandered into their territory. It had taken every single warrior in the pride to drive it off—and even then, most of them hadn't walked away unscathed.

"C'mon, Varg! We have to leap across the gorge!" Jonathan shouted, but Varg ignored him, and turned to face the direction of the incoming noise.

The raptobeast erupted from the jungle, and it was truly monstrous. Its body was covered in thick, scaly armor, like stone fused to flesh. Massive tusks jutted from its mouth, gleaming in the dim light. Its eyes were dark pits beneath a crown of bone as it charged. But still, Varg did not move as the raptobeast barrelled toward them.

"What are you doing? You can't fight one of those things on your own!" Jonathan protested.

"I am Varg. I do not move for anything smaller than a mountain," he said and squared himself to the charging behemoth.

Jonathan was starting to believe Varg could crush a boulder but probably couldn't spell it.

"You're about five seconds from your own funeral."

"Then I will punch the coffin open," Varg said with a sideways glance at the teenager. "Now run along, Little One. I've been waiting all day for someone bigger and uglier than me."

And then the beast and Varg collided.

Jonathan had known Varg was strong—he was the largest Malric he had ever seen—but nothing could have prepared him for what he saw next. The beast lunged, and Varg caught it.

He *caught* it.

With a roar, Varg sprang up to meet the charge, seizing the creature's tusks in both paws. The ground beneath him cracked as he planted his feet, muscles bunching like mountains. With a guttural snarl, he wrenched the raptobeast's head down, slamming it into the dirt.

He had stopped the charge cold.

Jonathan stared, awestruck. That was impossible. Even for Varg.

The raptobeast thrashed and bellowed, claws gouging trenches in the earth. Varg's feet slid—an inch, then another—but he held fast, shoulders and back straining like steel cables.

"You think you're big?" he shouted, locking gazes with the beast. "I've tripped over pebbles with more aggression!" He snarled into its face. "I hereby declare that your mother was a swamp toad, and your father was a squirrel!"

But the raptobeast, startled though he might have been at the result of his initial attack, was just getting warmed up. He shook and trashed, and as they struggled, the ground continued to crack beneath them. They twisted, the beast surging against him, and for a moment Varg nearly lost his footing—sliding dangerously close to the edge of the gorge. Panic flared in his eyes, but he recovered with a grunt, planting his feet and driving the creature back into the dirt.

"If that was your best, you should be ashamed. *And* extinct. My grandmother hugs harder than you—and she's *dead!*" He stared down the raptobeast who was preparing for another lunge, and Varg roared. "Try again. But this time, pretend you have bones!"

"Varg, you idiot! He can't even understand you!" Jonathan shouted. "Give it up!"

With a growl and a heave, Varg once again grabbed and tossed the raptobeast to the side, looked at Jonathan, and growled. "I will *not* cross the gorge here. Too risky!"

The raptobeast lunged a third time with a mighty bellow, and one massive tusk slammed into Varg's face with a sickening *crack*, snapping his head to the side and tearing a gash across his cheek.

"Bah!" cried Varg. "You call that an attack? I've passed gas with more violence than that!"

Then movement flashed at the edge of Jonathan's vision.

Another shape prowling through the trees. Jonathan turned, heart sinking.

A second raptobeast.

Then a third.

Then two more.

Jonathan didn't hesitate. He turned and ran, sprinting full tilt toward the edge of the gaping chasm. His muscles coiled and released, he manipulated the strands of gravity around him, and the act propelled him farther than any human had a right to.

For one brief, weightless second, he soared.

And then—impact.

He struck the far side of the gorge hard, and to his horror he found that the wall of the gorge was smooth, unbroken, and utterly without grip. His feet slid, sending him tumbling down the cliff face. Bark and loose dirt tore at his skin as he twisted mid-air, arms flailing. His hand shot out—desperate—and, miraculously, found purchase on a vine. His body screamed in protest as he jolted to a stop, hanging there above the darkness below. He hung for a breathless moment.

He blinked down at the chasm below, where the shadows twisted and shifted in the depths. His fingers tightened on the vine.

A sharp cry tore through the air, snapping Jonathan's head to the side.

"Jonathan—help!"

Jonathan's stomach dropped.

Apparently five raptobeasts was too much even for Varg, and he'd followed Jonathan across the gorge. But, like Jonathan, he hadn't made it in a single leap, and he now hung from the cliffside, claws sinking into the bark of the World Tree and the smooth man-made struts that lined its edge. His hind legs scrambled uselessly against the sheer surface, his eyes wide and wild.

"Help me, Little One! I'm slipping!" Varg growled, panic rising in his voice. His claws dug deeper into the bark, but his back legs were now dangling over empty air.

Jonathan's feet pressed into the rock face as he fought for balance. His grip on the vine trembled. The cliff above was too far to reach. He needed to climb higher, find something stable—but the vine in his hand was already fraying beneath his weight.

"I'll get to the top," Jonathan said, trying to keep his voice calm. "Once I do, I'll find something to help you. Just hold on."

"Little One," Varg called again. "What if there's water down there?" His voice was sharper now, nearly frantic. "You have to save me!"

Of course. That was what Varg was afraid of. Not falling to his death—falling into water.

Jonathan glanced up again, spotted a thicker outcropping of bark above him, and tensed his legs to leap for it.

His grip slipped.

Jonathan's breath hitched as his hand skidded down the vine. The rough fibers tore at his palm, and suddenly he was sliding backward. His feet scrambled, but the cliff face was smooth as glass. His arms flailed, but there was nothing to grab onto.

"There's water down there, I can smell it!" Varg screamed, his voice high-pitched and nearly hysterical. "Save me, Jonathan!"

But Jonathan was too worried about his own fate to concentrate on Varg. The vine was unraveling beneath his weight. He fumbled for another grip—anything—but there was nothing. He was slipping.

Falling.

A sudden whistle cut through the air.

Something heavy slapped against Jonathan's arm—a rope. Jonathan grabbed it as the last fibers of the vine tore away. His body jolted hard as the rope pulled tight, nearly wrenching his shoulder from the socket. But he held on, then planted his feet against the cliffside and pulled. Inch by inch, he dragged himself upward. His chest scraped over the rocky ledge as he swung his legs over the side.

Jonathan rolled onto his back, gasping. His eyes snapped open just in time to see Varg hauled up over the edge a moment later, a second rope in his own hands—claws scraping dirt, tail thrashing, limbs flailing—before collapsing in a heap beside him.

Varg stretched lazily, shook the loose dirt from his mane, and yawned wide.

"Told you I wouldn't fall," Varg rumbled.

Jonathan, still gasping, squinted toward the edge of the cliff. The rope. His gaze traveled upward—and then his breath caught.

CHAPTER 6
TIME RUNS WRONG

L ying on the ground was a drone—one Jonathan recognized instantly. He hadn't seen its like in over a year, but he would have known it anywhere. It looked exactly like the kind he used to operate as a Cloudwalker in Aetherium. It must have been the drone that deployed the ropes, saving him and Varg from the gorge. A rescue plan dropped out of the sky, silent and precise. But who had deployed the drone?

In answer to his unasked question, the drone whirred softly—and projected a hologram of a young girl he instantly recognized.

Selene.

She had grown since the last time Jonathan had seen her—probably close to twelve now—but she was still unmistakably a child. And though young, she radiated precision and confidence with a force that most adults couldn't begin to match. Her dark hair, cut neatly at her shoulders, framed a face that betrayed nothing. Even the way she stood—carelessly poised yet utterly in control—hinted at a quiet, unnerving authority, sharper than outright arrogance.

She was brilliant. She was also cold and calculating, and possessed roughly the same emotional range as a block of ice.

Which made it all the more shocking when her mouth dropped open and her eyebrows nearly jumped off her forehead at the sight of him.

"Jonathan, you're alive!" she said, paused, then frowned, her voice unusually thin. "You look… different."

Before Jonathan could respond, the hologram flickered.

"Jonathan is alive?!" shouted another voice—one he knew instantly—and a second hologram materialized beside Selene: a tall, stylishly dressed nobleman with gray eyes, perfect features and perfectly-coiffed dark hair.

Cedric.

Cedric's mouth fell open. His eyes widened to the size of dinner plates, his jaw working uselessly like a fish out of water. His gaze swept over Jonathan—face, shoulders, arms, the sword at his hip—then back up again. For a long moment Cedric just gawked at him, jaw slack, eyes flickering like he couldn't decide what to focus on first.

Jonathan glanced down at himself—and for the first time, really saw what they were seeing.

During his time with the Malrics, he had grown—but "taller" didn't really cover it. He had packed on at least twenty pounds of dense muscle, his lean frame hardened into something broader, heavier, scarred. His skin was tanned and roughened, his overgrown hair tangled and half-matted by sweat and dirt. His tunic—what was left of it—was little more than torn leather and hide stitched together from survival.

He wasn't just older.

He was wilder.

A creature shaped by Ydrathar, not Aetherium.

No wonder they looked at him like he'd just crawled out of a warzone.

After what felt like an hour, Cedric finally managed to close his mouth. He straightened his tie with a sharp tug, then pulled a slim crystal flask from his pocket and took a long, deliberate sip—an act which seemed to revive his usual noble composure.

A smile tugged at Cedric's lips.

"I see you've embraced the 'wild animal' aesthetic," he said, gaze flicking critically over Jonathan's torn tunic and scar-lined arms. "Joining the proud tradition of shirtless savages. Bold choice."

Jonathan scratched the back of his neck. He was suddenly very grateful they couldn't smell him through the hologram. "Yeah, well... laundry services are a bit lacking in the murder jungle."

Cedric's mouth twitched. "And here I was thinking you'd eventually follow in my shoes and become a true gentleman. But as it turns out, beneath the rough exterior lies... well, more rough exterior." His eyes flicked toward the torn tunic. "And animal hide? Really?" He sighed dramatically. "Well. I'm sure when I tell Valera, she'll be thrilled." He paused, then his face truly beamed. "And I must say, I cannot *wait* to see the Princess' reaction when she sees you. Please, please, *please*, for the love of everything civilized, do *not* change your outfit for that reunion."

The hologram flickered. Selene's gaze cut sharply toward Cedric. "We don't have time for pleasantries."

Cedric's eyes glinted. "I disagree. Drama is important."

Jonathan's heart tightened. He couldn't believe how good it felt to see Cedric again—sharp, polished, and humorously condescending as ever. His mouth curled, ready to fire back with something sarcastic—but Selene's sharp voice sliced through the moment like a whip.

"Focus," she demanded briskly. "We only have a short window before we lose communication. If you're done with the fashion commentary, perhaps we could move on to the part where we discuss how to stop the world from ending?"

The hologram flickered again, stabilizing as Selene stepped forward, her arms crossed behind her back in that sharp, composed way that always made Jonathan feel like he was about to be court-martialed.

Cedric gave a slight nod, and Selene began. Over the past year, she explained, the fall of the Chancellor had opened doors long kept shut, granting her access to extensive archival records: blueprints of Aetherium and the other sky cities, accounts of the ancient cataclysm, and long-buried reports about the surface world. In those records, she'd learned of the World Tree—its vast dangers, its strange wonders, and the factions that claimed it. In her judgment, it was the greatest hope left to Aetherium's survivors—a place that could become a new home. Even as the sky city continued its orbit around the globe, she and Cedric had managed to send drones down to the Tree, searching for threats, mapping terrain, and offering aid to any survivors they could find.

"The other survivors?" Jonathan asked, his pulse quickening.

"Elysra, Israel, Valera, and most of those you called friend who fell with District 145, they are alive. They were taken in by a human settlement called Arenthil. But they're in terrible danger. If they don't get help, they won't survive more than a few days."

At the sound of their names, Jonathan's heart kicked like a drum. For a year, he had lived with the weight of loss, convinced they were gone—swallowed by the fall, the jungle, the endless clouds. And now… they were alive.

And they were in danger.

Jonathan felt a cold feeling wobble through his guts, and Selene's gaze sharpened.

"During my research," she explained, "I uncovered something the Chancellor barely understood—and feared. The Tiger King. Whether he is Malric or something worse, I can't say, but his ambition is clear: to claim the entire Tree, even if it means killing it. His armies absorb every Malric into their ranks, and they slaughter every human on sight. And his powers of Rot are… immense. Making matters worse, he has turned his attention on Arenthil. The outer defenses have already been breached. The siege has begun, and the noose is tightening. They need every fighter they can get. I can show you the way—but you must move quickly, before the last routes are cut off. My sister, Valera, Israel; if they don't get help, they are doomed."

Jonathan stood frozen. His mind reeled.

They were alive. Valera. Israel. Fighting, bleeding, resisting.

And they were counting on him. It should have changed everything.

But it didn't…

The path before him remained, steep and dark and calling. He closed his eyes for a moment, steadying the storm inside.

When he looked up, his voice was firm. Steady.

"I'm sorry," he said. "But I can't help them. Not now. Me and Varg, we are going into the Hollow."

Selene blinked, as if she hadn't heard him right. Cedric's eyes raised in shock. "I beg your pardon—did you say *the Hollow?*" His eyes narrowed, sharp with equal parts confusion and anger. "Surely you cannot mean *the* Hollow. The festering abyss that swallows every man who sets foot inside? The cradle of the Tiger King himself? That charming little pit where the Rot remakes all it touches into something fit only for nightmares?"

"That's exactly where I'm going," Jonathan said.

Cedric froze, then drew a slow breath, pinching the bridge of his nose before shutting his eyes for a beat— breathing deeply, as if physically restraining the words that wanted to come out sharper.

"Did we get bad intel on this, or something?" he asked, turning to Selene.

Selene shook her head. "The intel was good. The Hollow is exactly as I described."

Cedric's glare swung back to Jonathan.

"Jonathan," he said, each word measured, as if addressing a stubborn child. "Unless Selene is wrong—and I can promise you, that doesn't ever *actually* happen—you must *not* enter the Hollow. Even the Jonathan I knew, in all his theatrical recklessness, would not indulge in something so suicidally absurd. Arenthil needs you. Your friends need you. *El* needs you."

Jonathan's jaw tightened. "I know. And that's exactly why I have to do this. The best way to help my friends is to win the fight. And the fight leads into the Hollow. And so that's where I'm going."

He started to say more, but Cedric cut him off. "Of course you are. Why save your friends when you could instead dive headfirst into a cursed death tunnel under a dying tree in search of some grand, pointless martyrdom?" Now there was anger in his voice now—raw and rising. Jonathan opened his mouth to protest, but Cedric silenced him with a sharp, manicured hand, the same way one might scold a misbehaving child. "Honestly, Jonathan. Into the *Hollow*? You would rather throw your life away chasing whispers than help the people who care the very most about you? The ones who bled for you? Do you have any idea how hard they have searched for you for the last year? Even though they all thought you were dead, they *never* stopped looking. They're the closest thing to family you'll ever have—and you'd abandon them for some half-formed quest for glory in the roots? Tell me, have you gone *completely* insane?"

"Probably," Jonathan said, a flicker of defiance rising in his chest. "But what I *do* know is that the Rot isn't just spreading anymore. It's evolving. Stronger, faster, more invasive. And it's not going to stop—not with the branches, not with the prides, not with Arenthil. Someone has to kill it. I don't see anyone else volunteering."

The air went still and Cedric's gaze turned ferocious, but he said nothing. Selene's expression tightened. "Jonathan... you *can't* do that."

"I've heard that before," he told her, meeting her gaze. "We'll find a way."

"No," she said, her voice sharpening. "I mean you *literally* can't. It's not that simple."

Her tone shifted from urgency to calculation, as if reciting hard data. "The Rot is fused with the Tree's life force. They've become... entangled. You pull it out the wrong way, and the whole system collapses. The Tree doesn't just *hold* the Rot—it's integrated into it. Like a second nervous system. Kill it without understanding how, and you won't save Ydrathar. Kill the Rot now, and you may well kill the Tree."

Jonathan stood frozen. He hadn't known. For a long moment, he said nothing as the wind rustled through the branches above.

It was Cedric's hologram that broke the silence next, his voice still laced with dry disbelief. "And let us not overlook the rather glaring detail that most of the Tiger King's army currently occupies the Hollow. By my count—which, I assure you, remains impeccable—there are precisely two of you. *Two.* Tell me, Jonathan, is there some brilliant stratagem you've yet to unveil?"

"Of course I have a plan. And it's very sophisticated."

Cedric looked unamused for several seconds as he studied the teenager.

"Your plan is to storm the fortress with two bodies and a prayer, isn't it?"

"You don't know that," Jonathan replied, lifting a brow. "Maybe I was going to try diplomacy first."

"You? The human wrecking ball?" Cedric scoffed. "I'll believe that when I see it."

Jonathan rolled his shoulders. "Yeah. Fine. I'm winging it. So what?"

"You have *wings*?" Varg interrupted, eyebrows raised in pure shock. "Why have you never told me you have wings?"

Jonathan felt his headache suddenly flare up. "Look. All I know is, the Tree is running out of time. If I turn around now, if I head to Arenthil, Ydrathar will be dead before I can make any difference. This is the only shot we have."

"It is true, we are all running out of time," Selene agreed. "And speaking of time… there's something else you should know."

Jonathan looked up, wary.

"The deeper you go into the Hollow," she continued, "the slower time moves."

"What?"

Her dark eyes sharpened, even through the distortion of the hologram, locking onto him with laser precision. For

98

several seconds, she said nothing—just studied him, not like a friend, but like a problem to be solved, a machine with moving parts that needed to be understood before it could be calibrated.

"There is compelling evidence, both theoretical and observational, that would indicate that time behaves nonlinearly within the World Tree. Specifically, the deeper one travels into its interior—closer to the planet's surface—the more time appears to dilate relative to the sky and upper canopies. In other words, a journey to the heart of Ydrathar that may feel like a week to those descending could correspond to several weeks or more passing up here. The cause is not fully understood, but gravitational field anomalies, temporal field distortion, and the energy signature of the Tree's Wellspring may all be contributing factors."

Jonathan frowned. "How different are we talking?"

"It's erratic, volatile, and utterly impossible to predict," Selene said, her voice crisp. "You might go deep into the Tree and spend days—weeks—down there, only to return and find nothing has changed. Or you could descend for a single hour and come back to discover a month has passed. And if the dilation is at its worst, you could return to find everything you knew in the canopy—Israel, Elysra, Valera—centuries gone."

Silence followed for several seconds.

Jonathan swallowed. "You're saying I might come back and find the world... changed."

Selene met his gaze, unflinching. "I'm saying you might come back and find it *forgotten you ever existed.*"

Jonathan stood still, Selene's words crashing over him like cold water. The idea that time itself could betray him—that he might return to a world where his friends were gone, where the world he knew was dead and his name a forgotten whisper—made his chest tighten. He'd known this journey into the Hollow was dangerous, maybe even suicidal, but this was different. This wasn't just risking his life—it was risking everything he belonged to. A future without Cedric's sarcasm, without Elysra's voice, without anyone who remembered Aetherium—it chilled him deeper than the thought of the Rot itself.

And yet, beneath the fear, the same resolve held steady in his gut. If the Tree died, none of that future mattered anyway.

Cedric's face filled with a deep empathy.

"Jonathan," Cedric said slowly, his voice gentler now, the usual sarcasm gone. "You are a… *passionate* individual. Admirable, if occasionally maddening. But might you, just this once, take advice from someone you once called friend?"

Jonathan didn't respond right away. The high stakes of his duty, of everything Selene had revealed to him, still lingered in his chest, dragging down his thoughts. He was committed to stopping the Rot—but the cost was suddenly, terrifyingly, higher than he'd ever imagined. Time itself was on the line. His future, his friends, everything.

Sensing hesitation, Cedric pressed on, his voice soft but urgent. "Make for Arenthil. Elysra and the others have made something there—something worth fighting for. But they need help, now more than ever. And if there's anyone who could turn the tide of a battle, it's you. And I *mean* that,

Jonathan, from the bottom of my heart. You've always been the spark that makes people move."

Jonathan's thoughts spun. The idea of seeing Elysra again—of fighting beside Valera, of standing next to Israel's giant figure—it pulled at him like gravity. And truth be told, storming a fortress with all of his friends to help him sounded far better than wandering into a dark unknown with only Varg at his side.

Cedric saw the shift in Jonathan's stance and leaned in, resolutely pressing his point further. "Jonathan, I love you like a son. But you don't even know what the Rot *is*, let alone how to carve it out of Ydrathar without killing the Tree. Go to Arenthil. Help them win. Then—when the dust settles—you'll have allies, knowledge, momentum. And when it's time to strike at the the Tiger King and his Rot, you won't be charging in blind." He paused, his voice steady. "You'll be ready."

It was tempting, no doubt.

But Jonathan knew what he had seen.

There was no going back—not for comfort, not for reunion, not even for love.

"I'm sorry, Cedric," he said at last, his voice low. He could barely believe the words himself, but they came with a terrible clarity. "But I have to see this through. You can spend the rest of this conversation trying to talk me out of it—or you can help me do the impossible."

Selene's expression didn't change. Calm. Unreadable. A mind already calculating ten outcomes ahead. Cedric, by contrast, showed everything. His brows drew tight in frustration, lips parting as if to protest—but no words came.

He raked a hand through his perfectly styled hair, the gesture more human than noble. For once, all the polish fell away. No wit. No flourish. Just a friend—scared for someone he cared about, and unable to stop him.

The silence stretched.

Then Selene spoke, quiet but firm. "There's one more thing, Jonathan."

He sighed, the sound heavy. "Of course there is."

He already felt buried—by duty, by expectation, by the weight of a mission that grew more impossible by the hour. Killing the Rot. Not killing the Tree. Navigating twisted timelines that might steal centuries before he resurfaced.

Selene's voice dropped. "At the heart of Ydrathar is technology similar to that of Aetherium, and I've been able to communicate with someone… or some*thing*… that lives there. I believe the Wellspring of Ydrathar—like the Core of Aetherium—was never just a power source. It's a prison. And the thing inside it… it's not fully free, but—"

She hesitated.

Jonathan stared at her. Selene didn't hesitate. Ever.

Her voice was quiet now. "It's *leaking*. A fragment of it has escaped. A sliver of thought. A piece of its mind, its will… whatever it is."

Jonathan felt his gut twist. "Leaking?"

She nodded. "Something has already escaped. And it's searching."

And somehow, he already knew what it was searching for. Somewhere inside, he'd already guessed.

"What's it looking for?" he asked anyway.

Selene met his eyes without blinking. "You."

And right on cue, the jungle behind them groaned— loud, raw, unnatural. Not a roar. Not a crack. Something else.

Something wet and alive and wrong.

CHAPTER 7
SILAS GREY

F rom the shadows at the edge of the clearing,
something slithered forward.

It was mostly black—but black was the wrong word.
It wasn't a color so much as an absence, a void where light
simply ceased to exist. Like peering into the emptiness of
space, or a black hole. Other parts of its body were metallic,
shimmering beneath the dim light, fluid and unnatural,
shifting in ways that made Jonathan's stomach lurch. It was
hard to tell where one part ended and another began.
Biomechanical patterns rippled across its sleek, chitinous
surface, crawling like living circuitry. Tendrils coiled and
unfurled from its sides, tipped with jagged, bladed edges that
hissed as they sliced through the air. Its shape was a
paradox—too fluid, too inconsistent—constantly shifting,
dissolving and reassembling itself with no fixed pattern.

The thing didn't walk—it simply changed location.

Limbs—if they could even be called limbs—unfurled
and realigned mid-step, moving with an arachnid grace but
none of a predator's natural logic. It didn't seem to obey the

rules of anatomy—more like an electric current given form. Fast. Too fast. Its limbs weren't even really *moving* in the traditional sense; they were simply in one location one moment, then in the next, without covering any ground in between. No transition. No blur of motion. Just sudden, impossible relocation. It glitched forward, a ripple of shadow and intent, gliding over the jungle ground like water hunting for a crack. Long and thin black tendrils twitched and flexed with an unnatural grace, their bladed edges hissing faintly as they sliced the air itself.

It wasn't just fast—it was wrong. A glitch in reality.

Then—it began to change.

The shifting mass slowed, folding inward, shape condensing like storm clouds thickening into a funnel. The chaos found form. Limbs straightened, spine stretched, and with a slow, unnatural precision, the pieces of something humanoid clicked into place—like a puzzle being solved.

It became a man.

He was tall—nearly as tall as Varg—but alarmingly thin. His frame looked like it could collapse at any moment, almost brittle, as if a strong wind might snap him in half… and yet something about him suggested he could cut through steel without lifting a blade. Jet black hair curled around his sharp, angular face. He wore a suit—black and neat and unwrinkled and entirely out of place in the jungle. It was the kind of outfit a bureaucrat might wear to a funeral… just before signing a contract with the devil.

The man stepped forward slowly, his eyes shining like dying stars.

"My name is Silas Grey. And I am here on behalf of the Lurker and the World Eaters." The man—if man he could be called—extended a hand to shake, pale and narrow, with fingers a shade too long to be human.

"Silas?" Jonathan raised an eyebrow, but did not take the offer to shake hands. "Yeah, no. I'm going with Twiggy."

The man smiled, and disturbingly, it seemed genuine. He withdrew his outstretched hand without offense.

"Jonathan Roe, is it not? May I call you Jonathan?"

"Sure," Jonathan said dryly. "But I'm still calling you Twiggy."

Silas's smile widened—too wide, like it didn't quite belong on a human face. "You've faced a great many trials. Betrayals. Ancient horrors. Powerful foes. The jungle, Malrics, even the Chancellor. I am… impressed. Truly. If your father were here, he'd be proud. If you were mine, I know I would be."

Jonathan tilted his head. "You're impressed, eh? Is that why you're about to threaten me?"

"Heavens, no, child," Silas said, and he laughed. Not a cruel laugh. A genuine one. Warm. Almost fatherly. "Quite the opposite. I don't kill. I *repurpose*. And you, Jonathan, are long overdue for a greater purpose. I see… tremendous potential in you."

Their gazes locked. For a heartbeat, Jonathan saw something behind Silas's calm—something that made his instincts bristle. Varg stepped forward and put his heavy paw on Jonathan's shoulder.

106

"Pay this creature no heed, Little One," Varg rumbled. "He is a beast of Rot. Wherever he walks, ruin follows."

Jonathan didn't look away from Silas. He heard Varg's warning—but he needed to hear this for himself.

"Give me one good reason why I shouldn't smack that ugly grin off your face right now," Jonathan said, voice careful.

Silas's eyes gleamed. "A new world order is coming. I offer you a standing in it. A position of power."

Silas studied him for a moment—too long, too knowing—like someone looking at an old, familiar possession rather than a person. There was no fondness in his gaze. No affection. Just recognition.

"The World Eaters are coming, Jonathan," Silas said softly, studying Jonathan. "It is inevitable. As certain as gravity. As certain as the death of stars. And the ranks of the Tide are always seeking new recruits."

He tilted his head, and when he spoke again, the warmth was gone, frozen away by something cold, so cold.

Varg made a grumbling noise and stepped toward the dark man. "He talks too much. Can I hit him now?"

Silas laughed again. And, to Jonathan's surprise, it was not dissonant or creepy, nor was it musical or pretty. It was just a laugh; warm, cheery and… human. Silas then looked at Varg the way a man might look at a candle in a hurricane—something fragile, quaint, and already doomed. "Peace, Child of the Tree. I have no quarrel with you."

Varg did not advance, but the anger never left his eyes. Silas turned back to Jonathan and spread his arms as if to ask for an answer.

"So this is a job offer?" Jonathan asked. "What happens if I say no?"

Silas didn't answer right away. He only looked at him—long and quiet, like a butcher deciding where to make the first cut.

Finally, he spoke.

"You won't," Silas said, his tone calm, almost bored. "Your intentions are irrelevant. Your beliefs mean even less. Because you are gravely mistaken about one thing."

Jonathan felt defiance slide into his words. "Enlighten me," he said.

Silas tilted his head, the faintest flicker of condescension curling at the edge of his mouth.

"You think what you do matters."

Jonathan started to tell Silas exactly what he thought of that—but the man flicked his hand, silencing him with the ease of swatting away a gnat.

"The end that waits here is not something you get to rewrite," Silas said. "It has already been written."

"Then why ask me anything?" Jonathan snapped. "If this is all set in stone—why bother trying to recruit me?"

Silas' expression oozed into something almost indulgent.

"Most resist the first time," he murmured. "But the ranks of the Tide are always growing. Willing… or otherwise. I suggest you reconsider, Jonathan Roe. Will you at least hear what I can offer?"

Jonathan met his too-dark eyes without so much as a flinch. His voice was steady, dry as dust. "Let me guess. Power? Fame? A ten-percent-off coupon for my first soul transaction?"

Silas chuckled, low and humorless. "The future is never fixed. It shifts, like water. But in nearly every future I glimpse, there is Jonathan Roe—brilliant, terrible, magnificent. You will lead armies. I would prefer they be mine." He stepped closer, not threatening, but not harmless either. "We are not so different. Much of our work aligns with your… values. Come with me for a single day. Let me show you what the Tide can offer. I believe you have potential; let me help you achieve the greatest version of it."

"Aww," Jonathan drawled slowly. "You say I have potential. But what you really mean is: you're afraid of me. Well, guess what? My answer still starts with 'no' and ends with 'you're out of your mind.'"

Silas' smile vanished.

His gaze darkened, the light in his eyes retreating to something far colder.

"I can make you," Silas said, and this time his voice was no longer smooth. It was final.

Jonathan snorted. "If you could," he said, "you'd have done it already instead of standing there looking like a butt nugget."

For the first time, Silas's composure slipped—only slightly. Something flickered behind his eyes, something sharp and alien, but it vanished too quickly for Jonathan to place it.

Jonathan frowned and reached for his sword. He didn't have any idea what the Lurker or the World Eaters were, but it didn't matter. Anyone who tried to bully him into joining their side had already shown they were on the wrong one.

The drone, which Jonathan had nearly forgotten about, came to float next to Jonathan. He heard Selene's voice quiet and faint, just loud enough for him to hear. "I know what you're thinking. But you cannot match him in battle. Jonathan, you need to get out of there."

Jonathan heard the warning—felt the weight of it— but he ignored it, planting his feet and squaring his shoulders to face Silas head-on. Silas—thin, ordinary, almost unimposing—radiated a quiet certainty, the kind that said he would not be beaten. And more than that, he *could* not be beaten.

But Jonathan could not help himself. There was only one way he knew how to deal with bullies.

"Counter-offer," Jonathan said coolly.

Silas's mouth firmed into a thin line. He did not look amused.

"Walk away. Go back to your cosmic prison. Lock yourself in nice and tight. And if you do that…" Jonathan shrugged, lazy and fearless. "I won't knock your teeth out one by one and smear what's left of you across the jungle floor."

Silas moved the instant Jonathan finished speaking, and he did so with unnatural speed, his right arm unraveling into a mass of metallic tentacles and black void-stuff—shifting, liquid darkness shot through with glinting, blade-like edges. It wasn't flesh anymore, it was a weapon. Tendrils of serrated shadow lashed forward, launching themselves at Jonathan like spears, slicing the air with a shriek.

But Jonathan had seen it coming.

He launched his counterattack before he even finished speaking, snatching the drone floating at his side and hurling it straight at Silas. And this wasn't some flimsy reconnaissance drone—it was the long distance type, and it was packed with enough fuel to do exactly what Jonathan needed: buy him a few precious seconds.

And before the blades could reach him, the drone smashed into Silas' shoulder.

There was a sharp, metallic crack, then a violent flash of heat and light as the drone's battery cell detonated. The explosion tore through the clearing, flinging Silas backward like a ragdoll and slamming him into the jungle floor with a heavy, wet crunch, the black mass of his arm writhing and twitching, struggling to reassemble itself.

Jonathan didn't wait to see if Silas got back up. He was already moving, sprinting for the edge of the clearing with Varg thundering behind him. Jonathan knew they couldn't fight a thing like Silas—not yet—and he highly doubted they could outrun him either. Which left exactly one option.

The cliff loomed ahead, a sheer drop swallowed by mist and shadows. Jonathan didn't slow. Didn't second-guess. He sprinted harder, drove his legs forward—and launched himself over the edge. Behind him, Varg let out a bone-deep groan that somehow conveyed all the fears he didn't say—then, reluctantly, hurled his massive body into the mist after him.

"Tigers were not made for flying, Little One!"

CHAPTER 8
SOUTHERN HOSPITALITY

Water engulfed them.

For one dizzying instant, Jonathan didn't know which way was up—only the crushing cold and the weight of a river swallowing him whole. The current wasn't fast, but the water was deep, dragging them downstream with slow, relentless force. Jonathan kicked hard toward the surface, sputtering as he broke through. He wasn't much of a swimmer—never had been—but he could float well enough not to drown, and right now, that was enough. Varg surfaced nearby with a snort and a violent thrash of his massive arms, sending a sheet of water cascading over Jonathan.

For a long stretch they drifted, carried helplessly downstream, until the river bent sharply and shallowed against a muddy bank. Jonathan fought his way toward it, muscles burning, and clawed his way onto solid ground, hauling himself onto the mud and gasping for breath. Varg followed, slamming one heavy paw into the earth to anchor himself, then heaved his bulk free of the water with a low, rumbling growl.

Both of them lay there for a moment, soaked, battered, and breathing hard—but alive.

"Only fools and fish trust water, Little One," complained Varg between sputtering breaths. "If this river had a face, I'd claw it off."

"The mighty Varg is afraid of water? I thought you said there was nothing in all of Ydrathar you couldn't defeat in battle," countered Jonathan.

Varg glared.

"I made no promises about fighting *stupid* things."

Jonathan pushed himself up onto his elbows, coughing river water from his lungs. Around them, the world had changed.

The jungle they had known—the vast boughs, the golden light threading through green and purple leaves—was gone. Here, inside the Great Hollow of the World Tree's mightiest branches, the world felt different. The air was warm, dense, and sweet with the scent of sap and damp wood. It was essentially a cave—but not one carved from stone. This was a cavern of living wood, the walls groaning faintly with slow, imperceptible shifts, and there were a dozen different caverns and tunnels, each carving a path in different directions. Trees and shrubs grew from the ground, walls, and ceiling of this vast, wooden cave, and the air buzzed with the soft hum of unseen life far off in the shadows.

The tunnel was dark—but not completely. Every twenty yards or so, metallic rings embedded in the walls pulsed with glowing circuitry, casting soft, rhythmic flashes of light, and clumps of pale moss clung to the inner bark, ghostly and bioluminescent, bathing the curved passage in a dim green-blue sheen that shimmered like light filtered through deep water.

Without speaking, they began walking. The direction was obvious: toward the center of the tree, where the Heart of Ydrathar was said to dwell. That meant downhill. They walked for days—deeper, always deeper—through the winding arteries of the World Tree. The further they went, the broader the tunnels became until they were so wide they could not see the far walls.

Time blurred into nothingness. There was no sunrise in this place—no change in light or sky to mark the passage of hours. Only the distant drip of sap and water, the low groan of bending wood grinding overhead, and the unshakable sensation that they were descending deeper with every step. They dared not light a fire—both out of fear of drawing predators and because most of their gear had vanished in the fall. They had no food; no equipment. Hunger gnawed at them like a second heartbeat.

And they were not alone.

Strange beasts slithered and skittered beyond the edges of vision. Winged things clung to the bark and stared without blinking. Twice, they had to go still, pressed against the slick walls of the tunnel, as something vast and nameless passed close by, its breath rattling like wind through a graveyard.

But worst of all was the Rot.

It clung to everything. Black rivulets oozed through the bark and dripped into cracks, pooling like tar in every crevice. It stained the leaves, warped the walls, fouled the streams. Even the beasts wore it like a disease—hides blistered and flaking, as if something had hollowed them out from within and left only skin to rot. The deeper they went, the worse it became. The very air turned sour, each breath tasting of rust and mold and making Jonathan's headache pound like a bass drum in his skull.

They passed the remains of a village—once home to small, clever creatures. Now it stood silent and sunken, its huts slumped like melting wax. No signs of life. Only black growth crawling over the walls like veins.

Varg slowed, shoulders tensing beneath his matted fur. His ears twitched as if catching something distant, unseen. "The Rot runs deeper here," he growled. "Which means the Tiger King will be near. Wherever he goes, the Rot follows."

"You've met the Tiger King?" Jonathan asked as he stepped carefully over a blackened root, keeping his voice low, but it was more of a statement than a question. "Is he as bad as the tales say?"

Varg didn't answer at first. His jaw clenched. Then he spoke, each word scraped from his throat.

"They say when he was a child, he wrestled a sky serpent from the sky and slayed it. They say he once broke the spine of a mountain lizard with his bare hands. That he hunted the storm apes of the northern canopies to extinction. They say the jungle bends to his will. Whole herds of razorbacks throw themselves from cliffs at his command. Even the roots move when he speaks. Through the Rot, he commands the World Tree itself—its limbs, its guardians, the dark things that dwell beneath."

His voice fell away, and a shadow crossed his face. Sorrow. Fury. And beneath it, something Jonathan had never seen in Varg before: fear. For a heartbeat, he looked older, heavier, his mane dimmed by the weight of memory. His claws flexed against his palms, curling tight before slowly releasing.

"I don't know if all the stories are true," he said at last, quieter now. "But I know this—his armies struck down my father."

Jonathan's chest tightened. The words trembled, almost breaking. And unless he was mistaken, there was a gleam in Varg's golden eyes—not just rage, but grief, brimming at the edges. His tail lashed once, sharp as a whip.

"When I meet him…" Varg's voice dropped to a growl, low and certain. "I will not stop until he has met the same fate."

A chill worked its way down Jonathan's spine. Varg's words rang with resolve, but doubt coiled just beneath, hidden like a snake beneath still leaves, and Jonathan knew: Varg did not believe his own words.

Still, they pressed forward, drawn on by purpose, and by the growing sense that something was waiting for them at the center.

Then, without warning, the tunnel walls simply vanished. One step they were in shadow, the next—open space. Jonathan blinked, momentarily disoriented by the sudden shift in scale. Before them stretched a vast, hollow chamber—so wide and so high it defied logic. The far end was lost in haze. The curved walls resembled the inside of a colossal ribcage—mostly wood, but veined with enormous steel girders, each one pulsing faintly with a rhythmic glow, as if tied to a hidden heartbeat. And there was a breeze—soft, constant, almost imperceptible. It took Jonathan a moment to place it. It wasn't just wind.

The World Tree was breathing.

In the center of the cavern lay a cluster of dark lakes, their still surfaces broken by the jagged outlines of decaying structures and tree growths. It took him a moment to realize he was staring at the remains of an ancient human city. Pieces of buildings jutted above the waterline—delapidated towers and rusted archways half-sunken bencath the dark water. The remains of the city had become part of the tree itself—a carcass the jungle had reclaimed and reshaped. Whatever lay at the true center of this place, it had not been disturbed in a very long time.

And along the shoreline, more Malrics than he'd ever seen in one place. Hundreds—no, thousands—an entire army gathered beneath the tangled canopy.

Varg and Jonathan stared for several long seconds, the creeping realization sinking like cold iron in their chests. Varg grunted. "Wait here, Little One. I will find a way into the Sunken City."

Jonathan opened his mouth to protest, but Varg's fur bristled and he shot him a sideways glare. "Your arms are small, and you couldn't catch a scent if it crawled into your nose and yelled."

Jonathan didn't like it, but he didn't feel like arguing either. He tried to follow Varg's movements as he watched his friend leave, but the tiger was shockingly stealthy for someone built like a walking boulder. Within moments, Varg had vanished into the dense jungle, swallowed by the vines and shadows.

Jonathan waited. And waited. And then he waited some more. He had never been good at that sort of thing. At first he found a patch of cover beneath a cluster of low ferns, forcing himself to stay still, to be patient. But the minutes dragged like hours. Eventually, thirst drove him to a narrow stream that threaded through a clearing wide as a training yard, the grass brushing his waist as he waded through it. He knelt by the bank and cupped the cold water to his lips. That was when he heard it—a voice behind him, deep and rough, carrying the promise of violence.

"Move, and you're dead."

Jonathan recognized the voice. He turned, hand instinctively tightening on the hilt of his sword—and froze.

A massive figure stood at the edge of the clearing, half in shadow. He was broad-shouldered, thick with muscle, and his bionic arm—a hulking construction of gleaming metal and exposed wiring—gleamed beneath the dim light. The man's face was harsh and weathered, his dark skin lined with the weight of too many battles, his short hair and beard threaded with silver and white. A jagged scar ran down one cheek, in the middle of which a glowing bionic red eye watched with a dangerous look.

Israel.

Jonathan's breath caught in his throat. For a long moment, they just stared at each other.

Israel's organic eye narrowed. His gaze raked over Jonathan, traveling from his tangled hair to the lean muscle lining his frame—the scars across his arms and shoulders, the sword resting easily at his hip, the animal hide tunic hanging loosely from his body. Jonathan could see the moment the recognition struck—when disbelief gave way to realization.

Israel's eyebrows nearly climbed off his forehead. "...*Jonathan!?*"

Jonathan's mouth twitched into a faint smile. "Hey, old man."

"Jonathan!"

Before Jonathan could say another word, Israel had closed the distance and pulled him into an embrace fit for a grizzly bear. But Jonathan didn't pull away for several seconds and struggled to breath.

Eventually Israel released him and his face lit up with a wide, animal grin. "Rust and ruin—you're alive!" His human eye sharpened, taking him in and his grip on Jonathan's shoulder tightened. "We thought you were dead."

A knot tightened in Jonathan's chest, sharp and sudden. For a year, he had lived with the uncertainty, carrying the faces of his friends like fading echoes, like ghosts—never knowing if they were alive or lost to the fall. And now, seeing Israel standing before him, real and breathing, a flood of memories rushed in—laughter in Aetherium's streets, missions to the Core together, late-night talks beneath the city lights, training for combat. Relief crashed into him, raw and overwhelming, nearly buckling his knees. After so much silence, after so many nights wondering, one thing was certain: he wasn't alone. Not anymore. The sudden wash of emotions and memories opened something in him. For a moment, he tried to hold it back, to stay steady—but a knot in his chest gave way. A year's worth of silence, of loneliness, of believing everyone was gone—it all crashed down at once. His face twisted, and before he could stop himself, he felt the tears well in his eyes.

Israel didn't flinch. He stepped forward and pulled Jonathan in again, this time not with the force of a warrior—but the care of a family member. Jonathan didn't fight it. He let the tears come. Let the weight fall. He was tired of carrying it.

"I'm so sorry, lad. I should've found you," Israel murmured. "I should've done more."

Jonathan shook his head into Israel's shoulder, voice muffled. "It wasn't your fault."

"I was supposed to be the one keepin' you safe. I made a promise to Jacky, and it's one I intend to keep." Israel's jaw flexed, the anger and disappointment in himself carving deep lines in his face. "We never stopped lookin', not one day. But I'm sorry for not finding you. For not doing more. We thought—" He stopped himself, shook his head. "*I* thought you were gone."

Jonathan pulled back enough to look at him, eyes wet. "You didn't leave me. I survived because of what you taught me."

That made Israel smile, and it was completely genuine. For a long time, neither of them spoke. But for the first time in what felt like forever, Jonathan didn't feel alone. He felt anchored. Home.

Israel's grin faded slightly, his gaze sharpening as he studied at the young man in front of him. Jonathan knew he looked different from the sharp-eyed, reckless boy he'd known. Israel didn't speak right away. He just looked at him—really looked at him—and his voice came quieter, rougher. "You look…" He shook his head, almost in disbelief. "...good."

Jonathan was once again suddenly aware of how rough and savage he must look. "There's a saying among the pride: get strong or get dead. I guess I wasn't ready to get buried."

"Whoa, easy there, Sky Boy. We get it. You lift," came a voice Jonathan didn't recognize—smooth, slow, and edged with an accent he couldn't place. There was a lazy confidence to it, like the speaker had seen everything twice and still wasn't impressed.

Jonathan turned toward the voice.

A young man stood just behind Israel, shorter than Jonathan and with a wiry build, with sun-warmed skin and dark eyes. His black hair was tousled but somehow still neat, and he leaned casually against a tree with the posture of someone who'd never been in a hurry his entire life. He was handsome, annoyingly so, with the kind of swagger that didn't need announcing. His grin came slow and lopsided, like even that took more effort than the moment deserved.

His clothes were strange—camouflage battle fatigues of a type Jonathan had never seen before, boots, and a jacket emblazoned with a strange symbol of an eagle, and the print *202nd Airborne*. A burnt orange hat with a large *T* on the front sat askew on his head, and the cocky smile curving his mouth said everything—it was the expression of a man who knew he was better than you, and was happy to let you know it.

Jonathan frowned. "Who's this?"

The man's stance was casual, easy. "Corporal Cody 'Blaze' Robe, Army National Guard, 1st Battalion."

Jonathan's brow furrowed. "I understood maybe three of those words. Are those… titles? You some kind of nobility?"

"You could say that," he drawled, all easy charm. "I'm 202nd Airborne."

Jonathan blinked. "That's supposed to mean something?"

His only reply was his easy smile widened even further. Jonathan couldn't figure out if he liked or hated the guy.

Before Cody could say more, the clearing was suddenly swallowed in shadow. Varg stepped out of the jungle, eyes narrowed, muscles coiled. Cody and Israel reacted instantly, hands going for their weapons, and Varg crouched low, fangs bared.

"Wait!" Jonathan shouted, throwing out an arm. "Easy, Israel. He's with me!"

Everything froze for a moment. Three warriors locked in mutual suspicion, one jungle boy acting as referee.

Israel's bionic arm flexed with a soft metallic hiss. "Can he be trusted?"

"I have not eaten you yet. That is usually a good sign," growled Varg.

For a moment that seemed longer than it was, Israel and Varg just… stared at each other. Two predators, sizing each other up. Varg's hide bristled slightly, the tension running through his massive frame, muscles flexing beneath his sleek coat. The air around him seemed charged, as if the raw animal strength beneath his skin was one breath away from unleashing itself. Israel, in contrast, stood mostly still. His bionic arm flexed with a faint hiss of hydraulics, the gleaming metal catching the dim light like a blade's edge. The air around him was taut, the weight of countless battles settling into his stance. He didn't bristle or growl—but there was something lethal in the stillness of his posture, like a drawn bowstring ready to snap.

Neither of them blinked. Neither of them moved.

Jonathan watched them, acutely aware that if this went wrong, the clearing might not survive the aftermath.

"He's with me," Jonathan said quickly.

But Israel didn't back down. It was clear he didn't like being towered over—and he especially didn't like being towered over by something with stripes. "Can he be trusted?" he asked a second time.

Jonathan hesitated, glancing between Israel and Varg.

"He's had plenty of chances to kill me. Never tried," Jonathan said.

Israel didn't look convinced. "Patient don't mean harmless. Patient just means he's waitin' for the right time to gut you."

"Yes, Israel, I trust him. I'd trust him with my life."

A moment passed—thick with tension, the kind that stretched between warriors weighing instinct against experience.

Jonathan hesitated, then frowned. It didn't sit right.

Sure, Israel had fought in the Malric Wars. He bore the scars—some visible, some buried too deep to name. But he'd never been the kind of man to judge others by how they looked. Jonathan had always admired that about him. Israel weighed people by their actions, not their blood. So why now? Why the sudden suspicion—just because Varg was a tiger?

"That's not like you," Jonathan said quietly. "You've never cared what someone was. Only who they chose to be."

Israel's jaw tightened, his gaze still fixed on Varg. After a long pause, he muttered, "A year at war with them, kid. Especially the kind of war we've fought… it changes how a man sees the world."

He glanced at Varg, then back to Jonathan. And when he saw the look in the boy's eyes—steadfast, unflinching, full of that maddening hope he'd never quite managed to shake—some of the tension drained from Israel's face. The hardness in his jaw softened. His shoulders eased, just a little.

He sighed, then said quietly, "Yeah… you're right. Burn me, you usually are. Maybe it's time this old soldier started listenin' to you first and saved us both the trouble."

"So. Does the skyscraper have a name?" asked Cody, eyelids half-lowered in an expression of terminal disinterest.

Varg placed a massive hand over his chest. "I am Varg, son of Drekkar. I have allied myself with the Little One. He and I mean stop the Rot, and save Ydrathar. And then, we will find the Tiger King. And together, we will kill him."

125

"Kill the Tiger King? Just the two of you? Sure. And I'm a unicorn that files paperwork," Cody said, shooting a glance at Jonathan.

"If you are a unicorn, where is your horn?" Varg asked, profound confusion on his face. "Or do you keep it... in a pouch?"

"He's jokin', right?"

"If I were joking, someone would be laughing. You are not laughing. Therefore, it is serious."

Varg glared at Cody, golden eyes narrowing in deep suspicion. "...If you are a unicorn, you are the ugliest one I have ever seen."

Cody blinked. Glanced at Jonathan. Then back at Varg. "Wait—you're jokin'. Right? That's your joking expression?"

"This is my joking face," Varg nodded solemnly. "It is also my battle face."

With a quiet groan, Jonathan buried his face in his palm.

"Well, I will say this, Jonathan," Israel interrupted before things could spiral further. "Your timing was perfect. We're in a world of hurt, and we could really use your help." He cast a glance in Varg's direction. "And who knows, if we pull this off, the pair of you might even get your chance to take out the Tiger King."

Israel filled them in.

Over the last year, Israel, El, and Valera had been living in the city of Arenthil—a fortified human settlement at the far end of Ydrathar.

"We've been at war this whole time," Israel said, his voice low, rough as gravel. "Held 'em off as long as we could. But three days ago…" His bionic hand clenched, servos whining faintly as metal met metal. "Three days ago, they came for Arenthil in full force. Never seen nothin' like it. The tiger folk fight hard, sure, but they're scattered—prides, not armies. Don't march, don't hold ranks. But the Tiger King… he pulled it off. Held 'em together. Thousands of 'em, movin' like one beast. An army."

He spat the words with venom, jaw tight. "They didn't care if they lived. Didn't care if they died. They just threw themselves on our blades, screamin' like they wanted it. Rage. Bloodlust. And it worked." His good eye darkened, shadowed with memory. "The outer walls fell. Arenthil's breached. And the Malrics… they took prisoners. Too many."

Jonathan's pulse quickened. "Who?"

Israel's jaw tightened.

"Elysra? Valera?" Jonathan pressed.

Israel's mouth twisted. He let out a heavy sigh, the sound edged with frustration and exhaustion. "I *hope* they were taken prisoner," he said darkly. "Chaos split us all apart. But it's either that or…" He trailed off, the implication hanging heavy in the air.

"The Malrics are big on prisoners," he went on, voice low, grim. "We don't know what they do with 'em. Nobody does. But the word is, they keep 'em in the Sunken City." He

127

jerked his chin toward the ruins—half-drowned towers jutting from the lake at the Hollow's center, their stonework choked in vines and shadow.

His one good eye hardened. He pointed. "All we can do now is hope they're still breathing. That's why we're here. We're gonna find them, and bust 'em out of whatever pit they're rotting in."

Jonathan nodded. "If what you say is true, then we don't have time to waste. How many of the people of Arenthil are here to help with our rescue operation?"

Israel's eyes gleamed. "You're lookin' at it."

Jonathan stared at him. "*This* is the whole team?"

Israel nodded.

A protest was already rising to his lips, but before he could speak, a sound echoed through the woods. A low, rhythmic thrum, like wood groaning under pressure… followed by a sharper crack, distant but distinct, like bark splitting open. Everyone froze. They crouched low, slipping behind a thicket. Through the leaves, Jonathan spotted them: a Malric riding atop a raptobeast, plus twenty more Malrics flanking him, marching like sentinels—broad-shouldered, armored, ready for war, and everyone of them tainted by Rot.

Jonathan's pulse quickened. *Twenty one of them.* Assuming Varg could battle the raptobeast to a draw, that still meant they were outnumbered seven to one, and every one of the Malrics looked battle hardened and hungry for blood. His hand tightened around the hilt of his sword.

If it came to a fight, he knew how this would go if they fought.

"Tracking party," Jonathan said darkly. "They know we're here. We should leave. We can lose them in the jungle; come back later. Our only hope of gaining access to the Sunken City is stealth."

Cody scoffed. "I can take 'em."

Jonathan's head snapped toward him. "There are too many of them. Including a raptobeast."

Cody's grin sharpened. "You think I'm scared of a pack of overgrown house cats?"

"It's not about fear. It's about math."

Cody tipped his hat toward the raptobeast, his voice low and steady. "You see that thing? It's got our scent, sure as sunrise. We ain't sneakin' off anywhere—they'll track us like bloodhounds on a hot trail. They'll hunt us down before you can say Bob's your uncle."

"Maybe," Jonathan said, trying to stay rational. "But if we're smart about it—"

"No." Cody cut him off, still grinning. "We can take 'em. *I* can take 'em."

Varg's grin stretched wide enough to show every fang. "I like you, unicorn man," he rumbled at Cody—trying to whisper, but failing completely. Then he turned to Jonathan, eyes gleaming with the joy of impending violence and he pounded one fist into the palm of his other hand. "Let's *smash* something."

Jonathan's mouth opened, but no words came out.

Cody leaned back, arms loose at his sides, his stance dripping with lazy condescension. "What's the matter, Sky Boy? You gone soft out here in the jungle?"

"I seriously can't believe that *I* am the one begging for restraint here, guys. That is such a terrible sign," Jonathan muttered to himself as he felt a tidal wave of frustration swelling inside of him. He looked at the tiger troop coming in their direction, then turned his gaze on Israel. "You want to weigh in here? Try and talk some sense into your friend before he gets us all killed?"

Israel rubbed his jaw thoughtfully. His bionic eye whirred faintly as it scanned the clearing. "Cody is right about the scent," Israel admitted. "We won't outrun them."

"Relax, Sky Boy," Cody drawled. His sharp smile widened. "I got this."

Jonathan sighed sharply, his gaze narrowing toward the Malrics beyond the tree line. Twenty-one against four. Terrible odds—

An explosion ripped through the clearing.

Jonathan hit the ground on instinct, his hands clamping over his ears as a deafening *crack* split the air. Two dozen more explosions followed in quick succession—rapid, concussive, each one tearing through the air like a thunderclap, each sound thumping against his headache like a hammer.

Jonathan's pulse hammered as he turned toward the source of the noise.

Cody stood with his feet planted, both hands braced around a strange weapon—part wood, part metal, smoke curling from the tip.

"What—" Jonathan's breath caught. "What was—"

"That," Cody said, and his mouth twitched into a lazy smile, "is what we refer to back home as Southern Hospitality."

Jonathan's gaze whipped back toward the tree line. Where the Malrics and raptobeast had once stood, there was nothing but broken shapes slumped across the ground.

"What…" Jonathan's mouth dried. "What did you do?"

Cody blew a thin stream of smoke from the barrel of the weapon. "Grandad's thirty-ought-six," he said. "At this distance, it's like takin' candy from a baby."

Jonathan's jaw tightened. His ears were still ringing. His gaze sharpened on Cody. "You just—"

"You're welcome," Cody said, flipping the weapon over his shoulder with a casual grace. "Everything's bigger where I'm from—including our kill count." He frowned thoughtfully. "Well, 'cept for the cats. Y'all definitely got bigger cats here."

With a smooth, practiced motion, Cody pulled several small golden objects—fat and cylindrical and about the same size as his thumb—from his pocket and began feeding them into the weapon with an unsettling ease. The action was so practiced it was almost casual.

"But you better hurry and come up with a plan real quick, Sky Boy," Cody said, and rolled his shoulders, his

131

arrogant expression reckless and unrepentant. "'Cause everything within a mile heard that gunshot."

Jonathan couldn't decide whether or not he liked the young man. But he shoved those thoughts to the back of his mind. Right now, he needed to focus on survival—because after that stunt, they weren't just in trouble. They were in catastrophe-level disaster territory.

Cody hadn't just drawn attention—he'd lit a beacon. Jonathan stepped forward and scanned the valley below. His stomach sank. The worst-case scenario was already unfolding. The Tiger King's army was on the move—rows of Malrics and raptobeasts shifting into formation, weapons drawn, eyes glinting in the mosslight as they charged in their direction. From the speed of their response, Jonathan guessed they had maybe two minutes—three tops—before the full force of the enemy was on top of them.

Running wasn't an option. The raptobeasts would hunt them down before they made it half a mile. Fighting was worse.

Fear, cold and brittle, gripped his spine.

His gaze flicked toward the tree line.

The trees.

That was their only advantage—the jungle. The canopy above was ancient and labyrinthine, a twisted maze of branches and vines. The Malrics, with their sheer size and bulk, would struggle to maneuver through the dense growth and tangled limbs. Their strength was an asset on open ground—but up there, it would slow them down.

Jonathan and his friends could slip through the gaps, climb where the Malrics couldn't follow. It wasn't much of an edge—but it was an edge. A slim chance to disappear into the tangled mess of the World Tree above them before the Malrics could surround them.

Slim. But better than nothing.

"The trees," Jonathan said. He started climbing without looking back.

"Follow me."

CHAPTER 9
STEP ONE: DON'T FALL. STEP TWO: YEAH, TOO LATE.

T he ascent into the trees was brutal. The canopy above wasn't just dense—it was tangled, a knotted, living maze of branches, vines, moss, and bark that twisted together like the strands of some ancient, gnarled ball of yarn. There were plenty of handholds—that wasn't the problem. The challenge was forcing their way through the sheer mass of growth, some of it soft as velvet, some of it barbed like wire. Jonathan moved like he was born in the branches. Cody and Israel kept pace with effort. But Varg... not so much. Here in the dense canopy he moved slower, heavier, his bulk clearly not made for canopy travel.

Jonathan felt incredible. Not just because Israel was alive. Not just because his other friends were too—probably. But because he was doing something he was good at. No— *great* at. The twisted canopy of the World Tree, with its vines like braided ropes and branches was a death trap to most. But to Jonathan, it was a dance. Every reach, every step, every shift of weight was instinct. The bark, the moss, the breathless heights—he moved through it all like a creature born to the wild.

"Where are you going?" Israel shouted from below. He was panting, slipping, his bulk and bionics not built for the canopy. "That's the wrong way! You're going *toward* the Sunken City. We should be running away!"

Jonathan didn't look back. "No. The city is our only hope. We can't outrun them."

"Shoulda never come to this murder jungle," he heard Cody mutter. "Back home, the scariest thing chasin' me was my ex-girlfriend."

The first arrow came without warning. A blur. It hissed past Jonathan's chest with the whisper of death, close enough to nick the fabric of his tunic. He froze—and looked down.

Far below, through the fractured weave of branches and tangled green shadows, a commander of the Malric battalion stood, and Jonathan knew: the Rot had claimed him. Black veins curled up his throat, spreading like cracks in scorched earth. His fingers looked brittle and diseased, the flesh darkened and shriveled like old bark.

One massive arm lifted, a silent signal to the tigers at his side. Around him, a dozen archers moved in perfect unison, their bows rising like a wave, arrows notched and drawn, all pointed toward the canopy.

Jonathan caught his breath.

For the briefest heartbeat, the captain looked up—directly at him. And their eyes met. The captain's eyes glowed like molten gold, blazing with unnatural intensity, but

135

they held no fury. No rage. No pride. Not even hatred. Just... emptiness. As if the thing inside had been hollowed out, leaving only the vessel behind. It wasn't the look of a commander issuing orders. It wasn't even the gaze of a predator preparing for the kill.

It was emptiness.

The absence of soul.

He dropped his arm in signal to fire, and another volley of spear-sized arrows rained down around them. Bark splintered beside Jonathan's face. One arrow tore through a vine beside Cody, sending him into a brief, panicked scramble.

Now they weren't just being hunted from behind.

They were being hunted from all sides.

The jungle all about them roiled with the movement of Malrics climbing after them—sharp claws, heavy breath, snarls echoing between the boughs. And from below, the archers turned the air itself into a killing field. Every step forward now came with a cost. Every handhold a gamble and Jonathan was forced to take cover.

"Well, good news," said Jonathan. "It can't get any worse than this."

"Rust and ruin, don't say that, lad! That's how it always gets worse," Israel said as he caught up a moment later, hauling himself onto the same branch Jonathan stood on, soaked with sweat and panting hard.

A sound split the air—a deep, shuddering groan that was more felt than heard. The kind of sound that made the branches tremble and the marrow in Jonathan's bones hum.

He froze, every muscle going still. Even the Malrics paused. The entire canopy seemed to tilt its head skyward, listening.

Then it came.

Slicing through the sky like a living storm was a colossal serpent—its body a ribbon of glistening scales and armored plates, undulating with terrible grace. It wasn't flying so much as swimming through the air, each movement silent and impossibly smooth for something so large. Its wings were translucent and vast, stretched membranes like sheets of living crystal, catching the fractured light and scattering it in a thousand broken rainbows. Horns like twisted obsidian crowned its head, and its eyes were endless pits of blue fire.

It opened its jaws and released another roar—this one sharp and thunderous, rippling through the World Tree like a sonic shockwave. Birds scattered in all directions. Even the jungle seemed to flinch.

"Congratulations, Sky Boy," Cody said between ragged breaths. He aimed his weapon and it belched fire and golden light several more times, and a pair of Malrics that were closing in on them fell to the ground. "You've officially made the top o' the local food chain's hit list."

Everyone, Malrics included, was forced to scatter or hide. Jonathan and the others ducked low, all four of them huddled together on a massive branch like mice hiding from a hawk as the serpent drifted overhead.

"The Malrics've been tryin' to kill that thing for two days now," Cody whispered. "Hasn't worked. Big one. Real angry. Claimed the city as its turf."

"I do not know how to kill that thing," said Varg. "But I would very much like to try."

"Don't," Jonathan said firmly. "Just… just don't."

The sky serpent twisted through the canopy above, its body coiling like a storm cloud made of scale and wrath. Its talons raked through the branches with terrifying ease, and in one fluid motion, it plucked three Malrics from their perches and swallowed them whole.

"I have changed my mind," grumbled Varg. "That is not something I want to punch."

Jonathan turned to Cody. "Will your weapon work against something like that?"

Cody adjusted his cap, then shook his head and whispered. "Nah. Too big. Armor like a tank, teeth like a bad breakup. Only thing we can do now is wait it out."

Another roar split the sky.

They didn't look—but the sound of it tearing into more Malrics below told them all they needed to know.

Jonathan didn't like it. He didn't like waiting. But he also knew there was no way they could fight such a thing. He moved to peer around the edge of the trunk they cowered behind, his eyes were fixed on the remains of the Sunken City—half-drowned, overgrown, and shrouded in mist. His mission lie in there. And his friends were in there. El. Valera. So close he could almost reach them.

He glanced toward the Malrics below. What he saw surprised him.

138

The tiger army was bold. Even with the sky serpent prowling above, their commander moved with ruthless precision. His massive arm lifted in a series of sharp hand signals, directing his warriors to continue encircling Jonathan's group. A few were taken by the serpent—snatched from the air like insects—but the captain barely seemed to notice. He would sacrifice as many as it took. His intent was clear.

He wanted Jonathan.

They had two minutes, give or take, before the Tiger King's soldiers overtook them.

"We can't wait here," Jonathan said, voice low. "Not with them closing in. We stay, we get boxed in. Or eaten. We make a run for the city. And it's now or never."

Cody arched a brow at him. "Correct me if I'm wrong, but weren't you the one—like ten minutes ago—saying we *couldn't* fight our way out o' this?"

"Yes," Jonathan snapped, eyes already raking the path ahead. "And I still don't think we can fight our way out of this. But things have changed. We now have a ten-thousand-pound monster tearing up the jungle. Clock's ticking. We don't fight our way out—we run through, straight into the city, before the fight catches us."

"Little One," Varg rumbled. "I have many abilities. Strength. Endurance. Handsomeness. Punching things... But perhaps now is the time to unlock the ability of invisibility. Let us not engage the flying murder lizard. Let us *observe* it... respectfully... from behind this very solid tree." He promptly flattened himself against the tree trunk—his massive bulk still very much visible from space.

Israel's jaw flexed. "As much as I hate to agree with the tiger, I think he's right, lad," he said, worried lines appearing between his eyes. "They outnumber us, sure, but we've faced odds this bad before. But that thing up there?" He gestured toward the canopy, where the serpent's vast shadow still slithered between the branches. "We don't even know if it *can* be killed."

He cracked his knuckles, the scent of oil and ozone thick in the air. "You rush now, you're feeding us all to it. We hold until it moves on. Then we go."

They waited, breathless, caught between two nightmares, frustration rising in Jonathan like a living thing. Before them, the sky serpent coiled through the canopy, its scales shimmering with every twitch, its shriek still echoing through the treetops. Behind them, the Tiger King's army was closing in fast. They had no cover, no easy way forward or back. They were surrounded. Hemmed in by fang and fire, by wings and war. It was the kind of place where heroes died.

"The Tiger King's soldiers aren't going to pause for the serpent to clear out. They will reach us any second now. If we stay, *none* of us is leaving here alive. And if that happens, we leave our friends and the entire World Tree to the mercies of the Tiger King and his Rot. And I am *not* going to do that. We have to go. *Now*," Jonathan said, looking them each in the eye. "If we go now, and with a little luck, our enemies might be too focused on surviving to see us slip through. It's our only option. Even if only one of us makes it."

Varg was still as stone as Jonathan spoke. But as the words left his mouth, something in the Malric shifted—his posture straightened, his jaw set, and the usual glint of humor in his eyes vanished. He looked deadly serious now. Resolved.

"Well, Little One," Varg said, voice calm but iron-hard, "I swore I'd follow you to the end."

Before Jonathan could respond, Varg stepped forward, his golden mane catching the light like a crown of fire. He gripped Jonathan's shoulders, turning him so they stood face to face. His massive hands were surprisingly gentle, but unshakably firm. There was something in his presence then—his mane wild, his muscles taut, the sheer majesty of him—that felt more like a force of nature than a warrior. A low growl rumbled from deep in his chest, and the ground seemed to hum beneath their feet.

"Kill the Tiger King and save your friends, Little One," Varg said. "I will do what needs to be done."

Jonathan suddenly realized what he intended to do, but not before it was too late.

"Varg, no!" Jonathan hissed.

With a sharp exhale and no further words, Varg dropped from the branch, wind whipping his golden mane. He landed hard, claws digging into the ground for balance, he sprinted toward the open jungle—away from the remains of the Sunken City.

The sky serpent's head snapped around, eyes glowing like twin suns swallowed in stormclouds. In a single whip-fast motion, it twisted midair and launched forward, ripping through branches and entire sections of canopy with horrifying speed. Four of the Tiger King's soldiers moved to block Varg's path. The giant Malric met them with a snarl and tore them apart like blades of grass. Without slowing he turned and vanished into the jungle at full sprint, a streak of fur disappearing into the trees, the monstrous serpent thundering after him.

And just like that… their path to the Sunken City was clear.

For half a breath, no one moved. Then Jonathan, Cody, and Israel exchanged glances—and ran.

They sprinted through the canopy, leaping from limb to limb as arrows cut the air around them and Malrics surged upward, climbing in pursuit. Cody fired behind them as they ran, his rifle barking fire and thunder, but it only slowed the tigers for a few precious seconds at a time. Below them, the massive lake spread wide and dark, swallowing light. One spire—massive, curved like a blade—rose higher than the rest.

Jonathan pointed. "There! That's our entry point!"

He veered toward it, heart hammering, feet slipping on moss-slicked bark.

Just as they reached the final stretch Jonathan knew they would never make it. The enemy were too many, and too close.

"I'll hold them off," Israel said suddenly, skidding to a stop mid-run, he turned to face the oncoming tide of enemies. His bionic arm snapped into place with a sharp hiss, plates locking as it shifted into a defensive brace along his side.

"Go," Israel said to Jonathan, voice rough but steady. "I've got this."

Jonathan spun around. "No. You can't—"

"I can!" Israel said, cutting him off. "And I will." Jonathan hesitated, but Israel stepped toward him and locked eyes. "This is what I do, lad," Israel said, quieter now. "This is what I'm for. You get them back. You save the ones I couldn't."

"There are too many," Jonathan countered, and he could feel tears in his eyes. He wasn't ready to lose Israel, not again. "You can't take them all—"

"I'm not trying to *win*," Israel said, eyes already tracking the charging Malrics. "Just trying to buy you enough time to do what matters." He stepped in close and gripped Jonathan's shoulder. "I made Jacky a promise. I failed her once. Looks like I've got a chance to do things right this time."

Jonathan's throat tightened. "I'm not leaving you."

"Yes, you are." Israel's voice was steady, but something flickered in his eye. "Because that's what leaders do. They leave the fight behind when it's not the one that matters."

A beat passed—one heartbeat, two.

Then Israel shoved him toward the spire. "Go."

Still, Jonathan hesitated. Cody grabbed him and started to pull him away. Arrows rained down all around them now, a miracle none of them were hit.

Israel gave him a look. The kind that carried decades of war in a single blink. He held out his flesh hand, and Jonathan gripped it tight.

"Go. Get Valera. Get El," Israel said, and then drew a massive hammer from his back. He met Jonathan's gaze.

There was no time for any more words—but something passed between them in that glance. A command. A promise. An urgent, wordless plea: *Don't waste this.*

"Now GO!" shouted Israel

Then Israel turned and charged.

The world erupted in a deafening clash of steel and fury. The hammer swung in wide, brutal arcs, striking like thunder against the incoming Tide. The enemy broke around him in waves, but still they came—swords flashing, claws raking, voices screaming beneath the weight of the onslaught. Jonathan hesitated for half a heartbeat—then turned and ran, forcing himself away from the heart of the battle.

He spun, sprinted, and leapt—and made an uneven impact against the sloped side of the spire. He slid down its surface, arms wide for balance, boots skidding over slick moss and rust-slicked metal, racing toward the drowned city beneath. The wind roared past his ears, and then he landed— hard—on solid steel.

Steel that felt familiar from another life.

Even overgrown with moss, half-consumed by the jungle, blanketed in centuries of grime and rot, it still pulsed with the same cold energy as had Aetherium. This place had once belonged to the same family as his former home—he could feel it. The same foundation, the same bones. And something else… something watching.

He ran, Cody pounding the metal just behind him.

Up ahead, nestled between two collapsed walls, they spotted it: a diagonal breach in the ground, jagged and gaping. Water spilled over its edge in a constant sheet, vanishing into the shadows like drool from the maw of a dying beast. Twisted pipes jutted from the crumbling stone like broken bones, and a thin mist clung to the edges, thick with the stench of mold and rust. Beyond the veil of water lay nothing—just blackness. Heavy, endless, waiting.

It reeked of Rot and abandonment.

Jonathan didn't slow, even as arrows hissed through the air around them, thudding into the ground like war drums. He sprinted for the threshold, skidding to a stop at the rim of the pit, the water soaking him instantly.

"Ladies first," Cody muttered behind him, breath sharp.

Jonathan didn't hesitate.

He jumped.

For a split second, the world blurred—wind howled past his ears, the roar of battle fading behind him. The familiar sensation of gravity claiming followed, and then he was falling.

Falling into darkness.

CHAPTER 10
TIME EXHAUST

J onathan landed in a soft puddle of mud and moss,
rolling instinctively before pushing himself upright. Seconds
later, Cody dropped beside him with a heavy thud. Together,
they glanced up toward the jagged shaft of light far above—
and froze. The opening they'd fallen through was already
closing, the city itself shifting as steel, roots, and branches
twisted together, sealing the way shut.

They stood still, breath held, ears straining for any
sign of pursuit.

But the silence held. Nothing came.

"So... we live here now," Cody drawled. "Dibs on the
least muddy rock."

Jonathan said nothing, and let his eyes relax to the
darkness as he scanned the shadows. The first thing he
noticed: the portion of the Sunken City in which they now
found themselves could've passed for one of Aetherium's
mid-districts—if someone had flipped half of the city
sideways and left it to rot for a few centuries. He stood on
what had once been a ceiling, and above him stretched

decayed steel, inverted streets, and buildings clinging sideways to the world.

The second thing: there was water everywhere. It poured from above in constant, silken veils—some from fractured pipes, others from impossible places. It flooded alleyways, carved rivers through shattered corridors, and spilled in cascading falls down crumbling staircases.

The third: this wasn't Aetherium. It wasn't even really a sky city any more—not really. For the jungle hadn't simply overgrown the city: it had merged with it. Bark fused with steel. Vines wrapped through wire. There were no borders now—no line between nature and machine. Trees erupted from walls and ceilings, roots threading through concrete and rebar. But instead of tearing it apart, they seemed to complete it. The city hadn't died. It had evolved.

It was impossible to tell where the jungle ended and the city began.

The whole place felt haunted. Not by spirits, but by memory. By the ghost of a civilization clawing its way back to life—through rot, and ruin, and root, giving Jonathan a sense of being watched by something long dead but not gone. As if the city itself remembered what it had once been, and mourned it. This place was a place that had fallen, and never forgiven the world for forgetting.

"Any idea which way?" Jonathan asked.

Cody's eyelids drooped in that casual way. "Far as I can tell, we've both got exactly zero experience spelunkin' through death cities, so… your guess is as good as mine."

He paused, then added, more seriously, "But if I had to bet, I'd say the Tiger King and his freakshow are parked

147

nice and cozy near the center of the city—probably sitting right on top of it. Whatever greasy, cess-pool magic he's cookin' up, that thing's the power source."

Jonathan exhaled through his nose. "Then I guess it doesn't matter much."

"Prob'ly not," Cody replied.

And so they gathered their resolve and began moving—guided more by instinct than certainty—toward what they hoped was the heart of the Sunken City. It was rough going, and the city was even more difficult to navigate than the jungle—whole streets swallowed by jungle, collapsed towers forming impenetrable walls of steel and stone. Other sections were simply missing, replaced by jungle or large bodies of water they didn't dare to cross. They ducked through broken windows, climbed warped railings, and crawled beneath twisted wreckage and dense foliage. The only constant was the sound of water—dripping, trickling, rushing—a steady heartbeat in a place suspended in hush and tension.

Jonathan found himself watching his new companion as they moved. Israel seemed to trust Cody—and that carried weight. But there was something strange about him. He didn't seem to care about much… at least, certainly not on the surface. Except maybe for fighting.

He seemed to enjoy that part a little too much.

"You don't seem to care about much," Jonathan said as they squeezed between two collapsed beams.

Cody gave him a lazy glance and shrugged, but said nothing.

"You also fight like a man with nothing to lose," Jonathan added.

"Well," Cody said, hauling himself over a massive, gnarled root, "that's 'cause I already lost everything."

"What do you mean?"

Cody offered a hand to help him up, and—surprisingly—kept talking as they trudged forward through the ruins.

"Well, truth be told, I was born more than ten thousand years ago, best I can figure. Everyone I ever knew—folks I loved, laughed with, hunted with, fought beside, broke bread with—they're gone. All of 'em are now dust. The boys I grew up with? Dead. Parents? Them, too. The girl I thought I'd marry? Probably bones in some forgotten corner of time. They're all gone. " He said it in a tone so dry it could've come from a desert—like he was listing off groceries, not the extinction of every friend and family he'd ever had. He glanced back at Jonathan, not with grief, but with a kind of weary amusement. "I'm not busted up 'bout it, not any more." He paused, frowned, thought for a second, then added, "Well, except for the dog. Still not over the dog, if I'm honest."

"Ten thousand years ago? That's impossible," Jonathan said.

They reached a dead end—a jagged drop-off swallowed by water and vines—and turned back the way they had come to find a new route.

"And yet here I am." He paused for a five count as they jumped over a large section of missing earth. "You really wanna hear my story?"

149

"As someone with a degree in Losing People, I think I'm qualified."

Cody took a breath, ducked under a fallen beam, and pushed through vines shot through with metallic veins.

"My old man was a scientist—some kind of big deal. Ma stayed home with me and my six brothers. She had her hands full, but she did her best. I was the oldest. Just got accepted into college."

"College?" Jonathan asked.

"Yeah—school for grown-ups. Super lame. All books and no explosions."

Jonathan gave a solemn nod, as if he understood completely.

"But that was the day," Cody said, his voice quieter now. "The day everything changed."

He paused as they ducked through a broken archway and stepped over a shattered piece of steel.

"The first thing to go was the power. Everywhere. Lights out, communication dead. But the power wasn't the worst part—it was the silence. The not knowing. No news, no updates, no one in charge. Just rumors. Panic. Chaos." He exhaled slowly. "My dad… they took him. Government types. Said they needed his expertise. Whisked him off to some secure facility. I never saw him again."

Jonathan stayed quiet as they climbed a collapsed stairwell. For several minutes they moved forward toward something that seemed to be pulling them in its direction before Cody continued the story.

"Power came back eventually. In flashes. Spurts. But every time it did, the rumors got worse. People said we were at war—but no one could say who with. Or why. Then came the day the East Coast just… vanished."

Jonathan frowned, confused.

Cody glanced over. "The East Coast was half a country. And not a little one, either. Imagine a place the size of a thousand Aetheriums, give or take, just… erased. Cities, forests, everything. Gone. Like someone scraped it clean with a cosmic ice cream scooper."

Cody's voice was flat, too flat—like a door shut gently on a room no one visited anymore. Not mourning. Just the silence of a story too old to cry over. Jonathan didn't respond. There wasn't anything to say.

"I was a soldier, and a good one. Seen my fair share of fights. Fightin' was prob'ly the one thing in all the world I was ever really good at. And my friends, when the fightin' started, they all went off to war. Said something about fightin' the World Eaters—and no, don't ask, I know basically squat about them. But next thing I know, I'm yanked outta the lineup and dumped at some secret squirrel facility, way out in the boonies. Middle of nowhere. Probably had more cows than people."

Cody scratched his chin like the memory itched.

"Pretty sure my old man had a hand in it, pulled some strings. Always said he had connections—turns out, maybe he wasn't full of it. So instead of going to war, I'm driving trucks and babysitting ammo dumps. Glamorous, I know."

"They had me doin' security detail on some hush-hush project. Whole thing was locked tighter than a banker's vault. Something 'bout a self-sustaining city—clean energy, no external inputs, whole deal. But no one would explain why. Just 'load this,' 'move that,' and don't ask questions unless you wanted to meet HR the hard way."

He paused, then added with a scoff, "Then one day I'm haulin' a truckload of ammo and artillery and some other fancy weapons, the world blinks out for half a second, and boom—I'm not stateside anymore. I'm in some nightmare jungle where the flies sound like chainsaws and even the moss hisses when I step on it like it wants to eat my bones for breakfast. Far as I can figure, that was about two years ago. I've been runnin' ever since. Until I met Israel."

He glanced at Jonathan, tone still dry but quieter now.

"You ever feel like the universe made a clerical error and put you in the wrong story?" he asked.

They reached a collapsed walkway choked with roots and debris and a massive beam blocking their path. Without a word, both dropped their shoulders to it, grunting as they shoved the twisted metal aside.

"Yeah," Jonathan muttered. "All the time."

"Figures," Cody said. "You've got that look."

Then, with the beam out of the way, Cody crouched and started crawling through the narrow gap. "C'mon. Hope you're not too attached to your kneecaps."

They wormed their way through, shoulders brushing the tight walls, boots scraping against tangled roots and rusted metal.

"Selene had a theory, by the way," Cody said casually, like they weren't squeezing through a prehistoric ventilation shaft of doom. "You know Selene?"

Jonathan nodded. "Yeah. She's a bright kid."

"Bright? I only ever met her hologram, but that girl's got neurons firin' like a firework finale. Anyway, she had this wild theory. Only thing that's ever made sense to me." He grunted as the tunnel dipped, then kept going. "She said every reaction—chemical, physical, kinetic—has an equal and opposite reaction. You rev up an engine, it gives you motion. But it also gives you heat, smoke, and noise, right?"

Jonathan grunted in agreement.

"Well, she figured the same thing happens with the sky cities. All that anti-grav energy it uses to float in the sky? She thinks it throws off something like... I think she called it 'time exhaust.' Like, leftover junk from the reaction."

Jonathan blinked. "Time exhaust?"

"Yeah," Cody muttered, scratching the back of his neck. "Little time bubbles—tiny pockets where everything slows down. Not enough to mess with the whole city, but step into one? Congratulations, you're livin' in slow motion while the universe sprints ahead. Wrong place, wrong time on an epic scale. And then—poof—thousands of years go by, the world moves on without me, Ma and my dog are both long gone, and the world decided to grow an epic forest right where my old home used to be. Because why not?"

Jonathan crawled in silence, trying to process it all. Time bubbles. Lost millenia.

Selene's theory sounded impossible—but so had everything else in this world, once.

The conversation faded, swallowed by the damp hush of the ruined city. Neither of them said much after that. The silence wasn't heavy—it was thoughtful, stretched thin between the crumbling walls and the creeping vines. Just the splash of their boots in shallow water, the hiss of wind through broken steel, the occasional crack of shifting debris. They pressed on, deeper into the drowned skeleton of the city.

For days they marched. Creatures prowled the darkness, and more than once they were forced to hide for long periods of time as corrupted Malric war bands moved through the Sunken City. And as they moved, a creeping unease began to settle at the edges of Jonathan's mind. It started small—an odd detour here, a street blocked by rubble or twisted growth there. Nothing unusual for a city this ruined. But then it happened again. And again. Every time they tried to divert—climb to another level, loop around a collapsed spire, wade back through a flooded corridor—they hit the same wall: impassable debris, stone shattered like glass, vines woven thick as armor. Paths that looked open at first would close just as they reached them, as if the city had changed its mind.

At first, it felt random. Just the chaos of a place long dead. But now... it didn't feel like chance anymore.

Because there was always only one way forward.

It was subtle, but undeniable—the city, or the jungle, or both, guiding them. Not with signs or words. With pressure. Like a hand on Jonathan's back, unseen but insistent. Pushing him. Herding him.

Deeper.

Toward something.

"You thinkin' what I'm thinkin'?" Cody asked, voice low and dry behind him.

Jonathan didn't stop walking. He kept his eyes ahead, unwilling to give shape to the thought. Saying it aloud might make it real.

Cody exhaled softly, then muttered, "We're bein' herded… like cattle."

Jonathan stepped into a long, narrow street—one of the old arterial roads that had once divided districts. At the far end of the street loomed one of the great steel gates—massive and half-sunken into the dark water of the Sunken City. Rust and root had claimed its surface, but it still stood. Still functioned.

Jonathan's pulse quickened. He could feel something behind it. Not hear. Not see. *Feel*—like heat radiating through a wall. Something watching. Waiting.

As he approached, the ground trembled faintly beneath his boots. Then the gate shuddered with a deep groan of metal and age, rivulets of dark water running along the edges. Giant pistons hissed and clanked, venting steam into the air. With a slow, mechanical moan, the doors began to open—just wide enough for a single person to pass through.

Jonathan stood frozen as the opening widened before him, like a mouth in the ruins.

Something wanted them to step through.

"All we need now is some ominous music and a thunderclap," Cody grumbled to himself.

Jonathan stared at the widening gate, its grinding echo reverberating through the drowned city like a challenge.

His instincts screamed at him to turn back—to vanish into the shadows, climb the ruins, disappear into the jungle before whatever lay beyond that door noticed he was here. He didn't like being led. He didn't like that the streets had funneled them to this point. And he especially didn't like the sense that something had been waiting for him the entire time.

But turning back wasn't really an option, was it?

He looked at Cody. "You don't have to come with me," he said quietly.

Cody checked his weapon with a flick of his wrist.

"Wasn't plannin' on living forever," he said with a smile. "Might as well go out doin' something half-interesting."

Jonathan stepped through the gates first, Cody a step behind.

Beyond the gates stretched a vast courtyard. Lining both sides of the courtyard stood a dozen towering figures—at first glance, statues. But not of stone or metal. They were trees. Or something that had once been trees, now twisted into the shape of colossal sentinels. Each stood several times the height of a house, their massive limbs gnarled like weathered oak, bark grown over what might once have been armor. Moss clung to their sides. Vines curled from their

156

shoulders like cloaks. Their arms were thick branches ending in clawed fingers. Their faces were carved by time, deep-set hollows and crooked ridges, as if the wind itself had sculpted them into grim monsters.

As Jonathan stepped into the courtyard, he felt it instantly—a shift in the air, subtle but unmistakable. Then came the sound—soft and unsettling. Wood creaked like old bones. Leaves rustled overhead, though the air remained still. Then, one by one, their heads turned.

Eyes blacker than coal blinked open across their bark-carved faces, fixing on him with quiet, unreadable focus. They did not move. They did not speak. They only watched. And waited.

In the center of the chamber, clustered around a crumbling stone platform, stood a dozen Malrics clad in full war regalia. Their armor was dark and jagged, etched with bone and claw, fur slick with blood, mud, and something far worse. Black veins snaked across their skin where it showed, pulsing faintly—marks of the Rot that now lived inside of them. Their weapons were drawn but not yet raised. One by one, they turned as Jonathan stepped into the room, gleaming eyes narrowing, the light behind them twisted and wrong.

The Malrics didn't move—yet. But the threat was there, woven into every tense muscle and silent breath. Their claws flexed. Armor shifted. They weren't here to parley.

They were preparing for war.

He began to worry he should've turned back. Regrouped. Found his allies before charging into a fight he couldn't win. A dozen Malrics—each a match for him alone. And the tree giants? Jonathan didn't need to fight one to know the outcome. They loomed like titans, limbs like gnarled pillars, bodies carved from bark and stone and filled with ancient power. They were monsters of a forgotten world, and even on his best day, he wouldn't last five seconds.

But he didn't run. He didn't move.

The Malrics stood in a tight ring around two small, bound figures—tied with thick vines, unmoving, facedown on the stone. Jonathan's heart slammed against his ribs.

One of them was small, bound and face covered, unrecognizable. The other, he knew. Even through the blood. Even in this nightmare.

Valera.

Bound. Gagged. Hurt.

They'd made one mistake—leaving her alive long enough for him to find her. He didn't know how, and he didn't care. But he was going to make them pay for every bruise on her body.

CHAPTER 11
CUB MINE

Jonathan knew it was insane—knew it defied logic, tactics, and every lesson he'd ever been taught—but a single thought surged through him: protect his kin. It wasn't noble. It wasn't rational. It wasn't even brave. It was something deeper, something older—a pulse that beat beneath thought, beneath training, beneath fear. It was rage and love knotted together into a single purpose, rising in him like a tide.

His mind screamed to plan, to think, to wait—but his heart overruled it all. That was *Valera*. That was his pride, his *family*. And if he had to carve his way through a dozen Malrics and whatever demons lived inside those trees, then so be it.

Before he could think better of it, Jonathan stepped forward into the center of the courtyard. His hand slid to the hilt of his sword. And with the steady grace of someone who had already made peace with madness, he drew it. Steel sang in the stillness, sharp and clear.

Behind him he heard Cody ready his own weapon, and drawl quietly, "Well, here we go. Just like Ma used to say—if you're gonna do something stupid, do it with confidence."

The Malrics turned as one. They moved with fluid precision, stepping between him and the two bound figures. They didn't snarl. They didn't roar. They simply stood, quiet and still, as if awaiting an order that hadn't yet come.

One of the tigers stepped forward. His fur, once a deep burnt orange, was streaked with grime and mottled by sickly patches where the Rot had taken hold. From his skull jutted warped antler-like growths of oozing black chitin. The sight was grotesque, yet regal—a crown of ruin that marked him as something both leader and monster.

He didn't reach for a weapon. He didn't posture or growl.

He simply watched Jonathan come closer.

And when Jonathan had nearly closed the distance, the great Malric tilted his head slightly, curious, and asked calmly, "Hmm... and what is it you think you're hunting, manling?"

Jonathan froze. There was no mockery in the tone. No challenge.

If anything... the Malric sounded genuinely confused.

"I'm going to take what's mine," Jonathan said, voice flat as stone.

The tiger warrior tilted his head, frowning, clearly confused by the statement.

"But you carry our blood, Skywarrior. You are one of us."

Jonathan took another step forward. He pointed toward Valera. "She is my kin. And I will have her back."

The Malric captain frowned, a low growl rumbling from deep in his chest. "I do not understand," he said, voice rough with genuine confusion. "If she is your kin, why would you deny her this gift?"

Jonathan stiffened.

Gift.

That was what they called it. But as he looked at the captain—at the black veins crawling across his throat, the dull sheen of decay in his fur—he understood. This wasn't salvation. Whatever they meant to do to Valera, she would be theirs.

He forced the rising dread down, his voice cold and sharp. "Yeah, I don't know what you *think* is happening here, but if you don't untie your prisoners and hand them over before I count to five, I'm going to start carving your theology into scrap."

The Malric captain's growl was laced with something almost pleading. "She must join us—join you. And if she is your kin, why resist? You should want this for her."

Jonathan didn't answer. He simply raised his sword and leveled the point at the Malric's chest. The steel caught the faint light, gleaming steady despite the war drum pounding inside his ribs.

"Five," he said flatly.

The Malric flinched, ears flattening behind the rotten spikes protruding from his skull, tail slicing through the dust behind him.

161

"I can't," he said. "You, of all people, should understand. The Tide's scent is already in you—I can feel it. You carry it. Its mark. You are the Chosen One! Why would you deny her the same gift?"

Jonathan froze.

The words landed like a blade, slicing somewhere unseen. *You carry the Tide's scent. Its mark.* His throat tightened. A cold pit opened inside him.

Focus, he thought, and he shoved the thought down, burying it beneath the heat of battle rising in his veins. Now wasn't the time. If a fight was coming—and every instinct screamed that it was—he needed to stay sharp. Stay alive.

"Four," Jonathan growled.

The Malric tilted his ruined face toward him.

"You may bare your teeth and thrash your claws, but it changes nothing," the tiger rumbled. "The End prowls closer with every step, and you are already in its jaws. You may struggle, but the jaws will close all the same."

Jonathan's hand tightened around the sword's hilt, and the blade responded like a living thing. The runes along its length blazed to life, searing green, pulsing with light and power. It felt... hungry. Wilder than before.

"Three," he growled.

The Malric captain moved. He drew a massive mace, nearly as tall as Jonathan. With a flick of his wrist, he gave a silent signal. The others responded instantly. They moved as one, stepping from the shadows like ghosts—silent, seamless, deadly. A dozen Malrics formed a tight circle around Jonathan, weapons drawn, shoulders squared. Their eyes gleamed in the half-light, and in their stillness there was a deadly calm. One breath, one twitch, and they'd strike.

Behind him, he sensed Cody step closer, weapon raised. "Perfect. Twelve-to-two. I was worried we might get bored."

The Malric then turned to Cody, took a slow step closer, voice dropping to something nearly seductive. "And what of you, human? You struggle alongside him. You risk your life. But for what? His cause? His burdens?" He gestured to the darkened cathedral around them. "Why fight and bleed for a dying world when you could rise above it? The Tide offers you more than loyalty. We offer power. Purpose."

Cody considered for a moment before drawling, "That's almost word-for-word what my ex said… right before she stole my truck and maxed my credit cards."

The Malric's antlers twitched, and a low ripple ran through his ruined face as if the Rot itself flinched in irritation.

"Two," Jonathan said.

He inhaled slowly. The breath caught in his chest. His sword stayed steady, a bright flare of green light pulsing from its runes—but inside, something cold uncoiled beneath his ribs. Doubt.

Could he take them all? Unlikely.

Could he even take one?

And what about the tree-creatures? The towering, bark-skinned watchers now loomed closer. Their leafy limbs stirred without wind, and Jonathan swore he could feel them breathing. The air around them was wrong—tainted, burdened with something more than rot. Evil rolled off them like mist.

But the worst of it wasn't the numbers. It wasn't the odds.

It was the question echoing in his mind:

What if it was true?

What if he had been touched by the Rot? What if the power thrumming in his limbs wasn't entirely his? What if every step forward had been bent toward its will?

The doubt cracked something inside him. But not the way they expected.

Because he still hadn't said "one," but he was done talking.

Jonathan roared—and attacked.

But not with his sword.

He reached inward—deeper than he ever had before—and found the threads of gravity, those quiet forces he'd spent a lifetime manipulating, and he unleashed. With every ounce of will and fury, he hurled that force outward— not with control, not with discipline, but with the raw, desperate violence of someone trying to tear gravity itself from the fabric of the world.

The power tore through the courtyard like a cannon blast.

All twelve Malric warriors exploded backward, lifted from the ground like toys caught in a cyclone. Dozens of yards they flew through the air, tumbling end over end, slamming into stone, bark, wall—whatever the jungle chose to offer in punishment. One crashed through a vine-covered column. Another skidded across the mossy floor, armor scraping sparks against the steel beneath.

Jonathan staggered, vision swimming, a high whine rising in his ears, and for a moment the headache he'd been feeling for weeks seemed to soften as his hold on consciousness weakened. The world tilted sideways—just for a second—but he forced clarity into his limbs. He moved. Stumbled forward, eyes locked on the two bound figures in the center of the courtyard.

He dropped to his knees beside the first. The larger of the two, Valera woke as he reached her side. Her hair, tangled and matted with blood and dirt, shifted slightly as he turned her over, slit-pupil eyes trained on him. Jonathan's heart nearly stopped at the sight of her. Bloodied, bruised, but unmistakably alive.

He fumbled for the knife at his waist, fingers still trembling with the aftershock of what he'd just done. The blade sliced through the ropes with a hiss of parted fiber.

She didn't wait.

The moment the last cord snapped, Valera exploded upward like a loosed arrow—gasping, spinning, crouching low with both hands raised, already in a fighting stance. Her eyes blazed, wild with frenzy and survival instinct, and for a heartbeat she didn't even seem to recognize him.

Then she blinked.

"Cub Mine," she hissed, baring sharp teeth. "You took far too long."

"Good to see you too," Jonathan muttered—just as the tiger warriors regained their footing and came charging.

But it was the other thing that made his blood run cold.

One of the tree giants had moved.

Not just shifted—uprooted. Its massive limbs groaned as it stepped forward, bark groaning like breaking bones. Eyes as black as rot fixed on the two of them. Cold. Intent. Ravenous.

Jonathan didn't need to guess what would happen if that thing got close. They wouldn't be injured—they'd be obliterated. Turned to pulp. Nothing left but memory and a red stain on the ground.

"Bring her," Valera snapped and pointed to the other figure on the ground. Then Valera dropped to all fours and began running, calling over her shoulders as she ran, "Follow me."

Jonathan hesitated.

The Malrics were coming fast—snarling, armed, eyes alight with violence. And something deep in his bones burned to meet them head-on. To make them pay. For hurting Valera. For threatening the ones he loved. For whatever it was they had done to this other girl—another innocent caught in the jaws of the Tide.

He wanted to stay. To fight. But he sheathed his weapon, reached to the ground, grabbed the tiny figure, and threw her over his shoulder.

He turned and ran after Valera, Cody right behind.

CHAPTER 12
THE ANCIENT STIRS

Jonathan followed Valera through a crumbling archway

that opened into a narrow tunnel choked with roots and debris. Behind them, the courtyard roared with movement—Malrics shouting, weapons clashing, the thunder of feet. He could feel them gaining. They couldn't outrun them.

They were going to have to fight.

With a grunt, Jonathan dropped to one knee and laid the girl down on the mossy floor. His hands moved automatically, cutting the ropes and pulling the mask from her head. He barely registered her face—there was no time.

He turned. His sword slid free from its scabbard with a hiss of steel, the runes along its edge already glowing, ready for blood. But before he could charge back into the fray, the world shifted. Roots began to grow—fast. Branches twisted from the walls and ceiling like giant snakes, thick and gnarled, weaving together over the entrance behind him. It wasn't a door in the traditional sense—it was the World Tree itself responding, sealing them off, cutting off pursuit.

Helping them.

The roots groaned and snapped into place, sealing tight.

But not fast enough.

A single tree-creature forced its way through, ducking low beneath the closing arch. It was massive, with bark-like armor and limbs like living stone. Moss sloughed from its shoulders. Eyes like burning coals locked on Jonathan.

The rest of the tree beasts were trapped. But this one had made it through, and one was more than enough. With Valera and Cody at his side, Jonathan raised his sword—and faced the impossible.

It came at them with the force of a landslide.

The creature moved like no tree should—fast, brutal, terrible. Limbs of gnarled wood slammed into the stone as it advanced, each step shaking the ground beneath its feet. Vines whipped behind it like serpents, and its face—if it had one—was a knot of roots twisted into a mask of malice.

Cody opened fire, pouring round after round of hot steel into its body. His rifle roared again and again—but the bullets punched through bark and vine as if striking water, leaving no sign of damage. Jonathan braced himself, sword raised, and Valera dropped into a low stance beside him, claws drawn, jade eyes flashing. But even as they prepared, he knew: this wasn't a fight they could win. This thing wasn't just strong. It was strength itself, the power of the forest, of earth, and Rot all packed into a monstrous form.

Even with Valera and Cody, even together—they would break before this thing did.

Then, just as the creature lunged forward, a voice rang out behind him. Sharp, fluid, spoken in a language Jonathan had never heard before. The syllables rose and fell like wind through a forest glade—beautiful and terrible all at once. He didn't understand the words. But he understood their weight. They were not a plea. They were not a question. They were a command, and the tree-creature froze mid-stride.

The thunderous stomp of its advance halted in an instant, as if time had stuttered around it. Its vine-limbs twitched in hesitation, the malice behind its movement drained away like breath from a corpse.

Jonathan turned, and his jaw dropped.

He had never seen anyone—or anything—like her before.

The girl they had rescued was tiny and thin, barely five feet even and a hundred pounds soaking wet—but she stood rooted like the earth itself. Her eyes were wide, glowing faintly with something elemental. Her feet were planted firm on the stone, hands not raised in defense, but in authority.

She was incredibly beautiful, yes, but she was more than that. Otherworldly, in a mystical, almost haunting way. Her hair was short, straight, and the color of the sky at midday and jungle leaves. Her eyes were such a dark green they were nearly black, and her ears—long and pointed—framed her face like the markings of some forgotten race.

Jonathan didn't know who she was, but she had just stopped a tree-giant with a word.

Jonathan's mouth opened and closed a handful of times before gaining control of it entirely. Valera cuffed him in the back of the head, and said, "Claws out, Cub Mine. Not hearts."

Jonathan blinked at his friend and mentor, as if his mind needed an extra second to believe what his eyes already knew.

A breath hitched in his chest, and for a heartbeat, the world blurred at the edges. It hit him all at once—like gravity doubling in weight, relief slamming into his ribs with the force of a hammer. He'd found her. Valera. After everything—the fall, the jungle, the fight against the Tide and time and fear—Valera was alive. Not just breathing, but still herself. Fierce. Sharp-tongued. Unshakable.

Without thinking, his arms closed around her, crushing her to him.

She froze for half a second, stiff as stone—then let out a low, irritated growl. But she didn't pull away. Slowly, the growl softened, melted into a deep, rolling purr that vibrated in his chest more than his ears.

"You stink like ten months of jungle rot, Cub Mine," she muttered, voice half-snarl, half-hug. "But I'll allow it. For now."

Jonathan choked on a breath and pulled back, blinking hard. The pressure behind his eyes built fast—tears, raw and uninvited. As if sensing it, Valera dropped to all fours and brushed against his leg with a deliberate nuzzle.

"Emotions are for later, Cub Mine," she said, her voice low and steady. She crouched, gaze shifting from him

170

to the girl across the courtyard—small, still, and very much watching. "First things first."

Jonathan nodded, voice tight. "Let me guess: you want me to do something dangerous?"

Valera didn't take her eyes off the girl with pointed ears and strangely colored hair.

"First things first," she said again, tone suddenly colder, darker. "We kill the girl."

The girl didn't flinch. She crouched low, arms raised in readiness.

"Even if you did manage to kill me—which, if you knew me, you'd know is next to impossible—you'd still have the Ancient to deal with."

Jonathan's eyes narrowed. "The Ancient?"

She tilted her head toward the towering tree-beast behind them.

"He's asleep," she said softly. "But the second I let go of him—even for a breath—he'll wake. And when he does, he'll tear you both to shreds and offer what's left to the Tide before you can land a single blow."

Valera growled. Her green eyes locked onto the girl. Claws curled into the dirt. Her muscles coiled, ready to spring.

The girl's eyes snapped back to Jonathan. "Look— just… hear me out, all right?" Her voice cracked slightly with urgency. "Call off your tiger. Let's talk. Just talk."

"Don't listen to its lies," Valera said, voice low and deadly. Her eyes never left the girl as she circled her. "Now is the time for hunting."

Jonathan's mind raced. He trusted Valera—her instincts were rarely wrong, and her sense for deception truly feline. But he also trusted his own gut... and something about what the girl had said rang true. The tree-beast behind them would tear them apart inside a minute, and if he died, he'd never be able to carry out his true duty, his true goal: to protect the people he cared about.

He glanced over his shoulder at the so-called Ancient. The massive tree-creature loomed, still motionless—but only barely. A thick, root-like leg twitched. The bark along its limbs creaked.

"C'mon, just call off your tiger!" the girl hissed, voice tight with frustration—and fear. Beads of sweat had begun to form on her brow. Her hands shook, her concentration clearly wavering. The Ancient behind them shifted again, a groan of wood and power reverberating through the courtyard.

"If you attack me," she warned, "we'll all die."

"I, for one, am against dyin'," Cody said, breath tight, eyes darting back and forth between the girl and the giant tree.

But Valera wasn't listening. Jonathan had trained beside her long enough to recognize the signs—she was only seconds from launching. He had to decide.

"Please," the young girl pleaded with Jonathan, beautiful eyes begging. " I can't hold it much longer."

Jonathan made his call.

"You hold it. If you want to talk, follow us. Valera—move."

But Valera's eyes were fixed on the girl. Her shoulders coiled, haunches tensed—ready to spring.

"Valera!"

She looked at him. There was a flash in her eyes—hurt, maybe, or confusion. But then she gave a subtle nod, trusting him.

Jonathan turned and ran. Valera and Cody followed.

They tore down a twisting stretch of crumbling architecture, ducking beneath root-woven beams and vaulting over fallen debris. A narrow hallway opened into a wider corridor, and still they ran, footsteps thundering in their ears. Jonathan didn't look back. Didn't slow. Minutes passed before he heard light footsteps catching up.

The girl.

Behind him, Valera gave a low, menacing growl. Either the girl didn't hear it or pretended not to. They pushed forward another hundred yards before the girl's voice cracked behind him.

"I—can't—keep running," she gasped, staggering to a stop. "Just… give me a second."

Jonathan slowed and turned. His eyes scanned the way they came, muscles tense.

"Is it chasing us?"

The girl leaned against the the nearest wall and shut her eyes, breath ragged. "No," she said at last, voice faint.

Jonathan didn't relax. He believed her—at least about that—but his hand stayed on the hilt of his sword just the same.

She stayed there for a long moment, gathering breath and composure. Then, slowly, she pushed herself upright, shoulders squaring despite her exhaustion.

"Thank you," she said, voice steadier now. "For saving me. If the Malrics had finished their ritual... I would now belong to the Tide. And if that happened—this war would be one step closer to being lost. And now, I need your help."

Jonathan's gaze flicked to Valera, searching her face for confirmation. She prowl-circled the girl on all fours, tail low, claws flexing.

"The witch speaks the truth," she said at last, reluctantly.

Jonathan's brow furrowed. "She fights against the Tide? Then why—why are we supposed to kill her?"

"So the Tide can't have her. Her power is great. And if the Tide gains such power, then all will be lost," Valera said and bared her teeth. "And also because I hate her."

"That's it?" Jonathan asked. "Not evil. Just irritating?"

The girl straightened, face flushing as she faced Valera. "I don't have to explain myself to you," she snapped. Genuine anger crackled in her voice. "I did what I thought was right. And if I hadn't, then my people would have paid the price."

Valera responded with a hiss, low and feral, her body tense, claws flexing against the stone floor. The girl didn't back down. She hissed back—shriller, defiant, her dark eyes blazing, and Jonathan noticed her canine teeth were sharper than any human's he had ever seen.

"This just got more tense than my cousin's third divorce hearing," he heard Cody grumble quietly.

Jonathan stepped between them. "Enough," he snapped.

Valera narrowed her eyes but didn't strike. The girl crossed her arms, lips pursed, but said nothing more.

Jonathan turned, first to Valera. "You don't trust her. Fine. But you do trust me. So let me do what you trained me to do—listen before I strike."

He looked at the girl. "And you—if you want our help, start talking. Now. But if either of you hisses again, I swear I'm throwing both of you in a tree and walking away."

"You want a speech? I'm out of breath, out of time, and out of patience. If you think I went through all that trouble holding back an Ancient just to betray you, you've got bigger problems than trust issues. And besides, if you want to survive, you're going to need me."

Jonathan remained unconvinced. He glared and said, "Convince me."

Their eyes locked. Despite her small frame and youthful face—he guessed she was near his age, though it was hard to tell, her race so unlike anything he knew—there was strength in her. Not strength of body, but of spirit. Quiet, heavy, immovable. Will carved into stone. Just standing there, she radiated it. Their gaze held like a clash of wills.

But it was the girl who looked away first.

A flicker of exhaustion passed through her features. She exhaled slowly, brushed damp strands of sky-blue hair from her face, and gave a brief glance toward Valera, who still crouched low, eyes narrowed and claws flexed. Then she looked back at Jonathan.

When she spoke, her voice was tired, but resolute. She held out her hand.

"My name is Aelowen." She said. "And if we're to survive what's coming, we'll need each other."

CHAPTER 13
THE HEIR OF A BROKEN PEOPLE

Jonathan took the offered hand. "Jonathan Roe."

Recognition flickered across her face, and then came the smile—radiant, disarming… and a little too pleased. "Awwww. Elysra mentioned you to me," she said, and looked him up and down. "I can see now she wasn't exaggerating."

The smile shifted—subtle, smoky, dangerous. She licked her lips and took a slow step forward, her gaze running over him like she was deciding whether to eat him or collect him.

Valera growled.

Aelowen paused, her eyes flicking sideways to the crouched tigress. Something in her expression cooled. She stepped back. Still, when her gaze returned to Jonathan, the smirk lingered. More guarded now. But not gone.

"My people are called the Ael'Shari. We didn't rule cities or raise armies—we listened. To the wind. The earth. To Ydrathar."

"Israel told me about her people," Cody said. "Called ya'll druids, if I remember right. He didn't seem keen on pickin' a fight with you—but I sure as rain know he didn't trust you, neither."

Aelowen shot him a glance—like she was deciding whether the fly in her soup was worth swatting—then turned back to Jonathan.

"Our magic came from Ydrathar herself," she said softly. "We were bound to her—every one of us. When she ached, we ached. When she flourished, we flourished. We lived as part of her rhythm, her breath. The Tree was not just a home to us—it was life."

She paused, her gaze distant, as if sifting through old memories. "But some time ago, things began to change. Subtly at first. The balance we once knew shifted."

Her voice dropped even lower. "At the center of Ydrathar lies the Wellspring—the beating heart of the Tree. It was the source of all life here: the strength of the roots, the breath of the leaves, the pulse of the branches. But there were those among us who believed it had been touched by something... Evil.

"A fragment of what lies sealed in the Wellspring has escaped. The Malrics call it the Rot, as if it were merely some sort of infection. But it is more than that. It can wear the shape of a man, but it is not one."

"Yeah, I've met the guy," Jonathan said dryly. "Calls himself Silas... something-or-other. Real charmer."

Aelowen's eyes sharpened, her body tensing. "You've *spoken* with him?"

Jonathan nodded once, feeling the weight of her sudden suspicion.

"Did you accept anything from him?"

"No," Jonathan answered and shook his head. "And when I turned him down, he tried to kill me."

She studied him in silence, her gaze narrowing further. For a moment, Jonathan half-expected her to strike.

Then she spoke, voice cold and edged. "He is evil itself, Jonathan. When he first emerged, the World Tree fought him. The roots rose, the branches struck—Ydrathar herself tried to destroy him. But he escaped. And since then, he has spread his corruption like a plague."

Jonathan's stomach twisted. "He's the source of the Rot?"

She nodded grimly. "He *is* the Rot. Shortly after he escaped his prison, everything changed. Our bond with the Tree... twisted. The Tree stopped giving. It started taking. It fed on us. Whispered to us. And those who listened too long—" her voice broke slightly, "—they changed. They were never the same again."

She glanced toward the roots coiled around the walls. "It infects everything. Trees. Beasts. Malrics. Even the Ancients. The Ancients were once guardians of the World Tree. They were made to protect us. But now… even *they* are starting to turn. And one by one, nearly all my people fell to it as well. Some fought. Most didn't. The bond broke them from the inside out."

Her voice caught for a moment, but she forced it steady. "My father—he was the last Druid Chieftain. Stronger than any druid in generations. When he saw what the bond was becoming, what it was doing to us, he did the unthinkable. He severed our connection to the Tree. He tried to save us. Tried to hold back the corruption."

She paused, a flicker of pain flashing behind her eyes. "But that was when *he* came."

Jonathan's chest tightened. He already knew who.

"The Tiger King," she said, her voice colder now. "Silas gave him power—more than any Malric was ever meant to wield. The Rot feeds him, twists him. It made him something else. Something beyond Malric. My father stood against him... and the Tiger King killed him.

"And when he did... most of our kind died. Others lost their minds. I don't know how many are left. Maybe none."

Her hands clenched at her sides. "Every day of my life since then, I've done nothing but run for my life—from Malrics, from the Tide, from anyone who thought killing me might save the world. But I'm tired of running. I don't want the Tree to die. I don't want the Tide to win. I want to stop it."

She hesitated—then said, quieter, "I want to find the others. If there *are* any left. I want to understand what I've become. And maybe... maybe I want someone to see me as more than a weapon."

"But most of all? I want to kill the Rot."

As the words left her lips, a flicker of raw emotion broke through Aelowen's practiced calm. Her eyes, once cool and guarded, flashed with something sharper—grief, fury, and longing twisted into one. Her jaw clenched, and a faint tremble passed through her—barely noticeable, but there.

This wasn't desperation. It wasn't even vengeance.

It was purpose.

And for the first time, Jonathan saw it clearly—not just the weight she carried, but the fire underneath. Not the scared girl holding back an Ancient, but the last heir of a broken people... ready to burn back the dark.

Jonathan looked to Valera as she continued to circle.

"You want to know why I don't trust her?" she murmured, voice barely more than a growl. She moved slow and deliberate, each step silent, each motion like a coil tightening. "She abandoned us. Arenthil. The Eastern Gate. She vanished. We bled."

Aelowen stood still, but tension radiated from her posture—spine straight, arms tucked close, hands clenched at her sides. Her breath was steady, but her eyes tracked Valera's every move. Not with fear—not quite—but wariness. Like someone standing still in the presence of a storm, not sure if it would pass or strike.

Valera circled behind her, then angled her muzzle toward Aelowen's still form and sniffed.

"And her magic?" Her voice dropped further, almost curious. She inhaled again, lip curling back to bare sharp white teeth. "It smells like ruin. Sweet. Rotten. Wrong."

"I don't blame you for hating me," Aelowen said quietly, eyes on Valera. "I've done things to survive. Things I'm not proud of. And the Rot is in my magic whether I want it or not, because it's in Ydrathar. But I didn't ask for this mantle. I couldn't give it up if I tried."

Her voice steadied.

"But I'm not your enemy. Not unless you decide to make me one."

Valera's lip curled again, eyes narrowing as her face twisted with malice. Her claws flexed.

"Hold," Jonathan told her.

Aelowen spared him a glance, then back to Valera. "If you're going to trust me, do it now. If not—then let's settle it here."

Jonathan turned to her. "What do you want?"

Aelowen didn't hesitate. "I want your help."

Valera's eyes flicked to Jonathan. Her voice was low, firm, the growl still coiled beneath every word.

"You owe her nothing, Cub Mine. Her people chose their path. Let her carry the weight of it alone."

She took a step closer, her tail lashing behind her.

"Your kin, our family, they bleed while we stand here. The She-Cub is among them. Come with me. They are taken—I know where they are held. We will free them. Leave this witch to her own fate."

Aelowen's glare lingered on Valera for a moment longer before she turned to Jonathan.

"You don't understand," she pleaded. "The Wellspring is failing. Silas came from the Wellspring, but he cannot control it on his own. He leads the Tiger King back into Ydrathar's domain, and together the pair of them are getting closer and closer every day. The Tree has been fighting them, but it will not be long before they reach the Wellspring, the Heart of Ydrathar. A Wellspring that is failing. It might already be dead. And if it dies, your friends, the ones you're trying to save? They die too. Doesn't matter how fast you run or how brave you are. If the Wellspring dies, we all fall."

Valera let out a low growl. "The She-Cub needs you, Jonathan. If we do not save them, then they will be sacrificed to the Tide, just as they were going to do to me."

Aelowen ignored Valera, eyes locked on Jonathan's. "If even *half* the rumors I've heard about you are true, Jonathan Roe… then you are exactly the kind of person I need. We are running out of time." Her voice dropped slightly, filled with quiet desperation. "I cannot face this alone. Help me."

Jonathan felt that familiar resistance tighten in his chest. He was already stretched thin, pulled in too many directions. When he said nothing, Aelowen reached out and grabbed his arm.

"You think I'm asking for help because I *want* to?" she asked. "I'm asking because I have no other choice. None of us do. The Rot is spreading. The Wellspring is failing. You can't save anyone if there's nothing left to save."

She took a breath, eyes locked on his. "And I'm the only one here who knows where the Wellspring is… and how to stop it from cracking open like an egg."

Jonathan looked from Valera to Aelowen.

He knew what he *wanted*: to save El, to save the Skyborn—his people. Heaven only knew what the Malrics had planned for them. Every second that passed put them further out of reach. Jonathan turned away, running a hand through his tangled hair. His heart pounded with too many choices, too little time. His heart screamed at him to move— save them, run, act—but he forced himself to be still. To think.

He looked at Aelowen. This strange girl—barely more than a whisper in the ruins of a forgotten world—had power threaded through her bones, and sorrow etched behind her eyes. She wasn't lying. He knew that now, the way you know when rain's about to fall. The Wellspring was dying and the Tide was coming. And if what she said was true, it wouldn't just take El. It would take *everything*.

Jonathan took a long breath, his hand settled on the hilt of his sword—not to draw it, but to steady himself.

He'd set out to save the Tree. It was his duty.

And that's exactly what he was going to do.

"Fine. We'll follow your lead," he said to Aelowen. "But if you betray us—if you even *think* about it—I'll cut you down myself."

Valera blinked slowly, tail flicking. Aelowyn gave a single, solemn nod.

And with that, Jonathan turned his eyes to the path ahead.

"Let's go save the world."

CHAPTER 14
BACK FROM THE DEAD

That night, after Aelowyn had fallen asleep, Jonathan sat beside the fire's dying glow. The cavern around them was carved of cold stone and coiled roots, a forgotten space buried deep in the World Tree's bones. Shadows pressed in from the corners, but the fire held a fragile circle of warmth—flickering, soft, alive.

Valera sat a short distance away, cross-legged and silent, drawing a whetstone down the edge of her blade. She didn't need to sharpen it, not really. But she did it anyway, the slow rasp of steel on stone the only sound between them.

Neither of them spoke.

Jonathan kept his eyes on the fire, but his thoughts had long since slipped elsewhere—back to the year they'd lost, the moments they should've shared, and the ache that had lived in his chest since the day he thought she might be gone for good.

He used to think all Malrics were like Valera: cold, practically wordless, brimming with demanding expectation.

But after his time in the jungle—time with Drekkar, Varg, with the others—he knew better. Valera wasn't typical. She was blunt, yes. Fierce beyond belief. But she carried something the others didn't. Something rarer. A quiet kind of loyalty. A sharp, unreadable soul. She was... herself. And that had always been enough.

He wanted to speak—say something real, something that captured the feeling of having her back after so long. But as often happened around her, the words stayed tangled behind his closed mouth.

So instead, he just let the silence hold.

He watched the fire flicker, watched the glow play across her stripes and the blade she didn't need to sharpen, and thought of how strange it felt to sit this close to someone he had mourned a hundred times in his dreams. She looked older, somehow, in the darkness, and more of her hairs had gone gray.

But she was here. Alive. Whole.

And that brought him joy—quiet and aching, but joy all the same.

"Foolish Cub Mine," she murmured, her voice carrying that familiar rasp of amusement. "So many words in your head, and none make it to your mouth. You sit like a rabbit—frozen, twitchy, waiting to be eaten."

Jonathan gave her a sidelong glance and resisted the urge to roll his eyes. He'd learned not to sass her unless he wanted a cuff to the ears—and she never missed.

When he didn't respond, she tilted her head slightly, blade still resting across her lap. "There's something chewing on you," she said. "Spit it out, Cub Mine."

He hesitated, then spoke low. "Aelowyn's right. If we can't save the Tree… then saving the others doesn't mean anything."

The whetstone paused. Valera's gaze lifted slowly, catching the firelight in slitted green eyes that gleamed like polished jade. She studied him without blinking, her tail twitching with calculation.

After a moment, she spoke, voice soft but pointed.

"Words like that are meant for yourself, not me. Your voice lies. Your scent doesn't," she said. "Convince yourself first, Cub Mine—then try me."

Then she resumed sharpening, slow and steady, like nothing more needed saying.

He thought about it—about everything. He hadn't wanted power, hadn't chased glory. He was only ever trying to do the right thing. And yet…

"If you're so sure I'm wrong," he argued, voice more petulant than he'd intended, "why not stop me? Why not do what you think is right instead?"

Valera paused. She turned and gave him a look—the kind only she could give. Half disdain, half affection. Like he was a cub who'd just tried to wrestle thunder.

"How does a cub grow," she asked slowly, "if he's never allowed to stumble? How can he learn to hunt if the mother never allows him to fail? If she always brings home the kill and never allows him to chase something bigger than he is?"

"So that's it?" he said, incredulous, and rubbed away the headache that was starting in his temples. "You're *intentionally* letting me make mistakes? You're willing to gamble my life so I can learn?"

Her ears twitched. "Wouldn't be the first time."

Something about that answer made him bristle. He opened his mouth to say something more, but she cut him off before the words could form.

"You are Cub Mine, and you always will be," she said firmly. "And I will stand beside you in every storm. And when you fall—because you will—I'll help you rise. That is the way of it."

He fell quiet, chastened. The warmth of her loyalty settled over him like a blanket pulled tight against cold.

But warmth never stayed long these days. His thoughts shifted, turning down paths he hadn't walked before. He realized with a strange ache that he'd lived among the tigers of the World Tree for nearly a year now. He knew their hunting calls, their rites of fire, their endless grudges.

And yet, about Valera—about *her*—he knew so little. Only that she was from a land called Malrica. Only that her father had been someone important, someone feared or revered, she never said which. Beyond that, virtually nothing.

He looked over at her, still sharpening her blade with those steady, patient strokes.

"Valera," he said softly, careful not to sound like a challenge. "Tell me about your home."

Her ears tilted back a fraction. For a long moment, she didn't look at him. Then she spoke, quiet but final.

"No. Not tonight. Tonight is for sleep."

He almost argued. The words were on his tongue. But then she gave him *that* look—the one that had ended every protest before it began. His mouth shut before he realized it.

She went back to her blade, her voice roughened by that familiar rasp. "Rest, Cub Mine. I'll watch while you sleep. Nothing will touch you."

The simple certainty in her tone eased something in his chest. Safer than walls, safer than iron, safer even than his own strength—Valera's word was a shield. It was enough to let his eyes grow heavy.

He shifted, stretched out beside the fire, and let the jungle floor cradle him. Just before his eyes slipped shut, he muttered, voice dry with a tired kind of humor, "You know… there aren't many people who, after a year apart—after both of us thought the other was probably dead—would make the very first thing they say to me a full-blown chastisement, followed by a lecture, followed by stern commands. I'm not exactly a kid anymore, you know." He tried not to sound petulant, but failed spectacularly.

Valera didn't look at him. She flexed a claw, inspected it with feline disinterest, then gave the faintest shrug.

"I always knew you were alive," she said, matter-of-fact. Then, after a beat—so soft it nearly vanished into the crackle of the fire—"But… it's good to have you back."

Their eyes met, and for just a second, she smiled.

"It's good to have you back from the dead, Valera," Jonathan said, matching her tone.

She gave him a flat look, rolled her eyes with theatrical exasperation. "Don't be so dramatic, Cub Mine, or I'll box your ears again."

For the first time in what felt like ages, warmth bloomed in his chest. Whether or not he was making a mistake, whether or not the path ahead led to ruin, he wasn't walking it alone. Valera was here. She always had a strange way of showing it, but she was with him. And somehow, that made everything feel a little less impossible.

But the feeling didn't last long.

The weight of the world crept back in, settling on his shoulders like a heavy beam.

And when he finally slept, it wasn't peaceful. The dreams came—twisted, jagged things that clawed through the dark. He ran through burning branches. Heard screams he couldn't place. Faces he'd failed. Voices he couldn't silence.

And always, just out of reach, the sound of the Tree weeping.

CHAPTER 15
GRAN'S TABLE

They moved in silence, deeper into the drowned skeleton of the Sunken City.

Jonathan followed Aelowen through a low arch choked with vines, ducking beneath the twisted branches. Aelowen was quiet as she led them, though he caught her glancing back now and then, as if she could feel the questions scraping against the inside of his skull. As if she knew the storm brewing in his gut.

Jonathan said nothing. He kept walking.

Because he'd already made his choice. And now, he would see it through.

Please, he thought, *let it be the right one.*

Slowly, the world around them began to change. The living walls of metal and vine began to break apart, giving way to signs of devastation. Scorch marks blackened the twisting roots. Shattered plating and shattered armor littered the ground. What had once felt like an otherworldly fusion of forest and machine now felt like the aftermath of war.

Eventually, they reached a great chamber, and Jonathan's breath caught in his throat as he stopped momentarily to take in the enormity of what it contained.

The air shifted—dense with smoke and the sharp tang of blood. The chamber ahead looked like the aftermath of a giant's fury, as if a storm the size of a world had torn through, leaving ruin in its wake. Fires burned in scattered pockets, throwing jagged shadows over blackened stone and shattered wood. The ground was split and cratered, torn open by blasts—gaping wounds between mounds of rubble and the twisted remains of the World Tree.

And everywhere—*everywhere*—there were bodies. Malrics. Ancients. Corrupted beasts. Hulking trolls, raptobeasts, humanoid ravens, jungle creatures Jonathan had only glimpsed in passing, and others he couldn't have imagined—all fallen. Some had been torn apart, others still clutched their weapons, frozen in final defiance.

As they moved deeper into the cavern, Jonathan noticed them—scattered among the wreckage of the Tiger King's army lay the unmistakable forms of Aelowen's kin. Druids with long ears and vivid hair, their elegant robes now singed and bloodstained, their lifeless bodies draped across the ruin. The sight pierced him. He glanced toward Aelowyn, but her expression remained unreadable, her gaze locked forward with a terrible, unblinking stillness.

And there, amid the dead, lay the destroyed guardians—more than Jonathan could have counted in a year, even if he did nothing else. They shared much of the same smooth, biomechanical design as the guardians that once stalked the halls of Aetherium: sleek plates of old metal combined with dark flesh, glowing battery cells half-buried in their chests. But these were different. These were built in the image of scorpions rather than spiders—bodies low and segmented, tails arched and bladed, massive pincers still locked in the echoes of battle. Their twisted forms littered the battlefield, silent and still, their armor cracked, burned, and blackened. An entire graveyard of machines that had once inspired awe and terror—now just ruin among ruin.

And in the center of it all, lay a Guardian.

Not small. Not sleek.

Massive.

It wasn't just a guardian. It was the capital-G kind.

Its body followed the same biomechanical design— sleek, seamless—but scaled to monstrous proportions. The scorpion-like tail was thick as a tree trunk, easily several times wider than Jonathan's torso. Its pincers looked large enough to crush buildings, and its armor gleamed even in ruin, plates over plates, each over a foot thick and forged from some impossibly perfect alloy. Jonathan could only imagine what it must have looked like in its prime—a glorious weapon of the Founders, built to guard something sacred.

Now, it wasn't just destroyed.

It had been cut in *half.*

Ripped clean into two perfect pieces. Not broken. Not shattered. Sliced with nearly perfect precision. Jonathan couldn't even begin to guess what kind of weapon the Tiger

King had used to do that… only that he never wanted to see it up close.

"The Everguard was supposed to be indestructible," Aelowyn said softly, her eyes lingering on the sentinel's shattered frame as they passed.

"If that thing was the bouncer," Cody muttered, eyeing the wreckage, "I don't wanna meet the guy who kicked down the door." He didn't sound afraid, but he gave his rifle a quick once-over and gripped the stock a little tighter.

Aelowyn's voice carried pain and sadness… and something colder beneath it. Fear. "The Tiger King's strength has grown."

Jonathan said nothing. He didn't know what to feel. But whatever it was, it wasn't hope. And it certainly didn't help his headache…

As they moved through the chamber, the flickering firelight reflected off the wreckage around him. He had come expecting a fight, expecting danger—but not this. Not the aftermath of something so total, so brutal, that even the most powerful weapons of the Founders had been reduced to scrap. He stared at the massive, broken Guardian in the center of the room, and something cold settled in his gut. The battlefield was also a message. Whatever had passed through here hadn't just won, it had dismantled sacred defenses like they were nothing. Jonathan had fought monsters. He'd faced a tyrant. But this… this was something else. Something beyond him.

A quiet dread began to bloom in Jonathan's chest. For the first time in a long time, he felt small—truly, crushingly small. He had no name for the force that had done this. No weapon to match it. He was walking into a war he didn't understand, trying to fulfill a duty he never asked for, and now, standing in the ruins of things meant to be invincible, he wasn't sure courage would be enough. He clenched his fists to stop the trembling. There was no room for fear now. But still—it lived in him. Whatever lay ahead was worse than anything he'd faced before.

Then, without warning, a light flared to life near the far end of the chamber. Not cold or harsh, but warm. Soft. Golden. It spilled out like morning sun cutting through a storm, casting long, comforting rays across the wreckage. For a heartbeat, it almost felt like Ydrathar herself was calling to them.

"What is that?" Aelowyn asked, her voice hushed.

They paused, all eyes turning toward the glow. The light pulsed gently at the far edge of the chamber, rising from a shattered wall where roots had curled back, forming a kind of natural archway.

Valera stepped closer, her ears twitching. Her tail was still, her claws uncurled. But she didn't reach for her blade.

"I do not trust many things," she said, voice low. "But whatever that is… it smells like… home."

Jonathan nodded in silent agreement, and together they moved in the direction of the golden light. They turned toward it, scrambling over the mounds of broken metal and burning wood, clambering past wrecked guardians and scorched stone.

As they drew near, the light flared once more—and something shifted.

195

A doorway shimmered into view, materializing in the steely wall like magic from behind a veil of golden mist and curling vines. It had been there all along, tucked into the curve of the chamber wall, completely untouched by the destruction around it. Somehow, impossibly, it had escaped the notice of the Tiger King and his army.

Unlike the rest of the chamber, it wasn't forged from metal or wrapped in circuitry. It was wood—simple, warm, and painted in soft, earthen tones. Faded blue. Hints of green. A weathered brass knob. Vines clung to it gently, their leaves glowing faintly. Jonathan reached out and brushed them aside, the tendrils parting like strands of silk.

It stood in stark contrast to the world around it. There was no ruin here. No scorch marks. No jagged metal or futuristic glare. Just a door—homely, quiet, and absurdly out of place. It radiated a kind of peace, the kind that didn't belong in warzones.

Jonathan looked at the door, then back at the others.

Cody gave a helpless shrug.

Jonathan took a breath, placed his hand on the worn brass handle, and muttered, "Here goes nothing."

Jonathan opened the door and strode through.

The room they entered wasn't grand or imposing. It wasn't a throne room or a temple. There could be only one way to describe the room they stood in... it was a home.

The charred steel and fires of the warzone gave way to smooth wood and soft light. The floor beneath his boots was polished from years of footsteps, worn smooth with love. Pictures lined the walls—smiling faces, distant mountains, children frozen in time. A narrow shelf held a collection of keepsakes: a clock with brass hands, a row of faded books, hand-carved trinkets arranged with quiet pride. A pair of worn boots sat beside a coat rack in the corner, and a window in the kitchen was open, through which blew an inexplicable, yet gentle, breeze.

The air smelled faintly of cedar and something sweeter—bread baking, maybe. The light glowed from nowhere and everywhere at once, golden and soft, like dawn spilling through linen curtains. It wrapped around them like memory. Like comfort.

This wasn't just a room.

It was a life.

A place where someone had loved. Lost. Tried to hold the world at bay.

And in the corner, nestled in the gentle rhythm of a rocking chair, sat an elderly woman.

She wore a simple apron over a faded blue dress, her white hair twisted into a tidy bun. Her hands moved with quiet grace, knitting needles clicking steadily as a blanket took shape in her lap. Her face was a map of deep-set lines—rivulets carved by time—one hundred and ten years old if she was a day. And yet, her eyes… her eyes were bright, sharp, impossibly green.

"Gran!" Aelowen cried, hurrying to her side and throwing her arms around her. The old woman embraced her gently, whispering something in her ear. Aelowen nodded and stepped aside.

Then she looked at Jonathan. The old woman smiled—a knowing, quiet smile—as if she'd been waiting for him for a very long time.

"Jonathan Roe," she said, her eyes returning to the steady rhythm of her needles. Her voice was ancient and soft. And yet, it was warm. Like a fire that had never once gone out. "It's about time."

"If you know who I am, then you know why I'm here. The Tiger King is coming. Help me stop him."

"You poor boy. So serious. So full of fire," she said and gave him a knowing glance over the rim of her glasses. "Always running headfirst into the fire, aren't you? Well, death's not going anywhere, darling, and the world's been ending since long before you were born. Why not have some tea before you chase it down?"

Jonathan opened his mouth to protest, but she raised a finger and cut him off.

"The end of the world can wait five minutes."

He scowled and tried again, but she didn't miss a beat.

"And don't give me that look, young man. I've raised boys just like you—full of noise and noble intentions. None as stubborn, perhaps, but close. And not one of them ever won an argument at my table."

Jonathan hesitated... then sighed. After a beat, he gave a sheepish glance to the others and stepped forward, easing himself into the chair across from her. The old wood creaked under his weight, but the cushion was warm, and the air oddly still—calm in a way that made the storm outside feel far away. She reached for a chipped porcelain teapot resting on a lace mat at her side and poured, steam curling up in delicate spirals. The scent of mint filled the air—cool, clean, and just like Jacky used to make. She handed him the cup with both hands, her warm fingers briefly brushing his.

The others followed his lead, all of them save Valera sitting slowly, eyes cautious but curious. Jonathan lifted the cup and took a sip of the tea, and something unexpected happened. Warmth filled his chest. Not just the warmth of heat, but of comfort, of something remembered. The kind of warmth that reminded him of home, of safety, of something older than fear. It took him several moments to regain his wits.

"You seem to know everything about me. Mind if we even the scales with a name?"

She smiled at him. "You already know it."

The others exchanged glances, uneasy, but Jonathan held her gaze. Her voice had the gentle tremble of age—thin and almost delicate, it was the voice of a woman who had lived a thousand quiet winters and remembered every one. Frail but sure. Kind, but carrying the weight of centuries. And somehow… familiar. Not from memory, not exactly— but from the rustling of the leaves on sleepless nights, from the hush of roots pressing through ancient soil beneath his feet, from dreams he hadn't told anyone about. It was the voice of the world itself, aged and aching, calling him home.

"Ydrathar," Jonathan said quietly. "You are Ydrathar."

She looked up, eyes twinkling like candleflame on antique glass, and gave him a smile that crinkled every line on her face. "Oh, my stars, it's been ages since someone's said it like *that*!" She gave a little chuckle and went right back to her knitting, needles clicking softly. "Yes, yes, Ydrathar I've been called—long before your great-grandmama's great-grandmama ever drew breath. That was me, dear. Or a bit of me, anyhow. Just a whisper with bones and a heartbeat."

She leaned in slightly, lowering her voice like she was sharing a secret. "But mercy, what a fuss of a name, don't you think? All those syllables. No need to wear your tongue out on my account." Her smile widened, warm and wrinkled. "You go on and call me Gran. Everyone always has, in the end."

"Gran it is," Jonathan said, and her eyes beamed at him. They were bright and impossibly green. And her smile felt like the first true day of spring.

But then, just as swiftly, the warmth vanished.

"I know why you've come," she said, and her voice cooled like dusk settling over warm stone. "And I know what waits for you behind that door."

With motion that trembled with age, she lifted her hand and pointed behind her—where a door stood that clashed with the charm of her home, all cold steel and humming light, edges too sharp, glow too clean.

Jonathan set his cup down gently, eyes never leaving hers. The shift in her demeanor stunned him. Where the tea had warmed his bones, her words now sent a chill straight through them.

"I don't rightly know how he managed it," she said, voice heavy with weariness, "but Khan has destroyed my Guardians."

"Khan?" Jonathan asked, the name catching like a hook in his throat.

Gran nodded slowly. "Yes. The Tiger King. He was once called Khan. I doubt he wants anyone remembering that—he prefers the legend, the title, the myth of having never been anything but what he is now. But he was once a small kit… one I should've bent over my knee and given a good thrashing."

She allowed herself a brief, bitter smile, but it faded as quickly as it came. Her eyes grew distant, shadowed by memory.

"Khan… he has destroyed my Guardians," she repeated, softer now. "Laid them low like they were ants beneath a boot. He has broken through the Outer Gates. Tore 'em clean open, he did—and he didn't come alone. Brought his pack of Malrics with him, and worse… other things. Dark things. Beasts bound to his will like dogs on chains."

She paused, folding her hands atop her knitting, the needles silent now.

"I fought him," she said simply, her voice like quilted thunder—soft, but not weak. "Oh yes. Fought with every trick I knew, every trap I'd tucked away in these old bones. And the Sunken City—bless her cracked ribs and stubborn spine—she rose up with me. We gave him trouble, I'll tell you that. Brought down more than a few of his beasts."

She paused. Just a breath. "But it wasn't enough. He's strong, that one. Stronger than any creature has a right to be."

"That's why we're here," Jonathan said, his voice firm. "We've come to help."

She looked at him with something between sorrow and admiration. "Bless your heart, child. Truly. I see… many different futures for you. In all of them, you are great. And in all of them, you die young," she added, the last part barely more than a quiet murmur to herself. Then she blinked, drew a breath, and went on, "And I know you mean to help. But it's not so simple as marching down and knocking on his door."

She leaned back then, settling deeper into the cushions like a grandmother about to spin a tale for the little ones gathered 'round. Her eyes turned inward, to places far older than any of them could grasp.

"A long time ago," she began, "before any of your histories were written—before your myths had teeth or names—the world was ending. The Founders saw it coming. Things that don't crawl from the dark, but *are* the dark. And they knew no army could stand against what was coming. So they built something that could," she said, her voice like wind stirring old leaves.

"Sanctuaries," she said softly. "Some were floating havens in the skies, built with science so strange it wore the skin of magic. But they also created the World Trees—seven of them. Vast, living sanctuaries rooted deep in the earth. And at the heart of each Tree… a Wellspring."

Jonathan frowned. "What exactly is a Wellspring?"

Her gaze dropped, voice growing quiet, almost reverent. "Think of them as seeds. Restorers. Failsafes. When all else was lost—when life itself had been scoured from the planet—the Wellsprings would awaken. Not to end the world… but to *begin* it again, to start life anew after an extinction event, to restart creation after collapse. Not destruction, but rebirth. For contained within each Wellspring is a vast reservoir of pure, unshaped life—raw potential, waiting for the world to need it."

Her tone shifted, colder now.

"But Khan… he means to take mine. To twist its purpose. To seed the next world in *his* image. Not renewal—*dominion.* Not life—*obedience.* The potential within the Wellspring is nearly limitless… and he's found a way to corrupt it. To bend it. To remake the next world in the likeness of the Rot."

"The Rot," Jonathan murmured.

She looked at him then, steady and sorrowful.

"Exactly. My Wellspring is bleeding corruption, you see, and he drinks it in. And in his hands, that poison has taken shape as the Rot. If he succeeds, the Next World will be born. It will be a nightmare—living, growing, and utterly *his.*"

She looked to each of those at her table in turn, eyes narrowing with gravity. Jonathan hesitated before speaking again. "Selene said the Rot can't be destroyed. That it's part of your system."

Gran inclined her head. "It is. You can't kill the Rot. Neither can I. But you *can* kill its anchor. Take out Khan, and the Rot will unravel with him."

Valera straightened, a growl low in her throat. "Then we stop him. We are four. He is only one."

Gran gave her a soft smile.

203

"Oh, fierce one… such spirit in you. But I'm afraid it won't be so simple. That room beyond?" She nodded gently toward the sealed door behind her. "It's not meant for the likes of most folk. I'm not rightly sure any of you could step inside and still come out whole."

A ripple of confusion passed through the group.

Gran Ydrathar gave a slow, solemn nod. "Once you step through that door, you'll understand. My poor Core, the Wellspring, it was never finished proper. They rushed it, you see—ran out of time, or sense, or both. Deployed it before it was ready. Before the seal was strong." She let out a breath like creaking floorboards. "And now the monsters inside? The energy? The singularity inside my Core? It's leaking, child. Just a trickle… but trickles become floods."

"A singularity?" Cody cut in, brows raised. "You mean like… a black hole?"

"Not technically," she said, "but I wouldn't get too cozy with the difference."

"That's impossible."

"Sure it is," Gran said dryly. "But someone out there doesn't care. And the result of all that leaking energy is the Pit."

She took a deep breath before continuing, her voice laced with quiet mourning. "The Pit isn't just a hole in the ground, child. It's the edge of an unstable gravity well. Space twists and folds down there for time and all eternity. Time bends. Light itself can't find its way out. You could fall forever and never land."

Gran took a sip of tea, then set down her teacup with a gentle clink, her hands folding neatly in her lap. The golden light in the room dimmed just a little.

"You've come to save the world, haven't you, my dear?" she said. "Brave as they come. A heart that lights up like a hearth at the first crackle. But unfortunately, the Pit and the Tiger King are only one of the problems you now face. And perhaps, not the worst. The world's not the only thing in danger, and yours isn't the only soul hanging in the balance."

She leaned forward, the rocking chair creaking softly beneath her. Gran spoke again—gently, but with the firmness of someone who'd raised a hundred boys just like him.

"There are two doors before you, Jonathan Roe."

"One," she said, lifting a frail finger and pointing once more to the door behind her, the door made of steel and glass and otherworldly light, "leads to the Wellspring. To Khan. If you go there now, you may stop him. I think it unlikely. He is too powerful, and you are young. But there is a small chance you are successful, and that chance is, in all likelihood, the only chance that I have to survive. Retrieve the Wellspring and bring it to me, and you may save me, the World Tree, and the branches above, and everything that still clings to life upon them."

She paused. Her eyes did not waver.

"But Khan is no fool. He gave orders. If he falls, every prisoner under his command is to be slain. No quarter. No delay." She let that settle. "El is among them."

Jonathan's breath hitched.

Gran sat back again, the chair rocking once, slow and steady. "Door two," she continued, and pointed to a door at the far end of the room. There stood an oak door that led in the opposite direction, "takes you *away* from the Singularity Vault. Toward the city ruins. Toward your friends. If you go now, you might reach them in time. Might save the girl. The others too. But if you do…"

She exhaled through her nose, quiet as falling dust.

"Then the Wellspring will be his to do with as he chooses."

Cody coughed, trying not to sound too hopeful. "We don't, uh, have reinforcements hiding nearby?"

Gran chuckled, low and dry. "You sweet boy. I'm afraid the reinforcements are already seated at my table."

She looked around at the others, then back to Jonathan—her eyes full of sadness, but never pity.

"It's a cruel thing, I know. But life rarely gives us tidy choices." She paused, took a deep breath. "There's a choice waiting for you, child," she said, softer now, though the weight in her voice didn't lessen. "One that only *you* can make. And once your feet set to that path…" Her gaze traveled slowly across each of them, her knitting forgotten in her lap. "Well, there'll be no turning back after that."

"So. What's it to be, dear heart?" Gran's eyes narrowed, studying him.

Jonathan looked at the sealed doors behind her. His throat felt dry. He'd been brave before. He'd faced monsters, storms, cloudfall. But this… this felt different. Bigger. He felt painfully small. Insufficient. Like a child pretending at

206

heroism. If Khan was even half as terrible as the stories made him out to be, there was only a small chance he was walking out of there alive.

He opened his mouth. Closed it again.

"Tick-tock, darling," Gran said lightly. "The world's not going to save itself."

Gran raised an eyebrow, a flicker of teasing dancing in her eyes despite the heavy silence that hung between them. With a small huff, she adjusted the blanket across her lap, the gesture both casual and deliberate—like a queen settling her robes before delivering a verdict.

Jonathan stood.

"No," he said.

"No?" she asked, her tone unreadable.

"No," Jonathan repeated. "I don't accept this."

She tilted her head slightly, the warmth fading from her face. "This is the choice, child. It's the only one there is."

Jonathan shook his head. "No, it's the choice *you* gave me. But it's not the only one."

He turned to Valera. "You and Cody—go. Find El. Save the others. Get them out."

Cody's mouth opened, ready to argue. "And you?"

Jonathan's eyes turned to the door behind Gran.

"I'm choosing *not* to lose anyone else," Jonathan said. "Not today."

He could barely believe the words as they came from his mouth.

"I'm going after the Tiger King. Alone."

CHAPTER 16
THE PIT AND THE KING

Valera stepped toward Jonathan, close enough that Jonathan could feel the warmth of her breath, hear the purring rumble in her chest. She reached for him, pulling him close until their foreheads touched—a gesture as fierce as it was intimate.

"Bleed if you must, Cub Mine," she whispered. "But you may not die this night. I forbid it. If you get yourself killed while I'm gone, I will hunt you through the afterlife and drag you back."

His eyes burned, but he pushed the tears down. She would not approve. He nodded, but the tightness in his voice prevented him from answering her.

"Watch her back," Jonathan told Cody firmly.

Cody tipped his hat. "Always."

Gran's gaze locked on Jonathan. Her eyes—still bright and green—seemed to see not just the boy before her, but every step that had brought him here. He had known that this moment would come. That he would have to face the Tiger King. He'd heard the stories whispered in the jungle, the warnings from Drekkar, the unease in Varg's voice when the name was spoken. And now... here it was. Not a myth. A door. Could he do it?

Alone?

Without another word, Jonathan turned his back on his friends, stepped around Gran Ydrathar in her chair, and walked toward whatever fate awaited him.

Aelowyn followed.

He opened his mouth to protest, "You shouldn't—"

"I don't care about your friends, Jonathan Roe," she snapped, cutting him off before the words could land. "I care about Ydrathar. And if following you gives us even a sliver of hope to save her, then I'm coming with you. That's all that matters."

He studied her for a long moment.

"Can I trust you?" he asked.

Aelowyn held his gaze, considering. Then, with quiet certainty, she answered, "You can trust me to help the World Tree."

Something of disappointment must have shown on his face, because when he moved to step away from her, her hand shot out and grabbed his arm. He stopped, surprised by the suddenness of her grip—stronger than he expected. She turned to face him fully, her striking eyes searching his for a long, silent moment.

"My priorities are *Ydrathar*, Jonathan," she said. "They always have been. Nothing else matters to me—not glory, not vengeance, not even you. If you stand in the way… if it comes to choosing between you and Ydrathar… I need you to understand—I *will* choose the Tree. Without hesitation." There was no malice behind her words, no heat—only that quiet, unshakable certainty that comes from absolute conviction.

"Aelowyn—" he started, but she shook her head.

"This isn't anger, Jonathan. It's reality." Her eyes softened, just barely, enough to betray the hint of a burden she carried. "I won't lie to you. You have your people to fight for. I have my priorities. If you stand between me and what must be done, you'll leave me no choice."

For a moment, they simply stared at each other, the silence between them taut as a drawn bowstring.

Finally, Jonathan exhaled. "At least you're honest."

He nodded once. She released his arm.

"I just thought you should know," she added, her voice softer now. For a fraction of a second, something flickered behind her eyes—something she quickly buried beneath her steady resolve, and she added, "It's better this way. It's... easier not to be torn between two things."

Jonathan turned and moved toward the door. It hissed open with a low, grinding groan. A breath of air escaped from the chamber beyond—thick, metallic, laced with the scent of ozone and old roots.

Things were happening too fast, and Jonathan felt like he was barely hanging on—swept forward by momentum he couldn't stop, like a pawn caught in someone else's game. It all felt wrong. Out of his hands. Out of balance. How had it come to this? One person, alone, facing a room full of monsters. No true allies. No plan. And yet here he was—walking toward the storm, one step at a time, because there was no other choice left.

Drekkar's words echoed in his mind: *There will be moments when you must walk the path of duty...*

Jonathan stepped through.

The change was instant.

Sound vanished first—consumed by pressure so dense it swallowed everything but the thunder of his own pulse. Then came the sensation of weight—impossible weight—pressing inward from every direction, like the air itself was trying to collapse him. He could feel it in his joints, behind his eyes, in the grinding of his teeth. Each step forward felt like walking into a storm of gravity and silence.

The Wellspring Chamber unfurled around him like a cathedral carved from madness.

The room was circular, a hundred yards across, with a walkway that spanned all along the outer edges, as well as half a dozen bridges that led to a small pedestal in the exact center of the room. And in the center of that impossible chasm, suspended on a narrow column of root and marble, floated the Wellspring.

It was shattered.

A great sphere of once-flawless crystal, now fractured in half a dozen places, pulsed weakly with flickering veins of green-white light. Cracks spiderwebbed across its surface, and orbiting its broken heart were jagged shards of crystal spinning slowly like moons knocked off course. Black roots wrapped around the Wellspring's base, twitching faintly, half-alive, feeding or draining—it was impossible to tell. For long moments, it went black entirely. And then, like a final breath in the chest of a dying animal, a faint flicker. And another. Then it went dark again, sputtering between life and death. It wasn't merely fading. The Wellspring wasn't just dying.

It was in its death throes.

And around it all, threading through every edge and surface, was the leak.

It oozed from the fractures in the Wellspring like ink through broken glass—slivers of the singularity bleeding into the air. They shimmered like heat haze, like pieces of space that refused to behave, curling and pulling at everything around them, then they plunged down into the Pit below, for beneath the bridges there was no floor—beneath him yawned the singularity, a vast and bottomless pit—a void that wasn't just dark, but empty in a way that hurt to look at. He peered over the edge. The Pit didn't look deep; it looked endless, a curtain of darkness that swallowed all light, all sense of scale. No sound. No impact. Just the quiet certainty in his gut that the pit had no bottom.

He had no idea what the Founders had built here— what impossible laws they'd bent or broken to carve this place into the heart of the Tree.

Jonathan stopped just a few paces into the chamber, his breath catching.

It was breathtaking. Terrifying. Beautiful.

213

But he couldn't admire it.

Every nerve in his body was screaming. The pressure on his chest made it hard to breathe. His muscles trembled from the effort of simply standing. His vision blurred at the edges. The Pit wasn't trying to kill him—it was unraveling him. Thread by thread.

He clenched his fists, focused.

The old power stirred in his bones—not loud, not flashy, but true. He wasn't immune to the singularity's pull—but unlike most everyone else, he could exist inside it. He could *withstand* it. And in that moment, he knew: the others could never have survived this. No one else would've made it past the threshold. This was not a place for humans.

He took a step along the bridge that led to the Wellspring. Then another. Not fast. Not confident. He stared at the Wellspring, just a hundred feet away, spinning slowly above a wound in the world.

An abrupt sound echoed through the Wellspring Chamber, and Jonathan turned to his left.

It was the Tiger King.

The largest Malric Jonathan had ever seen—taller and broader in the chest even than Varg. His fur was snow-white, broken only by stripes as black as spilled ink, slashing through his frame like clawed fissures in stone. But what struck Jonathan most wasn't the size. It wasn't the gleaming crown of ivory bone that curved atop his skull like a throne grown from his spine. It wasn't even the fact that he wore no armor, as though he had never needed it.

It was the absence of scars.

The Tiger King's body was a canvas untouched by war. No burns. No claw marks. No trace of blade or fire or fang. The fur across his chest and shoulders was pristine—unbroken, untouched, pure. Every soldier Jonathan had ever known had carried the memory of battle carved into flesh. Every Malric Jonathan had ever fought wore the story of their survival in wounds and ruin. But not Khan.

The Tiger King had never lost.

Not once.

Standing next to him was a creature that defied sense—tall, broad-shouldered, its skin slick and pale like something dredged from the deep, like a shark in the crude imitation of a man. Its head was smooth and finned, with rows of jagged teeth jutting from a mouth that split too wide. Its eyes were small, black, and hungry. Muscles rippled beneath its semi-translucent skin, and each step it took left a smear of moisture across the marble floor. The four of them stood still, each framed in their doorway—Jonathan, Aelowen, the Tiger King, and the shark-faced creature. For a moment, no one moved.

Khan pointed at the Wellspring and issued a command to the creature at his side. With a bubbly shrieking sound, it lunged for the Wellspring, legs propelling it forward in an eerie, loping sprint. It moved like a predator from some alien deep—arms sweeping low, body sleek and coiled, a strange curved weapon clutched in its webbed hand.

The creature had a head start and would reach the Wellspring before Jonathan could, but Jonathan didn't need to arrive first. Without thinking, he reached for the gravity beneath his feet, pulling it up through his limbs like fire through his veins. Here next to the singularity, where gravity thrashed around him like a wild storm, it was easier than ever before to control. He felt a strange release of pressure in his skull and the world around him tightened, focused. He extended one hand—palm open, aimed—and pulled.

The space behind the creature collapsed inward, and with a deafening *crack,* the creature was launched backward like a missile. It sailed across the chamber, limbs flailing, and slammed into the far wall with bone-jarring force. The impact echoed through the marble like thunder, and then the creature fell into the black void of the Pit beneath them. There was no sound of it ever hitting the bottom.

Jonathan lowered his hand, heart pounding, the Wellspring pulsing faintly.

If he was rattled by Jonathan's display, Khan didn't show it. Jonathan said nothing. He didn't even slow. He simply continued walking—deliberate, steady—toward the platform where the fractured Wellspring hovered, dying. The exhaustion from throwing around that much gravity seeped through his bones and muscles, but he refused to let it show.

Across the void, Khan mirrored his pace, silent as snowfall, his snow-white fur catching the dim green light. Each step they took echoed, each of them a predator circling a prize neither of them would surrender. The bridges creaked beneath them, ancient stone groaning as if straining to hold the weight of what was coming.

It was Khan who broke the silence first.

"That was hardly pathetic at all, human," the Tiger King rumbled, voice low and smooth, rolling across the chamber like distant thunder. "Tell me—who taught you to wield the world's breath like that?"

In answer Jonathan drew his sword, leveling it toward the king, placing himself between the giant and the Wellspring. Jonathan couldn't shake the primal edge of fear that gnawed at him. He had never stood so close to something that could, quite literally, eat him.

Aelowyn struck first.

She stopped just short of the center and raised her hands, her motions slow and precise, almost ceremonial. Magic answered her call; for indeed, magic was the only word to describe what happened next. Fingers traced glowing sigils through the air, weaving threads of light that shimmered and twisted like living script. The air thickened around her, charged and electric. Jonathan felt it—something waking. She was the World Tree's child. Its voice. Its fury.

The Tiger King looked at her.

"No," he said simply—flat, dull, emotionless, empty of malice or concern—just a decision, made and done, like closing a book.

Aelowen dropped like a stone, her body crumpling to the ground without a sound. The giant beast stepped forward slowly, his eyes fixed on Jonathan.

Jonathan raised his sword and prepared to fight.

And die.

Then the Tiger King did something strange.

Without urgency, without threat, he set his massive war axe down beside him. He removed his crown—a smooth, carved relic of bone and iron on which was set a glowing green jewel—and placed it gently on the ground. Then, with

217

almost unnatural grace, he lowered himself to the floor, sitting cross-legged across from Jonathan, their eyes level.

"She's wrong," the Tiger King said at last, and motioned to Aelowyn's still form. His deep voice was smooth, without a trace of menace. "But she knows she's right. And that makes her impossible to reason with."

Jonathan tensed, keeping his sword raised, shifting subtly to stand between the king and the Wellspring. He studied the figure before him—this monster cloaked in royalty—and despite the Tiger King's composure, Jonathan felt like he was standing in the eye of a storm that hadn't yet chosen to break.

"Couldn't the same be said about you?" Jonathan asked.

Khan's lips curled—almost a smile, but not quite. He said nothing for several seconds, simply studied the boy with unreadable interest.

"I killed your cousin, you know," Jonathan added coldly. "Raulg, something or other. Maybe I'll put you next on the list."

"You may have killed Raulg, but he is not dead. I assure you." He smiled then —broad, sincere, and utterly terrifying.

Jonathan's brow furrowed, confusion flickering across his face.

"Put down your sword," Khan said softly, and there was neither anger nor malice in his voice. "Come with me, and I'll show you."

Jonathan shook his head. "I've seen enough monsters to know that whatever you're offering… it isn't salvation."

"Monster?" Khan echoed, tilting his head with mild curiosity. "You and I want the same thing, Sky Warrior."

"I highly doubt that."

Khan gestured toward the pulsing Wellspring, its faint green light flickering weakly behind them.

"Look at it, Sky Warrior. The Wellspring is dying. Through no fault of our own, Ydrathar withers. And it has been dying for far longer than anyone dares admit."

He shifted slightly, his voice taking on the calm, heavy tone of a ruler speaking hard truths.

"I have led my people for a generation. And only a ruler knows what it means to rule: sometimes it means sacrifice. Hard, brutal, necessary sacrifice. Once I accepted that truth, I made my choice."

"To kill it?" Jonathan said, his grip tightening on his sword.

"To *save* it, Jonathan." The Tiger King's voice remained smooth, disturbingly patient. "Yes, some call it corruption. But it is still life. And all life evolves. Change is inevitable. The Tree is not dying because of me—she is transforming through me."

He locked eyes with Jonathan, voice dropping lower, heavier. "You fight to preserve what cannot last. I fight to build what must come next."

"But the Old Ways—" Jonathan started.

"The Old Ways are dead!" he snarled, and a flash of murderous rage sparked in the Tiger King's eyes as he bared his teeth. His chest rose and fell—once, twice—and just as quickly, the fury faded, his voice returning to that chilling calm.

"You and I are very much alike. You would stop at nothing to save your kind. So would I. How are we different?"

Jonathan hesitated, the weight of the words pressing into him. He could feel the pull—the temptation buried beneath the logic. And yet...

When he didn't answer, the Tiger King pressed on, voice growing heavier, the gentle rumble of a sleeping volcano.

"What you call the Rot does not represent death. Rather, it is evolution. The old world must fall. Its branches burned, its roots consumed, so something stronger may rise in its place. I am not the destroyer of this world—I am its purifier."

"You're such a good guy, sure. Is that why you kill all humans on sight?"

"True. I have always despised your kind," Khan admitted, his gaze narrowing. "Humans—parasites feeding on what they do not understand. Weak, greedy, blind. A disease upon Ydrathar's flesh." His claws flexed once against the stone, but his voice remained steady, almost gentle. "But even a parasite, when properly applied, can have its uses."

He studied Jonathan now, the weight of his eyes like a predator appraising prey that had unexpectedly grown fangs.

"You, for example," he continued softly. "You are different. The Tree's breath is in you. I can feel it. You could stand beside me. Not as a parasite, but as something greater." He gestured faintly toward the flickering Wellspring, as if illustrating the scale of the moment. "The world is changing, Jonathan. Forces older than either of us are awakening. Beings more powerful than you... and more powerful than me. They have offered me a place in what's coming. I merely do the same for you." Silk and honey dripped from his basso voice, smooth and rich.

Then it turned cold.

"But if you do not accept this offer..." His lip curled faintly, revealing a glint of fang. "Then I will continue my sacred task. I will cleanse this realm of your kind—those soft-bellied, sun-worshiping vermin who build cities atop branches they do not understand, who multiply like ants and feed like carrion eaters. I will burn your shrines, salt your lands, and erase every trace of your species from the bark of this world until the Tree forgets you ever touched her."

He leaned forward slightly, voice smooth.

"The choice is yours."

Jonathan let the words settle around him like ash.

For a moment, the offer hung there, heavy, almost tempting. Power. Survival. A place in whatever nightmare future the Tiger King envisioned.

And then Jonathan shook his head—once. Firm. Final. Anger flashed in Khan's eyes, and Jonathan met his gaze with equal intensity.

"You were meant to protect the Tree, but instead you enslave it. You were meant to lead your people—not conquer them. You were supposed to fight for your ideals, not burn them to the ground." His eyes narrowed, voice steady but burning underneath. "You call this evolution?" Jonathan said, his voice sharp and steady. "All I see is someone who surrendered to fear and sold his people's birthright to the highest bidder the moment things got a little bit hard."

The words landed like a slap. The Tiger King's expression darkened—rage blooming behind his eyes like a lightning trapped in a bottle. Slowly, deliberately, he reached for his crown and set it upon his brow. Then he stood. It was like watching a mountain rise. His massive form uncoiled to its full height, bone-white fur catching the greenish glow of the Wellspring. The room seemed to shrink around him. Without a word, he reached for his war axe—an enormous thing, brutal and timeworn. His paw, easily larger than Jonathan's entire head, closed around the haft with quiet finality.

The air thickened with menace.

"Have a care—" the King began, voice edged with warning.

But Jonathan cut him off.

"No." His voice rang sharper than steel. "You and I are nothing alike."

He raised his sword, steady despite the tremor in his limbs. "I'd rather spend eternity as your slave than stand beside you as a false king who betrayed everything he was meant to protect."

For a breath, all was still.

Then the Tiger King's eyes narrowed—no sound, no roar, just cold wrath winding tight behind his gaze like a storm held in leash.

"That can most certainly be arranged," said a voice Jonathan recognized—smooth, alien, and disturbingly familiar.

Silas.

CHAPTER 17
TWO CHAIRS AT THE END OF THE WORLD

T he air suddenly rippled—not like wind or heat, but like reality itself had caught a fever. A shape began to form. First a smear of darkness, then a swirl of oil and shadow, coalescing like ink in water. It pulled itself together slowly, almost lazily, limbs stretching, spine unfurling, until the silhouette of a man emerged from the distortion.

Piece by piece, he congealed—black fluid twisting into bone, muscle, skin. A face took shape last: too symmetrical, too smooth, too perfect. As if it had been sculpted by a liar. Thin lips curled into a knowing smile. Silas Grey stood in the chamber—fully formed now. His eyes, twin polished voids, studied Jonathan not with hatred, but with curiosity—like a collector inspecting something precious and unpredictable.

"Really, Jonathan," Silas continued softly, almost amused. "You do have a gift for choosing the most... inconvenient paths."

Then Silas turned to Khan. The two beings, each monstrous in his own right, locked eyes like eternal rivals on the edge of war. For a heartbeat, the air tightened. Jonathan felt it in his chest—an instinctive certainty that violence was about to erupt.

But the moment passed.

Without a word, the Tiger King lowered himself to one knee before Silas, head bowed in a gesture of submission.

Jonathan blinked, stunned.

"There," Silas purred, his voice velvet over poison. "That's better."

Silas didn't thank him. He merely extended a single finger and lifted the massive warrior's chin with casual arrogance, as if raising a pet from the floor.

"My faithful beast," Silas said. "It pleases me that you have finally learned your place."

Silas turned his attention back to Jonathan. His smile was faint, hollow, and cruel.

Jonathan knew he couldn't beat the pair of them—not like this. The Tiger King was a force of nature, unequaled brute strength and relentless purpose. Add Silas to the mix, a creature who bent reality like paper, and Jonathan wouldn't last long enough to speak their names aloud.

So he didn't aim to win.

He aimed to stall.

Buy time. Distract. Endure. Whatever it took. If he could keep them occupied—if he could keep them from the Wellspring—long enough for Valera to return with reinforcements, there might still be a chance. It wasn't glory he sought. It wasn't victory. It was time. A few more seconds. Just long enough for the others to arrive.

He set his stance and raised his blade.

"Hey there, Twiggy. Let me guess. You came here to surrender, right?" Jonathan said. "I accept."

Silas ignored Jonathan's statement and studied the teenager for several moments. Then, with a flick of his fingers, a table shimmered into existence between them—sleek, dark, and far too perfect to be real. Two chairs appeared, as if conjured from shadow. Silas moved to the nearest seat and sat down with the ease of a man who had all the time in the world. The Tiger King moved to stand behind Silas, silent and still— more monument than Malric, a white-furred mountain crowned in bone, exuding the quiet promise of unspeakable violence. The largest bodyguard the world had ever known.

The thin man in the black suit gestured to the empty chair with a slight tilt of his head.

"Sit. Let's talk," he said smoothly, as if they were old friends meeting for tea.

Jonathan didn't move at first. He stood there, weighing every option as he watched the bone-thin man wait for his answer. It couldn't hurt. Not yet. Besides, every second spent here was a second closer to Valera's return— and reinforcements.

Slowly, warily, Jonathan stepped forward and lowered himself into the chair across from the man and the tiger, crossed his arms and said flatly, "Is this the part where I have to listen to one of your evil speeches about how you're really the good guy?"

The man smiled—and disturbingly, it seemed genuine. Just quiet amusement, as if Jonathan had told a joke he hadn't expected to land. Silas sat back in the chair with a relaxed grace, folding one leg over the other like a man settling into a fireside chat rather than a meeting at the edge of the world. His fingers tapped lightly on the table, rhythmic and patient—measured, precise, almost thoughtful. Like a man listening to music only he could hear.

"I knew your father, you know. He was very much like you—sharp tongue, sharper instincts. Believe it or not, we were… quite close. Dear friends, once. In fact, it was I who gave him that knife you wear. A parting gift, you might say."

Jonathan's hand drifted instinctively to the small knife at his waist. He'd never given the blade much thought—just something his father had left him. A keepsake. His father had died when Jonathan was still a boy, and the knife had always been more symbol than weapon.

But now… Silas's words clung to the memory like mold. It felt wrong. Tainted. The handle beneath his palm seemed colder than it had moments before.

"Yeah, I'm sure the two of you were best friends," Jonathan said. He looked at Khan and said. "And I've seen what you do for your friends. No wonder you're so popular."

Silas sneered, then waved his hands as if to dismiss the small talk. "When the Unmaking Tide returns in full… the earth will *bleed*," he hissed. "The stars will scream. And *nothing* you do can change the outcome."

Jonathan arched a brow. "If the end's so inevitable—if you're so certain—your omniscience must be slipping, because you're trying to recruit me like it's an actual possibility, and I'm definitely about to tell you to go jump into a black hole."

And that was when he saw it—truly saw it—for the first time. That flicker behind Silas's carefully constructed calm, that strange weight behind his gaze. It wasn't rage. It wasn't divine wrath or ancient menace. It was the temper of a spoiled tyrant denied his toy. His smile was still in place, but it was forced like a mask struggling to stay on.

"For now, perhaps. But not forever. All things break, Jonathan. All things bend. Even you. The World Eaters *will* inherit this world. I will lay it at their feet like a gift long overdue. And I ache, Jonathan—I *ache* with the knowledge that it has taken me this long to complete what should have been accomplished long, long ago."

He leaned forward, eyes gleaming with cold certainty.

"You *will* kneel. It is not a matter of if—it is only a matter of when. No one can reject the World Eaters."

Jonathan didn't hesitate. "Watch me," he said flatly. "Go. Stuff. Yourself."

The Tiger King stepped forward, drawing his weapon—a massive axe carved from polished bone, its edge gleaming like moonlight on a blade. He raised it high, muscles rippling with anticipation.

"His throat, Master," he growled. "Let me have his throat."

Silas lifted a single, lazy hand. "'Heel, you dumb beast. You're drooling on my moment."

Khan hesitated, snarled once, but obeyed—taking his place at Silas's back like a chained storm waiting to be unleashed.

Silas turned his attention back to Jonathan, expression unreadable.

"I don't accept your refusal," Silas said, with the tranquil arrogance of someone convinced the final page had already been written.

Then came the smile again. Gentle. Nostalgic.

"Perhaps a game? Your father always enjoyed games. He was… quite good at them, you know. I rarely bested him—even on nights when I thought myself cleverest."

Jonathan hesitated. He knew Silas was not what he seemed; any game he offered would be a trap, plain and simple. Silas seemed the type who smiled too easily, spoke too smoothly, and offered "games" like they were doing you a favor. Silas didn't have an honest bone in his body… assuming he even had a body. But right now, Jonathan needed something even more than honesty: time.

Time to think. Time to breathe. Time for Valera to come storming back through the doors like the warrior she was.

"Honestly? I'd rather settle this the old-fashioned way—just me, both of you, and a big bloody mess," he said, and met Silas's gaze, voice level but laced with steel. "But sure. I'll bite. What've you got in mind?"

Silas drummed his long fingers on the table, slow and deliberate, like a ticking clock. "Before we play, let's establish the stakes, shall we?"

His gut told him to slow down. He ignored it. If he was already halfway over the cliff, he might as well see how far the drop went, right?

"Sure," he said.

"If you win," Silas said, "I leave this world. No strings. No tricks. I lock the door behind me and scatter the key across the stars."

Jonathan's breath caught. That was... big. Too big. Too easy.

There had to be a catch.

"And if you win?"

Silas didn't answer right away. Instead, he reached into the air—like slipping his hand between the seams of reality—and drew forth a shard of glass. It was small, no larger than a thumbnail, and perfectly ordinary in appearance. No glow, no runes, no hum of power. Just glass, fragile and sharp. Silas set it on the table before him.

"If I win," Silas said, his voice smooth and effortless, "You eat this."

Jonathan stared at it. "That's glass."

Silas nodded. "Core glass, to be exact."

Jonathan's body tensed. "What if I eat it... and then just decide I want nothing to do with you? What if I walk out the door and never look back? Will you try to stop me?"

Silas gave a soft chuckle. "If you eat the glass, Jonathan… I very much doubt I'd be *able* to stop you."

Silas placed the shard in his pocket, But Jonathan could still feel it—that object wasn't just a simple piece of glass. It was a throne. A leash. A crown of chains. It was power. All bundled up into a single piece of obscure crystal the size of his fingertip.

Silas tilted his head, then extended his hand. "Shake on it?"

Jonathan looked at the hand. That hand. Creepy. Off. The fingers were too long, too pale, like something that had never belonged to a man. Adrenaline surged through his body—useless here. This wasn't a battle muscles could win. And thought it wore the name of a game, he knew getter: this was war, dressed in pleasantries.

Jonathan reached out—and took the hand.

Silas' cold fingers curled slowly around his own, and with it, he felt it. A jolt—not electric, but binding. Like unseen chains snapping into place. The man's too-wide mouth split into something that might've been a smile, and he said, "Marvelous."

CHAPTER 18
KEEP, CHANGE, CUT

Silas reached into the space between them as if reality once again had seams only he could find. When his hand returned, he held a knife.

It wasn't large. The blade was no more than the length of Jonathan's palm, its hilt wrapped in something too pale to be leather, its blade impossibly sharp—thin, translucent, and shimmering faintly like it had been forged from solidified breath.

He set it gently on the table between them.

"The rules are simple," Silas said. "This is a memory knife."

Jonathan's fingers tensed near his sword, but he didn't speak.

"We take turns," Silas went on. "Each round, one of us asks the other a question—something personal. A memory. A truth. Something real. The one asked must place that memory on the blade."

The knife pulsed faintly, as if it heard and understood.

"Once it's placed, the other has three choices," Silas said, holding up his long, pale fingers. "Keep it. Change it. Or cut it."

He let that hang in the air a moment.

"If you keep it, the memory remains untouched. If you change it, the knife will rewrite it. The truth will bend. But if you cut it—" he smiled, just a little too wide, "—then the memory is gone. Wiped from your mind. Erased from your story. As if it never happened at all."

"If both players agree, between each round we may pause momentarily to discuss, but the game can never be stopped once started. If either fails to proceed, they forfeit the game, with resultant consequences." He folded his hands, gaze steady. "We play until someone yields."

Jonathan looked at the knife, the air suddenly colder around it.

A game of memory. Of truth. Of what you could live with—and what you couldn't. It hit him then, what he'd actually agreed to. The game wasn't just a game, it was a scalpel aimed at the softest parts of him. Memories were all he had left of some people. Of who he used to be. To gamble them… to let someone like Silas crawl around inside them, twist them, cut them away—change them—was a violation he hadn't truly considered when he shook that cursed hand.

And yet, he'd agreed. He was in. For better or worse. The trap was sprung, and the only way out was forward.

Either that, or surrender to the Tide…

233

Perhaps most terrifying of all, Jonathan instinctively knew, just by looking at him that Silas was the kind of man with very few memories he wouldn't gladly discard. There was no shame in him. No hesitation. No conscience to flinch. A man like that didn't fear loss. He welcomed it. Which meant Silas would play this game with surgical precision—and without mercy.

He would play until there was nothing left of either of them—memory by memory, carving away until the very center of who he was began to fray. That was the kind of man Silas was. That was the kind of game this was.

It's okay, Jonathan told himself. *All I need to do is borrow a little time. Valera and the others will save me.*

A slow smile oozed over Silas' mouth as if reading Jonathan's mind. "Oh, and one more thing," he said pleasantly. "We're in a time bubble, Jonathan. A little trick of mine. For the duration of this game, time outside slows to a crawl. Or stops entirely, depending on your perspective. No one will come to save you. We play until the very end."

And in that moment, Jonathan noticed that the Tiger King stood behind Silas, frozen mid-breath, mid-blink—like a statue carved from snow and fury.

"See?" Silas said with a tilt of his head. "No interruptions."

Silas then reached into the void around him, and with a flick of his fingers, an hourglass shimmered into existence between them. It stood tall and thin, filled not with sand, but something darker. Smoke? Ash? The grains tumbled impossibly fast.

"And the final rule," he said, eyes glittering, a pleased expression. "Each phase of the game is played in ten second increments. No stalling. No circling. No games within the game. If you fail to ask a question, your turn is forfeit."

He tapped the hilt of the memory knife gently.

"Now then… shall we begin?"

Jonathan swallowed, his throat dry, a queasy weight twisting in his stomach. He felt truly sick.

"Your turn," Silas said softly.

The narrow hourglass turned itself, inverting with eerie precision. Silver smoke-threaded sand began to fall in a slow, steady stream.

Panic clawed at the edge of Jonathan's thoughts. His body might survive this game, but if he lost all his memories—who would he be? Could a person still be himself if every piece of what made him was carved away? Jonathan's mind raced, clawing for a plan that didn't exist. His friends weren't coming. Time was ticking. And across from him sat a man who had no fear of the past. Who looked like he thrived on pain. How could he win a memory game against someone who had nothing to lose?

He opened his mouth and let the first question spill out before he could stop himself.

"Tell me the memory of how you survived the Breaking of the World."

Silas blinked—once, slow. And to Jonathan's surprise, the ever-present smirk didn't appear. A flicker of sorrow moved behind his eyes, old and bitter, like a scar that never healed.

The memory hit Jonathan like a wave.

Suddenly, he was there.

Not as himself, but through Silas's eyes—reliving the moment in perfect, brutal clarity.

He stood before a massive window, in a building so high that the sky itself bowed beneath him and he could see the curvature of the world. But there were no clouds—only smoke. The world stretched out below, and Jonathan soon realized it was a battlefield. No, not a battlefield—*The* battlefield. The end of an age.

The skyline had collapsed into ruin. Towers crumbled. Fires raged. The air was thick with ash and magic and the scent of blood burned into vapor. The very ground beneath them was scorched glass and bone. And in the center of it all—*it*.

Silas didn't know what *it* even was, but its body loomed across the battlefield, vast beyond comprehension—too immense to be seen in full by mortal eyes. It was alien, and even in death, its form defied physics. Its corpse bubbled and hissed, smoldering in places, cracking open to reveal things that should not exist. Limbs twisted in impossible geometries. Colors bled from the air itself. Reality bent around its carcass.

Silas turned away from the morbid scene.

Silas was in a military chamber—stone walls veined with conduit lines, timeworn banners hanging limp in the stale air. A dozen others stood in silence around him, their uniforms marked with dust and wear, their faces grim, eyes fixed forward. Silas' face was weary as he addressed them.

"I believe it is clear now: we cannot defeat them," he said. "Our armies are gone. Our ammunition spent. The Aegis Lance has done as much damage as good. We have destroyed a single entity, but *infinite* more will come. The world is already lost—the creature's body alone is rewriting the fabric of reality. It will spread, warp everything. There's only one path left."

He looked around the room.

"Deimos," grumbled an angry looking man. "We need to deploy the Weapon."

Silas shook his head. "No. We have not yet reached such dire straits yet... though its time may come."

A woman to his left swallowed hard. "*SkyWorld,*" she said.

Silas nodded. So did the others.

"SkyWorld... and containment," Silas said, his voice quiet but firm.

He turned to the crystal at the center of the chamber—a massive, green sphere suspended in a delicate frame of gold and steel, pulsing with an inner light that seemed to breathe. He immediately recognized it as the Wellspring, though in its youth; bright and healthy and filled with Life.

"This is the Wellspring," he continued. "Beautiful, isn't it?"

He circled it slowly, fingers brushing the edge of the containment field like a curator admiring a relic. "Most people think it's just a power source. A floating miracle. But that's not what it is—not really."

He paused, glancing over his shoulder.

"It's a prison."

Jonathan said nothing, watching through Silas's eyes as the room held its breath.

"In order for the Wellspring to function—to truly contain one of them—it needs more than crystal and circuitry. It needs a *Warden*. One mind. One soul. Someone willing to step into the Core's reality and seal the prison from the inside. The Architect, God rest his soul, he understood: to bind something as vast as the Lurker and the World Eaters, it would take more than machinery. It would take will. Resolve. The mind of an individual strong enough, steadfast enough, to hold the bars closed."

He paused.

"Once inside, the Warden stands vigil. Alone. Timeless. They do not age. They do not leave. They do not sleep. They simply... *watch*. Forever."

His hand fell to his side, the weight of it final.

"The Lurker and its kin... they don't die. We can't kill the dark. But we *can* bury it—in a dream so deep it forgets itself. And the Warden... is the anchor that keeps the nightmare asleep."

Silas looked to each of them in turn—one by one— his eyes lingering just a moment longer on the youngest among them. He swallowed hard. Then, softly, almost like a prayer: "Godspeed."

Emotion welled behind his stern gaze, but he didn't let it break the surface. Instead, he turned without another word and stepped away, shoulders stiff, spine straight—but

238

his hands betrayed him, twitching with the weight of what he was about to do. His eyes shimmered with tears that would not fall.

He walked to the Wellspring.

It glowed in the center of the chamber, a sphere of verdant light pulsing with unnatural rhythm—as if it had a heartbeat of its own, slow and patient and infinite. Silas stood before it, small beneath its looming presence. His hand hovered near its surface, fingers shaking. Not with desire. Not with glory.

But with fear. Raw, human fear.

He placed his hand upon it.

And the world began to change.

And then—

The memory ended.

"You were supposed to be one of the protectors of our world," Jonathan said bitterly, realization hitting him hard. "A Warden. But you betrayed us—all of humanity."

Silas's expression twisted instantly, fury snapping across his face like a whip. "You know *nothing* of what I endured," he hissed. His voice cracked—rage wrapped in pain. "No one… no one can."

His hands trembled—this time not from weakness, but from barely restrained madness. His eyes gleamed with something broken, something wild. Whatever it was that remained after being trapped for an eternity with whatever the Lurker was, it was barely human anymore.

239

The hourglass ticked. Sand spilled like smoke.

Silas was smiling.

Jonathan stared at the memory, jaw tight. He could feel the weight of it pressing down on him—not just what he'd seen, but what it meant. It wasn't just a story. It was a scar. And if he wanted to win this game, if he wanted to survive…

He had to be cruel.

He had to hurt Silas.

Jonathan's voice was low. Firm.

"Cut."

Silas exhaled—slow and long, like the breath had been buried in his chest for a thousand years. He leaned back in his chair, eyes fluttering closed for a brief moment.

"Thank you, Jonathan," he said quietly. "I will sleep better now."

He smiled again, more softly this time. "Although I must say… you're not very good at this game."

And then the memory dissolved—vanished in a whisper of light and smoke. Gone.

Erased.

The knife lay silent once more.

Silas turned his gaze toward Jonathan.

"My turn." He smiled. "Tell me your fondest memory of Jacky."

Jonathan froze.

The name hit him like a punch to the chest. His throat tightened. His mind recoiled, instinctively trying to shield itself from the impact. The question cut deeper than Silas could possibly know—or worse, maybe he did know.

He wasn't ready for this.

Not this game.

Not this opponent.

Not this cost.

He'd come to bargain for time, not to be broken apart piece by piece.

But the game didn't care.

And to his horror, slowly, like peeling back something fragile and already frayed, the memory came.

He was younger—maybe ten. The two of them had snuck away from the safety of the bunkers, past the guards, and all the way to the Edge. The wind was sharp that night, tugging at their clothes and hair, and the clouds below glimmered, stars scattered across the sky like a billion diamonds.

Jacky was sitting cross-legged beside him, her cane folded neatly on her lap. Her head tilted toward the open sky, her blind eyes wide and full of something far beyond sight.

"Describe it to me," she whispered. "All of it."

So he did.

He told her about the way the lights blinked in patterns, like a language only they knew. He described the colors of the sunset—orange and lavender and gold spilling across the vast ocean of clouds—how they bled into the rising dark like spilled paint. He described the stars above, the curve of the world at the edge of the clouds, and the shimmer of the moon like silver glass.

And she smiled.

Not politely. Not to humor him. But a real smile, wide and full of wonder. "It sounds beautiful," she whispered. "I think I can see it."

He hadn't spoken for a long time after that. Just sat beside her in silence, resting his head on her shoulder, her hand finding his and holding it like it was the only solid thing in the world.

That was the memory.

The knife glowed softly.

Silas didn't hesitate. "Now that you know the stakes, Jonathan, I ask: do you yield?"

Seconds in the hourglass fell down, each a subjective eternity. Jonathan's jaw clenched.

He was not prepared for a game such as this…

Silas tilted his head. "Do you yield?"

Jonathan felt the tears well in his eyes. But he shook his head.

"Cut," Silas said.

The knife flared for the briefest instant—then went still.

And then it was gone.

Jonathan blinked. A strange, quiet stillness pressed in around him. He searched for something—but what? A name? A face? A feeling? He wasn't sure. Just a hollow shape in his chest, like someone had carved out a piece of him with surgical precision and left the edges raw.

He tried to recall what he had lost. But there was nothing.

No image.

No name.

Just a profound and agonizing ache, like a phantom limb of the heart.

And sadness. Deep, unshakable sadness.

Though he couldn't explain why.

"Shall we pause?" asked Silas, his voice polite, almost kind.

Jonathan, still reeling from the experience, dazed by the eerie weight of what had just been taken from him, gave a slow, instinctive nod.

Silas folded his hands, that maddening calm never wavering. "A question, then," he said, the corners of his mouth tugging into something that might have been a smile. "How long do you think we've been playing this game?"

Jonathan frowned. "What are you talking about?"

"I mean," Silas said softly, "how many turns have passed? How many memories have been carved away—yours and mine? It would be very easy, you know, for me to take the memory of that, too. To take away the memory of previous turns. It might be we have been playing for hours. Days. A year. Who knows? I don't, and neither do you."

Jonathan's expression hardened. "If you think that's going to scare me into joining your side, you're more deluded than I thought."

Silas' smile remained, still and cold. "You think you can beat me?"

Jonathan stared at him—the inhuman stillness, the hollow darkness in his eyes, orbs so black it was like staring into the Pit itself. A chill crawled through him.

Maybe Silas was right…

Maybe this had all been decided before he sat down. Maybe the game was rigged, the ending already written. Maybe the outcome truly was inevitable. He didn't have Silas' power. Or his weapons. Or his army. So how could he possibly win?

Well… the way he saw it, he had exactly one thing Silas didn't.

Sheer, mule-stubborn defiance.

Suddenly he felt the corner of his mouth curl—not in amusement, but in something harder. The kind of smile born when you've been pushed so far there's nothing left but the will to push back. In a game like this, Jonathan knew he wouldn't survive without stubbornness.

And he had more of it than anyone he'd ever met.

And it must have shown on his face, because for a sliver of a moment—gone as soon as it came—he thought he saw a hairline crack in Silas' perfect composure.

Jonathan leaned forward, elbows on the table, eyes locked.

"Buckle up, creep," he said, his voice hard as tempered steel. "You should have killed me when you had the chance."

He tapped a finger on the blade's edge.

"My turn."

CHAPTER 19
BETRAYAL

And so it went.

Round after round, blow for blow—not of blade or fist, but of thought and soul. With each move, they tore pieces from one another, not with violence, but with something far crueler. Jonathan stole from Silas the memories of strategy—knowledge of the Lurker and the World Eaters, their strengths, their blind spots. Memories that, if he could win the game, would help him in his future battles.

But Silas' smile never faltered.

"I will be blessed for my loyalty," he whispered, even as his mind unraveled. "The World Eaters reward the faithful… even in madness."

And Silas always struck back, each round more painful than the last.

He reached into Jonathan's mind with fingers like cold fire and began to take. Not just thoughts—moments.

Joys. Faces. He stole Jacky's laugh, Israel's camaraderie, the exact sound of El's voice when she said his name, the warmth of victory after battle. Each memory peeled away like skin, and some he didn't just take—he twisted them. Turned smiles into sneers. Hugs into betrayals. Truths into lies.

The pain came in waves, growing sharper, more invasive with every round. Jonathan gritted his teeth until his jaw ached, trying to hold on, trying to remember what he was even fighting for.

But the memories were gone.

And the pain only grew.

And yet… somewhere beneath the torment agony, beneath the hollowed-out memories and fractured thoughts, a fire still burned. It was small, flickering, but it was his. And he would let it burn out until the end.

"I tire of this game," Silas said, his voice low and taut, like a thread drawn to its final stretch. His eyes burned—not with anger, but with a strange, hollow calm. "But you should know—every memory you steal from me makes me a happier man, Jonathan. I have no memories worth keeping. No joy, no peace; only regret. There is nothing you can do to me. How can you inflict a wound on that which is already dead?"

He reached into his pocket with deliberate ease, and drew out the shard of glass. He placed it on the table between them.

The same offer… but this time, it didn't seem quite so bad…

"I will ask only once more," Silas said, voice smooth again, almost kind. "Take the shard. Let the Tide make you whole. You've already given so much. This would be the end of pain. The beginning of truth."

Jonathan stared at it, chest heaving. His fingers twitched, aching to reach for it—just to end it. Just to feel *something* other than the hollow ache where his life had been.

And for a moment... he considered it.

Jonathan knew he couldn't last much longer. His thoughts were fraying at the edges, his body a trembling shell. He was running on fumes—on the last cracked remnants of willpower. *What was he even doing here?* A part of him wondered. What was the point of fighting someone who couldn't be hurt, couldn't be reasoned with, couldn't even *feel?*

Silas didn't seem so monstrous anymore. Just... inevitable. A quiet end to the screaming. An answer to the ache.

And what was he offering, really? Just an end to pain. *How could something that ended pain be so bad?* His hand moved before he realized it—slow, unsure at first, but gaining weight, gaining purpose. Fingers closed around the shard. Cold light pulsed against his skin. He lifted it.

The shard was smooth and cold in his hand, lighter than it looked, yet it seemed to hum with power. Its surface began to shimmer with colors that didn't belong, shifting in and out of view. As Jonathan turned it between his fingers, the edges caught the dim light and bent it, fracturing reflections that whispered in voices just below hearing.

But before he could raise it to his lips, a surge of raw panic clawed its way into his thoughts—wild, primal, desperate. Somewhere, buried deep in the fractured recesses of his mind, whatever was left of Jonathan Roe screamed in defiance. His hand trembled—then with sudden force, he slammed the shard back onto the table, its edges flashing with angry light.

He'd lost pieces of himself. Good pieces. Sacred ones. He couldn't afford to lose any more.

And through the pain he forced a clarity, and he realized three things. First, Silas was human—at least partly. That mattered.

Second, Silas was afraid. Afraid of failure. Afraid of rejection. Afraid of being denied the ending he thought he deserved.

Third, he felt. Not much. But enough. Enough for pain. Enough for heartbreak. Enough to bleed.

If Jonathan was going to win, he had to stop playing defense. He had to hurt him. Well. And truly. Jonathan leaned forward, eyes sharp as drawn steel.

"My turn," he said. "And this time, I own you."

Silas gave a slow, arrogant grin, folding his long fingers together. "Do your worst, Jonathan Roe."

Jonathan didn't blink.

"Tell me about the time you betrayed my father."

The grin shattered.

Silas's face flickered—first with confusion, then horror. His eyes darted, just once, to the side. His breath caught. The color in his face, already pale, drained completely.

"How did you...?" he rasped.

Jonathan shrugged, calm and cold. "Good guess."

The hourglass burned beside them, its smoke falling faster now—like time itself was trying to escape the room.

And the knife, waiting between them, began to tremble.

The memory rose—sickeningly vivid.

Silas was dressed in black, standing in a circle of half-shadowed figures. Before him, a man knelt. There was a bag over the man's head.

"Please, Silas. You don't have to do this."

Silas approached and tore the sackcloth from the figure's head. Jonathan didn't recognize the man. His father had died when he was far too young to remember his face. And yet—there he was. Young. Handsome. With features that mirrored Jonathan's own. But it wasn't the resemblance that struck him—it was the ache. An ache that felt older than thought, deeper than memory. A yearning that reached out like roots seeking water. He didn't recognize the man standing in this memory, not truly. But he *knew* him. The way a tree knows the sun. The way an eagle knows the sky.

He yearned to be near him. To hear his voice. To be told, even just once, that he had done well.

Jonathan's heart clenched.

His father.

Silas stood still. He didn't tremble. Didn't hesitate. Just looked down at the man before him with something cold in his eyes. For a moment, he whispered something to himself. Mercy. Necessity.

But Jonathan saw the truth, buried behind Silas' eyes.

It wasn't mercy.

It wasn't necessity.

It was envy.

Silas raised the knife—*his* knife—and brought it down, directly into his father's chest.

Across the table, Jonathan's hands clenched into fists.

The memory vanished, and the three dimensional representation of it hovered over the blade now, flickering like firelight. Waiting.

Jonathan felt the emotion well inside of him.

Silas opened his mouth, perhaps to justify, perhaps to deflect—but Jonathan didn't let him.

"Yield," Jonathan said coldly, voice low and sharp. "Or I change this memory."

Silas chuckled.

"Nothing could possibly make me happier."

"No. You don't understand. I won't erase it. I won't twist the truth."

He pointed at the flickering memory above the knife—the man kneeling, the blood on the floor, the knife in Silas' hand.

"I won't change the details. Not a single one. Every cut, every word—you'll keep them all. But I'll *bind* it to you."

Jonathan's voice was sharp as ice.

"The rules never said how I had to alter a memory. So I'll do this: I'll drag it out of the shadows and recesses of your mind, and anchor it in the very center of every thought. You won't be able to bury it in the far corners of your mind. You won't blink it away. This memory will burn through every breath you take, flash behind your eyes with every heartbeat. It will become your constant—your rhythm, your pulse, your curse."

He leaned in, voice falling to a whisper.

"You'll see it every time you blink. Hear his voice in every silence. Wake with it. Sleep with it. Choke on it. This won't be a memory—it will be your entire world. Your betrayal will be before your eyes for every waking moment. It will be your punishment. Your prison. You betray your best friend for power? Then I'll make sure that regret, that memory, is the *only* thing you remember."

He didn't raise his voice. He didn't need to.

"And *that*... is how I'll change it."

Silas' face drained of color. His mouth parted slightly, no words forming. Just the look of a man staring down a punishment even he had never dared to imagine.

The silence stretched, taut as a wire.

The hourglass tipped over.

"Yield," Jonathan commanded, his voice low but unshakable.

Silas looked around the chamber like a man searching for a door that wasn't there. His composure fractured, panic clawing up through his mask of calm. A sheen of sweat glistened on his brow. The hourglass bled, smoke swirling like a noose tightening.

"No. No, it can't be," Silas rasped. "You can't do this…"

"Yield!" Jonathan barked.

Silas shook his head, eyes wide. His breath came in gasps now—like a drowning man refusing to go under.

"You don't understand!" he choked. "You can't—this memory, I—"

Five seconds.

"Yield!" Jonathan shouted again, voice ringing like a blade across stone.

Three seconds.

And then something snapped. Hatred erupted across Silas's face, raw and venomous.

The spell shattered. The time-slowed chamber groaned as reality surged back into place. The hourglass vanished in a flash of black ash.

"Kill him!" Silas screamed, voice shrill and breaking, whipping toward the Tiger King. "Kill him now!"

CHAPTER 20
THE LAST CRY OF THE WORLD TREE

T he results of trying to cheat the memory game were instantaneous. All of Jonathan's memories came rushing back to Jonathan, pristine and untouched. But more importantly, before Silas could finish his statement, he began unraveling.

Silas had tried to cheat the rules, twist the knife, and break the binding oath of the game. And now it was breaking him. He fell to the ground and crawled backward across the stone floor, his long limbs trembling, the smooth arrogance drained from his face, replaced now with pale terror and something deeper—rage curdled into disbelief as he screamed.

With a sudden, deafening hum, the Wellspring flared to life, an explosion of blinding, radiant light that painted the chamber in gold and green. The air vibrated. The ground trembled. Energy surged outward in waves. Silas' form began to glitch, unravel, fragment—bits of shadow and static breaking away as the Wellspring drew him in. He clawed at the air, mouth moving in soundless protest, but there was no stopping it. With a final pulse of light, the Wellspring swallowed him whole.

No monologue. No last words. No drama.

Just gone.

And Silas Grey was no more.

But Jonathan barely saw any of it.

Because the Tiger King moved.

And when he did, it was like reality flinched.

Khan the Tiger King was raw violence incarnate. An avalanche of muscle and fury surged toward Jonathan with a speed that made no sense for something so massive. One second he stood still; the next, he was on him—claws flashing, axe whistling through the air like a thunderclap.

And even though he knew it was coming, Jonathan barely raised his sword in time.

The first blow was unlike anything Jonathan had ever felt before, and blocking the blow broke a bone in his wrist, and pain howled up his arm. Kahn's second strike was a hairsbreadth from killing him, and he barely managed to duck beneath the blade. The third—he didn't even see the third, and only managed to move out of the way on instinct alone.

It was as if several attacks came at once, each one a blur of motion and force. One moment the Tiger King's weapons were at his sides—the next, they were already inches from Jonathan's throat, as if the distance between them simply ceased to exist. And worse, he was precise.

Every move was honed by years of brutal experience, his strikes flowing with a terrifying mix of skill, knowledge, and unstoppable power. There was no time to parry, no space to counter. His power was monstrous. His speed—inhuman.

Not even against the Chancellor had Jonathan felt so utterly, hopelessly outclassed.

Jonathan scrambled backward and Khan surged forward. Jonathan didn't even see the blow coming—only felt the moment time ran out. One massive hand clamped around Jonathan's throat, lifting him clean off the ground. And in the next, something sharp pierced his shoulder. The breath left Jonathan's lungs in a silent gasp as the world went white.

For one heartbeat, he felt nothing.

Then it hit.

Agony. Fire in his nerves. Cold in his blood. The wet, red bloom of agony spreading across his chest.

The Tiger King then tossed him aside like broken debris. Jonathan hit the ground hard, a heap of torn cloth, blood, and breathless pain.

Khan didn't even look back.

Just another enemy dispatched. A task completed. A problem solved in the time it takes to draw five breaths.

Jonathan lay on his side, each breath was a ragged wheeze, pain blooming in waves through his body. The world was fading, shadows creeping in at the edges of his vision, the cold crawling up through his limbs. He watched through dimming eyes as the Tiger King turned, calm and unhurried, toward the Wellspring.

The green sphere loomed at the heart of the chamber, once brilliant, now barely flickering, its light like the dying heartbeat of something eternal and holy. Whatever power had lived inside it was sputtering now, shrinking inward, like a star on the verge of collapse.

The Tiger King circled it slowly.

Once.

Twice.

Three times. He studied. He stalked. A predator sizing up something wounded.

Through sheer willpower alone, Jonathan forced himself up to a sitting position. Every movement screamed in protest, pain flaring brilliantly in his nerves. For though he knew he could not stop what was happening, he had to see it for himself.

Then he lifted his head, blood streaked down his brow, eyes still defiant.

"Ydrathar..." Jonathan rasped, "spoke to me."

Khan froze mid-step, his massive form going still as stone.

"You lie," he said at last.

But his eyes betrayed him. Just for a flicker—a glint of hesitation, of uncertainty stirring in the cold furnace behind his gaze.

"She was begging for help," Jonathan whispered. "She wanted me to save her."

"Save her?" he snarled. " From what?"

"From you."

The words hung in the air like a blade.

For a moment Khan did not move.

Then something shifted—barely perceptible, but real. A tension in his jaw. A flicker behind his eyes. As if the words had struck something raw and buried, something long denied.

"That's not true," he said—too quickly, too sharp. "Ydrathar has not spoken in a generation."

But even as he said it, his voice faltered. The certainty cracked. The silence that followed was louder than any roar.

Jonathan locked eyes with him, bleeding, broken, but unwavering. "No," he said. "You chained her. You silenced her voice. You crowned yourself king over something that never belonged to you."

Khan took a step back. Not out of fear. But doubt. And for the first time, Jonathan saw it: He wasn't just fighting a tyrant. He was fighting a believer—a believer who had just been told his god wanted to be saved *from him*.

That was a blow that struck hard.

Jonathan tried to speak, to lift his head, to defy him—something—but his strength was gone. All he could do was watch.

The Tiger King studied him for a long moment, then added, almost gently, "You should rest now. It won't matter soon. And if it brings you peace, know this: The world will follow you into the dark."

Kahn turned his attention back to the Wellspring. With slow, deliberate purpose, Khan raised his arms high— his incredible weapon gleaming in the Wellspring's eerie glow. Then, in a blur of unnatural speed, he drove the edge straight into the sphere's surface. The impact was like the toll of a bell. A spiderweb of cracks burst across the glowing surface. The Wellspring flickered. Then groaned. Twice more he attacked the Wellspring, until a small hole in the sphere appeared.

Khan let the weapon fall with a hollow clatter.

He stepped forward and placed both clawed hands against the fractured shell—curved talons digging into the light itself—and began to pull. Slowly, impossibly, the Tiger King wrenched the Wellspring open like a sealed vault, prying the edges apart with brute, unrelenting force.

The sphere resisted. Light bled. Reality warped. But Khan did not stop. And inch by inch, the Wellspring gave way, the shrieking sound it emitted a stabbing agony of headache. And something moved inside it.

A slithering black substance began to leak from the wound—viscous and alive, rippling like oil with a mind of its own. It oozed out in long, ropy tendrils, gathering mass and shape. Jonathan's fading eyes widened in horror.

The black fluid rose. Limbs formed. A face—too smooth, too still—began to take shape.

And in that terrible silence, something stepped free from the broken Wellspring.

Silas Grey had returned.

He emerged slowly, unfolding from the black ichor like a shadow uncoiling, slick with starlight and ruin. His form shimmered with unnatural light, limbs too long, eyes too black. And his face—twisted, wild with hysteria and anger—looked nothing like the smooth-talking specter Jonathan had faced before. His face was rage and insanity.

"Lock me in that prison again with... with *him*," he finally snarled, hatred pouring out of him like heat from an oven, "and I will drag your entire race into the dark with me. One by one. Screaming."

"If you kill Ydrathar..." Jonathan croaked from the ground, voice barely more than a pained whisper, "may you rot forever."

Silas didn't speak. His eyes, wild and unblinking, burned holes through the room. Then, at last, he spoke—his voice cracked and brittle, like laughter wrapped in glass.

"Fool," he said, and turned away. "I'm not going to *kill* Ydrathar."

He approached the sphere—fractured, groaning, weeping threads of singularity. Without ceremony, he placed both hands on its surface. A sound like a thousand reversed heartbeats echoed through the chamber. The cracks began to close.

He was healing it.

Jonathan's breath caught. His thoughts scrambled to catch up. It didn't make sense. Silas looked over his shoulder. And for a moment, the fury in his eyes cleared— just long enough for something colder to surface. He approached Jonathan.

"I cannot say how long it has been since I abandoned my post as Warden, since I clawed free of that prison. But in that time, I have scoured the world. I have corrupted many Cores. I have destroyed others. Only few remain. I will not unmake the Wellspring. Not yet. First, I will seize it, bind the Tree to my will. With the Tree in my grasp, I will drag Aetherium from the heavens. And when at last I shatter the Core that holds it aloft… then the End of All Things will come."

"But why? Why abandon your post as Warden? Why would you… join them?" Jonathan asked.

Silas smiled, as if enjoying the moment. "Die confused," he snarled.

Jonathan was too tired to say anything more. Through dimming vision he watched as Silas reached into the air—no pocket, no sheath, just space—and from it drew a crystal as long as Jonathan's forearm. It pulsed faintly, a deep violet glow coiled in its center like smoke trapped in glass.

Wordless, Silas pressed it into the Tiger King's waiting hand. For a moment, he just stared at it. His broad shoulders rose and fell with a heavy breath. There was something in his eyes—something that didn't belong there. Not hunger. Not triumph. Something close to regret.

Then he turned. His lips curled into a low snarl, and with a roar that split the air like thunder, Khan drove the crystal into the Wellspring.

The reaction was instant.

At first Jonathan thought the entire room was screaming; later, he realized it had been Ydrathar. A blast of energy erupted from the impact point, a shockwave of light surged outward, then collapsed inward. The sphere buckled and imploded.

The Tree was crying. And then—he didn't know how he knew it—but Ydrathar was gone.

Gone.

It felt like watching a friend be murdered in cold blood.

The ground convulsed in a deafening rootquake as the World Tree's absence echoed through the bones of the earth. Massive tremors rippled outward, tearing ancient roots from the soil, toppling towers of vine and bark, sending entire canopies crashing down in sheets of emerald and ruin.

And then—

Jonathan slept.

CHAPTER 21
WHAT YOU'RE FIGHTING FOR

Agony came first. White-hot. Total. A fire in his shoulder that radiated out to every limb. A scream trapped in bone. It faded by degrees, and only as the blood drained from his body. Then came the darkness—thin and foggy at first, then thick, absolute. Like he'd sunk beneath the world.

But even there, there was no peace.

He floated. Or fell. Or both.

Then came the dreams. And even the dreams hurt.

Faces blurred. Names he should've known slipped through his fingers like smoke. Memories he should've held vanished like mist. Others—ones he wished he could forget—clung like thorns. He called out. No answer. Only the echo of his own voice, hollow and afraid. He wasn't sure if he was alive. Only that he hadn't died the way he wanted.

Not with honor. Not with purpose. Not with victory. Just pain. And silence.

He didn't know how long he slept. Hours. Days. Maybe longer. Time slid past in fragments—whispers, shadows, voices just out of reach. And somewhere in that haze, guilt took root.

He'd failed.

The Wellspring was broken. Ydrathar was gone. The enemy still lived. He tried to remember why he'd done it— what had felt so right in the moment—but the reasons felt thinner now. Paper promises folded into weapons he couldn't wield. He'd told himself it was the only way. That he'd only tried to do what needed to be done to end the war. But the war hadn't ended. And he hadn't saved anything.

In the darkness, his breath caught in his chest. And for a brief moment, he didn't feel like Jonathan Roe at all.

He felt like something smaller.

Someone... broken.

A hand on his face. Gentle. Real.

He flinched, let out a broken sound, barely more than a gasp.

"It's alright," came a voice. Soft. Familiar. "Calm down. You're safe."

Jacky? No. Not Jacky. His mind tried to make sense of the sound, to pin it to a face. But he couldn't open his eyes, and everything inside him was scrambled, memory and pain and dread mixed into a knot too tight to untangle.

"Shhh," the voice soothed. The hand stayed on his cheek, grounding him. "You're not dead, Jonathan Roe. Not yet."

Pain bloomed again—sharp and sudden—as something pressed against his injury.

He cried out.

"Sorry," she whispered. "I have to stitch it. It's bad."

He tried to reply. Only managed a groan. Another flash of agony, but still his eyes wouldn't open. But even through the pain, her hands never shook.

"Soon, this will all be a memory. And rest assured, Jonathan Roe, I will mock you mercilessly and endlessly for being such a baby about this."

But though she teased him, he could hear worry, thick and real, in her words.

Then he slept again.

He dreamed this time, but it hurt less. Jacky gave him mint tea after a bad day. Valera barked instructions while they trained beneath the humming light of the upper districts. He ran through jungle mist with Drekkar and Varg and Ruhn, laughter echoing through the canopy like thunder before a storm.

He didn't know how long he slept—hours, days, maybe more. Just flashes. Fleeting moments caught between pain and silence. A hand on his chest. A whisper in the dark. Memories and half-memories, drifting past like leaves on water. Water poured down his throat, and a girl's voice told him it was healing water from the Wellspring itself.

When he finally opened his eyes, it felt like sandpaper dragging across glass.

But even through the haze, even half-blind and dazed, he'd have known her anywhere.

El.

She sat beside him, knees drawn up to her chest, arms wrapped loosely around them. Her hair was longer now—tangled, uneven, even more wild than usual. Her violet eyes—those clear, sharp eyes—were locked onto his, wide with relief, rimmed with exhaustion. She didn't speak. Just stared, as if afraid that saying his name might shatter him. Like if she blinked, he might vanish.

When his eyes finally focused and found hers, she startled—just slightly—like she wasn't sure whether to believe it. Then a breathless laugh slipped from her lips, half disbelieving, half something else.

"Well, look who finally decided to wake up," she said, smirking. It was the kind of smirk he remembered—tilted, teasing—but it didn't quite reach her eyes. Underneath, he saw it: the worry she was trying to hide. The grief she hadn't managed to bury.

"Thought maybe you were just being dramatic."

"Hngh," was all he could manage.

"Still the eloquent wordsmith, I see," she teased. "Don't hurt yourself with all that poetry."

Jonathan rolled his eyes with an exaggerated grunt, flopping back against the moss-covered rock behind him.

El laughed—a light, magical sound that danced through the air like wind chimes on a bright summer day. "Wow," she said. "You sure know how to make a girl swoon."

Jonathan groaned, and closed his eyes. After a good five count he grumbled, "This is why I almost died. To avoid banter like this."

A quiet pause settled between them. The pain dulled. The moment softened, stretched.

"Besides," Jonathan murmured, cracking one eye open. "I had a reason to come back from the dead."

She met his gaze. He met hers. Something unspoken passed between them.

"El. I just... I couldn't die knowing you still owed me a plasma saw," he said, perfectly deadpan.

It took her a second—eyebrows lifting as the words sank in—then her expression twisted.

"You absolute idiot," she muttered, and punched him in the shoulder.

Jonathan's face scrunched up in pain. "Ow! That's my hurt shoulder!"

"Oh—sorry! I'm so sorry!" she gasped, guilt flashing across her face.

Then she realized it was the *other* shoulder that was injured.

She froze. Narrowed her eyes. Glared. "Ugh, you're *such* a jerk. You were totally faking that!"

Jonathan couldn't help a chuckle, even though it pained his ribs. Her glare sharpened with anger and disbelief that he'd dared to trick her—but it was all a flimsy disguise for the smile tugging at her lips, threatening to break through.

"You were worried about me. It's okay. I'm very lovable."

She punched him again.

And then she smiled.

Brilliant. Beautiful. Everything he remembered—and more. It lit up her face like sunshine after a storm, a rush of relief and something dangerously close to joy. But even through it, he saw the cracks. Her eyes shimmered with something unshed, and when she thought he wasn't looking, she brushed the back of her hand across one cheek, and the tear disappeared.

She didn't say anything for a long moment after that. Just sat there beside him, her shoulder barely touching his. The silence between them wasn't awkward. It was weighted and familiar, like an old blanket worn thin by years but still warm.

"How bad is it?" he asked finally, his voice a gravel scrape in his throat.

She hesitated. Then, softly, "Bad."

"The Wellspring?" he asked.

A crooked smile tugged at her lips, and she shook her head—part disbelief, part exasperation. "Of course. That is *so* like you. Inches from death, barely breathing, and the first thing you want to know is whether you managed to keep the world spinning."

"El…" he rasped.

Too much weight in just two letters. "I'm here," she whispered. "I'm not going anywhere."

Her hand found his—weaving through his as if anchoring him back to life. No ceremony. Just presence.

"You scared me, you know."

He tried for a grin. "I do that."

"I've mourned you like ten times now," she scolded. "It… sucked."

But this time there was no laughter behind it. No eye roll. Just the tremble at the edge of her words.

"Don't do it again." She was smiling, but only barely—and not in the way that meant she was fine. She was dead serious when she told him he wasn't allowed to die again.

The air between them seemed to tighten, weighted with all the things they couldn't say. All the things they'd lost. And all the things they still might.

Then—again—his voice dry, raw, but steady, "…The Tree?"

El rolled her eyes, but the gesture was half-hearted at best and she was still smiling. "Of course that's your first question. Not how long I've been here. Not, are you okay? Or for that matter, where have you been for the last year!" she paused, took a breath, and shook her head. "No. You want to know about the Ydrathar and the Wellspring."

"All of those things, yes. But first, the Wellspring. Everyone else. What happened?" he asked again.

She drew in a slow breath, as if bracing herself against the truth.

"Everything fell apart," she said, her voice low, distant. "Valera, Israel, Cody… we were right there. We saw the end of it. Khan left only a few to guard us, and Valera and Cody dispatched them easily enough. We took everyone who was able to fight, and we made it into the chamber just as Khan reached the Wellspring. I don't know how he did it—but he took control. Not just of the Wellspring… of the Tree itself."

She paused, swallowing hard.

"He turned it against us. The roots, the branches, even the stone—the whole city came alive. And it fought for him. We outnumbered him a hundred to one, but it didn't matter. The Tree made sure it didn't matter. I don't know what happened to the others. But I found you—barely breathing—and dragged you out before the whole place came down."

Jonathan tensed.

She shook her head, eyes distant. "We all got separated. One second we were together… the next, I couldn't hear anyone. Couldn't get back. I don't even know how far apart we are now. I don't even know where we *are* now."

Jonathan tried to sit up, but she placed a hand gently against his shoulder. "Don't," she said. "Not yet. You're not ready."

He slumped back down, his jaw clenched. "How long?"

Her lips pressed into a line. "Best guess? A week. Maybe more. It's kind of hard to tell this deep in the Hollow."

"A week…" he echoed, voice faint with disbelief.

"I've had a little food," she added quickly, "and there's water. We're trapped here, in this tiny place. But a stream runs through part of the room—cold and clean. I've been using it to keep you… stable."

Jonathan felt his strength ebb, the edges of his consciousness blurring. She gave him water—cool, careful sips from her bottle—and pressed a bite of something soft and bitter to his lips. He swallowed without tasting. Then the dark took him again.

Time passed. He wasn't sure how much. Hours. A day. Maybe more.

When he woke again, she was still there—curled beside him, watching, waiting. Dutiful and constant. Her jacket doubled as a blanket, her hair was tied back now, and shadows carved hollows beneath her eyes.

"Learn anything new?" he rasped, his voice still gravel.

"No." She snorted softly. "Kind of had my hands full keeping you alive."

He ate a little more that time. Drank more deeply. Then slept again.

And so it went.

The ache in his limbs dulled to a distant throb. The fog in his head began to lift. Slowly, steadily, his strength returned—muscles remembering their purpose, bones no longer protesting with every shift, hands growing steadier with each sip of water. His breath came easier. His mind, clearer.

Then, one morning—if it could be called morning in that near lightless tangle of root and stone—he sat up without help.

And he stood.

Wobbly. Slow. But upright, all the same.

Each time after that, she helped him reclaim a little more of himself. A few careful steps. A few more bites. A laugh, once or twice, when she said something dry and teasing just to test if he could still smile. His recovery came fast—unnaturally fast, as though some part of him had decided he no longer had the luxury of healing slowly. Jonathan suspected the Wellspring's water had given him a gift for regeneration; Elysra insisted it was nothing but sheer, bullheaded stubbornness.

And, trapped as they were, tucked away in that hidden cove of twisted branches, Jonathan had a hard time thinking of anything other than the World Tree that was now, in all likelihood, completely under the Tiger King's control. About Kahn and his next move, Valera, about Israel and the others, about how he could fix what had been broken. The weight of everything still pressed on him like armor he couldn't take off. But when he realized it would be days, maybe longer, before he was strong enough to fight again… he let himself stop. Just for a little while. He sat. He listened. He healed. And he talked to Elysra.

And he loved talking to her.

She had a way of melting the shadows. Not all at once. But piece by piece, word by word, smile by soft smile, the weight in his chest eased.

In their small, dim shelter—part twisted branches, part moss, part ruined bones of the Sunken City—they carved out a space for quiet. And in that fragile little cove, she told him everything.

She told him how, when their little portion of Aetherium had fallen, she thought she'd died. How the crash had stolen the breath from her lungs and left nothing but green and pain and silence. She'd seen him injured, but never found the body. They had never stopped searching. Eventually, they were taken in by the city of Arenthil.

It was nothing like Aetherium. And the Sky Born survivors of Aetherium had thrown themselves into the war effort. El had helped where she could. But she was no warrior. She was no longer even a princess. Her gifts, she explained, weren't made for war. No sword. No claws. But she'd learned medicine. Enough to be useful. Enough to help.

"I'm still an apprentice," she added with a sheepish grin. "But I can set a bone. Stitch a wound. Keep people breathing when breathing doesn't come easy."

And for the entirety of that year, they had searched for Jonathan. "We all figured the best way to find you was to end the war. Beat the Malrics, and maybe—just maybe—you'd be on the other side of it. And we searched for you every chance we got. Every patrol, every mission, every whisper through the trees—we hoped. I hoped. But I…" She trailed off, swallowed hard. "I thought I'd lost you, Jonathan. That I'd never get you back. We all did. Except Valera. She never wavered. She said you were alive, and if she hadn't believed that…" Her voice cracked. "I don't think I'd be sitting here."

Later, as Jonathan paced their tiny makeshift cove—his so-called "jail cell" of twisted roots and moss—he told her about his time with Drekkar, Varg and the rest of the Malric pride. The hunts, the rituals, the slow climb from slave to something more. She listened in silence at first, chin resting on her knees.

As he spoke, pacing slowly in their little alcove of moss and stone, El's gaze followed him. Not openly. Not directly. Her eyes moved with his gestures, with the rise and fall of his voice, like she was tracking something beneath the words. She said nothing for a while. Then, almost like a thought escaped without permission: "You've changed."

There was no weight to the words. Just quiet recognition. Like the way you'd acknowledge the wind had shifted.

Her gaze lingered a beat longer, soft with something she didn't name. And then she smiled, small and tired.

"Still, your new look is a bit dramatic," she teased. "You know, most people just get a haircut when they want attention."

"Yeah, well... I was going for tragic jungle prince. Pretty sure I nailed it," Jonathan said and gave a dry smile.

Eventually, all the resting turned to restlessness.

One morning—though down here, morning was only a guess—Jonathan opened his eyes to find Elysra already awake, arms crossed and one eyebrow raised in challenge.

"It's high time you found us a way out of here," she said. "Before I die of boredom or you grow roots."

He groaned, but the grin that followed came easily.

So they climbed.

It wasn't graceful. Or fast. His body still ached with every motion. But the strength he'd rebuilt was enough. Slowly, painfully, they began to work their way up—through twisted branches, splintered stone, and vine-choked ruins. The jungle didn't make it easy. Neither did the Sunken City. But they left their little cove behind, one step at a time.

A part of him was almost sad for the fact.

They found food—sweetfruit clinging to the high canopy, and Jonathan took small game once. It wasn't much, but it was needed since her supplies had nearly been exhausted and it was enough. And even with the threat of the Tide, with the Wellspring broken and the world teetering, something strange settled in Jonathan's chest. Peace. Quiet moments between the cracks of survival.

And despite everything still ahead—Jonathan felt… happy.

It was a dangerous thing to feel.

That night, with a small fire crackling between them and the scent of roasted game hanging in the damp jungle air, El looked at him across the flickering light and said quietly, "There's a reason you lost to Khan, you know."

"Yeah," Jonathan muttered, tossing a twig into the fire. "He's a thousand-pound monster with claws, an axe of bone that could cut through a building, and the personality of a sledgehammer. Hits like a meteor. That about cover it?"

She didn't smile.

"Well. That's *one* reason," she said. "But not the only. Maybe not even the biggest reason."

Jonathan glanced up, but she was still watching the flames.

"You do your duty," she continued. "Just like Drekkar said. You fight to win. You always have. But do you even know *what* you're fighting for?"

That silenced him.

"I mean, *really* fighting for?" she pressed. She paused a breath, then another, debating whether or not to press her point, before she finally continued, "You care more about the goal than the reason you even want to get there. Or why you even want to accomplish your mission in the first place. Why else would you charge straight into the Sunken City without even finding us first? You didn't even try. You didn't even look. Granted, I'm just a silly girl, but in my opinion: What's the point of saving the world if the people you care most about aren't even in it? Doing your duty is all good and fine… but do it for the right reason."

Jonathan looked away, jaw tight.

"And you're different?" he asked, a little more defensively than he meant to.

But the serious moment passed like a ripple, and her usual smirk slid back into place. "Absolutely I'm different, oh great *Sky Warrior*," she said, mock-bowing. "Everybody likes me."

His mouth opened, but nothing came out.

She leaned in slightly, eyes twinkling. "Also? I don't smell like someone who's been marinating in jungle sweat for a year."

Jonathan didn't sleep well that night.

El's words had struck a chord inside of him—gentle, cutting, impossible to shake.

At first, everything he had done had been about survival. About proving something. Maybe to himself. Maybe to a world that had never asked him to exist in the first place. In the beginning, his cause had been revenge—or pride—or just sheer, stubborn defiance. But somewhere along the way, Jacky's voice had reached him. Soft, kind, and unrelenting.

Make it worth saving, Jonathan.

So he'd clung to that. He'd made himself believe that fighting for a better world was enough. That doing the right thing—defeating the Chancellor, saving Aetherium, defending the Wellspring—was noble. That it gave him purpose. And maybe it had. For a time.

He always knew what he was fighting against. He needed to figure out what—no, *who*—he was fighting for.

The next day, they could tell they were getting close to the canopy.

The roots thinned. The stone grew softer, mossier. Shafts of light pierced the tangled canopy above, golden and dappled, filtering through the branches like the breath of something divine. The climb was still brutal—hand over hand, foot by aching foot—but Jonathan felt his strength returning fast. Faster than it should have. His muscles obeyed without protest, his wound barely twinged, and each movement felt more like instinct than effort. El, by contrast, struggled. She never complained—but he saw the way her breath came short, the strain in her arms, the tremble in her legs. She was brilliant, determined… but her body wasn't built for this.

So he helped. Quietly. Wordlessly. A hand here. A boost there. And she never objected. Never snapped. Just nodded once, each time, eyes full of stubborn gratitude.

They stepped through the last tangle of vines—and the world opened.

The canopy had once been a kingdom of life—colossal boughs arched like mountains, rivers spilling from root to root, leaves glittering with rain and light. Cities had clung to its limbs. Birds had sung in a thousand tongues. The air had smelled of flowers and storm-washed earth.

Now it writhed.

The branches were no longer branches. They twisted into shapes that shouldn't exist—spined, hunched, contorted like things caught mid-scream. What had once been trees now resembled corpses mid-transformation, as if the forest were being remade from the inside out by something cruel and patient. Black growths bulged like tumors—fleshy and wet, they clustered in impossible shapes: loops, eyes, mouths. Whole towers of wood and stone had been warped—not crumbled, but melted into grotesque silhouettes, displaying faces half-formed in the bark that stared without seeing.

Jonathan stood frozen at the ledge, eyes wide. It was still a jungle—but no longer anything he recognized. Every inch of it whispered corruption.

Elysra hauled herself up over the ledge behind him, breathing hard—but the moment her eyes took in the view, she went still.

"Oh no…" she breathed. Her voice was soft. "How? It's only been a week. Two at most."

Jonathan didn't answer right away. His eyes moved slowly over the devastation. It was like waking from a fever dream into a world already lost.

Then a memory surfaced. A conversation—quiet, almost forgotten. Selene's voice. *The deeper you go into the tree, the slower time moves.*

He closed his eyes. The pieces clicked together, heavy as stones in his gut.

When he finally spoke, his voice was tight. "It hasn't been a week up here," he said. "Not even close."

Elysra turned sharply toward him. "What are you saying?"

He swallowed. "I think we were gone for a long time."

They stared in silence, the breath stolen from their lungs by the sheer scale—and wrongness—of what lay before them. Jonathan had heard stories of the Rot, seen its manifestations in broken ruins and whispered nightmares, but never this. Never so close. It wasn't just decay. It was distortion. Infection. A sickness reshaping the world into something alien. His stomach churned.

"That can't be good," Elysra muttered, voice tight.

She pointed. Far in the distance—barely visible through the clouds—they saw one of the great branches of the World Tree rising like the arm of a colossal beast, twisting skyward. It was still growing, visibly, unnaturally, clawing higher with each passing breath. Its limbs curled around something massive, something suspended high above the jungle.

279

Jonathan's heart sank.

"It's Aetherium," he said.

"My sister!" El gasped, her eyes locked on the distant shape. She turned to Jonathan, voice cracking, "She's up there! We have to help her—now."

In that moment, Jonathan remembered why Silas hadn't destroyed Ydrathar—at least, not yet. They needed it. Ydrathar was the key to getting to Aetherium. They were using Ydrathar to bring Aetherium down from the sky. And once Selene and the floating city were broken... then they'd burn the Tree.

Jonathan's chest tightened at the desperation in her voice. He was well acquainted with what El felt in that moment: the helplessness of knowing someone you loved might be suffering, and being too far, too late, too broken to reach them.

But this time, she wasn't alone. And they weren't too late. Not yet. He could see the lights of the city's defenses glowing in the distance as Aetherium fought against its invaders.

He turned to her, voice harder than he'd intended. "I'm not very good at words, El," he said. "But I can promise you one thing: it's going to be okay."

Elysra turned to him, tears brimming in her eyes but not falling. "Really? How?"

He looked at her and managed a crooked grin. "Because now we're going to find our friends." He drew a breath, straightened his shoulders. "And then we're gonna kick some serious butt."

She laughed—soft, sudden, and warm as golden sunshine. Then her violet eyes lingered on him a moment longer, the smile still playing at her lips. Something shifted in her expression—barely there, but unmistakable. A quiet kind of pride. Like she believed him. Like she knew he could do anything. Like, for a second, he was everything that mattered.

Something turned over in his chest.

She wasn't the girl he remembered from the skies of Aetherium. Not anymore. She was older now. Stronger. Time and hardship had chiseled away much of the girl she'd been and had begun to reveal the woman underneath—stronger, wiser, undeniably more. Her face had changed—sharper in some ways, softer in others—but it was her eyes that held him—deep violet, full of thought. They were the eyes of someone who had walked through fire and chosen compassion instead of bitterness.

She was beautiful.

Not in the way of statues or paintings, but in the way a sunrise is beautiful—natural, radiant, impossible to ignore. Hers was a beauty born not just of appearance, but of presence. The kind that came from choosing to stand, again and again, when it would've been easier to fall. It lived in the warmth she gave freely, in the fierce loyalty she guarded like treasure, in a strength that had nothing to prove but everything to give.

Yes, her features were striking—the graceful curve of her cheek, the soft shape of her lips, the proud tilt of her jaw—but it was the way she carried herself that held him. The light behind her eyes. The quiet, unwavering fire in her spirit.

It wasn't just how she looked.

It was who she was.

She was someone worth fighting for.

CHAPTER 22
YEEHAW

They didn't waste time. For a moment, they considered heading to Arenthil—but it would take at least a week to reach it, and they didn't have that kind of time. By then, Aetherium might already be gone. Elysra told Jonathan that if any survivors had made it out, they most likely would've headed for an outpost not far from their current location. It was hidden high in the canopy, wedged between two of the largest boughs of the World Tree, abandoned long before the Rot had taken hold.

The climb was brutal. The terrain worse. Twisted branches clawed at them. The air grew thin. But they pushed on—driven by hope, desperation, and the faint glimmer of something waiting just ahead.

And eventually… they found them.

The survivors.

Huddled behind broken barricades and crumbling stone. Hollow-eyed. Gaunt. Weapons drawn at the slightest sound. Faces Jonathan knew—tired, worn, but unmistakably his. Valera. Cody. To his great surprise even Israel was there, sporting only minor injuries; as was Varg. A hundred survivors who'd once stood with him in the skies of Aetherium; twice that number of survivors from Arenthil. They looked like shadows of the warriors they had once been—battered, dejected, on the edge of breaking.

Jonathan stepped into view, Elysra just behind him, and something passed through the camp like a current. Eyes widened. Spines straightened. Jonathan wasn't sure what they saw—maybe not strength, maybe not certainty—but they saw him, and suddenly they weren't alone anymore.

After the initial commotion died down, Israel gathered everyone around the dim light of a salvaged lantern, his voice low but steady as he laid out the truth to Jonathan and Elysra.

"Aetherium's still up there," he said. "Barely. Its anchors are cracked, the Core is dead or dying, and the city's floating by inertia and prayer. But there's no way up—not unless we go through the canopy. The Tree's upper branches have latched onto the lowest levels of the city like claws, and that's the only path left."

He paused, his face drawn.

"But those branches are infested—crawling with corrupted Malrics, twisted beasts, and whatever else the Tide's unleashed."

He reached into a satchel and pulled out a battered datapad. "We got this just this morning. From Selene."

He tapped the screen. A grainy recording flickered to life—static, flickering lights, distant sounds of explosions. Selene's face appeared, pale and determined, bruises along her temple, the city's skyline trembling behind her. But still, she maintained a near otherworldly calm as she spoke, as if completely detached from the madness that was around her. "If you're hearing this… we need you. Most of the survivors have been evacuated to the Tree. We used the last of the drones to get them out. Cedric and I alone remain to protect the Core."

She paused, just long enough to catch a shaky breath. "We've held them off as long as we can. I've rerouted all Power to the defense systems that are still functioning, and for now, we're holding the line. But the Malrics don't stop. They don't sleep. They don't fear death. They just keep coming."

Her voice dropped lower—tight, but steady. "If the shield lines fall, we won't last more than a few days. A week, *maybe*. That's being generous."

"We've moved the Core to the Golden Spire. It's the most secure place left in the city. We're doing everything we can to protect it. But we can't hold forever."

She paused again, and for a moment, Jonathan saw it—beneath the analytical calm, the smallest flicker of concern tightening her features. And then: "If you're out there… we need help. Please."

The screen cut to static.

Israel lowered the datapad. "We haven't heard from her since."

Silence fell over the group.

Then Israel looked to Jonathan.

"If we're going to save her—if we're going to save what's left of Aetherium, including its Core—we go up. Through the branches. Through everything the Tide has waiting for us." His voice hardened. "And we go soon."

"It's a hopeless effort," said one of the survivors from Aetherium, Lord Smith. "Best to count our losses and move on."

Murmurs of agreement whispered around them. Jonathan glanced around the battered group. Faces hollowed by exhaustion. Eyes dulled by loss. They'd already given up—they just hadn't admitted it out loud.

But Jonathan was smiling.

He couldn't help it. Because deep down, he knew something they didn't.

There was still hope.

Cody squinted at him, eyeing Jonathan like he'd just grown an extra head.

"Boy," he drawled, voice full of dust and disbelief, "we're halfway dead, outta food, sittin' on a tree that's about to burn, and you're standing there grinnin' like a fella who just remembered where he hid the good jerky. Start talkin'."

Jonathan told them his idea. It was reckless. Dangerous. Ridiculous. It was so crazy it made his head hurt. No sane person would've considered it. El wouldn't talk to him the rest of the day after he proposed the idea. Cody had called it, "Suicide, but with extra steps."

But the truth was undeniable: if they wanted any hope of reaching Aetherium—of helping Selene and Cedric and defending the Core—they had only one choice.

Jonathan stood atop one of the highest branches of Ydrathar they could reach. Below, the jungle plunged into a churning sea of green and violet mist and jungle life, though the Rot was beginning to take hold here, as well. Above, the clouds parted just enough to reveal the distant, broken silhouette of Aetherium—still aloft, still glowing faintly... but ensnared.

Even from this distance, Jonathan could see the sky city struggling. Flashes of energy lit the sky, chased by fire and smoke. The great city swayed in the clouds, its golden spires battered, tilting as the World Tree's strangling vines pulled it down—inch by inch, breath by breath.

Down below where Jonathan and his friends waited on the ancient limbs of Ydrathar, the jungle pressed in around them—hot, humid, alive with the whine of unseen insects and the distant, haunting calls of hunting beasts. Sweat clung to their skin, trickling down spines, soaking into their clothes. It felt almost like one of his old hunts with Drekkar—poised, alert, waiting for the signal. Breath held. Eyes sweeping the trees.

But this wasn't buffalo they were stalking. Or antlered prey.

This was something far more dangerous.

Something that hunted back.

"Well," Cody muttered, running a gloved hand through his stubble beard, "if this ain't the dumbest hunt I've ever been on, it's at least top three. And the other two involved ATVs and a blindfold."

As usual, Jonathan had no idea what the man was talking about. But somehow, Cody's dry calm helped settle the pulse in his ears.

And then, they waited, watching the jungle rot around them.

Then—movement.

A blur of gold and black fur tore through the underbrush below, fast and precise. Varg. He moved between roots and boulders with lethal ease, a creature at home in the World Tree if ever one existed, and he was moving fast. He wasn't panicked.

But he wasn't happy, either.

"You scared?" Jonathan asked.

Cody tipped his hat back and squinted into the sky, then looked at him, eyelids drooping like he was halfway to a nap. "Naw. Where I'm from, I knew a hundred good ol' boys who'd pay oil-money just for the chance to shoot at something like that. And only half of 'em would've died trying."

Jonathan recognized it as a joke—at least, he thought it was. But he was too nervous to laugh. During his time among the tigers of Drekkar's pride, he'd heard several stories of Malrics foolish or bold enough to try and ride a sky serpent. Almost every tale ended in disaster. Crushed bones. Scorched remains. Swallowed hole. Vanishing into the clouds. But scattered throughout the centuries were whispers of success—one rider every hundred years, maybe less. No one knew how they'd done it. No names. No proof. Just myth. And Jonathan had a theory. And if he was right—if he was even half right—then he might have a chance.

A stupid, impossible chance.

But sometimes, those were the only ones worth taking.

The jungle exploded.

Branches snapped, trees tipped in waves, and the air split with a shriek that was less a sound and more a force—primordial, deep, like the tearing of the sky itself. The serpent crashed through the canopy, a tornado of motion and muscle and madness.

Its body was impossibly long, coiling and uncoiling with terrifying grace. Scales shimmered in shades of deep blue and gleaming silver, catching the dying sunlight as it twisted. Wings unfurled behind it in massive, translucent arcs, veined and luminous, like lightning trapped in flesh. Its head burst into view, jaws wide, rows of curved teeth flashing.

It had arrived.

And it was magnificent.

And it was death.

Varg darted below the beast's writhing mass, moving like a streak of golden light as the sky serpent gave chase. He was fast, but Jonathan knew firsthand, no creature on legs could outrun that thing for long.

Jonathan looked at the soldier and said, "You're up."

Cody cracked his neck, adjusted his hat and muttered, "If I die, I'm hauntin' you in your outhouse."

And for the first time since Jonathan had known the man, Cody didn't look bored. There was no lazy smirk, no tired drawl—just fire in his eyes

"Yeehaw!" he shouted. "Come and get some, you overgrown belt!"

And with that, he dropped from their perch like a madman from the heavens, twin pistols drawn. He fired mid-fall, bullets cracking through the thick jungle air, aiming not to kill—but to provoke.

It worked.

The soldier turned and ran—and in a blur of silver eyes and bared fangs, the sky serpent gave up the chase of Varg, and his head snapped toward Cody. It shrieked, coiled midair, and streaked toward Jonathan's hiding place. Jonathan crouched low, muscles coiled, breath held. He knew he should've been afraid—every instinct should've been screaming at him to run, to hide, to survive.

But instead, he grinned.

Because what he felt wasn't fear.

It was pure exhilaration. The kind that burned in his blood and roared in his ears. The kind that said *this*—this insane, impossible moment—was exactly where he was meant to be. As the colossal beast came closer, Jonathan stood on the branch, toes balanced at the edge, knees bent. There was no time for second-guessing.

He ran three steps and jumped.

Time slowed.

Air roared past his ears. The jungle dropped away beneath him. The serpent twisted, its spined back rising as Jonathan landed on its neck, only a few feet behind its massive horned head. Jonathan's hands found a ridge of bone or something like it. His legs slammed against its side, scrambling, slipping—then locking into place.

For one heartbeat, he was weightless.

Then—

The sky serpent shrieked.

When it realized it had an unwelcome ride along, it bucked, thrashed, wings beating against gravity, trying to shake the insect off its back. Jonathan clung tighter, teeth grit, legs burning. And very quickly, he realized just how far out of his depth he really was. This wasn't a Malric brute or a corrupted animal or even a raptobeast. It wasn't something you outsmarted, outmaneuvered, or outfought. It was a storm with a spine. A mountain wrapped in muscle. A hurricane with eyes. A meteor with fangs. You didn't *ride* a sky serpent. If you were lucky, you survived it.

And in that moment—straddling a giant beast, wind screaming, the world tilting beneath him—Jonathan realized something else:

He had made a mistake.

The pair of them, serpent and rider, screamed through the jungle, faster than an arrow loosed from a warbow, twisting through canyons of massive trees and exploding through tangles of vine and mist. Every shift of its body jolted Jonathan like a ragdoll. One wrong twitch, one loose grip, and he'd be a smear on the canopy.

The toll on his body added up quickly. His fingers were cramping, locked in place from gripping too hard for too long. The beast thrashed so violently it rattled his bones. His shoulders burned like fire. Muscles quivered, torn between holding on and giving up. The wound on his shoulder opened up and began to bleed again. The world tilted and spun and blurred around him, but he didn't dare close his eyes.

The sky serpent didn't just want him off. It wanted him gone. It wanted him *dead.* He could feel it, like heat rising off coals—its fury, its confusion, its primal need for freedom. And now, something *dared* to ride it.

Jonathan's grip faltered—

And then instinct kicked in.

He reached with his will. Not with his muscles. With that strange, impossible other sense—the ability that had occasionally let him float, bend gravity, move stone. And it answered.

Gravity tilted—not down, not sideways, but toward the serpent. His body snapped against its back like a tethered weight. His center of gravity aligned to the beast's axis, as if the world had suddenly agreed he belonged there. For a breathless second, he was part of the serpent. The serpent shrieked—a high, keening wail—and dove.

Jonathan barely had time to brace. The world spun as wings folded and the sky dropped away, and then—

Impact.

They crashed into Ydrathar's surface like a meteor. Branches shattered. Bark exploded. The force of it ripped

Jonathan from the serpent's back and flung him through the air. For a moment, everything was noise—leaves falling like ash, birds screeching as they fled, the dull ringing in his ears.

The serpent uncoiled from the crater it had made, silver-blue scales gleaming, wings tucked close to its body. Its eyes locked onto him and the beast hissed.

Jonathan groaned and staggered to his feet, blood in his mouth, dirt in his eyes. He had his blade. He had his bruises. And he had exactly zero good ideas.

So he met the monster's glare, lifted his chin—and growled anyway.

Then, the sky above both of them darkened.

A roar tore through the sky.

And then it came.

A second sky serpent burst through the canopy, the air shattering beneath its wings—and Jonathan knew at once this one had been claimed by the Rot. Its scales were cracked and crumbling, armor flaking in diseased patches. Half its skull was encased in a crown of fossilized sinew and fungal horns, and where its chest should've been, a hollow cavity gaped wide—filled with thorned roots and slick black ichor that wept tar as it spiraled downward. This wasn't a wild beast. It was a weapon. A Rotspawn abomination, twisted by the Tide, sent by the Tiger King to kill them both.

It struck the first serpent in a frenzy of fang and violence, and the impact shattered the glade. Jonathan was hurled backward, the shockwave slamming him into the earth as a wave of hot, fetid wind stole the breath from his lungs.The two creatures tumbled across the jungle floor, wings shearing through trees like blades through silk. The Rotspawn was far stronger—bulkier, with limbs that gleamed wet and raw beneath rotting scales—and for a moment, Jonathan was sure the fight would end in seconds.

But the silver-blue serpent was not so easily broken.

It struck back with shocking speed, fangs flashing as it sank them into the corrupted beast's shoulder. Black ichor sprayed, burning holes through the vines and leaves. The corrupted serpent shrieked in rage and clamped its jaws around the silver serpent's wing, tearing into it with a crunching sound.

Jonathan scrambled for cover as the battle barreled toward him. With a guttural hiss, the corrupted serpent reared back and spewed a cloud of red mist—boiling, acidic, sizzling as it scorched the earth. The silver serpent twisted away just in time and surged skyward in a blur of wings and fear—but it didn't get far. Massive talons clamped around its body, yanking it from the air. The Rotspawn slammed its prey to the ground with brutal force, pinning it beneath its bulk. The younger serpent thrashed and screeched, wings trapped, tail lashing like a whip. Blackened claws drove deep into its chest. The Rotspawn reared back, jaws wide, fangs dripping, ready to end it.

And in that moment, Jonathan struck.

He drew his sword and ran, launching himself into the air with a roar, angling straight for the Rotspawn's exposed neck. Time seemed to slow as he flew. He caught the stench of decay, the slick gleam of bone beneath flaking scales, the glow of eyes burning with madness. His blade found the gap just below the skull, driving deep between jagged plates. The corrupted serpent shrieked—a warped, splintering sound that shook the air. It convulsed violently, wings flaring wide, tail lashing violently.

Jonathan held on, his blade buried to the hilt in the creature's neck, riding the convulsions as it reared and staggered. He could feel it—his sword didn't relish this kill. The beast had once been magnificent. But now, twisted and maddened, it was a rabid thing that had to be put down. Jonathan didn't like it any more than his sword did.

The corrupted sky serpent roared, its death throes violent and wild. Its wings beat the air in spasms, flinging debris and gusts of wind across the ruined clearing. And still, it fought. Still, it refused to die quietly.

Jonathan's knuckles whitened around the hilt as the beast whipped its neck, throwing its body into a final frenzy. Muscles screamed. Gravity strained. His power flickered like a dying ember.

He held on.

He held—

His strength snapped.

There was a sudden wrench, a sickening jolt—and the world spun in a blur of smoke and sky. The roar of wind filled his ears, and the weightless drop punched the breath from his chest. Leaves tore past him like knives, branches reached like claws, and then—

CRASH.

He hit the earth hard, bouncing, skidding, rolling through wet loam and shattered bark.

He blinked up at the canopy, his limbs splayed in broken angles around him. His sword was gone. His vision swam.

But he was alive.

And so was the Rotspawn.

Even as black blood poured from its neck, it twisted with one last, monstrous burst of hatred. Its eyes, red-veined and blazing, locked onto Jonathan. It saw him. Knew him. Hated him.

And it lunged.

Jonathan scrambled, too slow, too battered—he had no sword, no strength, no time.

Then—

CRACK.

Fueled by pain and fury, and by the opening Jonathan's strike had given it, that moment of weakness had tipped the scales, and, with a snarl that split the air, the silver serpent coiled around the beast's neck, muscles rippling like steel cables. It drove the corrupted beast down with brutal force, wings beating the ground like thunder. Fangs sank deep into rot-black scales, tearing through corruption and bone alike. With a final roar, the Rotspawn collapsed. A mountain of malice made meat, crumpling into the broken earth with a crash that echoed through the clearing.

And then, at last, the corrupted serpent was still.

Jonathan stared, heart hammering, chest heaving, barely able to process what he'd seen. The silver serpent pulled away, body trembling, its flanks streaked with blood and torn scale—but it was alive.

And it had saved him.

For a long moment, it simply stood there, the rhythm of its breathing the only movement, eyes locked on his.

And Jonathan exhaled, his breath shaky, unbelieving.

"…Thanks," he rasped.

Jonathan went to the carcass and retrieved his sword, shoulders rising and falling with each breath, staring down at what had once been a truly magnificent animal. Even corrupted, it had been beautiful—terrible, yes, but beautiful. Its wings had carved the sky, its cry had shaken the jungle, and for a heartbeat, it had ruled the heavens. Now it lay broken and still, the last flickers of red light already fading from its veins.

Something in him ached.

This creature hadn't asked for any of it. It had been a thing of freedom, born to ride the winds, not to be shackled and turned into a weapon. Not to be used. Not to die like this.

And then the sadness burned.

This was Khan's work. The Unmaking Tide's poison. They didn't just kill. They defiled. They took the wild and made it obedient. They took the sacred and made it evil. They took life and made it… *not* life.

Jonathan felt something rising in his chest—hot and bright and so intense it was a pain inside of it. It was not guilt. It was not grief. It was rage.

Righteous and clean.

Let them come, he thought. *Let them send their monsters, their armies. I won't run. I won't bend. I will fight for the world as it should be—not the twisted ruin they want it to become.*

Then he looked to the young sky serpent—the juvenile beside whom he'd just battled and bled.

There was no more rage in its gaze—only something quiet. Mutual. A recognition forged not through words, but through survival, through the fire they'd endured together.

He didn't know what made him do it. Instinct, maybe. Or madness. Or something stranger still—trust.

Jonathan stepped forward, slowly, one careful pace at a time. His boots crunched softly over broken leaves and scales. The serpent didn't move. It only watched. Its eyes were too sharp—too clear—for a mindless beast. Jonathan had seen creatures driven mad by pain or hunger, seen animals reduced to nothing but reflex and fear. But this one... it wasn't like that.

There was intelligence behind those eyes. It was simply waiting—measuring him.

And for some reason Jonathan didn't understand, that made him feel like he had something to prove. It was watching him with thought. With caution. With intelligence. He stopped a few feet away, heart pounding like a war drum in his chest.

Then, slowly, deliberately, Jonathan lifted his hand...

CHAPTER 23
SUICIDE RODEO

Jonathan couldn't think. Could barely breathe. Riding the serpent wasn't flying—it was being strapped to the front of a living missile and hurled through a hurricane with no control, no logic, no chance to scream. Every wingbeat sent shockwaves through Jonathan's spine. Wind roared past so violently it stole the breath from his lungs and left his face numb, his eyes watering. He clung to the creature's jagged spines with frozen fingers, every muscle locked in panic, teeth rattling like loose stones in his skull. The world blurred. Branches whipped by below in dizzying streaks of green and gold and violet, and the clouds above twisted in ways that made no sense at all. There were moments—several—when he was fairly sure they were upside down. The serpent didn't care. It howled through the air like a creature that had never been tamed, and never would be.

They landed like a meteor strike. The ground shook. Trees cracked. The dragon's wings snapped open like sails, and its talons carved trenches into the jungle floor as it skidded to a halt, snarling steam and outrage. Jonathan was nearly thrown from its back. When he looked up, camp had gone silent. Survivors gawked, their expressions frozen between awe and horror. When he had left, few had believed they would ever see him again. Now he'd returned like a storm in human form, dragged in by madness and the jaws of a beast no one dared name.

They couldn't have looked more surprised if he'd ridden in on the back of the sun itself.

One by one, they stumbled to a stop—soldiers and scouts, techs and healers, the wounded hobbling on makeshift crutches, even wide-eyed children peeking from tents. A wave of footsteps pounded through the camp, rushing toward the landing site—and then, all at once, silence.

A little girl clutched her father's sleeve and whispered, "Is he real?"

A man near the front—Lord Smith, an elderly noble from Aetherium who'd sworn Jonathan would get them all killed—removed his hat slowly, like in the presence of something sacred.

Elysra appeared beside him, breathless from running, then froze when she saw him. Her lips parted, but no words came at first. She just stared—shocked, radiant, overwhelmed.

"You…" she started, then stopped. "You did it."

He blinked at her, eyes red from windburn. "Pretty sure I'm still doing it."

Varg let out a bellowing laugh that echoed through the clearing. "He rides the sky-serpent! *Mad!* Completely mad!" His fangs gleamed as he grinned. "I love it!"

Cody shoved his way through the crowd a few moments later, skidding to a halt in the clearing and staring with his mouth open. "Well dip me in gravy and call me breakfast. He actually pulled it off."

Without warning, the beast reared. Its wings snapped wide, blotting out the canopy. Its talons raked the ground like it was trying to tear apart the planet's crust. The roar that followed wasn't a sound—it was a force, vibrating in their bones, pressing against their lungs, and the sheer force of the sound sent a shockwave through the clearing, forcing everyone to clamp their hands over their ears.

Jonathan nearly slid from its back.

"What are you all waiting for?!" he bellowed. His voice cracked with strain. "I can't hold it! Now—or it's leaving without you!"

The spell broke. The camp surged into motion. Those who had volunteered bolted for the beast, scrambling up its flanks, clinging to anything they could grip. The serpent snarled, swatted the dirt with its tail, and hissed with mounting impatience.

Amid the chaos, Varg stood at the rear, eyes locked on the dragon's twitching tail. "I assume this is the entrance?"

Jonathan turned. "No, don't—"

But Varg was climbing fast. "So this is what it's like to feel like prey. Don't like it. 0 out of 10."

Israel and Cody each carried a massive box in their arms, the weight of them making their muscles strain as they climbed the sky serpent's back and tried to hold on. Valera, tense and withdrawn, looked so uneasy about the entire situation that she hadn't brought a weapon at all. Aelowyn had somehow procured a staff—ancient-looking and humming faintly—though no one dared ask from where.Then, before the last of them could climb aboard—

It launched.

"Hold on!" Jonathan shouted, but the wind ripped the words away.

And then they were airborne.

Jonathan still couldn't believe it had worked. Some part of him—maybe the sane part, or whatever passed for it—was convinced it shouldn't have. He was riding a sky serpent.

A sky serpent!

If Drekkar could see him now…

But there was no time to dwell on it. Riding the serpent was like riding a tornado. A tornado that very much wanted to kill everything in sight.

The first minute was pure mayhem.

The sky serpent surged higher, its massive wings pounding the air. The jungle dropped away beneath them— green, purple, and gold blurring into a vast, dizzying sea.

Jonathan leaned low, gripping a ridge of scales with one hand, the sword tucked awkwardly against his side, shouting wordless commands into the howling wind, trying to guide it by pressing against one of the horns that grew out of the back of its skull, to nudge it toward the colossal branches that spiraled upward toward Aetherium.

But it was like trying to steer a hurricane with a piece of twine. Every course correction was a battle of its own: a clash of wills between a stubborn human and a force of nature with wings. Jonathan gritted his teeth, as he forced it a few degrees to the left—only for it to jerk violently the other way, nearly throwing half the group from its back.

"Steady!" he bellowed, not sure if he was shouting at the serpent, himself, or everyone clutching for dear life.

Valera growled something under her breath and dug her claws deeper into the beast's hide. Israel grumbled angrily as his box almost slipped from his grip. Varg just laughed—*laughed!*—like a thing who'd made peace with the idea of dying stupidly.

Bit by bit, wrestle by wrestle, Jonathan inched the serpent's path toward the massive branch that would lead them to his former home.

And then they reached the base of the giant trunk.

A storm of noise and motion exploded below. Malrics—thousands of them—poured into view like a black tide, and the air filled with the shriek of arrows cutting through the sky.

The serpent didn't hesitate. It tucked its wings and dropped like a thrown dagger, a roaring silver bolt aimed straight for the mass of enemies.

Jonathan barely had time to react.

"No—*NO!*" he roared, hauling back on the jagged ridge of scales, pulling with every ounce of strength he had. The serpent resisted—screaming, flailing, rage burning through its muscles like wildfire. The world spun—up became down—and for a terrible instant, Jonathan thought he would be ripped free. And then—wings snapped open with a thunderclap. The serpent tore upward, skimming the treetops so close the branches whipped against their legs, a howl of broken air and chaos in its wake.

Arrows rained down around them, clattering harmlessly against the silver blue scales of the serpent's belly. A few glanced dangerously close, but thankfully, none of his friends were hit.

"If our plan is going to work, you have to get it higher!" Cody bellowed over the rush of wind. "Climb!"

Jonathan yanked on the jagged ridge of the serpent's neck, willing the beast upward. With a furious screech it relented, sweeping its massive wings downward and soaring higher, climbing, cutting through mist and whipping leaves— climbing up the colossal trunk of Ydrathar that clawed at Aetherium like a living noose.

Jonathan looked back the way they had come. They were high.

Really high.

"NOW!" Cody roared.

Israel dropped the heavy box he'd been clutching onto the massive trunk below.

Earlier, when they'd been hammering out the plan, Cody had described the contents of the boxes with a grin and a twang: "a big, Southern-sized birthday present for our kitty friends." Jonathan hadn't fully understood what that meant at the time—but Cody had been insistent that if he could get them over the trunk, his plan would work. If they could get

304

above the massive trunk and drop a box onto it, he said, it would be enough to blast Ydrathar's grip loose and give Aetherium a fighting chance.

The box tumbled down, spinning end over end, tiny against the monstrous scale of Ydrathar's trunk. For a heartbeat, nothing happened.

Then the world split open.

A flash of blinding light—white, red, gold—ripped through the mist, followed by a booming sound so loud it felt like someone had punched the air out of Jonathan's lungs. The trunk shuddered violently, weathered bark splintering outward in ragged fissures. Chunks of wood the size of houses flew in every direction. Vines blackened and snapped like burning ropes.

And then came the fire—cascading down the trunk in waves, devouring the grasping branches that had ensnared Aetherium.

The World Tree's grip on Aetherium loosened, and nearly all of Khan's armies were now trapped on a branch that would soon burn and then plummet.

Above it all, Cody's voice rang out as he clung to the sky serpent's hide, grinning like a maniac: "Yeehaw, you rotten salad! That's how we do landscaping back home, baby!"

But then the compressed air from the explosion slammed into them like a battering ram. The serpent flipped midair, wings wrenching sideways, nearly knocked from the sky. It tumbled once, stalled, and for a terrifying five counts they were in free fall—and it was all they could do to hold on.

Jonathan twisted around. His friends clung desperately to whatever they could grab. Jonathan's heart lurched when he saw Aelowyn's grip falter. She was lighter, smaller, and the blast had ripped her loose. For a terrible instant, he saw her tumbling backward, arms flailing, nothing between her and the endless drop below.

Cody moved first. He reached out and snagged the back of her cloak with one hand, then hauled her bodily back onto the serpent's back.

"Gotcha, kiddo," Cody muttered through gritted teeth, hauling Aelowyn back onto the serpent's back as it bucked beneath them.

They barely managed to right themselves—but the serpent wasn't finished. With a roar that split the air, it twisted back toward the battlefield, silver scales flaring, bloodlust rippling off its body in waves. Jonathan could feel it—the raw fury, the wild instinct to kill—thrumming through every coil of muscle beneath him.

It took everything he had—every ounce of strength, every drop of will—to wrench its path back toward Aetherium.

"I don't know how much longer I can control this thing!" Jonathan shouted, his arms burning with the effort.

"I don't think you *are* controlling it!" Israel bellowed back, clinging to the beast's spiked neck with both hands, eyes squeezed shut.

When they finally crested the ridge of Aetherium— what was left of it—Jonathan realized they were too late.

The city sprawled below them, but it wasn't the shining marvel he remembered. It was a ruin. A smoldering wreck. Maybe half a mile across now, the once-great sky city of Aetherium lay cracked and bleeding. The Golden Spire still stood at the center—pristine, untouched—protected by a strange shimmering forcefield. But everything else? Ash. Smoke. Twisted metal. Shattered towers leaning like broken teeth.

Worse still, enemies swarmed the ruined city like carrion birds. Ancients heaved their massive bodies through the wreckage, each step shaking the broken city beneath them. Malrics prowled in coordinated packs. Raptobeasts— hulking, fanged nightmares—battled through the wreckage, tearing apart anything that stood in their path. And all of them were corrupted, their bodies blackened by the evil disease. But worse than all of it, worse than the bodies and the smoke and the ruin, was what Jonathan saw next.

The Guardians.

The once-proud defenders of Aetherium—razor-edged, towering, deadly—were moving alongside the invaders. Shoulder to shoulder with Malrics and raptobeasts.

Which could only mean one thing:

Raz—which, by extension meant the very city itself—had turned on Selene and Cedric.

Jonathan felt the breath catch in his throat.

Behind him, Israel grumbled. "Rust and ruin."

Aelowyn gripped the serpent's scales, her voice sharp over the roar of the wind.

"We have to get to the Golden Spire—" she didn't get to finish.

Jonathan felt it first—the shift, the change.

The serpent's muscles bunched beneath him like a coiled spring ready to snap. It was done thinking. Done listening.

With a roar that shook the air itself, the sky serpent twisted violently, wings snapping tight to its sides, and plunged—a silver missile straight into the heart of the battle. Jonathan yanked on its frills, tried to steer, but he might as well have been trying to shove a mountain. It didn't take him long to realize it was pointless, and as soon as they were close enough to bail out, he shouted, "Time to get off this thing!"

Not that it mattered.

The serpent thrashed—a savage, whip-crack motion—and they were torn loose, flung like ragdolls into the smoke and chaos below.

Jonathan hit the ground hard, the impact jarring his bones—but somehow, miraculously, he rolled with it, coming up on one knee in the dust and smoke. His heart hammered against his ribs, blood roaring in his ears, but nothing felt broken.

He staggered to his feet just in time to see the silver-blue serpent roar in indignation and hurl itself into the enemy lines. It was a force of nature, all muscle and madness, tearing into the tide of Malrics and corrupted beasts with savage abandon. Steel and fang and claw collided in a maelstrom too chaotic to track.

Jonathan heard screams—human, inhuman, some too distorted to name—rising above the clash. But then the smoke thickened, the world twisted into a blur of ash and noise, and he lost sight of the serpent.

Through the swirling smoke, Jonathan caught the sound of laughter—wild, raw, a little unhinged. He turned to see Israel staggering toward him, eyes wide, dust and grime smeared across his face. His armor was dented, his clothes torn—but he was alive. Israel clapped a heavy metallic hand on Jonathan's shoulder that made a whirring noise as he did.

"One day, lad. One day you're gonna do something the easy way—and that'll be the day I keel over and die from pure disbelief."

The others found them quickly. They regrouped behind the broken remains of a toppled skybridge, panting, wide-eyed, every one of them stealing quick glances at the chaos around them.

Jonathan followed their gazes.

There it was: the Golden Spire.

It rose from the center of the ruined city like a final, desperate beacon—still standing, still untouched. But wrapped around it was a shimmering barrier, a dome of translucent blue shot through with cracks and flickers of weakening light.

"Granted, I'm no expert in magical blue forcefield thingies," Cody muttered grimly, wiping blood from his brow. "But I'm reasonably confident that shield won't hold forever."

Jonathan nodded in agreement. But what Cody said next took him off guard.

"So, what now, Sky Boy?" the soldier drawled. And to Jonathan's surprise, they all looked at him.

Honestly, I didn't think we'd make it this far, he almost said. But he bit it back. They didn't know he was improvising, when they looked at him, all they saw was someone who had just done the impossible. His mind snapped into motion.

"We can't kill them all," Jonathan said, his voice steady, grim. "Not even close. Which means we only have one option: get the shield down, save our friends, grab the Core... and then get off Aetherium before it all comes crashing down."

Cody barked a laugh—half amused, half despairing. "And how exactly do you propose we do that?"

But it was Israel who answered. "A big enough strike ought to do it. Don't you think?" He turned to Cody. "You got any more of those 'birthday presents' stashed in that fancy jacket of yours?"

Cody shook his head.

Before anyone else could speak, Aelowyn stepped forward. Her gaze was sharp as she studied the shield flickering in the distance. "The barrier's siphoning power straight from the Core," she said. "It's not stable anymore. It's overloading."

The others turned toward her.

"If we can divert or drain the energy—force it to bleed faster than the Core can replenish it—the shield will collapse on its own."

Jonathan blinked, a cold memory flashing across his mind. He lifted his sword slightly, remembering the last time he had struck at the city's mainlines of Power. "I tried that once," he said grimly. "The results were... unpredictable. Chaotic."

"I agree with Jonathan," Israel said, and crossed his arms. "You hit those pipes, we don't just drop the shield. We drop the whole city. Core and all. Everything goes down, including us."

Aelowyn's expression didn't waver. "Do you have a better idea?"

Jonathan felt the knot growing in his stomach. The sound of fighting was getting closer. They were running out of time. He had an idea—

But he hated it. Hated even *thinking* it.

It was reckless, desperate.

Sure, it was no crazier than anything they'd already done that day.

But somehow... it felt wrong. It felt like betrayal.

Not of his friends, not even of the world—

Of himself.

Like he was throwing away something good inside him, discarding a piece he might never get back. He could feel it, like a blade twisting just under his ribs. And still, he

311

knew he would do it. He would burn that part away, if it meant saving the ones who mattered.

Jonathan swallowed hard. "I know a way through the shield," he said. A vile, bitter taste pooled at the back of his throat.

"But none of you are going to like it."

CHAPTER 24
DUTY BEFORE DEATH

Jonathan led the others through the broken streets to a modest structure on the outskirts of what was left of Aetherium. Surprisingly, they made it without being spotted—Khan's army was too focused on bringing down the shield to notice a handful of rebels slipping through the ruins.

Jonathan pushed open the heavy door with a slow creak. No lights burned inside. No hum of power. In the background he could still hear the sounds of battle, but here in this place there was only silence. Only darkness.

He stepped forward without a word and the others followed. Inside, the blackness closed around them like a living thing. Jonathan drew his sword with a rasp of steel. The runes along the blade flared to life—a low, steady glow of ghostly green that cut a narrow path through the gloom.

They moved carefully through the darkness, every sound amplified, quiet but hurried, and it didn't take them long to find what they were looking for.

"If he's still alive," Jonathan said quietly, "he'll be in here."

Israel loomed at his side, his glowing red eye scanning the darkness ahead. His voice was a low rumble.

"You sure you want to do this, lad?"

"Actually," Jonathan muttered, tightening his grip on the sword, "I'm pretty sure I *don't* want to do this." He exhaled, steadying himself. He closed his eyes, gritted his teeth, and grumbled, "But it has to be done."

He turned to the others. "Wait for me here."

He stepped forward, raised his sword, and sliced through the barred doors with a screech of tearing metal. The heavy iron clattered to the floor in a shower of rust and dust.

Jonathan walked through. At the far end of the room, half-slumped against the wall, bound in chains thick as a man's arm, sat the Chancellor.

At first, Jonathan almost didn't recognize him.

The Chancellor looked like he had aged a century.

He was still tall, but his once-pristine robes were reduced to tattered rags, hanging from a frame that was now withered, borderline emaciated. His hair—once dark and immaculately kept—had grown long and wild, now mostly white and gray. A heavy, unkempt beard obscured most of his hollowed cheeks, tangled and matted like an abandoned banner left to rot. The lines on his face had deepened into harsh crevices, carved by exhaustion, defeat, and something worse. His eyes—Jonathan remembered them with a chill, twin glaciers of cold hatred—were now sunken deep into shadowed sockets. But there was no hatred in them now. Only emptiness.

The chains binding him creaked as he stirred, a faint sound in the heavy stillness. Slowly, the Chancellor lifted his head. His hollow gaze found Jonathan, but his face showed not even a flicker of recognition. Jonathan stepped closer, his sword casting a low, ghostly glow in the dark.

"I need your help," Jonathan said, voice flat.

The Chancellor leaned back against the stone wall, the chains binding him clinking softly. His dead eyes flicked to Jonathan—and to Jonathan's surprise, he said nothing. No sneer. No cutting words. Just a vacant, almost absent study.

"Not because I trust you," Jonathan pressed on. "And certainly not because you deserve it. But there's a fight coming—and if we lose, it won't just be Aetherium that falls. It'll be everything."

Still, the Chancellor did nothing. Only watched, silent, as if Jonathan's words drifted past him like mist.

Eyes narrowing, Jonathan gave a terse, clipped explanation of the situation—the Core, the shield, Khan's army tightening its grip on what little remained. He laid it out in as few words as possible. The Chancellor listened—or at least, his empty gaze stayed fixed in Jonathan's direction. But his eyes... his eyes seemed elsewhere. Distant. Far beyond this broken place.

Jonathan's patience thinned.

"Did you hear me?" he demanded, stepping closer, frustration bleeding into every word. "Can you help us or not?"

Still, silence.

Still, that broken, hollow stare.

Then, a sound—a rasp, low and harsh, like gravel dragged across dry stone. For a terrible moment, Jonathan thought the old man was dying, some final death rattle clawing its way free from his ruined lungs.

But after several seconds, he realized: the Chancellor was laughing.

It wasn't a clever laugh. It wasn't even a cruel one. It was a cracked, splintering sound that filled the darkness like smoke—the broken laughter of a man who had already lost everything, even himself.

Jonathan's gut twisted. A thousand emotions warred inside him—anger at the memory of everything the man had done, guilt for needing him now, revulsion at what he had become.

Jonathan tightened his grip on the sword, planting his feet like roots into the broken stone.

"Jonathan Roe," the Chancellor rasped, voice cracked but still laced with mockery at the edges. And then the Chancellor smiled—a real smile, jagged and weary, but genuine all the same. For the first time in Jonathan's memory, the old man actually looked... human. "You should thank me. Without my sins, you would have remained soft. Weak. Now look at you: a wolf pretending at mercy."

Jonathan didn't flinch. "You owe it to the people you betrayed."

The Chancellor let out a breath that might have been a laugh—or maybe a sigh—and the smile faded. The hollowness returned, the distant, vacant stare sliding back into his ruined face.

"I owe them silence," he murmured. "I owe them penance. I made my choices. Let better men fix what I shattered."

Jonathan gritted his teeth. "You think sitting here rotting in the dark is penance? You think dying forgotten is redemption?"

For a heartbeat, the Chancellor just stared at him, silent. And then—

The dam broke.

His chains rattled as he lurched forward. Glacial hatred flew into his eyes, the hatred Jonathan knew all too well, and the Chancellor bared his teeth as he roared.

"You think I don't know what I've done?!" he cried, the sound raw, splintering, loud enough to rattle the ruined walls. "You think I don't carry it? Every breath, every moment, every cursed heartbeat since the Core cracked beneath my hand—!" He stood, slammed his fists against the chains with a metallic *clang*, teeth bared in a snarl.

"I was trying to save us!" he shouted, spittle flying from his mouth.

His voice cracked into something savage, something closer to a wounded animal than a man.

"You don't understand! None of you ever understood! I gave everything!"

The malice spent itself as quickly as it had come. His chest heaved with ragged, shuddering breaths, the chains trembling with him. And in the hollow that followed, Jonathan saw it: Not just rage. But grief.

Bone-deep, unending grief.

A single tear came from one eye.

The Chancellor slumped back against the wall, spent. His next words came out as little more than a whisper: "I gave *everything*. And it still wasn't enough."

Righteous anger flared in Jonathan's chest, and for a moment he nearly lost control. His muscles tensed, blood burning hot in his veins, every instinct screaming to lash back. To let all the fury and betrayal boil over—the righteous fire he'd carried for so long.

After all, this was the man who had shattered Aetherium. This was the man who had ordered countless deaths, crushed lives under his heel without a second thought. This was the man responsible for Jacky's death—the person who had meant more to Jonathan than anyone in the world at the time. The grief still clawed at him like a splintered bone beneath the skin, never fully healing, and the very thought of working side by side with the Chancellor made his headache pound.

He *wanted* to yell. He *wanted* to demand answers, demand justice. He *wanted*—for just a moment—to hurt the Chancellor as deeply as he had been hurt.

But with a sharp breath, Jonathan forced it down. Such actions would accomplish nothing. And what was more, if he acted on such impulses, would he have been any different than the Chancellor?

Instead, he simply stood there, sword lowered, chest rising and falling with slow, intentional breaths.

And he looked. Really *looked*. Not at the Chancellor—the monster from his memory. But at the hollow man slumped against the wall. Broken. Defeated. Ruined from the inside out. And against all logic, against all justice, against everything his anger screamed for—Jonathan felt something else stirring in his chest: Empathy.

Because whatever the Chancellor had been… Whatever crimes he had committed… There was almost nothing left of him now but regret.

"I'm sorry," Jonathan said, his voice softer than he would have thought possible. "But you don't get to sit this one out."

Tears welled in the Chancellor's sunken eyes. His breath shuddered in and out. "I have no right to pick up a sword again," he rasped. "No right to stand on any battlefield."

"I agree," Jonathan said quietly. "You have no right. But this isn't about rights. It's about duty. About debt. Redemption. You don't get to decide when your fight ends— not when the cost of your mistakes is still being paid by everyone else."

For the first time, the hollow in the Chancellor's gaze faltered. Just a crack. A flicker of something old and buried deep—something not yet dead.

Jonathan stepped closer, the glow of his sword creating long shadows across the ruined cell. The Chancellor's head bowed, his shoulders sagging under the weight of everything unsaid. For a long moment, he didn't move, didn't speak—just breathed, ragged and shallow.

And then, slowly, something shifted.

It was subtle—barely there—but Jonathan saw it. In the hollow wreckage of the Chancellor's eyes, a new light flickered to life. Hope.

Jonathan took another step closer, then sheathed his sword.

"Can you help us get past the shield?" he asked.

For a heartbeat, the Chancellor said nothing. Then he lifted his head—and something changed. It was faint at first, like the first crack of dawn cutting through a storm. But it grew.

A glimmer of happiness touched his weathered face. Real happiness. The kind that could only come from finding some small, impossible scrap of purpose in the ruins. He smiled—a real smile, tired and fierce.

"I can do much better than that."

He shifted slightly, the chains clinking softly. "But if I'm going to help you, I think it's time everyone stopped calling me *Chancellor*."

Jonathan blinked.

"My name is Caelan," the old man said. It wasn't said with power, or pride, or menace. Just quiet resolve. "If I'm going to die today… I'd rather do it as a man than a title."

Jonathan held his gaze. Then he nodded.

"Alright, Caelan. Let's end this right."

CHAPTER 25
YOU WILL NOW FACE JUSTICE

T heir small band moved carefully through the skeletal remains of the scorched city, each step cautious, silent. From a hundred yards out, they watched the Golden Spire, the last unbroken monument in a sea of ruin. By some miracle—or perhaps sheer luck—none of Khan's army had yet noticed their presence.

They had a clear view of the battlefield.

In a wide, seething ring around the shimmering forcefield, Khan's entire army had gathered. Thousands strong. Malrics, corrupted Guardians, raptobeasts, and worse. And standing at the very front, pressed closest to the barrier, were the Ancients—giant tree-creatures, monstrous and relentless.

Their tactic was crude but devastating.

The Ancients pounded the shield again and again, using whatever heavy wreckage they could lift—chunks of fallen towers, shattered engines, beams of twisted steel. Each thunderous blow sent shockwaves and blue sparks rippling across the forcefield. The shield shuddered, blinked, and crackled in protest. Every impact seemed to weaken it, dimming its once-blinding brilliance.

It wouldn't be long now.

Jonathan watched in grim silence, feeling the clock ticking louder with each failing flicker of the barrier.

The time for planning was over. They were ready; they were all waiting for Jonathan to give the command.

Before Jonathan could speak—before the words of command could leave his mouth—a voice called out behind him.

"I would have a word," said Caelan.

Jonathan turned, clenched his teeth. Of all people. The others around him glanced sideways, uncertain, but Jonathan held up a hand. The moment stretched. He didn't answer right away. He didn't want to. Part of him still hated that Caelan was even here—standing among them, breathing the same air. Jonathan had been the one to bring him. And that knowledge clung to him like a stain he couldn't wash off.

But finally, with a low breath, he nodded. "Fine. Make it quick."

Caelan drew him a few paces aside, just far enough that the roar of the dying shield swallowed their words before the others could hear.

"I know we don't have much time, but there's a lot of ground to cover. How's your headache?"

Jonathan stopped suddenly, eyes narrowed. "I don't know what you're talking about."

Caelan gave him a knowing smile.

"I can feel it," Caelan said, eyes scanning Jonathan's face. "There's something waking in you. Something powerful."

Jonathan's brow furrowed, but remained silent.

"You know what I'm talking about. Don't play dense." Caelan's voice lowered. "You've used your powers before. You know what you're capable of. But you almost never do—and when you do, it's only in moments of desperation. As if you're holding back. As if you're afraid. And I can feel it. The power is building inside you. It's not going to wait forever, and it won't stay quiet. It needs a release, whether you're ready or not. The headache is a sign things are… about to blow, Jonathan. Use your powers now, or suffer the consequences."

Jonathan frowned, unsure what to say, and Caelan pressed his point.

"And just as important—that sword of yours? It wasn't meant to cut alone. It was forged as a conduit, a vessel to channel what lives inside you: your power. You've treated them like separate tools. They're not. The sword and the gift—used together—don't just add to each other. They amplify. Exponentially. Right now, you're holding a weapon that would've made the Founders weep with envy… and you're using it like a letter opener."

Jonathan said nothing, but something in his posture shifted—just slightly.

Caelan's eyes gleamed. "Besides. It's the only way you'll defeat the Tiger King. You might get close with one or the other. But to win? To stop him for good? You'll need both. That's what you were made for."

He paused, let the silence press in as Jonathan considered what Caelan told him.

"So why not now?" he asked softly. "Why not use your power in the battle?"

Jonathan looked away, jaw clenched. "For one, feels like cheating."

The Chancellor chuckled. His eyes glittered, cold and amused. "Of course you'd say that. Noble to a fault. But I've got news for you, kid—these things we're fighting? They won't hesitate to eat your face while you sleep."

He took a step closer, his voice suddenly quieter. "And honestly… I don't see how we win this. Not without help. It would be my… *strongest* recommendation to use every advantage you have."

Caelan held his gaze. "The lives of everyone you care about depend on this. Every last one of them. So ask yourself—what matters more? Fairness… or survival?"

Jonathan closed his eyes for a moment and considered what Caelan said. He'd never thought about that before, relying on his powers instead of the strength of his arm and skill with the blade. He'd used his powers occasionally, but it was always a spur of the moment decision. To do it tactically? To use it for violence?

But before he could follow the thought any further, Caelan was already pressing on.

"One more thing," he said, and glanced around, as if the shadows themselves might be listening, pausing as if regretting his decision to tell Jonathan. Eventually, voice tired and quiet, he whispered, "The Lurker... has taken one of the survivors from Aetherium."

Jonathan felt a fierce resentment flash through him at the accusation.

"That's impossible," he said, eyes narrowing.

Caelan shook his head slowly. "I felt it. I don't know who. But someone from your Rebellion—someone noble of blood—has been taken."

Jonathan's heart pounded. "What are you saying?"

"I'm saying," Caelan replied, "you need to look carefully. Trust your instincts. Because if I'm right... the Lurker already walks beside you."

Jonathan said nothing. He turned and walked back the way he'd come, Caelan falling into step beside him.

"Everyone know their job?" Jonathan asked.

"We know our job," Cody replied, flashing a grim smile. "It's not exactly complicated. Fight our way through an entire army at hundred to one odds, not in our favor."

Jonathan gave a small, humorless huff. "Guys, look," he said. "I'm not going to lie to you. This won't be easy. We might not live. The plan? Odds are, it won't even work."

"Wow. Great speech, boss," Cody drawled.

Jonathan managed a faint grin. "I get it," Jonathan replied and managed a faint grin. "But today, it's not about what we want. It's about what needs doing."

Varg cracked his knuckles, teeth flashing in a grin that was all fang and fire.

"Perfect," the giant tiger rumbled. "Wouldn't trust a plan that sounded safe. Lead the way, Little One. Let's go do something stupid."

They crouched low, studying the enemy arrayed before the great shield wall. A thousand at least stood directly between them and the barrier—and once the alarm was raised, Jonathan knew even more would come flooding in.

He tightened his grip on the sword, the old blade humming faintly in his hand. His whole body coiled with tension. It was a fool's charge, and he knew it—but knowing had never stopped him before.

And still, he raised the sword slightly, feeling the anticipation gather like a storm in his chest.

"On my mark," he said, voice low and steady.

Jonathan drew in a sharp breath, feeling the world tighten around him. The city, the shield, the army—they all blurred into a single, impossible wall ahead. His sword gleamed in his hand, pulsing faintly with power.

He raised the blade high, the signal they'd agreed on.

"Now!" he shouted.

The world snapped into motion.

He had reasoned Caelan might give them an edge. More than anyone there, he knew what Caelan could do. He had seen it first hand. But even Jonathan was not prepared for what followed.

Before their feet could move, a voice rang out— commanding, thunderous, shaking the very bones of the earth.

"Enemies of this world!" Caelan's voice boomed across the square, *"You will now face justice!"*

Jonathan spun, stunned. Caelan stood tall, arms raised like a conductor invoking a storm. His cloak billowed. His voice echoed. He thrust both hands forward toward the shield wall.

With a sound like glaciers breaking, twin walls of ice erupted from the earth—colossal, jagged, roaring outward in opposite directions. They split the enemy ranks clean in two, bodies flung aside like leaves in a gale. The ice tore through steel and stone, carving a perfect corridor straight to the barrier.

The path was clear.

But Jonathan knew it would not stay that way for long.

Jonathan turned, eyes wide, heart racing. "Move!"

He surged forward, legs pumping hard over the broken ground. He heard the others fall in behind him—felt them, their weight, their momentum—but he didn't look back. Couldn't. To either side, chaos erupted. Corrupted Malrics—black wounds and oil bubbling along their muscular flesh—clawed at the towering ice walls, trying to scramble over with snarls and fury, their claws scraping uselessly against the slick surface. Others hurled spears and blades, but the ice deflected them like glass. Ancients struck like demons, their powers battering the glacier with flame and force, but it held. Cracks spidered along its edges, but the center path—straight and true—remained.

The shield barrier loomed ahead...

Just as he neared the end of the corridor—mere strides from the shield wall—the air cracked like thunder.

The last section of ice gave way.

With a deafening roar, the far end of the glacier shattered into jagged shards. A tide of Malrics poured through the breach—snarling, leaping, blades flashing in the fractured light. Dozens of them. Then more.

Jonathan skidded to a halt, sword already rising.

"They're through!" Cody shouted, breath ragged.

All around him, the enemy crashed into them—Cody, still holding his massive box from the Before-Times could not fight. But Israel and Varg each tore into the enemy like wrecking balls, Valera carved through them like she was born to do it, and Aelowyn danced through them in arcing flashes of purple and green light. Jonathan fought forward, slashing and carving his way forward. Pain flashed in his side as something grazed him, but he ignored it, driving himself harder. Two more Malrics closed in on him from opposite sides. He didn't slow.

He ducked the first strike, twisted low, and let their own momentum work against them. His sword flashed in a clean, practiced arc—striking one in the side before it carried through into the second. Both went down hard.

Caelan reached the shield wall just as the ground trembled—and from the fractured ice burst a colossal shape.

An Ancient.

It towered in the air, its massive limbs formed from knotted wood, its body a twisted fusion of bark, root, and Rot. Moss clung to its sides like scars. Its face, if it had one, was a tangle of thorns and coal black eyes that burned in the gloom like black diamonds. Each of its steps made the ground tremble. Its arms ended not in hands, but in heavy, gnarled growths like living warhammers. As it advanced, vines writhed along its body, flexing and snapping, ready to strike. It was strength incarnate—and it was directly in their path.

"Hold that thing back!" shouted Caelan.

Jonathan charged, sword flashing in the flickering light. He leapt, aiming for the Ancient's center mass. A massive limb swung out with brutal force and caught him midair.

It wasn't even a contest.

The blow sent him flying, the world spinning in a blur of smoke and ruin. He hit the ground hard, the impact sending shockwaves of ruining pain through his guts and driving the breath from his lungs. He barely had time to roll before the Ancient's foot—a slab of root and stone the size of a wagon—came crashing down where he'd landed.

Jonathan scrambled to his feet. Before he could take a single step, roots burst from the broken earth and coiled around his legs like living chains. Another root shot up and coiled around his waist, locking him in place. Jonathan instinctively swung his sword, but before the blade could bite, another thick vine lashed out and seized his arm, yanking it away. He strained against the bindings, muscles burning with the effort, but it was like fighting the pull of the earth itself.

The roots tightened, crushing, unforgiving. His boots dug trenches in the dirt, but it was no use. He couldn't move. Couldn't even turn. He was pinned, helpless, the battle raging on just out of reach.

And the Ancient was already shifting its massive bulk toward him, preparing for the killing blow.

Suddenly, brilliant streaks of purple and green light lanced through the air, slamming into the Ancient's twisted form. Wherever the green lights struck, the creature's bark-like skin hissed and bubbled as if burned by acid. The purple streaks of light froze its limbs in place; others solidified its torso, turning flowing muscle and root into rigid, unmoving wood.

The roots binding him relaxed just enough for Jonathan to turn against the last of the roots just in time to see her.

Aelowyn.

Aelowyn, her feet sure on the broken ground, her hands raised in effortless command. Light poured from her fingers, tearing into the Ancient, binding it, burning it, breaking it. Her soft skin caught the glow of her attacks, making her look like something born of starlight and defiance, her dark eyes blazing with unshakable will.

The Ancient let out a thunderous roar and staggered backward, its massive body fighting against the purifying and petrifying force seizing it. It tore free with a groaning crack, roots and bark splintering—but even as it broke loose, more of Aelowyn's magic rained down, relentless, weaving a lattice of binding light around it.

Each step the Ancient tried to take was slower. Heavier. It thrashed, desperate to crush anything in reach, but every movement only sank it deeper into the web of light.

Jonathan watched as the impossible unfolded before him—the Ancient's twisted form stiffened, roots thickening and digging into the earth, bark hardening into knotted wood. Branches sprouted from limbs that had once thrashed with fury, and a heavy, unnatural stillness began to claim its body, like a monument being born out of rage.

Aelowyn approached the paralyzed beast, tears streaking down cheeks, exhaustion trembling through her limbs. And in that moment, she wasn't just powerful—she was beautiful in a way that had nothing to do with appearance and everything to do with spirit.

Then the arrow struck.

It drove into her shoulder blade with a sickening thud, and she collapsed forward into the dirt.

"No!" Jonathan roared, wrenching free from the roots that still clung to his legs, slashing wildly with his sword.

She tried to stand, but another arrow whistled down—another direct hit, and she fell again.

"Hurry!" someone shouted behind him. "We don't have time!"

But Jonathan didn't hear it. He didn't care. All he saw was Aelowyn lying broken in the mud, and he sprinted for her. But something seized him from behind and hurled him backward—straight through the open gap in the shield wall, thrown to safety by Israel's massive arms.

He stumbled, rolled hard across the shattered ground, panic lurching in his chest, and watched in horror as the energy field crackled and blinked back into existence.

He ran for her anyway, crashing into the barrier with a deafening impact.

The shield didn't budge. It held firm as steel.

Both Aelowyn and Israel were trapped on the other side of the shield.

"Hurry!" Israel bellowed, his voice rough with urgency. He turned without hesitation, planting himself between Aelowyn and the oncoming tide of enemies, his weapon rising in defiance.

And then, with a low, thunderous hum, the shield wall pulsed—and turned opaque. Jonathan slammed his fists against it, shouting their names, but it was like beating on solid stone. He could see nothing. Hear nothing. Only the swirling light of the barrier cutting him off from the ones he'd sworn to protect.

A hand gripped his shoulder. He turned. Valera stood there, her face grim, her green eyes filled with sadness but unwavering.

"No time for tears, Cub Mine," she said softly. Her voice wasn't unkind, but it brooked no argument.

"On your paws. Move," she said, and pulled him toward the Golden Spire.

CHAPTER 26
WHERE REALITY BREAKS

J onathan stared at the wall, disbelief churning in his

chest—but there was no time to feel it. The shock, the fear, the rising dread... all of it would have to wait. He turned and faced the looming Golden Spire ahead. It rose like a promise and a threat, wreathed in firelight and shadow.

No more time. Just forward.

Selene spotted him first. "Jonathan!" she cried, racing to his side. Her robe was scorched and torn, but her eyes were fierce with relief.

Behind her came Cedric—pale, wide-eyed, and clearly terrified. But somehow, impossibly, his burgundy-and-white suit remained crisp, his tie perfectly knotted, not a hair out of place. He looked like he'd just stepped out of a ballroom and into a war zone.

"You absolute lunatic," Cedric gasped, gripping Jonathan's shoulder.

Jonathan managed a weary smile, but before he could answer, Cedric looked at Caelan, and recognition flashed across his eyes.

"Jonathan... what have you done?"

Selene stepped forward, urgency flashing in her eyes.

"There's no time for reunions or scolding. Our entire world hangs in the balance of what happens in the next fifteen minutes," she said sharply, then turned to Jonathan. "Please tell me you have a plan."

Cody pushed forward. He opened his massive box and began handing out several small backpacks, one to each member of the group.

"We do," Cody said. "I can get everyone off Aetherium—but first, we have to get the Core."

Selene winced. "That's going to be... problematic."

She spun on her heel and took off at a brisk pace. "Follow me."

They moved fast through the rubble-strewn steps that led to the Golden Spire. She stopped just short of the entrance.

"No one goes in there," Selene said. "Not anymore. Whatever's happening to the Core... no one can survive it."

"I can," Caelan said and stepped forward, gaze steady. He turned to Jonathan. "And so can he."

Jonathan looked up, uncertainty flickering in his eyes. "Are you sure?"

Caelan gave a shake of his head. "No." Then a faint smile. "But even if I'm wrong—what choice do we have?"

A beat passed. Selene held his gaze. "No one who has entered the Golden Spire has come back."

Caelan inclined his head. "Whatever's happening in there, I can stabilize the Core. I can retrieve it. And once we have it—" he glanced around at the others, each one strapping on the gear Cody had handed out "—we get off this rock."

"Why should we trust you?" Cedric snapped. His voice was sharp, his eyes cold. Whatever goodwill he had for Caelan had clearly run dry.

Before anyone could answer, a strange, wet, syrupy *blurb* echoed through the air behind them—like the world's largest boot sinking into something it shouldn't. All eyes turned as a massive section of the shield wall began to warp inward, metal and energy screaming under pressure. The noise twisted into a groan, then escalated into a shrill, bone-deep whine. The shield held for a heartbeat longer… then imploded with a deafening roar, collapsing in on itself before exploding outward in a shower of light and shrapnel.

The shield was down.

They were out of time.

Jonathan reached for the pack that Cody offered him and slung it over his shoulders, then drew his sword in a practiced motion. No more plans. Just the final stretch of a road he'd been walking for a long, long time.

Varg turned toward the incoming Tide, bared his teeth, muscles bunching like mountains, and let out a thundering roar that echoed through the broken city.

"VARG!" he howled, voice shaking stone and soul alike.

Then he charged—headfirst, fearless—into the chaos, fur bristling, laughter rolling from his chest like thunder; no weapon save for his gleaming claws. And just in case the enemy hadn't gotten the message the first time, he bellowed it again, even louder: *"VARG!"*

Cody grabbed Jonathan by the arm, pressed a small spherical object into his hands and said, his voice somehow simultaneously casual but urgent, "In case it all goes sideways. Push the red part. Aim away from your face."

Jonathan nodded and put the object in his pocket. Cody turned toward the advancing army and opened fire— thunder and lightning erupting from his rifle in bursts of precise, unflinching judgment. It was clinical, detached, almost impersonal—the practiced violence of someone who'd done this far too many times to feel much about it anymore.

Valera lingered. Sadness in her eyes. And something else—acceptance. She gave Jonathan a small nod, and when their eyes met, there was more said in that glance than words could ever carry.

Jonathan felt the sting of tears press behind his eyes but forced them back down.

Caelan grabbed his arm and pulled him toward the looming gates of the Golden Spire. Together, they pressed forward. The doors opened with a hiss of displaced air and light spilled out from within, cold and strange.

Jonathan and Caelan stepped through the threshold—and reality collapsed around them.

There were barely walls. No ceiling. No floor in any conventional sense. The space warped and breathed like a living dream turned sour. Blackness stretched in every direction, but it wasn't empty—far from it. Stars wheeled in slow, impossible spirals, constellations he didn't recognize, blinking like the fading eyes of vast titans. Some were close—too close—so near he felt like he could reach out and touch them. Others burned cold at impossible distances. There was no horizon. Just madness.

The walls—if they could be called that—were shifting things, slick and half-organic, stitched together from vines and metal and wet, pulsing light. Tentacles slithered in and out of them, slick with some dark fluid that steamed in the cold air. They twisted without purpose or direction, flinching from the two men like snakes disturbed in their nest.

And at the center of it all, suspended in a jagged cage of bone-white tendrils and flickering energy, was the Core.

The Wellspring Jonathan had seen—the one buried in Ydrathar—had flickered like a dying candle, low and struggling, ancient and frail. But this one… this one teetered on the edge of eruption—a bomb with a frayed fuse, a volcano trembling at the seams, raw nuclear potential waiting for the smallest spark. Light so bright it nearly blinded them poured from fractures in its shell, and seething waves of molten gravity that twisted space around it in violent ripples.

338

Caelan's eyes widened in sudden alarm. "No, no—this is all wrong!" he shouted, voice sharp with panic. "It's unraveling! I have to contain it!"

He sprinted forward and threw himself toward the Core. The moment his hands touched the flickering sphere, a blast of light surged out in all directions—blinding, searing.

Agony tore across Caelan's face.

He didn't scream—but only because he didn't have the breath. His jaw clenched, eyes bulged, every muscle in his body locking tight as the energy coursed through him. Light poured through his fingers, into his veins, lighting him from the inside out.

And still Caelan held on.

Jonathan stood frozen, unsure what to do. The moment Caelan's hands met the Core, the entire chamber recoiled. The warped walls rippled like disturbed water, twitching with each pulse of unstable energy. Above, the strange stars—if they were stars at all—flashed with furious bursts, pulsing brighter with every second Caelan strained against the force threatening to erupt from within.

Cautiously, Jonathan stepped forward. The Core throbbed violently. Caelan let out a strangled cry but didn't collapse—he was holding it back, containing whatever lived inside. And then, for one breathless moment, it eased. The flickering softened. The tremors faded, ever so slightly.

Jonathan advanced slowly, weaving around flickers of searing light that shot through the air like silent lightning—missiles of energy that seemed to carry destruction beyond imagining. But Caelan was gaining ground. His fingers traced the surface of the Core in slow, concentric patterns, his expression taut with concentration. The glow dimmed. The chaos quieted. The storm was, to some degree, being tamed.

Jonathan reached the pedestal.

"Stay back," Caelan warned, sweat beading on his brow. "It's still unstable."

Jonathan opened his mouth to reply—then froze.

A voice slithered through the chamber, smooth as oil and twice as smug.

"Well, well. The prodigals return. And still pretending at power, I see."

Jonathan turned.

Silas Grey stood at the far end of the room, his sharp grin stretched too wide to be kind. And beside him, towering and silent, stood Khan—still as stone, eyes burning with quiet fury.

Jonathan raised his sword but said nothing.

"I'm growing tired of you getting in my way," Silas said, the smile fading.

"Then get used to disappointment."

Silas' gaze hardened. "You've already lost, Jonathan."

"Doesn't look that way from here."

Silas chuckled humorlessly. "The only thing standing between this Core and its own annihilation is your friend Caelan. If he stops for even a moment—if he lifts a finger to help you—the Core will explode. And with it? The locks break. The prisoners wake. The End of All Things begins."

Jonathan looked at Caelan. His face was still strained with concentration, maximum effort, muscles tensing beneath skin, sweat pouring down his forehead, too focused to even so much as acknowledge that Silas and Khan were present.

Jonathan's only reply was a low growl.

"You *can't* win," Silas went on, arrogance oozing in every syllable. "Even on your best day, you and Caelan couldn't have defeated the two of us. But now?" He gestured. "It's just *you*. Caelan moves, the Core dies. So fight, don't fight—it makes no difference. We win."

Jonathan smirked. It was probably true. "Fine. But if I'm going down… I'm dragging both of you with me."

Khan—snow-white fur now veined with thick lines of corruption crawling beneath the surface—loomed like a monument to inevitability. He wore armor now, a jagged fusion of deep green and crystalline plating that shimmered with unnatural light, each facet reflecting a twisted echo of the Wellspring's power. He didn't need to speak. He didn't need to threaten. His sheer presence did all the talking—a mass of coiled strength and regal violence, silent as a stormcloud before the break. The walls pulsed, the tentacles twitched, the stars flared—all of it in rhythm with his breath, as if the room itself bowed to his will. Jonathan's old wound throbbed sharply at the sight of him. It still hadn't fully healed—and in Khan's presence, he doubted it ever would. Not truly.

He raised his sword, hands steady despite the thunder in his chest. He wasn't under any illusion—he doubted he could beat either of them in open combat, let alone both…

341

But perhaps he could stall them. Perhaps he could buy Caelan the precious seconds he needed to stabilize the Core. Perhaps, against every law of sense and survival... he could make it matter.

A slim hope. Stupid. Suicidal.

"Just... remember what I told you," Caelan rasped, voice ragged with pain.

Jonathan closed his eyes for the briefest breath and reached outward—not with his hands, but with his sixth sense. That strange, other sense that had always whispered at the edge of his thoughts, now sharp and singing like a tuning fork struck too hard.

He felt them.

The gravitational fields radiating from both Khan and Silas—twisting, coiling, flowing around them like invisible armor. No, not armor. Gears. Systems. Strands of invisible force braided and stretched like puppet strings. And he realized: that was how they moved like phantoms—by manipulating the field around themselves, detaching from the normal flow of gravity and time. They weren't just fast... they were unbound, uncoupled from the rules of time itself.

That was their secret. That was their weapon.

His grip tightened on his sword.

"Then I'll just have to cut the strings," he muttered.

He didn't want to do it—didn't want to charge headlong into battle, to meet death with nothing but a sword and a scream—but he knew it had to be done.

So Jonathan charged first.

And he nearly ended the battle with his first strike.

He launched forward like a man possessed—driven not by rage, but by something sharper: courage, duty, purpose. As he moved, he unbound himself, just as his enemies had done—gravity shedding from him in layers, each one lifting his speed higher. At the same time, his senses reached outward, seeking the tangled threads of warped gravity that clung to Khan like armor—then yanked, *hard.*

In an instant, Khan was stripped of his unnatural speed. Robbed of the advantage he'd come to rely on. Disoriented, vulnerable, he barely—by the breadth of a single hair—managed to raise his weapon in time.

The clash shook the chamber.

Khan reeled back half a step—not from pain, but from surprise. And for the first time… Khan looked uncertain.

Jonathan didn't stop. He pressed the advantage, lashing out with strike after strike—raw, desperate, and utterly relentless. Every blow was fueled by fury, by grief, by the need to buy Caelan one more breath, one more heartbeat.

As he moved, he reached with that other sense—the invisible tether to the world's weight—and pulled with everything he had. He bent the gravity around Khan, locking him in place, robbing the Tiger King of his impossible speed. At the same time, he lightened his own relationship with time, sharpening his reflexes, turning momentum into a weapon.

It worked—briefly. Khan faltered.

Five more seconds and he would have bested Khan at his own game.

But before Jonathan could land a decisive blow, a black tendril lashed from the side—Silas.

Silas extended an arm, and it simply unraveled. Black tendrils of oily magic shot out like a viper. Jonathan rolled instinctively, narrowly avoiding the worst of it, but not before a blade-edge kissed his calf. His senses exploded with a flash of light as pain tore up his leg in a hot line. Not deep, but enough to stagger. He landed in a crouch, breathing hard, sword raised.

He was exhausted, and it took a moment to realize the reason: only moments had passed—but bending the world the way he had just done was already taking its toll. His lungs burned, legs trembled, muscles screaming for rest. He could fight like a man possessed, but he wouldn't be able to do it for long.

Silas stalked toward him now, coat flickering in the chaos, face delirious with rage.

"You locked me in a cell with a *mind-eater*," he wailed. "For a thousand years he screamed in my mind. A thousand years of rot and silence and torture and screams!"

Silas lashed out. A dozen tendrils exploded toward him, slicing through the air—but Jonathan was ready. He snapped the tendrils one by one with the precision of a blade master, defending against Silas' attack with a measure of will and a dozen flicks of his sword.

But his focus was on Silas—and Khan struck.

The Tiger King lunged. Jonathan twisted, just in time. He dodged the beast's mighty war axe, but claws raked across his ribs—shallow, but enough to draw blood. He staggered back. Khan pressed forward with terrifying speed and strength, every blow forcing Jonathan to retreat, each attack closer than the last. He fought the Tiger King to a stalemate of speed…

Until Silas raised a hand and snapped his fingers.

The air folded in on itself.

A ripple of gravitational distortion surged through the chamber—and Jonathan was flung like a ragdoll, slammed into a wall of twisting stone and writhing metal. Pain exploded through his back. The sword clattered from his hand. He scrambled for it, lungs heaving—but too late.

Tentacles, thick as his thigh and slick with some black, glistening secretion, uncoiled from the shadows and wrapped around him. Wet suction cups clamped onto his skin with sickening squelches. The moment they touched him, a burning sensation shot through his nerves—like fire poured through his bloodstream. Worse still, their presence pressed against his mind, a cold poison that clawed at his thoughts, twisting his sense of self, drowning him in whispers and howling agony. And with every struggle to wrench himself free from their grasp, the psychic assault intensified and the darkness pulled him deeper.

But still, he fought, struggling with all his strength against the otherworldly things that pulled him into the void. He didn't want to keep fighting. Stars above, every part of him screamed to give in.

But he had something worth fighting for.

345

Gritting his teeth, he reached out—bloodied, shaking—and called his sword to him. It leapt to his hand with a burst of light, and he lashed out, blade carving through the tentacles with a crackle of energy. The weapon sang with power, and he felt its strength surge through him.

He gasped, dragging in a breath, forcing himself upright. Every movement burned. They had only been fighting for perhaps a single minute, two, tops. But more had occurred in that minute than in a half hour of any other battle, more strikes, more counter blows, more heavy lifting and damage.

Silas stepped forward, his face twisted in something between disgust and exhaustion. "I am so thoroughly *sick* of you," he hissed, his voice vibrating with contempt. "Khan. Take care of him. I'm going to end this once and for all."

The Tiger King growled low, a sound like thunder rolling in his chest, and stalked toward Jonathan. In his hands, he hefted the massive war axe—its boney edge jagged with age, its haft wrapped in cracked leather. This was no ordinary weapon. It was the very axe that had cleaved Ydrathar's mighty Everguard cleanly in half. A weapon built to destroy the indestructible. And now, it was aimed at him.

Silas turned toward Caelan—toward the Core.

Caelan's eyes snapped to Jonathan, wide with desperation, his face slick with sweat, muscles trembling as he held back the chaos threatening to burst free of the Core.

"I've... almost... got it..." Caelan gasped, voice thin and breaking under the weight of effort. Behind him, the Core was changing—its violent pulses slowed, its storm-light dimming. Like a sea beginning to calm, the waves of pressure eased, the shrieking softened, and the bleeding energy began to seal.

"Jonathan—please," Caelan said, barely above a whisper, "I need more time. The Core can never fall."

But Silas was on the move.

His entire form began to unravel—his sharp-suited silhouette dissolving into that same awful tide of black oil and spinning blades. It rippled across the floor, a nightmare given form as it slithered toward the Core.

Panic flared in Jonathan's chest. Caelan was holding on by a thread. If Silas reached Caelan and the Core, it was over. All of it. The war. The tree. His friends.

The world.

Khan struck, and Jonathan engaged the terrible beast. Every strike carried the weight of survival, every counter a gamble against annihilation. But in the heart of it all, Jonathan felt his sword stir.

It began as sang a thrum that wasn't just metal or magic, but *life*. Wild, righteous, untamed. A weapon born of nature and force, and now… something more. The hunger in it was not for blood, but for justice. For balance. For preservation.

Jonathan didn't think.

He raised the blade—and with a roar from somewhere primal, somewhere true—he hurled it straight at Silas.

The weapon changed mid-flight. Green light burst from its edges, trailing vines and flame, its steel core sheathed in a writhing aura of luminous, living power. It wasn't just a blade anymore—it was a spear of the forest itself, the last warcry of a dying world given form.

Silas turned, tendrils whipping around to meet the attack. A dozen black limbs crossed in front of him, alien tech and dark magic combining to form an X in a defensive gesture.

But even before blade met barrier, Jonathan knew—

Silas was no match.

The blade was like a comet made of spring itself, and it pierced clean through shadow and steel, carving a path of light through the black mass like sun through fog, the shield unraveling strand by strand as the living blade screamed toward its mark. The sword struck Silas in the center of his mass, and for one blinding instant, it was like watching a dam collapse. Green light poured into him. And Silas Grey—or whatever passed for him—screamed and flew backward.

For a breathless moment, even the chaos paused.

The Tiger King stopped mid-step, his massive frame rigid as he turned to watch the spectacle. Silas twitched in the rubble, black tendrils spasming, the last of his form unraveling in flickers of dark static.

And then—

"Jonathan."

The voice came from behind. Jonathan turned.

Caelan. With a low hum, the Core in front of him pulsed—slower now, steadier. The cracks had disappeared from its surface, the beams of light emitting from its center all but ceased, now merely vibrating in quiet rhythm—contained, at last.

Caelan stood before it, barely upright. His shoulders shook, his breath came ragged. His face, pale and hollowed. His hands trembled as he slowly stepped back from the Core. He turned to Jonathan, eyes rimmed with fatigue, but burning with something fierce and final.

"It is finished," he said, voice tired but firm. Then louder, called "Now get out of here before they kill you!"

With what strength he had left, Caelan reached for the Core—his fingers glowing with residual force—and wrapped his hands around the orb and as it responded to his will, it reformed, smaller now, a pulsing sphere the size of a heart, cradled in his hand.

Then Caelan took the Core in one hand, and with the other made a slashing motion through the air. Reality stretched—warped like pulled cloth—before tearing open into a shimmering portal. Caelan turned back just once, met Jonathan's eyes with a look full of purpose.

Then he stepped through the portal—

—and was gone.

CHAPTER 27
OBLIVION

Jonathan blinked.

One second, Caelan was there—worn down, barely standing, clutching the Core like it was the last ember of warmth in a frozen world. The next... he wasn't. Just a shimmer, a ripple of torn reality, and then he was gone. No goodbye. No plan. No portal for two.

Jonathan stood frozen, staring at the space where Caelan had been, mouth slightly open.

"Seriously?" he breathed. "You just—?"

He turned slowly back toward the center of the chamber. Silas was already recovering, his body forming into something less than human. And the Tiger King was still standing—alive, breathing, eyes burning with hatred.

He looked once again, as if hoping it was all a trick and Caelan was coming back, but he knew he wasn't.

"Jerk move," Jonathan muttered. He once again called his sword to his hand, the blade snapping into his grip with a familiar hum. Even that small effort made his knees wobble and his vision blur. "Total jerk move," he added, breathless, as if sarcasm alone might hold the world together a few seconds longer.

He blinked, and the warped realities—the swirling stars, the trembling walls, the unnatural sky, the tentacles lining the walls—began to dissolve like mist in the morning sun. The air steadied. The shadows softened. Gravity felt... normal again. Slowly, like peeling back layers of a fever dream, the world resolved itself into something familiar. The walls straightened, stone and gold reasserting their form. The madness faded.

And then—he was simply there.

Back in the throne room of the Golden Spire of Aetherium.

The vast, crumbling chamber greeted him with silence. Shattered stained glass still hung in fractured frames. Dust motes drifted through the golden shafts of late light, falling on scorched marble and quiet ruin.

He grimaced, rolling his shoulder as he raised his sword again. It felt heavier than ever. Khan was already moving, circling like a great jungle cat. No wasted motion, no sound. Just the quiet inevitability of something built to kill.

And if Khan was a predator, Silas was a madman.

He rose, twitching with static and fury, his form barely human anymore. His eyes were wild—wide and glassy, rimmed with black veins and flickers of something savage beneath. He staggered, then lunged forward a step, teeth bared, voice cracking like glass under pressure.

"You..." he hissed, staring straight through Jonathan. "You dared lock me up with him. And now you steal the only thing that could have redeemed me?"

Jonathan's sword didn't waver, but his knees trembled. He knew he couldn't keep this up for long.

Silas kept speaking, his voice rising into a tremble. "Do you even understand what that place is? Time slows to a trickle; what was for you a few moments was, for me a thousand years—a thousand years! A thousand years, he tortured my mind. There is nothing left of me now, boy, but madness and rage."

Jonathan blinked through the sweat and blood in his eyes, lips dry and cracked. His sword sagged slightly in his hand, but he didn't let it fall.

"Poor Silas," he rasped, voice flat. "A thousand years in a magical time prison? Boo hoo. Did you not get enough hugs from the void monster?"

Silas's face twisted, part fury, part something worse—hurt.

Jonathan didn't care. He was beyond tired. That last attack had hollowed him out. His muscles burned. His vision swam. Every heartbeat felt like dragging a mountain uphill. Only a miracle—and sheer, mule-stubborn will—kept him upright.

Silas laughed again, a sound like splintered glass scraping a rusted pipe. "You think you've seen madness, boy? You dropped me into the abyss and locked the door."

"Then maybe don't be such a jerk next time," he muttered. "See how that works out for you."

He didn't want to fight anymore. Not really. He wanted to lie down and sleep for a week. But Khan and Silas were still there—standing between him and the only exit: the door back to the Golden Spire. He knew it was a long shot, but if he could only get through that door, there was a chance his friends were still there, waiting for him. Perhaps they could help him survive…

Two monsters. One barely standing kid.

He was too tired to be afraid anymore—and if he was too tired to fight, well… he sure wasn't about to let *them* figure that out.

"I can do this all day," Jonathan said, flashing a cocky half-smile he absolutely didn't feel. His voice was hoarse, his arms trembling, and he was fairly certain a stiff breeze could knock him flat. But they didn't know that. And he wasn't about to tell them.

Silas' manic composure faltered. His twisted grin twitched, eyes narrowing with something like hesitation.

The Tiger King, who had yet to take a wound, frowned. Just slightly. But for a creature of his stature, even that was meaningful. He'd expected Jonathan to break. To fall. To crawl. Instead, the boy still stood. Bruised, bloodied, broken… but unbent. And for just a moment, the predators paused.

Jonathan couldn't help a smug smile. "Alright, freaks," he muttered. "Who wants to lose first?"

They all moved at once—Silas with a shriek of rage, Khan with a roar like splitting stone—but they never reached him.

The entire room lurched.

A deep groan echoed through the throne chamber, followed by a low, shuddering vibration that rolled beneath their feet. Jonathan staggered, catching himself on trembling legs. He realized it at the same moment they did: the Core was gone.

The Power that had kept Aetherium floating—its lifeblood, its anchor—had vanished.

Without it, the city would fall.

Not all at once, not yet. But the descent had already begun—slow, almost gentle, like the first breath of a coming storm. But it would crescendo soon. The spires would crack. The girders and beams holding it up would shear.

They would fall.

He had to get to the exit…

With a ragged cry, Jonathan surged forward, sword raised high. Silas and Khan moved to meet him, twin forces of ruin. The Tiger King lunged first, his axe a flash of bone and fury, but Jonathan slipped beneath it, rolling low. Silas was fastest, and his tendrils lashed out, warping into jagged blades mid-air. Jonathan deflected one, dodged another, but the third sliced across his shoulder, opening his old wound with a fresh line of pain. He countered with a blast of force from his palm, knocking Silas back just long enough to spin and clash with Khan again.

It wasn't a fight. It was survival. Every second was chaos—dodging a claw, countering a tendril, striking blind and praying it landed. Jonathan was outmatched in strength, outclassed in speed, but he had desperation, and it burned hot in his veins. But he knew: he wasn't going to make it out of the room. He could feel it—every step slower, every breath harder. He wasn't fighting to win anymore. He was fighting to survive. To delay the end. The exit loomed behind his enemies, but it might as well have been a world away. He was too busy staying alive.

Suddenly, the throne room began to unravel. Cracks spiderwebbed across the marble floor, pillars groaned, then split, raining debris from above. The ceiling buckled. The walls bent inward. The Golden Spire—or what was left of it—split into a dozen pieces and began falling.

Jonathan lost his footing in the chaos. Pain exploded through him—first as Khan's claw raked across his ribs, splitting flesh to the bone, then again as one of Silas's tendrils slammed into his back like a spear, driving him to his knees. Jonathan choked on a cry, vision swimming, blood soaking into the stone beneath him.

Jonathan staggered, tried to rise—but Khan was already there. With a brutal kick to the chest, the Tiger King sent him sprawling. Jonathan's sword clattered across the broken floor, skidding out of reach. Before he could crawl toward it, Khan grabbed him by the throat, lifting him into the air like he weighed nothing. Jonathan's legs dangled, kicking, vision blurring as the pressure closed around his windpipe.

Khan leaned in close, breath hot and reeking of smoke and blood. His eyes burned with wild hunger, pupils narrowed to slits, the look of a predator not just eager to kill, but to savor it. His snarling lips pulled back over gleaming fangs, and the muscles beneath his fur coiled with terrible power.

"You fought like a king," he growled, his voice low and full of lethal promise. "But you die like the rest."

Jonathan's vision tunneled as the flow of oxygen to his brain ceased, the edges darkening like frost on glass. Khan's grip crushed tighter around his throat, and the last reserves of strength bled from his limbs. His legs dangled, his sword lost. His lungs screamed. He was slipping—slipping fast.

But then… a flicker.

A memory.

Cody's voice, casual but urgent. *In case it all goes sideways. Push the red part. Aim away from your face.*

With his last trembling effort, Jonathan's hand fumbled toward his pocket. His fingers closed around something smooth and cold—a circular object, no larger than his palm. He pulled it free with numb fingers. The device gleamed faintly in the flickering light, polished metal wrapped around a single red button.

He didn't know what it would do.

He didn't care.

He pressed it.

Hatred and malice twisted across Khan's face. He leaned in close, eyes wild with triumph and rage, and roared loud enough to shake dust from the broken ceiling. The sound hit Jonathan like a wall of heat and hate.

Jonathan didn't flinch.

Instead, he threw the grenade straight down the Tiger King's throat.

Khan froze.

Just for a second.

Then his eyes widened.

Whatever force had empowered the Tiger King—whatever ancient magic or monstrous strength he'd drawn from—must have shielded him, because the blast didn't kill him outright.

But it apparently hurt.

A lot.

The explosion cracked like thunder, fire and kinetic force blooming from within his chest. Khan staggered back, as if struck by a building-sized asteroid. He let out a sound unlike anything Jonathan had ever heard—part roar, part scream, part wounded titan—and his grip on Jonathan faltered. He dropped him.

Jonathan crumpled to the floor, coughing, eyes wide, the air burning in his lungs. Khan reeled backward, smoke curling from his jaws, one hand clawing at his throat. Silas surged forward, a blur of rage and blades—but he was too late.

There was no one Jonathan had ever met who could beat him in a footrace. Not on even ground. Not when it counted.

With everything he had left—blood in his mouth, pain screaming in every limb—Jonathan ran, calling his sword to his palm as he did. Straight to the fractured edge of what remained of the Golden Spire. Wind tore past him, howling through the collapsing throne room as it came apart.

And then, without hesitation, he leapt off of Aetherium and into cloudfall.

The wind tore past his ears as he fell—lashing at his face, tugging at his limbs, howling like a living thing. For a heartbeat, the world dropped away completely. The feeling was madness. Beautiful, terrifying, exhilarating. For a fleeting moment, he forgot the wounds, the war, the weight of everything he'd just survived. He was falling, yes—but he was free. And for a small moment, he was just a Cloudwalker…

Jonathan spun slightly in the freefall, stabilized, and the world tilted into impossible perspective.

To his left, the World Tree rose like a monument, so massive it defied logic. From his vantage point, it was incredible. Massive branches stretched outward, woven with moss and ruin and flickers of golden light and green life, and rivers of glowing blue pulsing deep within its flesh. He saw remnants of cities clinging to its limbs like barnacles on a whale—some flickering with life, others half-swallowed by roots or overgrowth.

Directly beneath and to his right, nothing. No horizon. No end. Just cloud—rolling, sunlit, endless. A yawning chasm of blue and gold, bottomless, terrifying, beautiful.

His stomach dropped. But his chest ached with something else.

Awe.

He had seen wonder before. He had fought monsters, stared into the face of the abyss, defied ancient powers. But nothing—nothing—compared to this. It was the vastness of it, the raw truth of how small he was in the scheme of everything. And somehow, that didn't feel crushing.

It felt... peaceful.

At the last possible moment—his heart pounding, wind screaming in his ears—Jonathan reached back and yanked the cord on his backpack Cody had given him.

The effect was instant.

With a snap and a jolt that nearly wrenched his shoulders from their sockets, the parachute exploded open above him, billowing into a wide canopy of fabric. The sudden drag yanked him upward, slowing his descent from terminal madness to something just shy of manageable.

Cody had called it a parachute. Jonathan had called it "probably death in a bag." But now, as the violent drop shifted into a gliding drift, Jonathan laughed—half from relief, half from sheer disbelief that it had actually worked.

Around him, the sky was filled with falling wreckage. Slabs of stone. Shattered towers. Screaming Malrics. The golden glint of Aetherium's spires tumbling end over end. And somewhere among it all—Silas, the Tiger King, and the ruins of a broken kingdom.

To his surprise, Jonathan found he could steer. By shifting his weight and pulling on the cords, he angled the parachute toward the distant silhouette of the World Tree, its vast branches stretching like arms through the clouds. It wasn't precision flying, but it was enough to aim for home.

He hit the ground and collapsed in a heap, the impact knocking the last of the strength from his limbs. Dirt, leaves, and the scent of moss filled his senses. He was asleep before he could even take off the parachute—before he could roll over or even wonder if anyone had seen him land. Just one long breath… and then darkness.

CHAPTER 28
GOOD ENOUGH

Jonathan later found out he had landed in the dead center of Arenthil—quite literally. Right in the main square, flat on his back, parachute tangled around the statue of a long-forgotten Founder. Since no one had witnessed what had happened to the Core, rumors swirled in his absence. Some said he'd destroyed it. Others claimed he'd merged with it. A few believed he'd been vaporized and reborn. Eventually, after much arguing and two fistfights, the general consensus became this: whatever he'd done, it must have worked. The world hadn't ended. With Khan vanished into whatever lay beneath the clouds, the Rot's hold collapsed almost overnight—fading like mist in sunlight. The Tree still stood. Arenthil was still here.

So… good enough.

When they finally untangled him from his parachute, unconscious and still clutching his sword, he was rushed to the infirmary. Bruised, burned, bloodied almost beyond recognition—but breathing. Barely.

He slept for two full days. The nurses said he mumbled nonsense in his sleep. Something about tigers not flying and jerks stealing his Core.

The first thing Jonathan heard as he clawed his way out of unconsciousness was a voice—low, rough, and unmistakably irritated.

"Get up, Cub Mine. You've slept long enough."

His eyelids fluttered open. Blurred shapes slowly became a ceiling. A pale light. Then a silhouette looming over his bed, broad-shouldered and bristling with golden fur.

Valera.

She stood at his bedside like a disappointed coach. One hand on her hip, the other holding what appeared to be a wooden practice sword.

"We begin training at once," she said matter-of-factly. "These so-called *doctors* wouldn't know a healing balm from raptobeast urine."

Jonathan blinked. His body ached in places he hadn't known could ache. "You're not serious…"

But Valera was always serious.

Before she could shove the stick into his hands, a familiar voice cut in from the foot of the bed.

"Oh for light's sake, let the patient breathe," Elysra said, walking in with fresh bandages and a glare. She wore the blue sash of an infirmary nurse in training and a look that promised she was seconds away from stabbing Valera with a thermometer. "He just survived two monsters, a city-wide

362

destruction, and a six-thousand-foot fall. He doesn't need a duel. He needs rest."

Valera hissed softly, tail flicking. "Rest is for the nearly dead."

"He *is* nearly dead!" Elysra snapped. "And you're scaring the nurses again."

Valera growled under her breath, ears flattening. "Good. They need to toughen up."

Jonathan sank deeper into the sheets with a groan. "Please don't fight. I'm too tired to referee."

Elysra rolled her eyes and turned to the door. "I'll go get the doctor. He's terrified of her, but he might grow a spine if he knows you're awake."

As she left, Valera huffed and sat down heavily beside him, her expression somewhere between annoyed and... relieved. Jonathan fell asleep again.

To Valera's great annoyance—and the doctor's visible terror—she wasn't allowed to spar with him. But that didn't stop her from staying. She remained perched at his bedside like a brooding sentinel, arms crossed and eyes constantly scanning for danger or incompetence. She growled at nurses. Hissed at the doctors. Sent more than one intern into tears.

Even Varg, who visited with a basket of strange jungle fruit, took one look at her and decided to come back later.

But despite the chaos, Jonathan couldn't help but feel... safe.

Valera never left his side.

And even though she claimed it was because he'd attract assassins in his weakened state, or might try to sneak out like an idiot, Jonathan wasn't fooled. She stayed because he was hers. And deep down—though he'd never say it out loud—he was glad for it.

Speaking of Varg, he arrived the next day, striding into the infirmary like he owned the place—never mind the nurses who scattered at the sight of him. If he was remotely aware of how the locals felt about tigers, he didn't show it. Or more likely, he didn't care.

He was chewing something when he entered.

Jonathan blinked at him. "Uh… what is that?"

Varg paused mid-chew. "Kneecap."

Jonathan's face scrunched up in a disgusted look.

"What?" Varg said, and raised his hands innocently. "It's not mine." He gave Jonathan a deeply offended look, then went right back to chewing.

He loomed at the foot of Jonathan's bed, arms crossed, tail flicking behind him, a distinct sourness in his expression.

He was in a notably foul mood.

"I haven't punched anything all day," he said darkly, pacing a slow circle around the bed. "It's making me… something… not good."

"That sounds," Jonathan paused, searching for the right word. "Dangerous."

Varg leaned in, studying his face so closely Jonathan could smell his knee-cap breath. "Would you like to go hunting?" Varg asked.

Jonathan, still bandaged from clavicle to shin, croaked out a weak, "No."

"Would you like to fight?"

"No."

"Do you know of *anything* I could punch?"

"No."

Varg sighed and crossed his arms. "Pity."

Varg huffed, clearly annoyed by this complete lack of productive violence. Then, with a grunt, he reached out and patted Jonathan's shoulder—far too hard.

"You have earned a new name. You are no longer Little One."

Jonathan braced himself. "Oh yeah? What now?"

"Tiny Madman."

"Thanks?" Jonathan offered, unsure if that was a compliment or a warning.

Varg gave a sharp-toothed grin. "You and I, little brother, will do battle again, side by side. That much I guarantee." He smiled wide at the thought, flicking his tail like punctuation. "And that will be a *very* good day."

And with that, he turned and strode from the room, muttering something about how the rations tasted like moss and disappointment. Jonathan watched him go, then let his head fall back onto the pillow.

Israel came later that day, wheeled in by a quiet nurse. The big man looked worse for wear—his bionic arm was busted and burnt, and the rest of him didn't seem to be faring much better. Jonathan's breath caught when he saw the wheel chair.

The once-indestructible wall of a man was paralyzed from the waist down.

But Israel... was smiling.

Not the tight, forced kind Jonathan had seen in broken men. A real one. Calm. Content.

"Don't look at me like that, lad," Israel said, his voice low and weathered, though there was a calm patience behind it and he smiled with a relaxed, patient quality. "I've had a good run. And all things end eventually."

Jonathan felt the sting behind his eyes—hot, burning. He wanted to say something, anything, but a sharp ache rose in his throat and the words lodged there. He looked at his friend and realized, for the first time, that Israel was old.

He'd always seemed indestructible. Stoic. Eternal. It had never occurred to him that Israel was old enough to be his grandfather. His hair was grayer than Jonathan remembered—more white than gray, if he was being honest—and it made the grizzled soldier look older than ever. But at the same time... he looked good. Peaceful. Like the weight of his armor had finally been lifted.

"You're stronger than I ever was," Israel said, locking eyes with him. "I've said it before, and I'll say it again: I'm proud of the man you've become. Jacky would be, too."

Jonathan swallowed hard. Still, the words wouldn't come. Israel smiled and reached out, gripping his shoulder with a hand that had steadied many.

"I kept my promise to Jacky, God rest her soul. I don't think we'll be fighting together again," he added. "But… I'm alright with that."

And strangely, Jonathan believed him. Not just the words—but the stillness in them. After a lifetime of battle, Israel had found something close to rest.

"Just don't screw it all up," he said with a crooked grin.

Jonathan managed a faint smile through the haze in his eyes. "No promises."

Even Drekkar's old pride was doing well. The next day, Jonathan received word that they had been taken in by another clan deeper in the Ydrathar jungles, and they were doing well—strong, healing, rebuilding, though it had taken several days for the message to actually be delivered to Jonathan. The Malrics and humans weren't openly at war, but after everything that had happened with the Tiger King, no one in Arenthil seemed eager to trust a tiger.

Which, as far as the Malrics were concerned, was perfectly fine.

EPILOGUE

Nestled in the farthest corner of the World Tree, Arenthil was the kind of city that looked like it had been carved from a storybook.

Its towers rose in graceful arcs—not jagged or defensive like fortresses, but elegant—ivory spires crowned with banners that danced in the ever-present breeze. Castles and keeps clung to the floating cliffs like ivy, their walls veined with flowering vines and climbing roses. Marble courtyards glowed under golden lanternlight, and marvelous stone bridges arched between hovering districts like threads of a vast, airborne tapestry. In the distance, mist-veiled farms and orchards rolled along the horizon, adding a pastoral serenity to the city's grandeur. The whole place shimmered—like something half-dreamed and wholly impossible.

And somehow, Jonathan Roe had become its favorite son.

Overnight, he'd turned into a focal point—part hero, part myth, all legend. The teen who had timed a daring strike, tamed a sky serpent (albeit briefly) and used it to defeat the

Tiger King's army, and saved Ydrathar itself. The boy who battled Khan in single combat. Who struck down Silas Grey and helped rescue one of the last remaining Cores. Arenthil had been fighting—and losing—the war against the Tiger King's Malric forces for years.

Jonathan had ended it in a day.

So when he finally gathered enough strength to venture into the city, he was unprepared for the chaos that followed. Cheers. Handshakes. Gifts and roses and hugs. If it hadn't been for Valera stalking protectively at his side—snarling at anyone who got too close—he figured he would've suffocated to death under an avalanche of praise long before the Tiger King ever got the chance.

One day, the king of Arenthil announced he would be holding a feast for the heroes that had fallen from the sky. Or a banquet. Or possibly a ball? Jonathan wasn't entirely sure what it was called—only that he was fairly certain it had been custom-designed to make him miserable.

A battalion of tailors swept into his room like a military operation—armed with measuring tapes, pincushions, bolts of fabric, and opinions sharp enough to draw blood. They clucked and fretted and barked commands, tugged at fabric and fussed with lapels, circling him with the intensity of surgeons.

All of this, of course, unfolded under the gleeful command of Cedric, who oversaw the chaos with the smug satisfaction of a stage director on premiere night. He flitted between tailors like a maestro, offering commentary, adjusting collars, and radiating pride. He was dressed immaculately—black and white tuxedo with a silver cravat, hair slicked back to the exact angle of perfection that

369

somehow defied the wind. Jonathan could only imagine what life sequestered on Aetherium must have been like for a man who craved such pageantry, and he was pretty sure that now, amongst the nobility after a year away, Cedric had never been so happy in his life.

"If a world can't host an event where a man gets to wear a tuxedo," Cedric declared grandly, arms spread as if delivering a sermon, "then tell me, Jonathan, what was the point of even saving the world?"

Jonathan, halfway through being cinched into a double-breasted jacket with at least seventeen buttons, gave him a flat look. "To stop a war? Save lives?"

Cedric waved dismissively. "Secondary benefits. The *true* reward," he gestured broadly to a line of shoes polished so perfectly they may have contained alternate realities, "is tailoring."

Jonathan groaned. Somewhere in the corner, Valera smiled at Cedric.

Which he was pretty sure meant the world was probably ending.

Jonathan sighed. "Where's Cody? Doesn't he have to go to this thing, too?"

Cedric, perched on a velvet chaise like a smug falcon, didn't even look up from where he was approving fabric swatches. "Last I heard, he was out showing Selene his 'truck,'" he said, making air quotes with silk-gloved fingers. "It's filled with some sort of military tech he brought with him from the Before-Times. Although—" he paused, selecting a swatch with unnecessary flair, "—she did want me to pass something along."

Jonathan raised an eyebrow. "Yeah?"

Cedric finally glanced up. "Apparently, that Wellspring water you were given after the injury? It didn't just save your life. Selene believes it changed you. Long-term. You'll probably always heal like that now—fast, unnatural. Regenerative, even."

Jonathan blinked. "Like, forever?"

Cedric smiled thinly. "Well, until you explode into vines or mutate into a glowing tree-thing, yes. Forever."

A pause. The tailor tugged at his sleeve again. Jonathan finally swatted the hand away.

"What about Aelowyn?" he asked, more serious now. "I haven't heard anything since... well, since the fall. Just that she's alive. I never even heard how she survived after getting trapped on the other side of the wall."

Cedric's posture shifted. He sat up straighter, and the smile faded from his lips.

"She's alive," he said quietly. "But after the Tiger King breached the shield wall and entered the throne room, his influence over the Ancients shattered. The moment it did... she took control of them. She turned them into her own personal army. Marched them through Khan's forces like her enemies were children's playthings. Used them to rip the Malric warbands apart—systematically. Brutally." He exhaled through his nose. "She's a scary one, Jonathan. You watch out for her."

A heavy silence settled over the chamber. Jonathan didn't answer right away.

371

Cedric leaned against the wall, arms crossed. "Soon as we touched back down on the World Tree, she vanished. Didn't say a word to anyone. Just made her way back to the center—to the Wellspring. With Khan's forces shattered—most of them dead in the fall—there was no one left to stop her. She reclaimed it. Took it back like it was hers all along."

Cedric studied him for a moment, then wordlessly reached into his coat and pulled out his silver flask. He unscrewed the top and handed it over.

Jonathan took it without hesitation, tilted it back. "It's water?!"

Cedric smiled faintly. "You looked like you needed it."

Another pause. The tailors had drifted away for a moment to argue about lapel widths.

Cedric stood, brushing invisible dust from his sleeves. His voice dropped slightly. "There's one person you haven't asked about, Jonathan…"

Jonathan looked up sharply, something tightening behind his eyes.

Cedric said nothing else.

The gala—or ball, or masquerade, or torture chamber (take your pick)—was… kind of fun.

Jonathan hadn't expected that.

The king of Arenthil turned out to be quiet but nice enough, though he mostly seemed to do whatever his wife told him to, and the queen insisted Jonathan try every type of honeyed pastry Arenthil had to offer. Cedric was in his element, proudly parading Jonathan around like a prized painting. "Yes, yes, this is *the* Jonathan Roe—fought a demon tiger, saved the world, has excellent cheekbones."

Israel was in good spirits too, parked comfortably in a wheeled chair beside the dais, laughing with old knights and entertaining young ones with stories. Varg arm-wrestled the guards, an activity that went exactly the way one would imagine it would, and he never stopped laughing nearly the entire night. Even Valera... well, she wasn't exactly smiling, but she stood at Jonathan's side without scanning the exits every three seconds, which was as close to "relaxed" as she got.

And then Aelowyn was suddenly there.

He turned, and there she was—bright eyes, long ears, she looked radiant in a flowing druidic dress. There was something almost otherworldly about her. She stepped forward and wrapped her arms around him in a fierce, unexpected hug.

"Thank you," she whispered in his ear, voice thick with emotion. "For everything."

He returned the hug—stiffly at first, but it softened quickly, settling into something real. When they parted, Aelowyn's eyes lingered on his, searching for something neither of them could quite name.

A quiet beat passed.

"So... where will you go now?" Jonathan asked.

"The king says I can stay," she replied, her voice quiet. "He offered me a place. A home. Said my people could stay too." She hesitated, then gave a small shake of her head.

"But just because you're welcome doesn't mean you belong."

Jonathan nodded slowly. He understood that all too well.

She looked at him, brow furrowing slightly. "Gran told me something, before all this ended. She said... our paths are intertwined." Her voice was soft now. "I guess I'm still trying to figure out what that means."

She hugged him once more and left.

Jonathan weaved through the crowded ballroom like a man on a mission—or more accurately, like a man trying not to get pulled into another conversation about military strategy by someone wearing a three-foot feathered hat. He scanned every cluster of guests, every swirl of silk and armor and color, looking for her, but never could find El.

She found him.

He made it to the food table and had just reached for something that looked vaguely like meat on a stick when a hand seized his arm with startling force.

"I've been looking for you all night!" he yelped, nearly hurling the skewer across the room. "How did you find me in this giant place?"

"Please," Elysra said flatly. "Use your brain, Roe. I knew I'd find you by the food."

He turned, and his heart pounded out roughly a hundred beats in three seconds—not from the ambush, but from the sight of her. She wore a deep red gown, somehow both elegant and wildly untraditional. Her violet eyes sparkled with mischief, and her hair—long, golden, loose, and wind-tossed even indoors—looked like it had absolutely refused to be tamed for royalty.

"I—uh—I don't really…" he began.

"You don't know what you're doing, I know," she said, pulling him to the dance floor, then spinning around him, violet eyes beaming. "Your dancing is about as elegant as my swordplay."

He fumbled for a comeback, blinking. "I—uh—well—"

"And your wordplay," she added with a smirk, "isn't much better."

They danced.

Jonathan said nothing—too focused on not stepping on her toes, or his own. Especially with the bruises and bandages still hidden under his formal clothes. His ribs ached with every spin. His shoulder twinged when he turned. But Elysra didn't miss a step. She moved like water, flowing around him with a grace that made him feel even clumsier by comparison. She guided without seeming to. Danced without demanding. And for once, he let himself follow.

Then—he stumbled.

Just a tiny misstep, half a second off the beat. Her hand tightened briefly on his, catching him, steadying him. Her laughter bubbled up, soft and bright and entirely unjudging. When he looked up, their eyes met and the world slipped away. The ballroom, the music, the hundreds of guests in glittering robes and golden armor—gone. Just her, smiling at him like he was the only one in the place.

And even after everything he'd endured in the past year, the wave of pure emotion that slammed into him was stronger, fiercer, more overwhelming than anything he and El had faced since falling from the sky, a tide that stole the very breath from his chest. For a moment, Jonathan could only stare, undone by the staggering realization of who she was—what she was. Elysra wasn't merely beautiful, or graceful, or brilliant beyond compare. She was everything—light and laughter and strength woven into one breathtaking whole. In that instant, Jonathan knew with a certainty that burned straight through him: she was the most incredible person he had ever known. And he knew—utterly, irreversibly—that Elysra Sel was—

"Jonathan Roe," came a voice behind him.

Everything froze. The dancing. The music. Even El's laughter faltered as she looked past him, her smile replaced by concern.

Jonathan turned. The king stood there, flanked by a ring of armored guards. The mood in the ballroom shifted instantly—silken conversation shriveling into silence, golden music breaking against the stone edge of authority.

"Your majesty," Jonathan said, and bowed deeply.

The king studied Jonathan for several seconds, his face an unreadable mask, but his eyes betraying something very close to fear.

"Come with me," he said. It was not an invitation.

Jonathan knew better than to protest. He let himself be led away, down glittering halls and shadowed corridors, the guards closing ranks around him. Only once they were far

376

from the revelry did he finally mutter, "All this muscle to protect you, Majesty?"

For a long moment the king said nothing, and the only sound to be heard was the scuffle of their boots over marbled floors. The king's expression was carved from stone, his silence heavier than words. After several minutes they arrived at their destination.

"Please forgive me, Jonathan. I had no wish to harm you. Nor to steal you from your celebration. But your friends are very… persuasive."

The king stopped at a door and pushed it open, but did not step inside. Jonathan didn't hesitate. He walked through, and the king shut the door behind him.

The room was plain and severe—stone walls, a single table at its center, and a handful of chairs arranged around it. No banners, no decorations. Just the kind of place soldiers used when talk mattered more than appearances.

Jonathan crossed to the table and sat. Minutes passed in silence. His thoughts drifted—back to the ballroom, to the dance, to what came next… when suddenly the air shifted. No knock. No sound of hinges. Only the shadows stirring, and suddenly someone was there. Sitting across from him.

Caelan.

Jonathan shot to his feet.

"You," Jonathan growled.

Caelan didn't so much as flinch. He looked faintly irritated, like someone pulled from a dull book at the worst possible page.

"Jonathan Roe. You could no more defeat me now," he said, voice flat as stone, "than a goose could fly through a black hole."

Jonathan's hand moved on instinct. One blink and his sword was there, green fire erupting along the blade.

"You sure about that?" His words came out like ice.

For the briefest instant—just a flicker—something uncertain touched Caelan's eyes. Then it was gone, his composure unbroken.

"I'm not here to fight you, Jonathan. I'm here to warn you."

Before Jonathan could reply, a soft voice cut through the tension.

"Oh, for stars' sake."

Gran was suddenly standing beside Caelan—no footsteps, no announcement, just... there. She looked like herself: apron, bun, warm eyes. But there was something different now. Not less kind. Just... heavier.

Caelan glanced sideways at her with something resembling unease.

Caelan held out a book. Small, bound in cracked brown leather. He extended it to Jonathan.

"This is the journal of the Architect himself," Caelan said, his tone grave. "Read it, and you will uncover truths you may wish had remained buried. But you cannot ignore them. The Lurker grows in power, and the battle ahead will not forgive ignorance. You must be prepared."

"Don't open it tonight, dear heart," Gran said gently.

Caelan scoffed. "He should open it now. There's no time for—"

"Let him have one night of peace," Gran said, her voice still soft, but with an edge that could cut glass.

Caelan opened his mouth to argue—

Gran didn't touch him. She just lifted a hand. And with a flick of her fingers, Caelan's jaw snapped shut with a comical clack. He stared at her in outrage.

"You could no more hurt me," Gran said sweetly, "than a goose could fly through a black hole."

Jonathan blinked at both of them. Then looked at the leather bound journal in his hands.

"Sleep now," Gran said, her voice suddenly warm again. "Tomorrow gets harder." And just like that—she was gone.

Caelan studied Jonathan for a long, quiet moment.

"Ydrathar isn't on humanity's side," he said at last, voice firm. "She is not to be trusted."

Jonathan frowned. He didn't trust Caelan—not even a little—but something in his tone made him pause. So he listened.

"You're saying she's evil?" Jonathan argued.

Caelan's eyes flashed. "Don't be absurd. She isn't evil—far from it. In fact, in many ways, she might be the closest thing to good this world has left. And she serves the

Wellspring—Life itself. *All* life. Human, animal, everything that breathes or grows. And that's the problem."

His voice dropped, laced with bitter certainty. "To protect it, she'd sacrifice anything. You. Me. This entire world. Every last human who ever lived. If she thought it necessary, she'd burn us all and smile while the ashes fell. Because to her... starting over is always an option."

Caelan glared, opened his mouth—and then thought better of it. He vanished too.

For a long time Jonathan sat in the moonlight streaming through his window, the gloom of the new information pressing around him like fog. The book rested in his hands—ancient, weathered, still warm from where Caelan had held it. He didn't move. Not at first. Not for a long while.

His fingers traced the edge of the worn cover, the leather cracked like old bark. It felt heavier than it should've—heavier than any book had a right to be. Maybe because it wasn't just a book. It was truth. It was burden. It was choice.

A thousand thoughts clamored in his mind, and his heart hammered so powerfully in his chest it was literally painful. He was exhausted—soul-deep, marrow-deep—but he knew he wouldn't be able to sleep. Not yet. His body ached, his eyes burned, and still he sat there, staring down at the thing that had outlived empires, that had passed from the hands of monsters and visionaries alike.

He wasn't ready for what came next. Not really. But duty, however heavy, could not wait. Slowly, he opened the journal.

Inside, a single photograph of three individuals and a baby.

His heart lurched to a stop.

He knew them. His mother—her face blurred by the haze of childhood memory, almost lost to him, yet still sharp enough to strike straight through his chest. The soft curve of her smile, the warmth in her eyes—he remembered fragments, lullabies, fleeting touches—but here she was, whole again, immortalized on faded paper, holding a baby, holding *him.*

Valera, too. Even frozen in an old photograph and several decades younger, she radiated that same fierce presence, the gravity of a warrior in every sense of the word. To see her younger, standing there as though she belonged to another life, another world—it twisted something deep inside him.

But it was the figure at the center that unraveled him. Jonathan's breath faltered. The man's face was very nearly his own, carved older, sterner, shadowed by burdens Jonathan could only guess at. The resemblance was inescapable—jawline, eyes, even the subtle tilt of his brow. It wasn't recognition that came to him, but revelation—sudden, thunderous, impossible to deny.

This wasn't a stranger. Not some relic of history.

It was his father.

And not just his father—the Architect of Aetherium.

ABOUT THE AUTHOR

Dane Stewart

Dane Stewart is a surgeon living in the Rocky Mountains
with his wife and children.

www.ingramcontent.com/pod-product-compliance
Lightning Source LLC
Chambersburg PA
CBHW070907260626
47162CB00007B/2579